On a Darkling Plain

a novel by

R. P. Burnham

 The Wessex Collective, 2005

On a Darkling Plain © 2005 by R. P. Burnham

ISBN-13: 978-0-9766274-5-6
ISBN-10: 0-9766274-5-0

Published by   The Wessex Collective
P.O. Box 1088
Nederland, CO 80466-1088

Web: http://www.wessexcollective.com
contact: sss@wessexcollective.com

Acknowledgements
The zenlike tale told by a character on page 168 was originally published in a
slightly different version and under the title "Connections" in *Parting Gifts* in 2000.

Distributor: Wilson & Associates, Alvin, TX

Cover photograph by Kathy FitzPatrick

Printed by Thomson-Shore, Inc., Dexter MI

The Wessex Collective, publisher of progressive books:

If literary fiction (story telling) is the way that human beings can understand and
describe what history feels like, we believe it should be relevant to universal
and historic human experience. We believe also that literary fiction provides an
opportunity to recognize, with significant impact, the problems of societies as
well as individuals. At The Wessex Collective we are publishing books that
demonstrate an empathy for human vulnerability and an understanding of how
that is important to the larger society.

Contents

durch Mitleid wissend...
–Wagner, *Parsifal*

The Witness

The fall day was perfect. The air beneath the clear blue skies was just pleasantly crisp enough to require a light sweater. It was still and peaceful, the quiet of the woods only occasionally broken by the sweet songs of migrating birds flitting about in the high branches. The trees were a glorious mixture of reds, rusts, yellows, browns and greens, so beautiful they made one glad to be alive. For one of the first times since his enforced early retirement at age 56 last June, Samuel Jellerson was, thanks to the tranquility of the fall day, beginning to feel at peace with his situation. He had recently taken up bird watching, and it was this new interest that had led him to the woods. He and his dog, Old Boy, were strolling leisurely in the extensive woodlands behind his house in the country outside Waska, Maine, when he stopped at a steep rise and scanned with binoculars the land below him.

He was looking for clear views of the migrating birds he could hear, and this was a good place to view a very large area. The steepness of the rise caused erosion, and consequently the poor soil below supported only scattered spindly birches and scrawny pine trees for two hundred yards or so in front of him before the ground leveled off into thick groves of evergreens the size of Christmas trees. Then a movement near those trees caught his attention. Looking closer, he saw a man dressed in clerical garb doing something to a little boy.

Or rather he saw and did not see, for he could not believe his eyes. He gasped, stepped back, aghast to be in the presence of something so perverse, so unclean. His sudden movement caused a small stick behind him to snap loudly. At the same time Old Boy sniffed his fear and let out a single bark that ended in a whine. The man in the clearing looked up sharply before almost instantly ducking behind the living Christmas trees. Though it was only an instant, it was long enough for Jellerson to think he recognized the face that stared back at him in panic. He had seen this man occasionally around town and his picture was sometimes in the paper. Father Mullen was his name. He was one of the priests at the Irish Catholic church in Waska.

For another long moment Jellerson stood absolutely still as he tried to compute what he had seen. Then his body, independent of his will and his disbelieving eyes, made him do a very strange thing: he too panicked.

He panicked and ran headlong down the backside of the hill so wildly and precipitously that his momentum almost caused him to fall when he would suddenly have to dodge a bush or a rock. Branches slapped his face, but he hardly noticed the stinging. Once on level ground he ran more under control, but still as fast as he could. Old Boy, with his tail between his legs, kept pace. All the time he was running he hardly had a verbal thought: he saw trees to be dodged, rocks to be leaped over, branches he'd try to duck away from, but the force propelling him forward, the fear and panic, resided in his belly. Only when he got to the old dirt fire road and the pounding of his heart and his side gripping at him like a taloned claw forced him to stop, did something like human consciousness return.

He bent forward, hands on knees, and panted while Old Boy, hanging his head, did the same. While he gasped for breath the panic was still in him, but gradually the gasps changed to deep breaths that calmed him. Then, almost without a transition, he found he had passed from a state of acute panic to extreme embarrassment. Did the man—the priest— hear him crashing through the woods? And if he did, did he think him a fool? Out loud he said, "Why didn't you just greet him as one man does another?"

Old Boy, thinking he was being addressed, ambled up to Jellerson and whined a tiny bark. His long tongue hung from his mouth as he stared with his soft brown eyes at his master.

"Yes, poor Old Boy. And I would have spared your old bones a trauma, wouldn't I?" He shook his head. "We're neither of us getting any younger."

He started walking. The road here was bordered by thick pine groves so that the effect was like walking between two high fences. His pace was unhurried now, all sense of urgency having passed. His embarrassment, still waxing strong inside, had the effect of lessening his belief in what he had seen. As they came around a bend in the road and could see the fields behind his house ahead, that was what he tried to tell himself. But when he reached for finality—when he tried to scoff at the panic and say it was based on a chimera—he found that he could not.

The fields behind his house—the last remaining unsold land from the family farm—were starting to revert to forest. Small trees and bushes grew randomly, and the grass was very high except in the path. To his left, on the other side of a rail fence, was a large field of stubble corn, and on the other side, enclosed by a barbed wire fence, was an open field filled with scattered cylindrical bales of hay left to dry. They looked like a herd of brown cows. Though Jellerson had spent a lot of time here as a child visiting his grandparents, more than forty years had passed since then. It was all very lovely and he was glad he owned the ancestral home, but he still couldn't look at the land without wishing he was back at his school teaching history.

Once inside the house Old Boy went straight to his bowl beside the stove and lapped up a drink of water; then he sank down on his side and closed his eyes, looking very much like the tired old dog he was. Jellerson felt the same way, but he was too restless for a nap. What he desperately wanted to do was to think his way to clarity.

Though it was only three o'clock, an hour earlier than his usual time, he poured himself a glass of cream sherry and got ice cubes from the freezer compartment of the refrigerator. Shaking the glass and listening to the clinking of the ice cubes as he walked to his study, he found that the sound had none of its usual pleasant associations, and for a moment he debated putting it back in the refrigerator. But in his mind he pictured again the scene he'd witnessed in the woods, shuddered, and carefully placed the glass on the coaster on the small table beside his leather easy chair. Then he went to his pipe rack and cleaned the pipe he had taken with him to the woods by reaming it with a pipe cleaner and scraping the sides of the bowl with his pipe tool. Next he chose his favorite meerschaum pipe and carefully packed it with tobacco from his pocket pouch. Lighting it with a wooden match, he sat down and looked forlornly at his sherry. He puffed, picked up the glass of sherry and sipped, then put the glass down, dissatisfied. Was it really possible he had actually seen a priest sexually molesting a boy? Even to form the question in his mind awakened the panic he had felt. He took a deep breath. He was not unaware that such things happened, but surely not in Waska, surely not behind his own house. He took another sip of sherry, and still finding the taste of his favorite drink unsatisfactory, he sighed.

He thought back to an incident that happened at Hartley Academy, the private school in Connecticut where he had taught for thirty-two years until last June. Fifteen years ago two boys were discovered to have been homosexually involved, and he had been on the committee that voted to dismiss them. He knew and liked both boys, but he felt at the time the affair had ended satisfactorily. A problem had been perceived and a solution offered. Now out of the safe, orderly and structured world of the school, he felt lost.

He remembered what the French teacher, Monsieur Duclos, had told him when they were saying their farewells last June. Duclos was a short, dark bald man with thick glasses and continental ways who reminded everyone of the actor who played Hercule Perot in the PBS series. He had said with a little enigmatic smile, "Of all of us, my dear Monsieur Jellerson, of all of us who have taught here for many years, you will be the one who is, how do you say? The fish out of water." Jellerson had smiled and mumbled something about how on the contrary he was looking forward to early retirement, but even as he spoke he knew that Monsieur Duclos had anatomized him exactly. For the past four months he had been a fish out of water. The change in his life had been that traumatic, and he was still struggling to adjust to a different rhythm. After thirty-two years, from the time he left college to the closing of the school this year, his every thought, his every action, his every move, had revolved around the microcosmic world of Hartley Academy. He lived in a house near the campus, spending one night a week and every fourth weekend in a small apartment in one of the dorms when he was the faculty member on duty. His days were filled with teaching and faculty duties, his nights devoted to preparing classes and correcting papers. The little spare time he had was spent on extracurricular activities like the history club or helping coach the school's lacrosse team. It was no exaggeration to say that every waking thought was to some extent related to the school.

Then to have the school close through an act of folly that he foresaw and struggled mightily to avert was twice as devastating to him. The worst day of his life was the September day last month that would have been the first day of classes. Only with the greatest difficulty was he able to refrain from tears, but he did at one point pound his desk with his fist in frustrated anger as he thought of the events that had cut him off from his life.

Hartley Academy was quite consciously modeled on English public schools and as such had a policy of compulsory chapel on Sundays. As time went on and American demographics changed, this policy became more and more difficult to implement. Though the founder's will had specifically mandated the practice—he was a staunch Puritan of the old school and a pillar of the Congregational Church—first

9

Catholics, then Jews, and later students from Muslim, Hindu and Buddhist traditions sought exemptions. They were usually though perhaps begrudgingly granted by the headmaster. But finally a fall day at the beginning of a semester came when the number of exemptions reached crisis proportions. Almost thirty percent of the students asked for the exemption from mandatory chapel, and this figure did not include the large number of non-Protestants who attended chapel as it were sub rosa. When these facts were brought to the attention of the board of trustees (including the fact that even many of the Protestants sought to avoid church attendance), a crisis developed which quickly evolved into a question of institutional identity. First they tabulated the students, finding that only about a quarter of them were actually Congregationalists, and only sixty-two percent of the 420 students were Protestant. Catholics comprised twenty-five percent of the student body, Jews eight percent and the rest were put in the category of other. At board meetings and faculty gatherings these numbers were discussed and compared to the founder's will endlessly. Then in one of those irrational self-destructive impulses that drive committees as commonly as mobs or individuals, the board passed a motion that from now on no exemptions from chapel were to be granted. Almost instantly letters and phone calls inundated the administration. Many parents withdrew their children, the campus was in turmoil, and the media began running stories about the bigoted private school in Connecticut. All this happened five years ago. The school hung on with half empty classrooms and dorms and ate up its endowment for those five years before finally folding last June.

And so a day came when Jellerson found himself, age 56, without a job, too old to get another one, and in despair. At first he believed the only way to hold his life together was to continue living in their house next to the campus, but his wife Millie talked him out of that idea. The entire school, campus and buildings, was sold to a private health care group who planned to turn it into a private sanitarium where wealthy drug addicts and alcoholics could recover from their chemical dependency. Millie argued first that it would distress him to see this ignoble transformation and secondly that it was better not to try to live in the past. She suggested they move back home to Waska, Maine. Financially and emotionally he had to admit her arguments made sense. Between a small annuity he would get from his teaching job, income from some stocks and bonds they owned and the money they could get from selling their house, they would be able to live reasonably comfortably even before he became eligible for Social Security. And they already owned a house in Waska. Almost ten years ago he had, together with his brother, inherited the family farm when his mother died. Though his brother lived in California and he in Connecticut, they could not bring themselves to sell the place since it had been in their family for seven generations. For a few years they rented the fields to a neighboring dairy farmer while the house stood empty; then they did two things more or less strictly for their own financial benefit: they had the house renovated so that they could rent it, and they sold the fields to their neighbor. Three years later his brother died, divorced and childless, and the farm devolved to him alone. Thus when Jellerson conceded to Millie's arguments, he gave his tenant nine months notice, and they moved into the house themselves.

Their plans hit one slight snag when they were unable to sell their house in Connecticut before they moved; thus Millie got a job at the local bank in Waska to help stabilize their finances while they waited for it to be sold. Just last month their broker had informed them that a buyer had been found; Millie, however, found she liked working and had no plans to quit.

One particular aspect of his background troubled him as it pertained to what had happened in the woods. Jellerson was aware that many people in Waska knew about the negative publicity associated with the reason the school closed. If he accused a Catholic priest of molesting a boy, many people would suspect his motives. Thus in yet another way he felt poisoned by the bad decision of the board. And yet not only had he opposed its suicidal decision; he had also objected to its intolerance and small-mindedness. He believed in the old boy values of honor and rectitude, duty and honesty, fair play and compassion, and he respected and treated anyone who displayed these values well. As long as a student did well academically and conducted himself honorably, he did not care what his private beliefs were. He thought it was ridiculous to close the school simply because it had ceased to be a purely Protestant place. The members of the board were simply misguided. Even if the will was explicit, it was written 160 years ago and surely its mandate could be changed. He knew personally several students who were Catholic or Jewish who perfectly fulfilled the ideals of a Hartley Academy student. They were diligent in their studies and superior scholars; they were honorable in their personal behavior; they were good sportsmen on the playing fields. When they became seniors and positions of responsibility accrued to them in the dorms or in student government, they did their duty perfectly. And when they became old boys it was obvious that they loved and cherished the school as much as any former student could. The best student, both as scholar and as a gentleman, Jellerson had ever had in his years at the school was an Indian boy of the Hindu faith.

While he was thinking with pleasure of this former student, now an old boy, his namesake came into the study, his claws clattering on the hardwood floor even with his slow, deliberate pace. Instead of settling into his wicker basket with the green plaid blanket, he came up to Jellerson and laid his head on Jellerson's knees, then stared at him mournfully.

Jellerson reached down and scratched the dog's ears. "I know, Old Boy. I'm thinking about it too."

Old Boy emitted a tiny whine. He was still tired from the precipitous run they had made.

"What would your fellow old boys think if they saw me now? Jellerson whispered.

He was famous at the school for being a hard but fair taskmaster who always insisted on following the rules. Though hated by many students when at the school, at later reunions and visits he was always the teacher the old boys were most glad to see, and he had heard many successful old boys say he had changed their life. So when their old dog, actually their son Bennet's dog, died eight years ago and they got another one, Millie had suggested they name him Old Boy. "That way," she said, "we will always have with us a reminder of what the school means to us." He had replied rather tartly that it was not very likely that while he still had breath to draw he would ever forget Hartley Academy, but still he was pleased with the name and it had stuck.

Now looking into Old Boy's soft brown eyes and contemplating his unconditioned faithfulness and love, it seemed to him he was most appropriately named. Students came to the school as strangers, but the teachers were expected to take a fatherly interest in their well being. Their duties, that is to say, entailed far more than merely teaching facts to the boys: their duties were based upon a human trust that nurtured the boys' character and moral development. When that trust was fulfilled, the old boys became fully rounded human beings and citizens. But contrasting that ideal with the implications of what he had seen, or might have seen, in the woods, Jellerson felt sick at heart. He wondered if the world he had witnessed today was the real world and whether or not his entire life was some kind of Victorian illusion.

His pipe was finished. Tapping the bowl into the ashtray, he felt a wave of tiredness pass over him. Old Boy, just settling into his wicker basket, must have felt the same way, for he was yawning. Ordinarily Jellerson cleaned his pipes immediately after using them, but his eyes suddenly felt heavy and draining his sherry, the glass seemed equally heavy. He almost dropped it putting it back on the table. He closed his eyes, thinking in a languid, serendipitous way about Hartley Academy and teaching, and soon he was fast asleep.

He awoke when he heard Millie's key in the door. He was momentarily disoriented, mostly aware only of a pain in his neck where he had slept awkwardly, and while he was still gathering his thoughts he found Millie before him. She was removing her coat and leafing through the mail she had picked up from their mailbox at the beginning of their driveway.

"Well, well," she said. "I don't see that very often."

"That?" He knew what she meant, but he spoke sharply in resentment. He had just remembered what he had seen in the woods.

She was looking at a catalog and didn't seem to notice his tone.

He stood and gathered up her coat. "Yes, I suddenly found myself a bit tired."

She glanced at him, saw what he was doing. Her large blue eyes narrowed behind her round glasses. "I was going to take care of that. I just wanted to see if the sweater I want to get Beverly is in this catalog."

Jellerson nodded on his way to the hall closet to hang her coat up. Returning to his study, he picked up his pipe and got his cleaning tools. Millie still stood by his desk leafing through the catalog. She kept flipping back and forth between two different pages trying to make up her mind. Finally she turned to her husband. "What do you think of this one?" she asked, holding the catalog up for his inspection. "The blue one. I think Beverly will look good in that."

Jellerson, intent upon reaming his pipe with the pipe cleaner, barely looked. "Sure, that will be fine," he said.

But Millie was not going to be satisfied with passive or indifferent assent. She clucked her tongue. "This is for your daughter's birthday. I would think you'd take a bit more interest. Honestly, Sam, can't you let that pipe be for a minute and really look?"

He stopped and stared at her. After deferring to him all through their married life, Millie had lately become rather assertive, and he still was not used to it. They had been married in the summer before he started teaching at Hartley Academy, so for the entire 32 years of his career she had fulfilled the role of a faculty wife, a role analogous to that of a minister's wife. Though having no official capacity she was expected to be totally dedicated to the institution. This meant a plethora of sundry duties—everything from organizing faculty teas and Christmas parties to inventorying the linen in the dormitories or the silverware in the cafeteria. She had done all these things conscientiously and without complaint. Only when the well being of their two children (and his neglect of them in concentrating on the school) would sometimes become at issue would she demur, and then only in the most halfhearted and tentative way. Having grown used to that Millie, he was almost shocked every time she revealed her newfound sense of freedom and selfhood. He remembered the facility with which she would organize faculty teas with perfect settings and exquisite cakes and sandwiches, the cheerful smiles with which she would greet each guest and the particular attention she would pay to the Headmaster Dr. Willoughby, and he felt betrayed. It was as if he didn't know her anymore. And in fact she even looked different. As helpmeet at Hartley Academy, she was plump, matronly, and wore full old-fashioned dresses; but now she wore her gray hair in a ponytail; her glasses had changed from a narrow horn-rimmed frame to a round gold-wired one; she had lost weight, applied light touches of makeup to her eyes and lipstick to her lips; and she wore either blouses and knee-length skirts or pant suits. Today it was a conservative charcoal gray pant suit. For a woman of her years she was now very attractive. But was she fixing herself up for him or just because she was enjoying her new life of independence so much?

Thus when he answered her a lot of anger and resentment found their way into his tone. "She's the one who moved to California. I didn't want her in San Francisco."

"And you know why, don't you? I used to try to tell you that expecting perfection from children might work in the classroom, but it's disastrous in parenting. *You're* the reason Beverly moved so far away. Between your mania for orderliness and your strictness, you've alienated both Beverly and Bennet."

He stood and brought his meerschaum pipe back to the pipe rack. Replacing it, he turned to her, "What's that supposed to mean?"

Millie put the catalog on the desk and sat down on the chair. She looked at her husband for a moment before beginning. "I mean simply this. I think your fastidiousness and high expectations drove them both away. I used to try to tell you this, but you wouldn't listen. But why do you think Bennet dropped out of college six weeks before graduation? Because he wasn't going to earn honors. As a result he's wasting himself in the Navy now. And I don't have to guess about Beverly. She told me in so many words that she moved to California to have room to breathe. Right now I was just trying to get you involved in your daughter's life, and instead you find it more important to clean a pipe. But the pipe or this desk"—she pointed to his perfectly arranged desk with pens and pencils in a cup, phone neatly in the corner, and not so much as a stray piece of paper out of place—"well, it's unnatural to be so neat. The world isn't orderly but spontaneous, and things cannot be mapped out like a lesson plan. Hartley Academy is gone. The reason it failed was because it maintained an absurd degree of order and tradition. It was inflexible. Last June I vowed I was not going to allow that inflexibility to rule my life any more. We have to change now, Sam. Without the school we're only a family. That's what should be the center of our life."

Jellerson listened to her in silence. The only indication that her words struck home was that his face became flushed. Taking a deep breath and looking her in the eye, he said, "I don't know how to defend myself against what you say. I know I used to concentrate on teaching so much that I probably was more of a teacher than a father—at least sometimes. I feel bad enough about that myself not to need any reminding"—he rather glared at her as he said this but otherwise he spoke calmly—"and I know I have the tendency to be orderly and fastidious. But my study of history long ago taught me that the chaos and darkness of the world, both inside the soul and in the outer world, have to be struggled against. Civilization is the triumph over chaos. I can't help being like my forefathers in thinking like this. But please don't accuse me of being indifferent to the children. Haven't I dedicated my life to nurturing the next generation?"

Millie nodded solemnly in assent. "Of course," she murmured; then gesturing with open palms, she added, suddenly conciliatory, "Look, honey, I don't want to criticize you or argue with you. I suppose I had what they call a bad day at work. It took almost an extra hour to get my receipts to balance. But I know it's a difficult time you're going through. I just think that now you're not teaching it's time for your family to become even more important." She got up and reached for his hand. "The trouble with arguing is that you concentrate on something that's bothering you. But I don't forget that I think you're a wonderful, honorable man and that I love you." It was hard to remain angry after she said that. They embraced, and he promised he would make more effort to reach out to the children.

So the argument passed away. He still felt betrayed a little bit, or more accurately, confused. She had adjusted to their new life because she had a role ready-made for her in her new job while he…well, what was a teacher called who didn't teach anymore? Yes, confusion, that was his lot. But until he could see his way clear, he would keep the incident in the woods to himself. Maybe he would have kept it to himself even if they hadn't argued. He was a man who liked to be sure before he spoke.

That night they had a quiet supper, then went shopping for a new microwave oven. When they got home from the store they watched television for an hour or so, then retired early. He was quiet throughout the evening, only speaking when spoken to; but since this was the way he behaved himself lately, it was not likely Millie noticed anything out of the ordinary was bothering him.

The next day he did not go to the woods for his walk. Instead he got the leash out and took Old Boy for a walk along the road in the morning, then spent the early part of the afternoon trying to read a new history of Waska by Cliff Dalton, a man whom he met on the finance and affairs committee of the Congregational Church in town. It was well written and exhaustively researched, but he was not really in the mood for reading. The truth was, he couldn't get what he had seen yesterday out of his mind. Though he had fallen asleep last night convinced that he had not seen anything untoward in the woods, in the morning his certitude had vanished.

Feeling restless, he drove downtown to deposit a check at the bank and do a few errands. He saw Millie, who told him she needed some cosmetics at the drug store, so from the bank he walked the two blocks up Main Street to get these items and also to pick up a paper. While in the store he also examined their selection of pipe tobacco. He was fond of an English mixture readily available in tobacco shops but only occasionally seen on the shelves of less specialized stores. He talked to the manager when he couldn't find it and elicited a promise that they would start carrying the brand. With his business completed and his purchases made, he walked out of the store and down the street toward where the Most Holy Trinity Catholic Church stood. He was across the street from it, but he stared almost involuntarily in its direction, and then stopped when he saw a group of boys going up to the door. The same panic began stirring when he saw the door opening and Father Mullen coming out to greet the boys.

Jellerson started walking, but not before he exchanged a glance with the black-clad figure.

There was mutual recognition and more: from the priest a look of startled embarrassment and from Jellerson, besides stirrings of the same panic he had experienced in the woods, the sinking feeling that he was about to enter into hell.

At home he waited impatiently for the end of the day and Millie's return. He was not sure how he would tell her about the priest, but tell her he would in some way.

He simply had to share the burden of his knowledge with another human being. As soon as he heard her car in the long driveway, he poured her a glass of white wine and himself some sherry and had it ready for her as soon as she walked in, but first she had to get dinner started. He had already made a salad and had the rice dish ready to go, but not knowing anything about cooking, he had to defer to her for the main dish. Thus he stayed in the kitchen, foregoing his usual pipe, and waited for the right moment.

He sat at the kitchen table and watched Millie preparing a marinade for the chicken they were having. She was squeezing a lime into a bowl already containing ginger, soy sauce and cooking sherry when he asked, "Did you order that sweater for Beverly?"

"Not yet," she said, giving the lime a final squeeze. "There's some nice sweaters in the L.L. Bean catalog too, so I want to think about it for a day or two more. Besides, I'm also thinking of getting her something for her apartment."

"Suppose I buy her a TV," Jellerson said. "Last time she called didn't she say something about her old TV being shot?"

Millie went to the refrigerator to get the chicken breasts. "She did, but it would be hard to know what would be right. Her place is small."

"That's another reason I wish she lived nearer. Then we could see her place and know what she needed."

Millie's eyes flashed momentarily, making him wish he hadn't brought up that particular subject, but she was intent upon placing the boneless chicken breasts in the marinade and didn't say anything.

"Suppose I sent her the money to buy her own? You don't think that would be too impersonal, do you?"

She smiled at his uncertainty. "Well, under the circumstances it might be the best way. It's the thought that counts, you know. The cliché is true."

Old Boy ambled into the kitchen, looking from Jellerson to Millie, then sat on his haunches. His actions prodded Jellerson toward his duty. He took a deep breath. "You know, Old Boy and I saw something in the woods yesterday that was rather disturbing. That is, I think I saw something. I've been going over it in my mind ever since and am still very confused. I don't know what to do."

Millie was washing her hands. She turned and grabbed the hand towel from the rack below the sink. Her face, expressing concern, was the face of his old helpmeet, and instantly Jellerson felt comforted, less estranged. He was not alone anymore.

"What do you mean?" she asked. She came over, sat at the table, and reached for her wine. "Tell me about it."

"You know that Catholic priest, Father Mullen? The one whose picture was in the paper with Rev. Covington's a few weeks ago? I saw him in the woods yesterday with a little boy, and…"

"And?"

"And it looked as if he might have been abusing the boy."

Millie took a gulp of wine. "Good God! What do you mean?" she asked, her face a mixture of surprise, shock and intense curiosity.

"I mean it looked as if he was sexually abusing the boy, that's what I mean. The trouble is, I only saw it for a split second, and then I was so… so embarrassed, I turned away… I left."

"This is very serious, Sam. Did you see the boy clearly?"

"No, that's the trouble. I've gone over it in my mind so many times that I'm not sure of anything anymore. Right now I'm just barely sure I even saw a boy. I keep asking myself, did you see it or did you imagine it? It was only a split second. It happened so quickly. I was shocked. I think—I know—I panicked I was so shocked." Millie stared at her husband. Taking another sip of wine, she considered. "Well, with something like this you've got to be sure."

"I know. I can't accuse a man without some kind of certainty. And the fact he's a Catholic priest, after what happened at Hartley. It would be awful."

"Tell me this. What is the basis of your certainty and uncertainty. We've got to sort it out."

Jellerson nodded. "One thing that helps confirm my suspicions is that I saw Father Mullen this afternoon. After I left the bank I walked by the Catholic church and he was there. He recognized me when we exchanged glances and he looked guilty."

"That's still not much to go on."

"I know, but most of my effort for the past twenty-four hours has been to try to convince myself I really didn't see what I saw. But I think I did see it because my memory simply won't let me be convinced that way, and Father Mullen's behavior today seems to confirm it."

Millie turned and stared at Old Boy for a long time. He was resting on his side now, though his eyes were open and he was watching them. "What time was it you saw the priest and the boy?"

"It must have been about 2:30. I was too shocked to actually look at my watch, but when I got home it was a little before three o'clock. But why do you ask?"

"Because the boy you think you saw should be in school at that time. Do you think you could recognize him if you saw him again?"

Jellerson stroked his chin and looked far away. "I don't know. If I saw the priest for less than a second, I saw the boy even more briefly. Father Mullen ducked down behind a small pine tree. I think before he did that he shoved the boy down."

"You said you thought you saw sexual abuse. Can you tell me what you saw?"

Jellerson nodded, feeling embarrassed. Hesitantly he said, "I think you would call it homosexual rape."

The word seemed to make Millie angry. She frowned. "If that's true, we certainly owe it to that boy to try to prosecute the priest." She finished her wine with a long swallow. "One thing we could try to find out is if any boy was out of school at that time, but—"

"I know," Jellerson interrupted. "How do we find that out? We're not detectives."

"Well, one thing we can probably depend on is that the boy goes to a parochial school."

"But, remember, there's only the French-Canadian parochial school in Waska. The people who go to the Most Holy Trinity send their kids to the public schools."

"Then I don't know what to think. A child could only be let out of school with his parents' permission."

Jellerson stood and took both of their glasses to the sink to rinse out. Looking out the kitchen window, he could see the woods across the field in their backyard. "I want to do the right thing," he said with his back to Millie, "but you can see the difficulties. I can't see that there's anything to do. It's frustrating. I wish to God I could be sure."

They talked some more but could not reach any definite conclusion, since doing the right thing and being sure seemed an irreconcilable conflict. But as they sat at their rather quiet and subdued dinner, during which both were going over in their minds a way out of the impasse, Millie suddenly brightened. "I have an idea," she announced. "You really can't go to the police, but I think both of us find it intolerable that we would do nothing if in fact that poor boy is suffering."

Jellerson put his fork down and said, "There's certainly nothing we could do legally. A judge would just say it's too vague. So what can we do?"

"Considering the alternatives, I think you should talk to Rev. Covington about this."

Jellerson pondered for a moment. Rev. Covington was the minister of the First Congregational Church in Waska, which they had rejoined upon their return home (it was the church in which they were married thirty-two years ago). He didn't know the minister well enough yet to feel comfortable talking about such a thing, and he felt himself being forced into doing something he didn't want to do. During his years of teaching he had had to deal with plagiarism cases. They had always made him feel almost physically ill. The same distaste at having to confront dishonest, desperate and disorderly lives that he felt then he felt now, with this difference: now it was a hundred times more distasteful. He almost wished he hadn't told Millie his suspicions. Trying to be noncommittal in his response, he said, "I don't know. He probably doesn't know much about Father Mullen since he just became the minister here last year. And I don't want to sully a man's reputation if I'm wrong."

"Well," Millie said, not at all pleased, "you'll have to be discreet, of course. But you could obliquely broach the subject. In the meantime I could try to find out a few things from one of the women I work with. She goes to Father Mullen's church."

Millie's inquiries garnered no information about the father, so all depended on what Jellerson could learn from Rev. Covington. He had no chance to speak to him after services that Sunday, but as the minister shook hands with the departing congregation filing out of the church, he did invite Jellerson to join a birding trip to the Rachel Carlson National Seashore the following Saturday. The outing was planned by the informal church group comprising three or four experienced birders and up to a dozen beginners that Jellerson had joined in a conscious effort to enrich his retirement. Since this decision inevitably led to his being in the woods on the afternoon he saw Father Mullen, he had wished hourly for the past several days that he had never heard of the group. At least, he thought, as he bid good-day to the minister and promised he would come, the cause of his misery would now offer him a chance to extricate himself from his dilemma. After his initial reluctance to talk to the minister, he had grown desperate enough to look for relief from any quarter. Only one thing was devoutly to be wished: that his doubt, one way or the other, would cease.

Thus after a bad week Saturday arrived and Jellerson found himself riding to the coast with Mike Adamson, a high school biology teacher, Ray St. Cyr, a surveyor before he retired a few years ago, and Ray's wife Eleanor. She was the birder in the family; Ray was only going along for the company and didn't even have a pair of binoculars. Millie had also been invited, but as she was not really interested in nature, she elected to spend the day with her sister. The group made several stops to look for different birds in different ecosystems; they started on the rocky coast, went next to a beach, and followed that with a visit to a salt marsh dotted with tidal pools. Many birds were seen, but Jellerson, intent upon looking for a chance to speak privately with Rev. Covington, scarcely got involved in the excitement of the group when such rarities as a harlequin duck were seen. The only time he did lose himself was at the beach where they discovered a sandling with a broken wing. The small shore bird was running on the beach and periodically attempting pathetic efforts to fly, all of which ended with it falling on its side and laboriously righting itself on its feet again. A few of the birders started walking down the beach toward it with the idea of capturing it and bringing it to the Maine Audubon Society for treatment, but before they got to it a less disinterested pair of eyes had spotted the bird. A great black-backed gull swooped down just after the sandling had made another attempt to fly and plucked it from the sand before it had a chance to right itself. They could see the small bird still making frantic efforts to escape even as it was firmly clamped in the gull's bill. Only during this incident was Jellerson able to forget his ulterior motive for coming on the trip. He watched predator and prey with an emotion approaching horror. Where loons, grebes, sea ducks, shore birds and phalaropes could not capture his imagination, death could.

An hour later his chance finally came. The group, having exhausted the possibilities at the salt marsh, began walking down a dirt road to a promontory that jutted out to the sea when Rev. Covington stopped to reload his camera. He had a telephoto lens on a rifle shoulder mount with which he had been taking photographs all day. He yelled to the group to go ahead—he would catch up directly. Jellerson lingered behind, and after a false start where he inanely remarked about the weather and how tired he was getting and read a certain look of impatience in the minister's face, he got right to the point.

"Rev. Covington, I've been meaning to ask you about Father Mullen, one of the Catholic priests in town. Do you know him well?"

The minister was concentrating on lining the film up with the sprockets. He looked up briefly. "Not well, but I do know him."

"Well, I saw him in the woods behind my house last week. It was rather strange."

"Hmm. He's not a bird watcher, if that's what you mean, Mr. Jellerson. I suppose he was taking a walk or something."

"But he was with a young boy." Despite his effort to appear casual, his voice broke. "I just wondered why he would be in the woods with a boy."

It was obvious that Rev. Covington caught the urgency of Jellerson's voice, but not wanting to be gossiping about a fellow clergyman, his response was guarded as he pursed his lips and considered for a moment. "I really don't know. You aren't implying something sinister, are you?"

"Probably not. I mean, I guess a little bit. It's just that he acted guilty when I saw him. What kind of a man is he? I mean, is he a good man?"

Rev. Covington eyed Jellerson suspiciously. "A good man? Well, personally I find him a bit of a cold fish, actually. I've only met him at meetings of local clergy where he's quite businesslike. If I see him on the street he just nods. I think he loves music. He's the choir director at his church. That probably explains why he was with a boy, now that I think of it. But is he a good man? I can say he's a stickler for doing the right thing. He strikes me as a man who is only comfortable within the confines of the rules. I think he observes all the minutia of his vocation as a Catholic priest. But this may be just my perspective. Protestant ministers are probably not the ones who can accurately judge the life of a priest. But a one-word answer to your question is yes. Yes, I think he's a good man."

As he was speaking Jellerson was watching the other birders out on the point. One of them looked back at them, causing him to speak quickly. "So you think he may have acted strangely when I saw him because he's not comfortable with people?"

Rev. Covington nodded. "That sounds like him. As I say, he's a bit of a cold fish.

Probably he's just shy."

Jellerson liked this answer. "Shy, you say. Maybe that's why he appeared so embarrassed. He clearly didn't want to talk to me. He ducked away, in fact."

The minister started walking toward the others. "That sounds like the behavior I'd expect from him."

So Jellerson's mission was successful. What Rev. Covington told him was just what he wanted to hear. For the next several days he was able to convince himself—and to a lesser degree, Millie—that he had only imagined that he witnessed evil in the woods. When in the dark recesses of his consciousness he would begin to enter the woods, the comforting, reassuring words of the minister would act as a barrier, and he would think: the priest is a shy man, and that is why he acted so strangely. The rest, he told himself, he imagined. Millie, much bothered by his easy resignation, once went so far as to suggest he call Father Mullen and confront him about what happened in the woods, but she didn't put up much of an argument when Jellerson said that was impossible. Without actually lying to her, he managed to suggest that his conversation with Rev. Covington was franker and more explicit than it really was.

Another week passed during which Jellerson was more or less free from the nightmare incubus that had been weighing him down. He had successfully argued the father's innocence with Millie because he was really convincing himself. Then one day at the end of the week he ran into his uncle, Walter Pingree, downtown. His mother's brother was sitting on one of the park benches on Main street with another elderly man, and Jellerson stopped to chat with him. He hadn't seen him in years, and in fact they were not close, but still there was some catching up to do. While they were talking a woman and young boy got into a car down the street. When they drove by, she waved at Pingree.

"Who was that?" Jellerson asked.

"That's Mercy Harmon," Pingree said. "She's the woman my son was going to marry before he was killed in Vietnam."

Jellerson licked his dry lips. "And the boy?"

Pingree looked up at him, his eyes narrowing in curiosity at his nephew's interest. "The boy? That's her son."

Jellerson took a deep breath, trying to quiet the rising panic he felt. He saw the scene in the woods as clearly as he saw it when he was there. The boy in the car was the same boy he saw with Father Mullen.

Mother and Son

Mercy Buckley stood in the kitchen washing the lettuce in preparation for dinner. With her was her sister, Hope Harmon, who was sitting at the kitchen table poring over a book of wallpaper designs. She had delivered Mercy's son Jason half an hour ago, and wanting advice on redoing her own son Robbie's room, she had stopped for a glass of wine and a talk with her sister. Jason, whom Mercy could see through the space below the cabinets and above the counter, was in the living room of their small house. He had the TV on, but instead of watching it he was standing in front of the window and staring blankly out into the street. Dusk had already descended, so whatever he was looking at was not in front of him. Mercy, frowning thoughtfully, didn't hear Hope at first. She turned. "What's that you say?"

"I said Robbie keeps telling me he's too old for duckies on the wallpaper. He says all his friends laugh at it now." She looked down at the wallpaper book at a design of blue paper with gold coronets, then held it up for Mercy to see. "What do you think of this one?"

Mercy squinted her eyes and looked. "It's okay," she said rather matter-of-factly.

"Okay!" Hope repeated incredulously. "You wouldn't have this kitchen if you were so casual."

She waved her arm, taking in the whole kitchen with one sweep. The decorative touches here, as in the whole house, were always subtle and sure. The satin off-white walls and antique white cabinets with leaded glass were accented by touches of sky blue everywhere. It was predominantly seen on the row of stenciled flowers across the top of the walls; then it was picked up in various designs on the crockery stored on the counter holding flour and so forth, the blue sailboat that decorated a large urn in one corner and which contained exotic dried plants, even on the blue magnets that held up various of Jason's school papers and notes on the refrigerator. The phone was blue; a trivet hung above the stove was blue ceramic; even a framed watercolor of sand dunes and sea grass displayed the blue in the painting's sky. The only nonblue decorative touch made a perfect contrast: it was a framed 1945 newspaper front page with the huge headline JAPS SURRENDER above a photograph of the ceremony on the U.S.S. Missouri, where MacArthur accepted the Japanese surrender. Mercy and her ex-husband had found the newspaper in the attic when they first moved in, and she had decided to frame it. The round oak table at which Hope sat (and which had blue place mats) had also been stripped and refinished by Mercy. She had done the entire house in the same careful way: every detail was always carefully considered for its relationship to an aesthetic whole. Mercy cared about beauty; she subscribed to several magazines of design and home decoration; everyone in the family asked her opinion before one brush stroke was made or a single curtain rod was mounted. "Okay" was simply not an acceptable or expected response to a question of design.

So again Hope repeated in an incredulous tone, "So what do you mean, 'okay'? Come on, is that all you have to say?"

Mercy couldn't help smiling at the look on Hope's face. Picking up a cucumber and beginning to peel it with a potato peeler, she said, "Why don't you just paint the room."

"Are you kidding? I vowed years ago never to go through the hell of removing wallpaper ever again."

"That wallpaper wouldn't be hard to remove. It's vinyl."

"Well, even if that's so, I want wallpaper. I like wallpaper."

Mercy, having finished slicing the cucumber, put the knife down and walked over to the table. "Let me see that blue wallpaper again. You'll have to turn the pages. My hands are wet."

They began looking through the book, discussing the merits and demerits of several designs. It was hard for Mercy to concentrate, not only because she could still see Jason looking forlornly out the window from where she stood, but also because she was in a hurry and too polite to say so. She was having Bill Ricker over for dinner but made no mention of it because Hope did not like him. Hope was a strong feminist. Unlike Mercy she had kept the family name when she married, making her one of only half a dozen or so women in Waska who dared to defy the conservative conventions of the town. From her perspective Bill didn't pass muster. Mercy was coming around to that opinion herself, but having naively once told her sister she could reform the man, she didn't really want to get into the reasons she now found that transformation unlikely. The one step she had taken was to stop deferring to him. She was going to serve a broccoli and chicken pasta dish tonight. Bill, like her former husband Brian, liked red meat (what was it about men, she wondered, that made them think only beef was food?). If this small step led to further deterioration of their relationship, then so be it. With all these thoughts and Jason too going through her mind, she wasn't too much help to her sister.

It was Jason, though, who interrupted their perusal of the wallpaper book. His listlessness was beginning to seriously worry her. "Just a minute, Hope," she finally said. "I've got to talk to Jason."

He turned around suddenly when he heard her coming. He was so lost in thought that her entering the room had taken him by surprise. She could see him composing his face as if he were putting on a mask.

"It'll be an hour and a half before we eat, Jason," she said. "If you want to go out and play, you can."

He looked up at her, his eyes questioning her in some fathomless way.

"You could shoot baskets. Just turn on the spotlight. Or you could play the piano if you want."

He turned and started walking toward the door. "Okay, I'll shoot baskets."

He didn't sound very enthused, but that was the least of it. The way he was looking at her, as if he didn't see her but was looking at something beyond her, pierced her like a wound. And the business of composing his face was something she had just started noticing lately.

"Just a minute, Jason."

He stopped, turned, looked at her, through her, at… at what? At something only he could see.

Her hands positively tingled with the need to hug him. She stepped forward, caressed his cheek. "Are you okay?"

He nodded. "Uh-huh."

"You're not feeling sick?"

He shook his head. "No."

"But you did feel sick Wednesday when you missed choir practice."

His face darkened. "I don't want to do choir anymore. I don't like it anymore."

He spat the remark out like something that tasted unpleasant. It made her heart well up, and she could have cried for him. When even music, the joy of his young soul and the gift that life had bestowed, when even it caused such palpable pain and distress, then she did not know how to reach him. She leaned down and kissed the top of his head.

"We'll talk about this later," she said. "Jason, you know your father and I love you very much, don't you?"

He stared at her, his eyes making some inchoate appeal. He inclined his head slightly, his hand on the door knob. "I know," he said in a whisper. Then, to hide the tears in his eyes, he quickly went out the door.

Mercy walked slowly back to the kitchen. She was almost numb from what had to be the strangest conversation she had ever had with her son. Now was no time to try to keep her fears from Hope, sitting at the table waiting for her. The book was still open, but clearly she sensed something was wrong.

"Did you hear that?"

"A little."

"Have you noticed he's been acting funny lately?"

Hope looked down at the wallpaper book. She frowned as she thought for a moment. "Well," she said after a time, "he's been quieter lately. Almost morose."

"Yes, that's it exactly."

"Today, for instance, I gave him and Robbie some cheese and crackers and milk, but he didn't eat much of it. That happens once or so and it's no big thing, but I suddenly realized today that he hasn't shown much appetite for a couple of weeks. Then they went out and practiced hitting hockey shots, but I could tell he wasn't really into it. He didn't block any of Robbie's shots, and he usually stops over half of them. Do you have any theories why he's acting this way?"

It was Mercy's turn to frown and think before she spoke. She was perfectly sure what was troubling Jason—she was positive his sad lethargy was a delayed result of her divorce, and it made her feel guilty. She had heard many times that divorce was always harder on boys. She had heard it so often that she realized she was waiting for this to happen. She could even see why his reaction was coming now when he was twelve years old and entering puberty instead of instantly after the divorce when he was eight. Her ex-husband Brian was a good father, conscientious about spending time with Jason. He would take him for weekends, go camping with him in the summer, take him to events like minor league baseball in Portland or the Red Sox in Boston, even to musical events like choral recitals. Just recently, however, he had become involved with a woman who had made it quite clear that she was not interested in baby sitting a child. Mercy had to admit that Brian was struggling manfully to be a dutiful father at the same time he was attempting to nurture the love affair. She knew that if a line were drawn in the sand, Brian would choose Jason, and she also understood his need to find mature love and fulfillment. She wasn't blaming him, but still of late the visits had become more irregular and of shorter duration. All this went through her mind before she said, "Yes, it's the divorce and the fact right now Brian hasn't been able to spend as much time with him. But what really hurts is that I blame myself. I feel guilty even though it's nothing I've done. Or rather, it's not anything small I've done—only the one big thing of getting divorced."

Hope nodded her head sympathetically as she listened. "I know the feeling. To be a mother is to feel guilty. It's the main attribute of the job. A kid goes bad and they blame the mother. He flunks a test, and she says, 'Where did I go wrong?' Sally Barclay was telling me a month or so ago about something that happened to her when she was pregnant with her first child. One day she was taking a rest and suddenly became aware she couldn't feel the baby moving. She called her mother in panic, and her mother told her two things. First, she said it was normal, and secondly she told her to get used to worrying. You will worry about your children until the day you die. To be a mother is to worry. That's what guilt is."

They went on exchanging anecdotes like this for a while, but neither of them could come up with any solution for Jason's feelings except time and the hope that Brian would straighten out his relationship with his friend Wendy. They parted both feeling somewhat dissatisfied. Mercy at least found little satisfaction in knowing she was not alone with her guilt. It seemed selfish, a way of stroking her ego when her thoughts should be outer directed to Jason.

It was in this frame of mind that she called Brian soon after Hope left. She dialed his home phone and waited for four rings, then hung up before his answering machine came on. She checked her watch and then redialed, this time calling his cellular phone number. Brian had a very successful hot-topping business that had recently expanded beyond driveway jobs to getting state and corporate contracts for roads and parking lots, and the cellular phone was just one sign of his new prosperity. During their married life they had often struggled through months when he got little income and her salary supported them. But neither their marriage nor its breakup had anything to do with economics, so in divorce, which by and large was amiable, she had no regrets. The only interest she took in the money he made was that it would insure Jason would be able to go to a good college.

After five or six rings he answered.

"Brian, working late again, I see."

"Oh, hi, Mercy. Yeah, we're doing the new parking lot at the hospital. My men are just finishing up now."

"Listen, I haven't heard from you yet. Are you going to take Jason for the weekend or not?"

There was a pause before he spoke that told her already what he would say. "Well, I wanted to. I had a chance to get tickets to the B.C. game. I thought we'd spend the weekend in Boston, but Wendy, well, you know."

Mercy did know. A flash of anger rose, only to be suppressed. Calmly she said, "You know Jason is going through a bad time now, don't you? I mean, like, he's depressed and listless. I'm concerned."

Again there was a silence on the line while Brian did some thinking. "I've noticed it too," he finally said. "Last weekend he wasn't too enthused about the car show we went to, and I know he doesn't like Wendy. We had an argument about him last night in fact. But look, I was going to call you when I got home. I thought Jason could come for the morning and through lunch. Maybe we could go and buy one of those dinosaur models he loves and spend the morning constructing it. That's what I was thinking."

"I suppose Wendy won't like that either."

He clucked his tongue in irritation, whether at her or his girlfriend, she couldn't say. He chose not to comment, however, and calmly Mercy explained her position. "You know I never interfere with your life. It's just that I'm very concerned about Jason. Awhile ago he was on the verge of tears. I saw it. It broke my heart."

"It breaks my heart too, Mercy." He took a deep breathe. "I promise you I'll never let that boy down. I love him too. I don't know how things will turn out, but I'll make you one more promise while I'm at it. Wendy and I have had a pretty good go of it so far, but you may be sure my first priority is Jason. Give me a little more time to try to bring Wendy around. That's all I ask."

While he was speaking, Mercy walked to the window with the cordless phone and watched Jason. He was standing, holding the ball, and staring straight ahead. "That sounds fair enough," she said, and after making arrangements for tomorrow, they hung up.

She got the rest of the meal ready for cooking; then she went to the door and called Jason in. She was glad to see he looked a bit better. "Your father will pick you up tomorrow morning. He'll have to bring you home after lunch, though."

Jason received this communication with a silent nod as she escorted him to the couch and sat down. "I've been so busy getting supper ready for Bill I haven't had a chance to talk with you about your day. What did you do in school?"

"Oh, the usual stuff. In science we studied the solar system. We learned that the inner planets—that's Mercury, Venus, earth and Mars—are solid, and the big outer planets like Jupiter and Neptune are gaseous. Jupiter was the planet that comet crashed into. We saw slides of it. And we found out if it had been just a little bigger Jupiter would have been a star."

"That's interesting."

"Yeah, it was. It made me think it'd be fun to be an astronomer."

"And not a musician? Music makes you special. You have a real gift for it, you know."

"I know. But my voice will change. They always do. I mean it, Mom. I don't want to sing anymore."

"Well, if you don't want to…" She looked over at the piano. Above the keyboard was some sheet music on which was printed in large boldface, SCHUBERT. "But your piano lessons, what about them?"

"Piano's okay. It's the singing I don't like." He looked up at her in sudden panic. "Please, Mom, don't make me go to choir practice anymore."

She stroked his blond hair. "I don't want to make you do anything you don't want to do. Your father will be disappointed, though. I'll have to argue the point with him."

"He doesn't really like the music, you know. He just likes it because I do it."
Mercy smiled at the accuracy of his perception, but she said, "That may be true.
But he certainly is proud of you."
She stood, feeling better that the conversation occurred. He seemed calmer now,
more himself. "Bill should be coming in half an hour or so. I've got to take a shower.
If he gets here early, let him in. Do you want to do homework or watch TV?"
"It's Friday, Mom. No homework. I think I'll do some stuff on the computer."
Upstairs she removed her clothes and went into the bathroom where for a moment
she stared at herself in the full-length mirror. She was forty-eight now, and in her
opinion she looked it. Everyone else she knew said she looked ten years younger and
that she was still very pretty. The center of her face was a freckled pug nose above full
lips. She had dark soulful eyes and sandy hair with touches of gray almost invisibly
blending in with the blondish strands. Thanks to the long walk she took with Hope
three mornings a week, she was still in excellent health and shape. Surveying her
naked body, she still felt the weight of years. If Bill, whose one undeniable merit was
prowess in bed, was not right, there would not be many more chances for love.
But she could still be a mother with Jason the center of her life, all else
circumference. The merest memory of how she felt when she saw Jason's faraway and
alienated eyes gave the lie to such externality. In ways she doubted even Hope could
understand, the intensity of her love for her son burned with the purest flame past all
understanding.
Even before his extraordinary musical talents were discovered, Jason was a
special child, a miracle, light in darkness, hope born of despair. In such terms was
Mercy ever prone to think of him, the reason being that for twelve years Brian and
she tried unsuccessfully to have a baby. Through those years of miscarriages, false
hopes, innumerable visits to doctors and specialists, an oppressive gray deadness
struggling for life was her dominant reality. At one time she tried to talk Brian into
adoption, but he was adamant in insisting that he was only interested in having his own
biological child. And it was during these twelve barren years that Mercy acquired the
skills in decorating and home renovations for which she became the acknowledged
expert among her family and friends. She learned all about painting, stenciling,
applying plaster to ceilings and joint compound to walls. She learned to strip and
refinish furniture so that their house, despite their relatively modest income, became
a treasure trove of beautiful bureaus, commodes, wardrobes, tables and cabinets. She
learned caning and refinished and recaned a magnificent set of oak chairs which she
had purchased at a barn sale. On weekends when Brian would go fishing or to sporting
events with his friends, she would drive through back roads all over southern Maine
to find and rescue old pieces of furniture at barn sales and estate closings. With her
brother's help she even knocked down a wall in their upstairs bedroom to make it
larger, then built a walk-in closet and connected the bathroom, which she also redid,
to what became the master bedroom. People said of her that not only could she be an
interior decorator; she could just as effectively be a general contractor. Plumbing was
the only building trade that she never undertook herself.
Those twelve fallow years could never be forgotten, not when the whole house
was a reminder of her desperate need for a child. There was nothing frivolous in
refinishing furniture or stenciling walls when the force behind these projects was the
longing for a baby. In the beauty of every detail pain lived; the enormous effort to tear
down a wall and redo a bathroom was an outlet for a frustration so intense that she was

often reduced to tears.

Sometimes when she marveled over how she could have lived through those years, in her mind she likened her condition of being childless and wanting with every ounce of her being to be a mother to being trapped in an underground cave where a rock slide had cut off escape and the air grew progressively staler and more stifling so that she could barely breathe. There, imprisoned in utter darkness without hope, she could expect only death for deliverance.

All that changed the moment she was pregnant with Jason. She took six months off from her secretarial job at a law office in Bedford and became so sedentary during the pregnancy that she and Brian joked that their baby would be a flower born of a plant, not a human baby. For sure when he was born he was as beautiful as the loveliest flower that ever lived, as beautiful and as fragile. Out of the cave and into the sunlight, she felt every minute of a joy so intense as to obliterate the full twelve years of pain. Breast feeding him was the deepest, most thrilling experience of her life. Her whole being, waking and sleeping, was filled to bursting with him. It was as if she were incomplete unless he gurgled happily at her breast.

As Jason grew and filled the house with his presence, the gain in love engendered corresponding loss. Inexorably Brian and Mercy began drifting apart. What had kept them together through all the miscarriages and barren years was the desire for a child. When the child came, when Jason was born and grew into a boy, both of them focused all their love onto him so that a day came when they found they had no love left for each other. In hindsight there were many signs of incompatibility—he liked to be with people, to have parties and gatherings; she liked to be alone and live quietly: he watched TV; she read: he liked meat with every meal; she had tendencies towards vegetarianism: he was Catholic; she Protestant: he grew conservative, even reactionary and racist; she was by inclination liberal and humane. The actual first sign of a problem, unrecognized at the time, came when Mercy wanted to name their son Kermit after Kermit Pingree, her high school sweetheart and the man she had planned to marry. He was killed in Vietnam, and on the rebound Mercy had met and married Brian within two years of receiving the terrible news of Kermit's death in the jungle. Mercy was surprised at the vehemence with which Brian opposed that reminder from the past. Heated words were exchanged before they compromised on the name of Jason.

The inevitable divorce was delayed a few more years by a wondrous discovery. First they found out he was very precocious. When she read children's stories to him, he was so interested in the printed words that she started teaching him to read and do rudimentary mathematics with the result that he went directly from Kindergarten to the second grade. Then the music teacher in the second grade discovered that Jason had perfect pitch, and from that discovery a whole sequence of events followed whereby Jason learned to read music very quickly and play the piano even more quickly, and he could sight read within a year of learning to read music. His voice was found to be a perfect boy's soprano and he began singing in the choir of the Irish Catholic church in Waska. Father Slipkowski, the associate pastor and choir director, even started comparing Jason to the young Mozart.

All this was very heady stuff for the proud parents, and nothing was spared in fostering Jason's talents. The piano they bought him and the music lessons caused actual economic hardship for them, but they did not care. Mercy even began going to mass each week to hear Jason sing. At the time of her marriage she had started to take instruction, but had found the priest so unctuous, pedantic and smugly assured of the absolute rightness of his beliefs that she had quickly dropped out, only promising Brian that their children would be brought up Catholic. Now she was in weekly attendance, though of course she took no part in the mass, only maintaining a respectful silence during responses and remaining in her seat during communion.

Both she and Brian took care to bring Jason up as a normal boy, one who played baseball, soccer and basketball, and did all the "boy" things. He developed a love of dinosaurs and had a large collection of books, models and posters to decorate his room. He liked fishing and being outdoors. Once or twice he got into fights with bullies who called him a sissy for playing the piano, and though Mercy and Brian sternly lectured him on the evils of fighting, both of them were secretly pleased.

They divorced when he was eight, Mercy getting custody and Brian having Jason for weekends, school vacations and a month in the summer. His musical career, though not able to save a marriage, continued to flourish. He even began writing songs and making compositions for piano. They weren't quite Mozartian, but musical people said they were good. Two years ago Father Slipkowski was transferred and replaced by Father Mullen, who had degrees in music and had taught it at a small Catholic college in the Midwest. He quickly concurred with his predecessor's opinion on Jason and new arrangements were made. Twice a month Jason was excused early from public school to have three hours of private lessons with the priest.

Much of Mercy's life after the divorce was absorbed in Jason, but she had had some half dozen relationships during the four years, most of them quite short-lived and none of them satisfactory. The reason for her dissatisfaction was never perfectly clear, but she did recognize that partly it was because in a secret place in her heart, and shared with no one, she regarded Jason as the reincarnation of her first love Kermit Pingree. If anyone who knew Kermit were ever to learn of this feeling, he or she might possibly laugh. In every surface characteristic they were opposites, Kermit being muscular, extroverted, a poor student, inartistic, a star football player at Courtney Academy, while Jason was introspective, brilliant, artistic and intellectually inquisitive. But no one except Mercy understood the secret of Kermit Pingree: he was a dreamer, and like mythic heroes and poets he had paid for his dreams with his life.

Someone had once told her in high school that the day after you die the sun will rise. She thought about that remark on the day she heard Kermit had been killed in Vietnam and for many days afterwards. Indeed, she really never forgot it; often she was haunted by the strange feeling that she was living a posthumous existence, that the life she had been meant to live had been stolen from her by fate. She hated this feeling and tried futilely to shake it off; ultimately she was able to master it only after she began seeing Jason as a continuation of the spirit of Kermit.

Of course in sober hindsight she saw that he would probably never have risen very high in the world. He was so focused on sports that he neglected his studies with his grades correspondingly reflecting that neglect. He would not have been able to go to college. But scoring the winning touchdown in the state championship game and thereby actually living his dream made him think dreams were easy and that they didn't require work to fulfil. But the most wonderful thing about him was that he did have dreams, dreams so real and so heartfelt that she was swept away by them. They were going to have a beautiful house with a white picket fence and a large backyard for their children to play in. They were going to be successful because life was like football and once you learned the rules your natural ability would make you excel. When he decided to join the Marines, he wasn't planning on being a time server. He volunteered for the front lines so that he could be a war hero, saving his squadron, perhaps, or single-handedly capturing a whole VC regiment like a modern-day Sergeant York. He got this stuff from movies, of course. They'd share these dreams parking on some back country road after making love in the back seat. He'd point to the moon where men had walked and say with a kind of breathless enthusiasm she loved, "We live in exciting times. Anything is possible." It was easy to see where he got this confidence. He was an only son, born late in the marriage of parents who worshipped him and concentrated all their hopes on him. Now those hopes lived on in Jason's music.

Even though she had lived beyond Kermit and his dreams and saw that he had the advantage of being forever young, still she measured every other man by his impossible yardstick. She knew, as the squabble over Jason's name had shown, that one reason her marriage had failed was the ever-present shadow of her first love. And most of the other relationships that had followed her divorce had been eclipsed by the same source. Frequently, though, real or imagined similarities with Kermit were all it took for her to be interested in a man. Such was the case with Bill Ricker. She thought the most wonderful thing in the world was human aspiration, the ability to project into a future yet unrealized but that could be glimpsed in a vision. Anyone who appeared to possess this divine spark instantly interested her the moment she perceived it. Her first impression of Bill was not, however, at all favorable. They met at a party at her brother's cottage on a lake up country. She could tell he was immediately attracted to her but something about the way his dark eyes darted about uneasily prejudiced her against him at first. Then later when an innocent remark led to a somewhat heated argument about feminism, he alone of the half dozen men there sided with the women. One of the other men had argued in that false, jocular way many men use in addressing this issue that women belonged in the home, and Bill had said as smooth as the polish on his sports utility vehicle, "I think a woman's place is wherever she wants it to be." Later he had argued that men should share the housework and that equal pay for equal work was the only fair way. These and like remarks changed Mercy's perception of him, and for the rest of the party they spent most of their time engaged in deep conversation together. Soon they were dating and getting along nicely, and soon after that they were sleeping together.

Bill was wonderful during the period when a couple is getting to know each other and each is on his or her best behavior. For two months their relationship played like a romantic love movie, filled with clichéd shared experiences like a walk on a moonlit beach and a rained-out picnic that turned into a high-spirited lunch in the steamed-up car. Almost always Bill would say the right thing on these occasions ("That moon's worth all the gold in China." "The importance of a picnic is who you share it with.") so that for a time Mercy was sure she was falling in love with him. But as summer turned to fall, little by little Bill began to reveal other aspects of his personality. On several occasions she found out he liked to have his own way, and when he didn't get it his face would momentarily flush with anger before being followed by a store-bought smile. Other times he would tell tasteless jokes about ethnic and racial minorities, and when Mercy would remonstrate, he would say with a shrug, "Hey, it's only a joke." In the meantime Hope began relaying to her rumors she had heard. One was that the women at the discount chain store where he worked as an assistant manager despised him as an arrogant, sexist pig; another was that after his divorce he had almost nothing to do with his three children. And despite the large capital he had gained on that first afternoon arguing for a humane, liberated view of the world, she found out that he was not really communicative. He never shared his real opinions on anything. He talked a lot about sports, politics, his work, but never about his feelings. Though he always projected a bluff and hearty bonhomie, Mercy was beginning to fear that he was a cold man, essentially self-involved. It was this conclusion that she wanted to test.

Still, she took time to dress carefully and attractively after her shower, donning a lavender V-neck sweater that accented her figure and dark hose under a tan knee-length skirt. A touch of perfume behind each ear completed her toilet, for she rarely used makeup.

She found Jason engrossed with his composition software on the Macintosh. He was composing a piece that sounded somber and foreboding from the snatches of it she could hear, but he seemed happy. "I'll call you when dinner's ready," she said, and that too seemed to please him. It was interesting, though hardly a coincidence, that he liked neither Wendy not Bill. She thought of Brian's remark about Jason being his first priority. That seemed right. He was hers too.

Downstairs she put on a CD of Schubert's piano music, knowing that Bill, who preferred rock 'n' roll, would not like it but that Jason, who was learning Schubert now, would. That too seemed right.

She went into the kitchen and began sautéing the boneless chicken breasts in butter and olive oil, turning the heat to low when they were almost cooked. When Bill came she would complete the cooking and add the lemon and spices as the pasta cooked. The pasta water was boiling now, so she turned that down too. Glancing at her watch, she saw that Bill was now officially late, but since one virtue he consistently maintained was punctuality, she expected him any moment.

Five minutes later a rain squall suddenly came up just as Bill pulled into the driveway. He dashed from his vehicle to the door holding his tan jacket over his head. Mercy held the door open for him as he ran in.

"Oh, baby! It's really coming down," he said by way of a greeting.

"Yes," she said with some coolness, "it's raining hard."

If he heard her tone, he chose to ignore it. He followed her into the kitchen and went directly to the refrigerator for a beer.

"I thought we'd have some white wine with the meal," she said, glancing at him from the stove. She turned up the heat on the burners for the chicken and the pasta water.

He crinkled his mouth disdainfully. "You know beer's fine with me." Before she could reply he cocked his head and listened intently for a moment. The sounds of Jason's music on the computer could be heard above the Schubert. His face dropped. "Hey, is Jason here?"

Without turning, she busied herself sautéing the chicken. "Uh-huh." She never let him make love to her when Jason was at home. She could feel his disappointment without even looking at him. This too was another test.

Bill sat at the table, noisily moving his chair to show his displeasure. "What the hell's going on with Brian anyways? This is the third time."

"I know. He's having trouble with Wendy. He tells me one way or another the problem will soon be resolved."

"Jesus, you'd think so. Does he realize how he inconveniences me?"

Mercy turned and glared at him. "I don't know."

After that the supper was not a success. Bill ate his chicken with the sullen air of one who had been grossly imposed upon, and Jason sat tiny and still at the other end of the table, refusing to even raise his head from his plate.

After the meal Jason disappeared upstairs, and Bill and Mercy went into the living room. He suggested they rent a movie, but he didn't put up much of an argument when she said she'd rather talk.

For a long time she listened to his troubles at the store. Some accounts weren't balancing, and if they couldn't get straightened out soon headquarters was going to send their own accountants in to look at the books. This made Bill very nervous because any black mark against him pretty much ruined his career as far as any further advancement. He railed against the company and the electronics department of his store (the main problem seemed to be there) for an interminable time, but after a while Mercy barely listened.

Finally after his third beer he suddenly changed the topic. "Doesn't your sister know Wendy? Don't they work together?"

"They used to."

"But they're friends, right?"

"I wouldn't call them that—they know each other, that's all."

"But maybe Hope could talk to her. Bring her around, if you know what I mean."

Mercy stared at him. He really had the most extraordinary notions. Hope was a part-time nurse at the hospital. She worked on Mondays and Tuesdays and sometimes as a substitute when one of the regular nurses was sick or on vacation. Years ago she had worked at the walk-in clinic where Wendy was a receptionist. From this tenuous connection Bill assumed Hope had influence over Wendy and her feelings about her boyfriend's son. Did he think women belonged to some secret cult? Did he have even the faintest idea how human relationships worked?

Thinking of these questions, she was silent for some time. Finally he prodded her. "Well, what do you think? Couldn't you talk to Hope?"

"No, Bill. It doesn't work that way. If Wendy got to know Jason, it might lead to something. He's an extraordinary boy. Most people know that."

Bill's eyes narrowed. "You're implying something, aren't you?"

She folded her arms across her chest and leaned back, feeling apprehensive. "Only this. I was thinking that if anyone should talk to her it's you. You feel about Jason just about the same as she does."

"Hey, I like the kid. He's A-OK."

"But you've never made any effort to be his friend. You regard him more as an obstacle than a human being. That's exactly Wendy's position."

Bill drained his beer and stood to get another one. On the way to the refrigerator he said, "Call Jason down here. I'll show you I like the kid."

Mercy could hear Bill stepping into the downstairs bathroom, so she went to the bottom of the stairs and called up to Jason. When he came to the head of the stairs, he looked apprehensive when she explained what Bill wanted. "It's just for a minute, Jason. Bill wants to tell you something."

Apprehension momentarily grew to the panic that she had seen earlier in the evening, but he looked at her with trusting eyes as he came down the stairs. "You'll be here, right, Mom?"

She put her arm around him and gave him a squeeze. "Of course, sweetie."

He sat on the couch nervously waiting. When he heard the toilet flush he started involuntarily and didn't seem too soothed when Mercy said, "Don't worry. He just wants to talk to you."

Bill, his fresh beer in hand, walked over to where Jason was sitting and leaned down, his hands on his knees and the beer bottle tilting precipitously. Jason made an involuntary movement that looked to Mercy's eyes like a cringe. Her stomach suddenly went heavy. She felt a surge in her heart and watched the two intently.

"So what do you say, Jason. Would you like to go fishing with me sometime? Bill spoke with fake bonhomie and was trying to smile and appear genial.

Wordlessly Jason shook his head.

Mercy started to rise. "What, you fish?"

Bill looked over his shoulder at her. "Sure." He turned back to Jason. "I know we couldn't go now, but later, or maybe some ice fishing next month when the lakes ice over."

Jason remained silent and stared at him with growing panic in his eyes. He gave an inarticulate shake of the head. He was unconsciously wringing his hands and drumming his foot.

"No? Why not?"

"I don't want to."

"But your mother says you like fishing. She says you're a normal boy, not just a musician."

Jason kept looking at Mercy with desperate, suffocating eyes that begged her to rescue him. His whole body, not just his eyes, communicated his šense of betrayal.

By now she was as tensed up as he was, but still Bill didn't seem aware of the effect he was having on the boy. "Come on," he coaxed, "just the two of us. It'd be fun."

"No! I don't want to!" Jason shouted.

Bill stood and turned away abruptly. His face clouded and for a moment she thought he might actually strike Jason. Trying to appear calm, he said to Mercy, "If the kid doesn't want to, he doesn't have to. I was just trying to be friendly."

Mercy wasn't looking at him. She was eying her son, wanting to hug him, comfort him, love him. She didn't understand his fear, but she wanted it to end for him. "Jason, I'm sorry. You can go upstairs now. I'll be up soon to tuck you into bed."

She had already resolved that later she would tell him she would never put him through such an ordeal again. Something was terribly wrong. Tomorrow she would find out what troubled him, no matter what the effort, what the cost. And at that precise moment the probationary circle that Bill had unconsciously been running was completed, and she forever shut him off from the center.

The rest of the evening passed most unpleasantly.

The Pupil

About a week after Jellerson learned the identity of the boy in the woods, he screwed up his courage for a return visit to the scene that had obsessed his mind ever afterwards. The road where he had been walking he found tiresome. Cars drove by going sixty miles an hour, kicking up dust and necessitating restraining Old Boy with a leash. Sometimes teen-aged boys yelled unpleasant obscenities, which Jellerson found beneath his dignity to acknowledge. Often it was hot and the glaring sun bothered his eyes. But before abandoning the road, he first took a walk across it to the woods on the other side as a kind of preliminary exercise. There he found a lovely brook meandering through pine forest so thick that only its banks, trampled by innumerable fishermen in search of trout, allowed easy progress. It was a good walk, a peaceful walk, a healthy walk. Back home, however, he realized that the panic he had felt on the day of witnessing was in danger of growing into a superstitious fear unless he faced it, and the very next day he resolutely turned his steps towards the woods behind his house and followed the lumber road to the ridge. As they got closer to it Old Boy became agitated, whining plaintively and keeping close to his master. In reassuring him, Jellerson found himself reassured. He got to the edge of the ridge without his heart quickening or his breath growing short. Before him was merely the nonhuman world, differing from his previous visit only in that defoliation from the advancing fall made the woods more open. They stood for some time staring down at the clump of small pine trees. Old Boy, seeing that no repetition of their precipitous flight from the woods was going to occur, even sat contentedly on his haunches as Jellerson scanned the area with his binoculars. He watched a band of chickadees accompanied by some titmice and a lone nuthatch for a while; then he descended the ridge to examine the area behind the clump of pine trees. He found nothing to either confirm or disprove what he had seen. There was nothing but dead pine needles and leaf litter, nothing but a tenuous memory of a fleeting moment. And doubt.

So he returned home to his pipe and sherry feeling that he had faced his demon, but still vaguely discontented that nothing had been vanquished. Perhaps that is why the next day he decided to take his walk along the road again. He was later than usual because he had to stay home to wait for the furnace repairman who was going to check out their unit to make sure it was ready for the winter. Thus the sun was already low in the sky when he and Old Boy, safely leashed, set out on the rough shoulder of the two-lane country road. He hadn't gone very far before a car slowed down and the woman driver waved. Reflectively, Jellerson waved back before recognizing his neighbor, Mrs. Turcotte. She turned into her driveway and stopped her car to get her mail at the rural mailbox. There she waited for him to walk the hundred yards to her.

"Mr. Jellerson," she said apologetically, for though neighbors they had never met face to face and had only occasionally waved to one another from their cars, "I'm afraid I've been a very negligent neighbor in welcoming you to the area. A half mile is no excuse. I'm Elaine Turcotte."

She extended her hand as Jellerson in turn introduced himself and said he was pleased to meet her. He asked her if she liked living up country, and she said, "Well, my husband had to talk me into it. I didn't want to at first. But now I love the peacefulness of it. And it's often beautiful."

Both of them looked across the fields to the low sun, which made everything, the trees, the bales of hay, the house, a kestrel hovering in the air, and above it the roseate clouds, everything both natural and man-made, luminous and exuding a contentment with the earth. Jellerson said that he too didn't want to live in the country at first when Hartley Academy closed, but with a sweep of his hand he added, "The peacefulness does grow on you."

Then they talked for some time about the neighborhood. The Turcottes' large colonial house was of recent construction upon land that in Jellerson's youth was part of the Colburn farm. He shared reminiscences of what the area looked like half a century ago when he was a little boy and would visit his grandfather's dairy farm, and she told him things he already knew from Millie—that her husband was a lawyer with an office in Bedford and that she designed catalogs for the same mail order firm his fellow parishioner at the Congregational Church, Cliff Dalton, worked for. He found her a pleasant woman, an attentive and polite listener, and best of all a proper lady, wearing a white open-throated silk blouse under a dark gray blazer, a neat gray skirt of a lighter shade than the blazer, hose and high heels, all of which apparently was her everyday wear. He approved, believing that the larger world should follow the example of Hartley Academy and have a dress code. He himself rarely wore a tie nowadays, but even in his rambles in the woods he never wore jeans or sneakers. Thus he was predisposed to like Mrs. Turcotte.

She also showed very proper social instincts by politely turning the conversation back to him after several minutes of listening to him describe the history of the land for her benefit. Without any sense of prying and solely to demonstrate that she took an interest in him, she asked him if he missed teaching.

He recognized the politeness of the question was analogous to asking "How are you?" and replied honestly but in a neutral tone, "Oh yes, that I do. It still feels strange that here it is the beginning of November and I'm not busy teaching, preparing for classes, dealing with students or getting them ready to take the SAT's in the spring."

"Yes," she said rather absently, "it must be quite an adjustment for you." She looked down at her mail, then surveyed the road behind Jellerson watching a car drive by before making eye contact momentarily. Hesitantly she said, "Did you say you prepared students at your school for the SAT's?"

"Yes. I did do that. Students who came to Hartley were of course hoping to get into good colleges and universities. We had a very intense curriculum to prepare them for the rigors of college, but some time ago—it must have been twenty-five years actually—we found that some students we knew were excellent scholars didn't always have their abilities reflected in their SAT scores. Often it was because they were unfamiliar with the kinds of questions and expectations of the tests. So I got a voluntary program together that helped coach the students. I'm proud to say it made a big difference too."

Mrs. Turcotte listened to his explanation attentively, though her face still wore the same expression of discomfort. "That's very interesting," she said. "You see, getting my daughter Michelle into a good college is my goal too. We're thinking of Bowdoin, Harvard or Yale. The trouble is, she didn't do as well as we hoped on the verbals in the sophomore year practice SAT's. You don't suppose—"

Jellerson, now seeing where her thoughts were leading, grew excited and reached down to pat Old Boy to collect himself. Quickly under control, he looked up and said, "Yes?"

"Well, I was thinking that you perhaps might like to…though I don't know if…" She smiled at her own awkwardness. "I'm trying to ask you if you'd like to tutor Michelle once a week, but I don't know if compensation would be required or if you'd be insulted. We'd be glad to pay any price to help Michelle get into a good school, you understand. But if you—"

He put up his hands and waved off her delicacy of feeling. "Believe me, Mrs. Turcotte, it would be a pleasure. No compensation would be required. You have no idea how much I miss teaching."

He spoke feelingly this time and could see the sympathetic light in her eyes that told him she understood. He felt immensely grateful to her for that understanding. Something like hope that he could make himself a new life after all lightened his spirits, and jokingly he added, "Of course your daughter may not be so happy. I always had the reputation of being a hard but fair teacher. Being an old dog like Old Boy here"—he reached down and scratched his faithful companion's ears—"I don't think I can learn any new tricks."

She laughed and politely said, "You don't look old, Mr. Jellerson. And discipline is something Michelle needs. She's very intelligent and does well in school—she skipped the sixth grade in fact, so she's younger than her classmates—but I do have to keep after her. And you'll find she has a mind of her own. I was an art major in college and Marcel was a French major as an undergraduate, but she's not interested in following us in the humanities. She wants to be a doctor."

He nodded his understanding of the situation without betraying any of his old-fashioned notions of a woman's proper sphere. When Mrs. Turcotte asked him if he would like to meet his pupil, he smiled and said he would be delighted. He strolled up the driveway and tied Old Boy to the wrought-iron fence by the front door while she put the car in the garage. The house was painted bright yellow with white trim and black shutters. On previous walks he had thought the colors garish—he himself had always lived in houses painted white—but with his newfound respect for his neighbor he revised his opinion.

Presently Mrs. Turcotte came from the garage carrying a large portfolio, which she explained contained preliminary mock-ups of the catalog she was working on, and further explained, mostly to his incomprehension, that the catalogs were actually done on computers but that she and her superiors still cut and pasted layouts while deciding on the look they wanted to develop.

She opened the front door and invited him into the hall. He just had a chance to glimpse the leather couch and chair and the luxurious rug of the living room before she called upstairs to her daughter. Only then did he become aware of high-pitched female voices giggling and talking excitedly, indicating that his pupil was not alone. It took a second call, sharper and tinged with impatience, for Michelle to come to the head of the stairs.

"Michelle, come down here, please. There's someone I want you to meet."

She turned and said something to her companions before descending. The person who appeared both surprised and dismayed Jellerson. He had expected a gawky, studious girl with thick glasses and found instead a poised young woman with hips swaying and breasts displaying their full maturity. She wore tight jeans, a yellow tank top that exposed her midriff and navel, and was bare foot. Though not really pretty, she had a pleasant, intelligent face, with dark eyes and hair, a large thin nose and a milky complexion. He made an instantaneous decision to concentrate on her face and avoid looking at her body, remembering even as he felt very uncomfortable and knew he showed it, that for years Millie had been telling him that young women dressed differently now and that he should not read into it any necessity to make moral judgments.

Mrs. Turcotte didn't seem to notice his discomfort. "This is our neighbor, Mr. Jellerson. He's a teacher, and I've asked him to help you prepare for the SAT's next spring. You remember we've talked about your needing to work on this. Well, Mr. Jellerson is an expert in the field and has offered to help. Shake hands and thank him."

She did as requested, though without any obvious signs of enthusiasm, and then, having shaken his hand, she stepped back to put distance between them.

"Your mother tells me you're a very good student," Jellerson said. He kept his gaze level, still not daring to be caught looking at her navel.

"I guess so." She sounded doubtful and turned to her mother, who was betraying signs of impatience.

"She gets straight A's, so I would say she's a good student," she said to Jellerson. To her daughter she added, "When would be a good time for you, Michelle? I think Wednesdays are the day you don't have any activities. Is Wednesday okay?"

"I guess so." Again the same tone.

In the cool air in front of the open door her nipples began to show. Jellerson, seeing them, quickly turned to Mrs. Turcotte. "Does Michelle have any preferences as to reading material?" he stupidly asked.

"She likes the life sciences. Is that okay, Michelle?"

"Oh, I don't mind. Anything is okay. We're reading *Silas Marner* in English now. I like it." She said this to her mother, only looking briefly at Jellerson. Afterwards she turned towards the stairs in response to a loud though muffled laugh from the bedroom. Her eyes searched her mother's for permission to rejoin her friends.

"Yes, I've got to go too," Jellerson said as if answering her mute plea to her mother. "Old Boy will be getting restless."

After Michelle safely escaped upstairs to her room and friends, the two adults made all the arrangements as to the time and so forth and then parted, though not before Mrs. Turcotte apologized for her daughter's lack of enthusiasm and friendliness. "I didn't realize she could be shy," she said. "Usually she's very outgoing and sociable."

"I quite understand," he said, folding his arms and regarding her with a knowing look that effectively hid his discomfort. "She's being asked to do extra work that she hadn't planned on. I'm not surprised that at first she's not enthusiastic. In my trade we get our thanks later after results are achieved. I hope that's the situation here. At Hartley we were able to add an average of a hundred points to both the mathematical and verbal scores."

With that they said their good-byes, and he and Old Boy walked home without completing their walk. Of course he had left unsaid the main thought in his mind—that he hoped very fervently that the next time he saw Michelle she would be more properly dressed. The thoughts that her casual and revealing clothing gave rise to frightened him in a way he dared not confront.

Such thoughts he was able to put aside as soon as he got home, for luckily time constrictions helped concentrate his mind. The chance meeting with his neighbor occurred on Thursday, leaving him less than a week to get ready. He located all his materials for teaching the SAT's in his file cabinet when he got home and spent all day Friday going over the papers, books and notes as he formulated a plan to fit his student's needs. On Saturday morning he and Millie went to the Maine Mall where he purchased a small blackboard on casters. He planned to use his first-story study as the classroom, and when not in use the board could easily be stored in his large closet. He also purchased two copies of the latest edition of the SAT preparatory book he always used at Hartley Academy. During the rest of the weekend he was unusually cheerful for the simple and obvious reason that he was pleased and happy to be doing work related to his profession again and because he was channeling all his thoughts into this serendipitous venture. For the first time in weeks he hardly thought of the boy at all. But Sunday night after they returned from an afternoon at Millie's sister's house, their daughter called and after that all his cheerfulness was gone.

It was gone because he talked to her.

The conversation took less than two minutes and came after Millie had talked intimately for half an hour. Saying good-bye and "I love you," she had ended by asking, "Would you like to talk to your father?" There was a pause while Millie listened closely, said "yes" twice after short interludes, and then handed the phone to him.

"Hello there, Beverly," he said with forced cheerfulness.

"Hi, Dad."

"Did you buy a new television?"

"Uh, yes. I got a nineteen-inch portable."

"It fits okay? You like it?"

"Oh, yeah. Thanks very much. It's great."

"You're welcome…Your place is very small, isn't it?"

"Yeah, real small. But the TV fits."

"Well, let me know if there's anything else I can get you."

"I will."

"Do you want to talk to your mother again?"

"Oh, no. We already said our good-byes."

"Okay, then. Bye. Take care of yourself."

"I will. Bye, Dad."

After he hung up he saw in Millie's eyes the exact gauge of his parental failure. She didn't say anything, but she didn't have to. The conversation was all-too typical of their interactions—polite and superficially friendly while both of them kept their distance. Every time he talked to her he promised himself that the next time would be different, and every time the next time was no different.

He was immediately depressed; the rest of the evening was the color of dead leaves, the taste of dust, and following it he didn't sleep well. At first he obsessed about the phone call, trying to think of ways he could have said something to open up his locked mind and express his love for her, but his inability to see any way to do this led him to start thinking about his equally inhibited relationship with his son Bennet. They received a letter from him last week, and something about it had vaguely bothered him. Now listening to Millie's quiet breathing, he saw what it was. Like all Bennet's letters home, the salutation said "Dear Mom and Dad," but this letter made clear that the face before his eyes as he wrote was Millie's, for he had unconsciously made this explicit when he wrote, "Tell Dad I saw Lawrence Carrington in Naples. It turns out his ship was in my squadron. He's been the same places I've been for the past year and I didn't even know it. He says he still remembers Dad as one of the best teachers he ever had and that he still loves Hartley Academy." Stupidly (he now saw) Jellerson's first reaction when reading this was not to see the slight implied in being addressed in the third person; rather he simply started recalling Larry Carrington—for he remembered almost all of his former students by face and by name—and reflecting that he was one of the last students he would have guessed would enter the military. In school he was small, quiet, studious and definitely not athletic. Other students bullied him. Jellerson recalled one time he had come upon the boy beset by two older boys and how grateful Larry was that he was rescued. It was only now, deep in the night and feeling lonely and small, that with a feeling of pain he realized his son's words conveyed a second message of continuing estrangement.

He knew he wouldn't dare write to his son Bennet about being hurt by his last letter just as he didn't dare tell his daughter of his love and didn't dare expose the priest as a child molester. Momentarily his mind rested, and he was conscious that the image of the nubile body of Michelle kept wishing to materialize in his mind, but he fought the impulse, though it fueled his self-anger as he berated himself for a coward. Millie was right last month when she said he had driven their two children away. He was a bad father, a conclusion that led to a further deduction: with human failings of such devastating proportions, he was no different than Father Mullen and therefore no better than him. He had no moral high ground from which to judge the man. He was purposely being hard on himself in reaching this conclusion, trying to spur himself to betterment; but even so it was an unfortunate conclusion because it opened avenues back to the nubile body of his new pupil. Now it was impossible for him to stop imagining her breasts and thighs. Like a man inadvertently exposed to a pornographic movie, he bore witness as his exhausted mind played him numberless scenarios of him exploring her body and her uninhibited responses. The intensity of his fantasies frightened him, but they were so powerful he couldn't stop himself. Is this how it started with Father Mullen? he asked himself. Even to pose the question seemed to imply the answer. He felt disgusted with himself, ashamed. No, he was no different than the priest. How could he say he had a restraint that Father Mullen lacked when his diseased mind pictured Michelle doing with him the very thing he'd witnessed the boy being forced to do? A year ago, a month ago, he could say that the priest was a perverted monster and he a respectable man, but no longer.

After that long and dark night the morning's light finally came as a blessed resurrection. Though demons do not willingly show themselves in the day, he still faced an inner struggle of heroic proportions. That he won the battle and was able to concentrate on his pedagogical preparations still came at the terrible price of narrowing his mind almost to a tunnel. For the first time in his life he was confronting the difference between rationally knowing something and having a gut feeling about it. He knew he was different than Father Mullen, but he felt the man was some evil Doppelgänger, the very sign and image of his fate. No sensible or sane idea he could muster could drive this feeling from his mind. Hartley Academy, instead of being the arena where his true self was expressed, had simply hidden his own nature from him all these years. He knew he would never molest Michelle, but he felt he was capable of it because he could visualize it so vividly. And so it was with every belief he ever held, the existence of God and the goodness of life, the cohesiveness of society and the indivisibility of personality—all were doubted, nothing was certain and sure.

And when the night came again, once more he was visited by demons, once again almost destroyed by lust and shame and self-loathing. Tuesday proved to be a repetition of Monday's inner battle, which once again he won, though at an even greater price. Thus when the night came he secretly took a sleeping pill, and whether from exhaustion or from its effects he slept the whole night through.

On Wednesday morning, however, he did not wake refreshed. Immediately upon opening his eyes he felt uneasy, and as the day wore on he became so tense he could hardly eat his lunch, and yet during the afternoon the tension built even more, so that he was almost shaking. Simultaneously time was unbearably slow. He both dreaded and wanted the moment to come when he would be alone in the house with his pupil. He saw the school bus go by at a little before three and tried to go over his lesson plan one more time. Then he paced for a bit and took several deep breathes to calm himself. It worked, at least a little, for when the door bell rang without his seeing her come up the driveway, he did not panic. Old Boy made one bark and ambled to the door, with Jellerson right behind him. Here was the moment, and it was Old Boy who made everything right. She was dressed slightly more modestly—she had on the same tight jeans but now a light grey sweater covered her torso. She greeted him politely when he said, "Hello, Michelle," and explained with a giggle she had walked across the fields to get to his house. Then she saw Old Boy and instantly turned her attention to him. She knelt down and patted him, murmuring little nothings to Old Boy's delight, and her face took on all the innocent sweetness of a girl. Instantly Jellerson found himself calm and in control of himself.

"He's an old dog, isn't he, Mr. Jellerson," she asked, looking up at him.

He smiled. "He is indeed an old dog. But he's a good one. His name's Old Boy. We called him that even when he was a puppy, so I guess he was destined to be an old dog."

She smiled back at him and said, "I wish we had a dog."

So for now everything was all right. He led her into the study and began by asking her a series of questions to get some sense of her academic capabilities while Old Boy settled himself in his wicker basket and went to sleep. Despite her focus on science, Jellerson was pleased to find his pupil liked to read. She'd read a lot of Dickens and Hardy, *Jane Eyre* and *Wuthering Heights*, as well as numerous popular novels for girls. "But I know," she said with a girlish giggle, "that *Tiffany Goes To the Sock Hop* is not great literature."

Next he had them do some sample SAT questions. She had been sitting very primly on his leather couch while he stood by the blackboard, but now as she relaxed he could feel the first nudging presence of the nighttime demons at the edges of his mind. He looked up from his book, momentarily making eye contact with her. Before his eyes returned to the page he saw her draw up one leg and rest one hand over her knee while her other held her book close to her eyes. A stab of panic like an alarm bell sounding in his mind told him to avoid the center of her tight jeans. He stared at the page before him waiting for it to cohere into logical form. There, just there. "You can usually eliminate two of the choices out of hand," he said. "Look at the example again."

She raised the pages even closer to her eyes; at the same time he found himself involuntarily stealing a glance at the forbidden area. Quickly looking back at the page in front of him, he read aloud:

> The prosecutor conceded that the accused man
> couldn't _____ between right and wrong.
>
> a. eliminate
> b. categorize
> c. discriminate
> d. extirpate

"Which do you think can be quickly dismissed?" he asked. "Remember, almost always two of the choices can be easily eliminated."

She studied the page for a moment, then said, "A and D."

"Good. That leaves 'categorize' and 'discriminate.' Which is right?"

"Doesn't 'discriminate' mean to be prejudiced?"

Jellerson nodded. "It can. It rather depends on the context. The more you read the more you get a feel for words. In this example does 'categorize' feel right?"

Michelle glanced from the page to him. "I don't think so. I think the 'between' makes it sound funny somehow. So is 'discriminate' the right answer?"

"Is it your answer?"

"If I was doing the test it probably would be. So yes, that's my answer."

"If I were," Jellerson said.

She looked at him quizzically. "What do you mean?"

"If I were doing the test," he answered. "'Were' is used for the subjunctive in English. But anyways, 'discriminate' is the right answer."

She giggled, reminding him of how young she was. "I would have gotten it right, but not because I knew the word." She put her hands behind her head and leaned back pensively. "Seems kinda silly."

She was a lovely girl, and her breasts, accented by her action—but he cut the thought off and with great effort managed to stay within the tunnel. He went over to his desk and got some papers. Glancing through them, he stopped and read something on the page, then said, "The prefix 'dis' can mean 'not, absence of, opposite of, deprived of, remove.' 'Crimen' is the Latin word for accusation. If you discriminate, you remove an accusation. You distinguish something from a fault. So 'discriminate' means to make a clear distinction. This is the positive sense. The sense in which it means to exercise prejudice is a derivative usage of the word. Do you see that?"

She nodded. "Sure."

"One disadvantage of concentrating on the science curriculum is that you aren't able to take Latin. I'm a great believer in every student studying the classic languages. Not only does Latin put English grammar in perspective for you, but it also helps in the SAT's because much of the verbal test involves what you young people call fifty-cent words, almost of all of which come from Latin and Greek."

She rolled her eyes ambiguously. "Well, it's too late now for Latin. My senior year is already filled with what I want to take, and next semester I have only one elective."

"Yes," Jellerson said, "I know that from your mother. But one thing we can do is something I used to do at Hartley Academy with students who didn't take Latin. One of my duties was to prepare students for the SAT's, so I made up these lists."

He handed her a sheet of papers and watched her for a moment as she glanced through them. "What they are are lists of Latin and Greek prefixes, suffixes and roots. If you learn them, you'll be able to figure out the meaning of many words just as we did with 'discriminate.' Let's look at another example. Look at the list of prefixes. See 'contra'?"

He waited for her to locate the term, then said, "If you know the word 'diction' refers to speaking, you could make an intelligent guess from four choices on the exam and choose "denial' if asked to define 'contradiction.' You see how it works?"

She nodded and leaned forward, studying the lists with undisguised interest.

After that example they did another half dozen, using the lists as a reference, and then the hour was up. He gave her her first assignment, which was to memorize the lists, and then dismissed her. Old Boy accompanied them as he walked her to the door. She leaned down and patted him before leaving, and the last thing she said before he closed the door on her was also encouraging: "Thank you, Mr. Jellerson," she said.

He went to the kitchen and put a casserole Millie had made in the oven as she had asked; then he got his cream sherry and ice and brought it to his study. He put the blackboard away, but before having his sherry and pipe he paced for a while. He wasn't sure, but his impression was that she was pleased with the session and found it valuable. And away from her friends, she was much more friendly and approachable. These thoughts brought a certain amount of relief, but he was still restless with the weight of his uncertainties. He had gained enough insight into his mental struggles the last three days to know that the tutoring was desperately important to him. If it worked it would offer him a way to escape the demons lurking in the dark forest of his mind. He was also aware in moments of clarity that what had unhinged him was witnessing the priest and the boy in the woods, but even that would not so oppressively be eating away at his core self-conception if he had not been forced to leave Hartley Academy and become the fish out of water that Monsieur Duclos had predicted he would be. Several times in his battles the thought of death as a relief had come to him unbidden. He knew, surely and instinctively, that he was actually struggling for his life, that if he didn't free himself from his doubts and recover his self-respect the only alternative would be to die.

Nevertheless he had gained something he could build on. He had successfully tutored his pupil for an hour in a professional and helpful manner. She had even shown signs of appreciating it. He decided, as now he sat down and lit his pipe, that if he were in a battle for life and death then he would fight to win. If insecurity and uncertainty dominated his mind and unhinged him, then he would work at ways to lesson the doubt, weaken the insecurity. Thus resolved, he was able to enjoy his pipe and sherry and to go on to enjoy a pleasant dinner with Millie as he told her all about the tutoring.

He even slept well that night without the help of a sleeping pill. The rest of the week went fairly well with only occasional episodes of dark fantasy, but on Sunday he received another setback.

He had determined that one way to start his recovery was to free himself from his social isolation. One step was already taken in his tutoring, but he also needed to expand his adult relationships. At Hartley Academy he had had a full social life. There were monthly faculty teas and frequent banquets, sometimes with parents and students, sometimes with alumni; the headmaster would have them to dinner once a semester; and with other faculty couples they would go to New Haven and Yale University for cultural events and sometimes to New York City. Even his monthly duty in the dormitory was a kind of social event. Since their return to Maine, however, their social life had been curtailed to almost nothing. They had gone by themselves once to a concert by the Portland Symphony Orchestra and occasionally they exchanged dinners with Millie's sister and her husband. With the exception of the after-church coffee socials and a few birding trips, that was the extent of their social life.

But since his isolation contributed to his brooding, and since Millie was enjoying her job too much to consider quitting it, he knew he had to find independently a life of his own, and he decided that the church offered him the greatest arena for this expansion. Perhaps, though, there was too much desperation invested in this scheme, perhaps he was too vulnerable to any slight, real or imagined, for this scheme not to fail. At the coffee and rolls social after services that Sunday, at any rate, he went out of his way to chat with Cliff Dalton, whom he had chosen as a likely candidate for friendship because he too was a trained historian and had written a book on the history of Waska. He thought that telling this man of his method of tutoring SAT's would impress him and win his respect. Instead he found that his doubts extended even to his intellectual beliefs, and after their conversation he felt like a foolish schoolboy.

Cliff, it turned out, preferred Saxon English and scoffed at Latin. One of the examples of what he called the idiocy of trying to impose Latin grammar on a Germanic tongue was the split infinitive rule. In Latin the infinitive was one word (he used the example of laudare) and therefore could not be split. To try to force English to follow this "rule," he said, was like trying to fit a round piece of wood into a square hole. Latin was a synthetic language that showed syntactic relationships by word endings. English, in contrast, was an analytical language, one that showed syntactic relationships by word order. Since the infinitive in English was indicated by the preposition "to," it was absurd to say one could not split it. "To easily split an infinitive took no effort whatsoever," he said to Jellerson, who of course did not appreciate the joke. Nor was he finished. "If you look at the great poets in English, it's mostly plain words from the Saxon they use because that's the language closest to the heart and to common life. Only pompous windbags use Latinate words when a simple English one would do." Here he provided an example. "It's absurd," he said, "to say, 'His proclivity for prevarication denoted a systemic personality disorder' instead of 'He was an untrustworthy liar.'"

Jellerson had heard such examples before. In the past he had criticized them for being absurdly exaggerated statements that no real person would use. But in his present condition he found he didn't have the wherewithal to argue. Instead he meekly acquiesced to Cliff's position and parted from him a beaten man.

He was morose and depressed following this failure, which meant of course that his doubts returned with increased ferocity and he had more bad days leading up to

Wednesday. But by his usual procedure of tunneling his mind, he managed to get by, and instead of dreading the tutoring session he looked forward to it as the one time during the week that he could be the teacher he was. Even here his tattered beliefs received yet another blow, though it came more as a discovery and didn't hurt so much as surprise him.

The lesson was going well. Safely dressed in a heavy woolen sweater and long skirt, his pupil proved to be every bit the first-rate student her mother had said she was. She had memorized the lists and got virtually every question right in the exercises they did. They next started some reading comprehension exercises, and here especially he was impressed with her quick and lively intelligence. Towards the end of the hour, however, and after he had praised her and told her he could foresee she was going to do very well on the examination next spring, she looked at him strangely for a moment so that he stopped and waited expectantly.

"Can I ask you something?"

Jellerson, deciding this was no time for a lecture on the difference between "can" and "may," inclined his head slightly, indicating she could.

"You keep telling me that the SAT's are important to get into a good college. My mother and father say the same thing. But…" She hesitated and looked at him, waiting for a green light.

"But?"

"Well, a lot of my friends don't really care about learning things. It's like you say. They want to get into a good college, that's all. But to me it's almost like cheating to do extra work. Does that make sense?"

Jellerson folded his arms and looked out the window. He felt vaguely uncomfortable. "How is studying cheating?"

"I don't mean cheating like that. I mean they want to know what you've learned in school, but if you can learn tricks to get a higher score, then aren't the ones who've got money to learn these tricks at an unfair advantage?"

He didn't know what surprised him more—her moral complexity or her naiveté. He could honestly say that he had never before thought of the unfairness of money buying advantages in terms of the SAT's. Once she said it, however, he instantly recognized what she was getting at. "Well," he said, carefully choosing his words, "it is an advantage. That's true. But you still have to study and make an effort. It's still you who makes the difference."

She nodded, though he could see she was pretending to accept his rationalization rather than really accepting it.

"What made you think of this?"

She smiled nervously. "One of my friends is poor. She can only afford to go to the University of Southern Maine as a commuter."

"She can still get a good education there."

"If that's so, then why is it important to go to a name school?"

He thought for a moment, feeling challenged by this young girl's inquisitiveness. The advantage would be the contacts made, but he couldn't bring himself to say this. "The school's reputation carries weight in the world," he finally said, once again carefully choosing his words. "It opens doors. And if your friend is a good scholar, maybe she could get a scholarship somewhere. I'd be glad to help her."

Michelle said she'd tell her friend of the offer, and then they got back to business and finished the day's lesson.

Later at dinner Jellerson said to Millie, "Michelle is really a remarkable young lady. Today she told me that she thought it was unfair that people who can afford to learn tricks to get higher scores are allowed to do it."

"Tricks?" Millie said, crinkling her nose. "What does she mean by that?"

Jellerson smiled, feeling good that he shared his pupil's insight. "Well, simply being tutored as she is to some extent is a trick according to her. And think of the implications. She never mentioned Hartley Academy, but it was a school dedicated to giving its students advantages to get into ivy league colleges and so forth, and it certainly wasn't a place poor people could afford."

Millie laughed, and when he looked at her with raised eyebrows, she said, "Her parents are progressives, aren't they? They've trained her rather too well. Before long she'll see the hypocrisy of their wanting her to get into a good college."

But Jellerson didn't see it as a joke. He was thinking of Michelle's friend, hoping he would get a chance to help her.

He also wanted to help himself, and on the next week he finally saw his way clear to do this. He was tutoring Michelle, doing readings this time. One of the passages was about Clara and Robert Schumann, and after they finished the workbook questions, Michelle mentioned that she took piano lessons and had had to learn "Träumerei."

"Do you play it well?" Jellerson asked.

She giggled. "No, not really. It's my mother's idea that I learn the piano. She wants me to be, you know, well rounded. And besides, I learned a long time ago that no matter how much I practiced, I would never be as good as Jason Buckley. At the recitals we have every year the rest of us just stand around and look sheepish when he plays."

Jellerson stared at her intently. "Jason Buckley? You know Jason Buckley?"

Responding to his urgent tone, she smiled nervously. "Everyone knows Jason. He's a musical prodigy. He plays music on the piano perfectly. He even writes his own music. Some of it's really good, my mother says. And he's the lead boy soprano at church."

"That would be the Most Holy Trinity Church?"

"Uh huh." She looked at him suspiciously. "How do you know Jason? And how come you're so interested?"

"Well, I don't know him personally, but as you say, he's a prodigy and I've heard of him."

He tried to act nonchalant, but he acutely felt the role-reversal of the situation. She, or her question at least, made him feel like a naughty schoolboy while she spoke from a position of authority. For he did have something to hide, and he could feel the blush come to his cheek at the same time he knew she saw through him. She seemed to have an instinct for ferreting out hypocrisy. But he recovered himself. "I saw him last month in a rather strange place and with a rather strange person, so I was curious. But let's go on to the next reading, shall we," he said in the voice of authority.

That strange person and the memory of that strange place haunted his mind after she left. That two people he knew in turn knew Jason Buckley didn't in itself surprise him—Waska was a small town—but that one of those two was intimately connected to his strivings for a new life and rebirth he took to be almost a mystical sign for him. For months and particularly during the last few weeks he had been struggling with ways he could free himself from his uncertainties. As he smoked his pipe and drank his sherry, with Old Boy, his coconspirator, beside him, it occurred to him that he would never be

43

free from doubt and would never regain his self-respect until he did something to help that boy. He couldn't in good conscience free himself while he knew a vulnerable and intelligent little boy was living in a hell of degrading bondage. He had been basing his inactivity on the legalism that what he saw was too fleeting and insubstantial to ever convict a man in court, but ethically a legal technicality bore no weight. He had to confront Father Mullen, he concluded.

He did nothing for two days, though he thought constantly of ways he could act. Then on Friday afternoon the phone rang. It was Millie. "Have you seen the evening paper yet?" she asked.

Her tone suggested something monumental. Guardedly he said, "No, it hasn't arrived yet. Why do you ask?"

"Father Mullen," she said and then paused dramatically, "has been arrested for child molestation."

The Priest

As he had been doing frequently for the last three days, on Monday afternoon Father Jerome Mullen was staring out the window of the parish rectory. Before him was a bleak November day of steel gray skies, naked trees and blanched lawn. To his far right he could see the traffic on Main Street moving slowly and the pedestrians, their shoulders hunched against the cold wind, going freely about their affairs and errands. They all looked innocent enough, but he knew that if he ignored the directions of Father Tombarelli from the bishop's office in Portland and walked among them and was recognized, they could quickly turn into a mob, even stone him as Stephen, the first martyr, was stoned. So watching them, he reflected that he hated every last one of them, and, further, that he hated Maine. It had never been home, never been a place where he could feel comfortable, though neither did New Jersey, the state where he was born and raised, nor Indiana, where he last served the Church. No where was there a place on earth that was home.

He thought of this without self-pity and in fact with some satisfaction since it verified his deepest belief about himself, that he was a stranger on the earth, that he was here as it were almost by accident—that he was really too good for this world.

A knock on the door interrupted his ruminations. He turned from the window and said, "Yes?"

The door opened. "It's me, Father Mullen." The speaker was Elaine Smith, the woman who did the cleaning and cooked lunch and dinner for Father Riley and him. A childless widow, she worked nine to six Monday through Saturday. On Sunday they were on their own. Father Riley generally dined with parishioners that night; Father Mullen usually either ate leftovers or bought take-out.

"I've come for your lunch tray, Father." She spoke with cold formality and avoided his eyes as much as possible. He in turn stared directly at her while she trained her eyes on the lunch tray. "Are you through with it?"

He kept staring at her, forcing her to look him in the eye. When she did, he folded his arms across his chest and turned back to the window. "Yes, you may take it away," he said, making sure to be just as coldly formal as she.

Her coldness, and particularly the way she emphasized "Father" as if he had no right to such an honorific, infuriated him, and for a few moments he glowered, clenching and unclenching his fists. The police last Friday had interrogated him with the same cold formality, some of them using the term "Father" with obvious contempt. It didn't matter, of course, for even had they been polite he had nothing to say to them. "So, Father, you like boys, do you?" "How many times did you abuse the boy, Father?" "Did you do it in the church?" "How long have you been doing this, Father?" To all their questions he had either refused to speak or had answered evasively in monosyllables.

At the remembrance of the cops' insolence, suddenly his anger surged with the ferocity of a lightning bolt splitting a tree. He would teach this silly woman a lesson in respect.

She was almost out the door when she was arrested by his voice. "Mrs. Smith, one moment."

She turned and looked at him before dropping her eyes. "Yes, Father."

"You're a good Christian, no doubt."

"'I hope so, Father."

"And you've been trained to respect priests and the leaders of the Church. The pope, for instance. You love the pope?"

"I pray every day for the Holy Father."

Father Mullen nodded grimly. Pointing a pudgy finger at her, he asked, "Can the Holy Father be wrong?"

"Of course not, Father. He's God's spokesman." She looked as if she wished to cross herself to punctuate the point but was frustrated by having the tray in her hands.

"So you agree God has chosen the pope?"

"Of course, Father." This time she frowned.

"And you agree that it is not for the likes of you to question what the Holy Father does."

Mrs. Smith's frown deepened, but otherwise she remained speechless.

"Well, then, just remember that God may choose others for his divine purposes, and you should reserve judgment."

Still wearing her frown, Mrs. Smith replied in a barely audible voice, "Yes, Father."

"All right, then. You may go."

Once alone again he stared out the window. He knew by her sullen frown that he hadn't vanquished her, but at least in the future she'd show more respect. For a moment he was troubled by the thought that he could only command external respect, but then he thought, what did it matter. So what that all of them—the cops, the people on the street, Mrs. Smith, even in a hidden, secret way his colleague, Father Riley—treated him with either open or barely disguised contempt? What were they but his grandfather again? Like that miserable tyrant, they also did not understand that ordinary rules did not apply to him. He didn't pick out the boys; God did. The world didn't understand, but God did.

God had been understanding him for a long time. When he was nine his parents, his sister, two cousins, and his uncle and aunt were all killed in a horrendous head-on automobile accident. The driver and passenger of the other car were also killed. He alone survived by ducking down in the back seat and having his parents land on top of him. His grandparents, his only living relatives, raised him after that. But whether because he somehow blamed the boy for surviving or whether because as an old man he thought he deserved freedom and rest from child rearing, his grandfather resented his presence in the house and in a thousand ways made life hell for him. When his grandfather was really angry, he would beat him; when only slightly displeased he would withhold his allowance; but the vast number of transgressions of the middling state were punished by confinement to his room. His grandmother tried to be kind to him, but she too lived in terror of the tyrant of the house and was unable to protect him. It was from her he gained his lifelong contempt for weakness and vulnerability.

Banished alone in his room throughout his childhood, one thing especially he learned—he learned how to survive by convincing himself that he was special and chosen. Even before he found in himself any particular talent or trait to justify this opinion, he could tell himself that God spared him in the car accident and see it as the proof that allowed him to endure his grandfather's tyranny. Sometimes he would even egg the old devil on just to display his independence and superiority. Then the priest who taught music at the parochial school introduced him to Bach, and it was as if a comet lit up the night sky. He had taken music lessons with his mother, who was an accomplished pianist, but he had been indifferent to the popular tunes and light classics she loved. With this priest everything was different. Music was exciting, and he had a special friend with whom he could share his discovery. The priest became his family, the music of Bach his mark of distinction. Because of the priest and because he already knew he didn't fit into the normal expectations of the world, he decided he too would become a father in the church of St. Peter. And because of J. S. Bach, who belonged to a different church and a different order of things, he would specialize in music. It was the music that allowed him to express that deep-seated feeling of being special; the priesthood would be the visible emblem of it to the world and to his grandfather.

Thus for him life was very simple: from his grandfather he had learned the world was filled with hate; from God he had learned he was special and had license to bring love into this world of hate. And for that, of course, the world hated him even more. He would not be surprised, not dismayed. He would show them! His only real worry right now was that they would defrock him, but that hadn't happened the last time in Indiana, so even on this score he was fairly confident. He was better than all of them put together, and he would prevail.

With this resolution, he sat at his desk and worked for a while on a manuscript on choral music he was writing, but not making much progress, he stood and paced before deciding to sit at his piano and play.

But first he examined his hands, raising them in front of him and splaying the fingers. He thought they were very beautiful and often admired them. They were impeccably manicured, with smooth, white and unblemished skin, and though pudgy (for he was overweight) the digits were long and elegant as suited a pianist. His aesthetic inspection over, he started playing, randomly at first but after a while Bach's The Well-Tempered Clavier became his focus. He loved the piece and played it often.

As he played he found himself thinking of the boys. Gregory Hanrahan was a small dark-haired boy in the choir who had a slight stutter that disappeared when he sang. He lacked self-confidence, however, and before every mass in which he sang his nerves had to be soothed. It was from this nervousness that their special relationship grew. His mother, a widow whose husband died in an industrial accident, wanted desperately to have her son grow in confidence and self-reliance after he became fatherless. Father

Mullen suggested he could work with the boy in private tutoring, carefully explaining to the mother that if Gregory could become a confident singer his psychic wounds would heal. The mother had agreed with this arrangement and was always grateful to him. Though it was she who brought the charges against him, Father Mullen imagined family members, and in particular an uncle of Gregory's who had long been hostile to him, were behind the affair. This uncle had once last spring made known to Father Riley that he didn't approve of the close relationship between the priest and Gregory, even hinting that there was something irregular about it. Whoever was behind it, however, Father Mullen did not blame the boy. He envisioned a scene wherein the poor child was made hysterical and forced to say things he did not believe.

As he admired the beauty of his hands on the keyboard flawlessly playing the C major variation, Father Mullen wished he could have a few moments alone with Gregory. He would soothe away all the mental turmoil and make the boy so grateful for his love that the charges would have to be dropped. He had a way with that boy and he knew it.

Of course love in a world of hate was a very complicated thing. Despite his deep adoration of Gregory, with his voice beginning to change Father Mullen had known for several months now that the day was coming when they would love no more. That is what led God to choose Jason for him. He too was adorable, though Father Mullen could not help but acknowledge to himself that he did not love him the way he had loved Gregory. To the latter he had never had to say that God would be very angry and wrathful if he told their secret to anybody, but for Jason he felt it necessary, even reminding him that God at any moment could take his life or his parents' lives away if He were displeased. But he certainly could sing like an angel, and as an angel was twice as lovable. Had this uncle of Gregory's—or whoever poisoned the boy—not interfered, the natural progression of things would have been for Gregory to disappear into the past and Jason to become the adored one. Eventually he would have seen that God chose him.

But it was not to be. The world of hate had meddled with and profaned a bright spot of beauty. The thought caused him suddenly to lose interest in the music he was playing. He stood and began pacing, and then tried working on his manuscript, again with little to show for it. He was staring out the window sometime later when he heard another knock on his door.

This time it was Father Riley.

He had made several visits since the arrest last Friday morning. Always wearing the woebegone expression of a deeply troubled man, he would come into the room, ask vague questions about Father Mullen's spiritual state and hint that he was available for spiritual consolation, all of which questions and hints Father Mullen would deflect. This time, however, Father Riley looked less woebegone and more determined. His jaw was set and he strode into the room like a man who was bent upon doing his duty. Despite his best efforts, however, his eyes still betrayed his nervous uncertainty, making Father Mullen smile contemptuously.

"What can I do for you, Father?"

Father Riley appeared to have rehearsed a speech, for he began in the artificial manner of an after-dinner speaker. "I wish to confer with you about the shadow that falls across our church, Father Mullen. I want to—"

Here Father Mullen decided to spare the poor man and interrupted. "What in particular troubles you, Father?"

He stopped in confusion, colored, then after a deep breath blurted out, "I'm worried about our church. The people are confused. During the weekend masses I was sorely tried seeing the questions in their eyes. I told them it was a sad time for our church and we must pray for guidance. But I did not know what else to tell them. We have to discuss this matter."

Father Mullen curled his lip and frowned. "Tell them nothing! What business is my private affairs to them?"

Father Riley's face registered shock. His lip quivered and his withered cheek, much to Father Mullen's disgust, twitched in agitation. "What do you mean, it's none of their business? We are a community. Of course it's their business. Can I tell them you are sorrowful and repentant? Would you like to unburden your soul in the confessional?"

"No!" he answered with an emphatic wave of the hand. "I would not. You are not my confessor, Father Riley. And I repeat, it's none of their business."

"Well, be it so," the old priest sighed. "But right now we could still pray together and humbly ask God's guidance."

"Humbly? Father Mullen sneered, "Why humbleness?"

Father Riley was a very mild-mannered man, so much so that Father Mullen had no real respect for him, but to his surprise the old man's face darkened and he frowned angrily. He took a step towards the door as if he were so angry he was going to storm out of the room, but he stopped abruptly and turned back. "Why humbleness, you ask? Because of all the gifts bestowed upon a priest, humbleness is the greatest. We serve humanity by interceding for them with God. To be in that position absolutely requires humbleness. It requires selflessness. We are here strictly and only to serve. *That* is why humbleness is so important. Remember your vows, Father Mullen." He spoke sharply and his face was still flushed.

"Well," Father Mullen said in a conciliatory tone, "I didn't mean any disrespect. You'll excuse me, Father. I really do wish to be alone." He turned his back on the old priest and looked out the window.

After getting rid of him he took his shoes off and lay down on his bed for a rest. He was a man who only needed four hours sleep a night, but because he slept so little he usually took a nap each afternoon if conditions and his schedule allowed it. However, he had been having bad dreams about his grandfather since his arrest and his sleep had been far from refreshing. So he lay on the bed trying not to fall asleep but merely rest, and he kept his mind occupied thinking about Father Tombarelli from the bishop's see in Portland. He had a degree in civil law and was in fact the lawyer for the diocese. Where Father Riley was a weak, pious man who hated to offend, Father Tombarelli could not offer a more striking contrast. He was a strong, imperious man. Father Mullen was actually afraid of him.

It was he who rescued him from the insolent cops. He came into the station extremely businesslike and authoritarian, and easily cowered the policemen by asking them if they had read Father Mullen his rights and had informed him that among those rights was the availability of a lawyer, then chastised them for their slovenly procedures when they rather sheepishly admitted their faults. But when he was alone with the lawyer-priest, it was his turn to be cowered. In the small conference room they had been given for a consultation, Father Tombarelli had said, "I haven't got time for details right now—in fact I will be returning to Waska next week to confer with you on the legal aspects of the case—but right now I want to know if the charge is true."

49

Father Mullen, staring nervously at the table in front of him, had answered, "That boy had a special relationship with me and—"

The lawyer-priest had cut him off. "I don't want an explanation now," he had said peremptorily. "I want a yes or no."

So Father Mullen had been forced to say yes.

"And the boy's name?"

"Gregory Hanrahan."

"Do you know if the family plan to sue in civil court for damages as well? The bishop will want to know this."

Father Mullen had said he did not know, whereupon Father Tombarelli had frowned at him as if he were dealing with an idiot and had said, "All right. We'll find that out soon enough, though I'm pretty sure you're going to cost the Church a pretty penny. Until I see you again what you have to do is simple: stay in the rectory. Don't talk to anyone, particularly anyone from the press. Do you understand?"

Father Mullen had nodded meekly. "Yes, perfectly."

After that they had gone to the arraignment and he was released on personal recognizance. Father Tombarelli had gone back to Portland, and Father Mullen had been driven to the rectory by a very troubled and silent Father Riley. Since then he had followed the lawyer-father's instructions, even doing him one better by voluntarily confining himself to his room instead of the whole rectory.

Then in reliving the time he spent at the police station, he fell asleep and had a bad dream, only this time Father Tombarelli was tyrannizing over him instead of his grandfather. He woke disoriented an hour later to another knock on his door. "One moment, please," he said while he hastily put his shoes on and tried to rub the sleep from his eyes. He expected it to be Father Tombarelli, come for the consultation, but when he opened the door he was both surprised and relieved to find Father Riley, still wearing a troubled look on his face, once more before him.

"There's a man who would like to talk to you, Father Mullen. His name is Samuel Jellerson. He says he saw you in the woods last month and you would know him."

Father Mullen scrutinized his colleague, trying to learn if any unpleasant information had been given to him. An image of a terrified face came into his mind, and despite trying to appear casual and indifferent he almost snorted. He saw a skinny bean pole with a craggy Yankee face that looked like the farmer in Grant Wood's American Gothic and remembered the man stared at him later the following week from across the street. Here were small potatoes, here a craven monument to human weakness. He felt positive glee in his misanthropy. Whatever else was besetting him, he was not afraid of this man.

"Well?" Father Riley said.

"Well?"

"Do you know him?"

"Never heard of him," he said airily. "Did he say what he wanted?"

"No. He just said it was urgent. He's not a parishioner. He's with Rev. Covington of the Congregational Church, though he says he wants to see you alone."

Father Mullen pondered for a moment. The minister would be there for moral support. That fit. A cowardly and weak man would not be able to initiate a confrontation by himself. Then he grew angry. This man, this Samuel Jellerson, had been discussing him with the minister. He felt positively sullied that these two profane, prying men dared to judge him.

"What? Two Protestants here to see me? What an honor."

Father Riley, responding to the sarcasm, colored. "Your beloved Johann Sebastian Bach was Protestant. You don't have to be contemptuous."

He smiled at Father Riley, thinking that the old priest was really getting feisty. "Yes, but Bach was a genius. These two I'm quite sure are not."

"They're human beings and therefore deserve respect. Father Mullen, I hope you are not yourself. These remarks do not befit you." While his colleague scowled at him, Father Riley continued, "But the question right now is, will you speak to Mr. Jellerson?"

Father Mullen, thinking that Father Riley had now clearly revealed himself as his enemy, did not answer at first. Then he looked at the old man and said dismissively, "Of course not. I won't speak to anyone I don't want to speak to."

Father Riley nodded slightly and left the room without a further word. It remained for Father Mullen to close the door of his prison cell himself.

Giving Thanks

Walt Pingree almost always woke up before four A.M. every morning. In the dark he would lie in bed thinking about his long life. The best times were when he worked in a print shop as a typesetter. The money was good. He liked the work and did it well. His son, Kermit, was a star football player for Courtney Academy, and his wife Eleanor was happy. Together they could still dream about owning a house. The world held possibilities, and that is why he now realized they were his best days. And back then there were things you could depend on—a place in society, a steady paycheck, leisurely weekends to unwind. Then computer typesetting came in and he lost his job and with it any hope of ever owning a house. A succession of poor-paying jobs followed—in a shoe factory, in the stock room of a department store, and as a delivery man. In those later days there were no possibilities anymore. So just as often as he relived his son's triumph of scoring the winning touchdown in the state championship game and remembered how he didn't feel cold in the freezing rain of a late November afternoon but only pure joy that flesh of his flesh, blood of his blood, was idolized by every citizen of Waska, just as often he remembered the bad times.

Like the day he was visited by a military officer who told him his son had been killed in Vietnam.

Like the two years before he was eligible for Social Security and he couldn't find any work and Eleanor had to get a job doing clerical work for a charity at little more than minimum wage and sometimes they had gone hungry.

Like the day Ellie was sitting in her chair and had suddenly froze. She started to raise her arm, but it stopped, quivered and fell, and she followed it down dead from a stroke.

Like the lonely days that followed and the deterioration of his body. His sight, his hearing, weakened and failed him. He was stiff and sore all the time and when he first walked in the morning his bones snapped like the drum section of a marching band. It made him sometimes wish he didn't have to lie in bed and think about the good and the bad times of his life.

This morning he thought about that touchdown and his wife's death and many another bygone day, but he also thought about the argument he'd had yesterday with Tom Belcher. They argued often, and with such gusto that it wouldn't be too much of a stretch to say they enjoyed it. But this time Belcher had gone too far. He had hit him below the belt. It began with another discussion about the local priest accused of sexually molesting a young choir boy. The story had been in the papers for over a week, and Belcher had already become obsessed with it. Everybody knew he was a gossip and a busybody. He had elaborate theories about the identity of the boy and the motives of those who made the accusation. Yesterday, though, a letter to the editor by a supporter of the priest had led Belcher to the conclusion that the priest was an innocent victim of an insidious plot hatched by the Protestant clergy of the town, an idea that Pingree thought stupid. That led Belcher to opine angrily that it wasn't stupid at all. All you had to do, he said, was accept the fact that Catholic priests simply didn't do such things.

"Catholic-smatholic," Pingree scoffed. "The guy's a man. He's as liable to sin as anyone else—probably more so since he's put in such an unnatural situation."

Belcher's face grew darker and darker as he listened. He didn't like to be contradicted. "What do you mean, 'unnatural'? He's serving God. That ain't unnatural."

So off they went. In no time they were shouting so loudly that Foss, the landlord, finally had to tell them to pipe down, though not until Belcher got in one final zinger. Pingree's argument was based on certain assumptions about human nature, but Belcher discounted them by saying, "What do you know. You're nothing but a lonely old man."

He might as well have kicked him in the you-know-whats. Pingree had felt his face grow as red as Belcher's nose habitually was. Even now, thinking about it fifteen hours later, it still felt like a slap in the face. "I am not. You have no right to say that!" he'd shouted then and repeated now in an angry tone.

Then, feeling that to talk to oneself rather proved Belcher's point, he quickly retreated back into his thoughts. It was the saying of it that he resented. He resolved to be standoffish to Belcher in the future. At some point Belcher might begin to understand that there was some things you didn't say.

It was still dark, but thinking about the argument was making him too restless to stay in bed. He leaned over and felt for the light on his bed stand. He almost knocked it over in his fumbling before finally snapping it on. He swung his legs to the floor and stood. It was cold outside the covers, and he shivered in his sweatshirt and long underwear. Quickly he donned a woolen shirt, his trousers and boots. Next he walked over to the radiator and felt it, but it wasn't news that it was cold. Murray Foss was a cheapskate when it came to heat. He turned it way down every night except in the coldest weather. The middle of November, though, was no time to pamper the tenants.

Now dressed and feeling warmer, Pingree stood by his bed and tried to collect his thoughts. Stiffly he walked over to the window and then back. He did this several times, trying to work the stiffness out of his bones. His walk was of necessity constricted, though. He lived in a one-room apartment, the type classified ads always described as an efficiency.

One wall had a sink and small counter with a hot plate and a toaster on it. Above was a double cabinet in which he kept his few plates and utensils and the canned goods he mostly ate. A small beige refrigerator was shoved up against the counter. On the other side of it was the door leading to the hall and downstairs. In front of the counter was a small, square wooden kitchen table and one chair. The other chair, one with a rickety back leg, was propped against the wall near his one window. The paint in his place was in pretty good shape on the walls but the ceiling had numerous brown stains, some of them quite large, from when the roof leaked a couple of years ago.

Most of the furniture came with the room. The antique inlaid chair against the further wall opposite the door that Eleanor had loved, that was his. And the TV and its metal stand were his too. Furnished apartments never included a television of course. But aside from these two things, the rest of the stuff was Murray's. Pingree had sold off all his stuff years ago.

The bureau against the same wall where the antique chair was had an attached mirror. On one corner of it was taped a picture of his son in his soldier's uniform, and a gold-framed wedding picture of him and Ellie leaned on the surface. It showed him looking distinctly uncomfortable in his thin lapelled suit and Ellie with her yellow hair in a bun under her wedding bonnet smiling happily. He kept some of Eleanor's things next to the picture, a small jewelry case, her hair brush, a sewing kit. They helped him remember, even though he always remembered, always carried her and Kermit with him. It was just that he was afraid he would forget.

Once he had walked the stiffness out of his bones as much as possible, he went to the sink and put his false teeth in. He had lost a lot of weight during the last ten years, and they did not fit very well. That in turn made eating certain foods difficult and so he lost more weight. He couldn't afford a new set, though. It was just one more thing he had to put up with. He thought about that as he went out into the hall to use the bathroom. He shared it with his neighbor, a young man named Gene Leterneau who always seemed to have money even though he didn't seem to have a job or any obvious source of income. Belcher thought he was a drug dealer, but he had no evidence.

Back inside he left the door unlocked.

He got bread from the refrigerator and put two slices in the toaster. He reminded himself to watch them carefully since the machine had long ago stopped working automatically. He made a cup of coffee from hot tap water and powdered coffee. He flavored it with a teaspoon of sugar and powdered artificial cream. He preferred real milk but had run out of it. He could only keep a quart because it spoiled too quickly. He told himself to remember to get some milk when he was shopping later. Then he smelt the burned toast and realized he had forgotten to concentrate. He scraped the blackened parts off and then thickly spread raspberry jam over the salvaged bread. He turned the TV on and sat down close to it to accommodate his weak eyes. He ate his breakfast and sipped his coffee, only half listening to a discussion of events in faraway China. He would go shopping later. He had to plan for it. He had to do it carefully. He had to buy what he needed without anyone getting suspicious. He needed to think of several other items. The milk, yes. Bananas if they were cheap. A can or two of beef stew. Maybe some soup and crackers. The frozen turkey dinner had to be lost in the midst of those other items. But the other items had to be things he needed. He couldn't waste money. In his wallet he had over twenty dollars. He could afford these things.

His thoughts were interrupted by a knock on the door, followed by Murray Foss busting in. "Here's the paper, Wally. Did you see the Celtic game last night?"

Pingree frowned and muttered an affirmative. He'd lived here eight years and had never got used to the way Foss knocked and entered. Once he'd brought it up, but Foss had just shrugged and said, "It ain't like you're on top of a woman when I come in. Besides, you could lock the door." The trouble with that was Pingree didn't like the door locked. It made him feel isolated, stifled. At the same time he didn't like Foss busting in unasked. He wanted it both ways.

But except for this flaw and the penny-pinching business with the heat, Foss was a pretty good landlord. Saving the paper for him was just one of the extras he did. He'd illegally run the cable TV up to Pingree's room so that his TV got the cable channels. He also kept the rent low for him and Belcher. He only raised it for new people who came and went in the other three apartments.

Thus Pingree never let his frown linger. "Yeah, I saw it. Can't say I heard much of it, though, what with Leterneau playing rock music all night. But they're pathetic, ain't they? Wish they still had someone like Bird."

"I've talked to Leterneau about the loud music. He's a young buckaroo so it's like talking to air." Foss rubbed his stubbly beard and cleared his throat. "Bird wouldn't make much different with this crew," he added emphatically, and they went on discussing the shortcomings of the once mighty Celtics and the virtues of the up-and-coming Patriots for the next fifteen minutes. Before they could get to the Red Sox, though, Foss had to leave to go to his daughter's house. "Hafta fix a leaky faucet—gotta pay for Thanksgiving dinner, you know."

Pingree nodded and felt his face redden. He was perfectly aware that today was Thursday, one week before Thanksgiving. "Okay, thanks for the paper," he managed to say.

Once alone, he set the newspaper flat on the table and got out his magnifying ruler so that he could see the print. He didn't start reading, though. Instead he thought back to the time three years ago when he'd helped Foss redo the upstairs bathroom. Mostly he was a gofer and assistant—sanding copper pipes with Emory cloth to get them ready for Foss's soldering, things like that. For his help he got a week's rent free, so that even though he never actually saw the money it was still the last time he had earned his way in the world.

His eyes glanced over to the bureau. In the third drawer down, hidden under some old shirts and pants, were Eleanor's engagement and wedding rings. They meant a lot to him, but not so much that if he ever needed to raise money to buy a new TV or whatnot, he was prepared to sell them. For sure he would never work again. You could say those rings allowed him to read the paper without feeling depressed at the ads for things.

Just as he finished with the paper he heard a loud knock on the door. He thought it was Belcher and quickly decided that he would forgive him—if he was abject enough, that is. But it was only Leterneau. He was going to use the shower and wanted to make sure Pingree didn't need the bathroom. After that he felt a bit disappointed, lonely even. He moped around for a while, then from nine to ten he watched one of the local talk shows he liked on TV. After it was over, though, he was still a bit lost. Usually this was the time he would go downstairs and talk to Belcher and, if he was there, Foss. In the summer they'd go to one of the benches on Main Street, and in the winter they'd just sit in the hallway. It was big and had comfortable chairs. But Foss was gone and he certainly was not going to be the first to talk to Belcher. Later he was going to do the grocery shopping, but that was his afternoon task.

He flipped through the channels on the TV but found nothing to his liking. He

tried the radio next, but the sports talk show he sometimes listened to was yapping
away about the Bruins and he didn't like hockey. It too got flipped off. He would read
the Bible, he decided. It was something he had been doing daily for the last two or
three years. In the past he was never what you call a religious man. He still wasn't, but some
changes were happening. Ellie used to get him to go to church occasionally, but after
his son died he'd never gone again. The only time he had prayed through all those years
was at Thanksgiving, and at first that was only to humor her. She always maintained
that she felt Kermit's presence on that day and she would pretend he was with them
and gave thanks to God accordingly. Somehow her fervor started convincing Pingree,
or at least a little bit. The rest of the time, though, he was angry with God. Then
three years ago a fundamentalist had knocked at his door. More than once he'd sent
Mormons and Bible thumpers packing, but this young man was different. He was shy
and seemed almost reluctant to make a pitch, yet he was sincere and had an honest
face. His yellow hair and freckles, in fact, reminded Pingree of his own boy. Even
so, he didn't give the young man much satisfaction, but he had accepted a large-print
Bible from him and promised to read it. Ever since he had too. He read for about half
an hour every day.

The bible (it was the King James Version, the book of his childhood) had one
of those indexes with headings such as "When You're Lonely" or "When You Have
Doubts," followed by a list of passages you could read. These two categories of the
fifteen or so listed were in fact Pingree's usual reading. This time he saw the Twenty-
Third Psalm under the lonely category and turned to it. The Lord is my shepherd...He
restoreth my soul...Yea, though I walk...surely goodness and mercy...dwell in the
house of the Lord forever. The words were so familiar he hardly had to read them. But
he did read them. Three times and aloud.

He got up and walked to the window. His building was about half a block from
Main Street, and he could see cars and pedestrians going about their affairs. That is to
say he could see their hazy shapes with his weak eyes and filled in the rest from his
memories of the days he was young and one of the people going about their affairs.
Was the Lord his shepherd? That wasn't so obvious as the people and cars he could
see, nor even as obvious as his memories. What would he do, he thought, if Belcher
didn't apologize? He felt almost scared. But another voice asked him what he would
do without the remaining scraps of his pride?

No, he wasn't going to take the first step. Belcher owed him an apology and would
be his enemy until he did. Come what may.

Still there was not silence inside. Yet another voice would be heard even though
he tried to resist it. He wanted to believe that he was in God's hands, but the inner
voice kept asking, If God looked out for you, would you feel this way?

Faith and doubt. An old man wasn't immune, he had discovered. He would keep
reading and maybe some day he would find peace. But enough for now.

He went back to the television and turned it on. He watched some old comedies
until noon, then had a can of soup and some crackers for his lunch, followed by a
nap.

He didn't really sleep. Instead he planned his shopping trip. The afternoon was the
least busy time at the store. So at two he got his cloth bags with the shoulder straps out
of the cabinet, put on his coat and hat, and went out.

Downstairs he saw Belcher sitting in one of the chairs. His enemy was peering out one of the narrow windows on the side of the door. The single word "busybody" formed itself in his mind. He bristled. Belcher would want to know what was in his bag when he got back. He wasn't going to find out.

"Going out?" Belcher asked.

"What does it look like?" Pingree replied angrily. He swept past his enemy with his mouth set in cold determination and his eyes staring straight ahead.

"My, aren't we huffy still," Belcher said.

Pingree turned at the door. "I'm minding my own business. You can call that huffy if you like. It's no skin off my teeth."

Belcher said something but the door slammed on his words. Outside it was cold, and he stuffed his hands in his pockets as he slowly walked the three blocks to the in-town shopping center where the grocery store was located.

A few random flakes of the year's first snow storm were falling, an observation that brought no joy to his heart. He had to walk even more carefully, that's all. Last year he'd slipped on some ice and broken his wrist, and the doctor told him his bones were brittle. The result was that he'd spent much of the winter cooped up in his room like a pigeon in a cage. The thought was unpleasant, and to get it out of his mind he forced himself to go over his shopping list again. His twenty-three dollars was the boundary. Bananas if they were cheap, milk, cans of soup, a can of beef stew, two if they were on sale, crackers, bread and the frozen turkey dinner—they all wouldn't come close to eating up all his money. He could get another frozen meal. That would be better. He could put it on top. The spaghetti dinner, maybe. He thought these thoughts and watched where he was going. One step at a time. Where the snow covered the pavement he stepped gingerly. On bare sidewalk he walked with more confidence but still carefully. At the street crossing he stopped. Cars more than a hundred yards away were just blobs of color. He had no confidence that he could judge their speed. He waited until the street was clear for over a block each way. At the next crossing he could see the green light that he knew said WALK. He looked both ways and crossed.

The in-town shopping center used to be a field where he played baseball as a boy. Where he walked now with the slow, shuffling gait of an old man he used to race like the wind to shag fly balls. The thought reminded him of a poem. A boy's will is the wind's will. He had to memorize it in the eighth grade. He forget the rest, forgot the title, the author, remembered only a boy's will is the wind's will. Sometimes it amazed him that his eighty-three year old mind was still throbbing with the same life as that long-gone boy. In his mind he could still grab his glove. It was his decrepit body and weak eyes that failed him.

Suddenly a car door opened and he almost walked into it. He had been unable to see someone was in the car he was passing in the parking lot.

Sorry," a man's voice said.

Pingree nodded and hurried away feeling embarrassed. There was his mind wandering again—and just at the time he should be concentrating. Thus chastised into awareness, he entered the store and got a cart. More people were shopping than he expected, and he found the going slow. Basically he relied on memory to know where things were, but since he had to put his face right next to the shelves to see the prices, he often had to wait for other shoppers to move out of the way. Besides, he didn't like people observing his poor vision. Sometimes he tried to wait for an entire aisle to be empty. His plan being to get the frozen dinner last, he had begun in the produce section. Apples were on sale, so he got them instead of bananas. Next came the canned goods. He had trouble finding the beef stew and spent quite a lot of time here. From the canned foods he went to the dairy case to get a quart of milk, and then he got bread and crackers. He was just proceeding to the frozen food section when he was arrested by a familiar voice.

The voice that said, "Walt, how are you," belonged to Mercy Harmon, the girl who had been engaged to his son.

For a year or two after his son's death they were very close before she started finding a new life and drifted away. Even for another year or so she was still very friendly and treated Ellie and him like second parents, but the visits started becoming rarer and then stopped altogether. She got married and had a son. The years passed and now he only saw her on the street or, like now, in the store every few months or so. And whenever he did see her he saw two Mercy Harmons. He saw her as the slender, winsome girl with the shy smile and gentle eyes, and he saw her as the careworn, middle-aged divorced mother who was struggling to bring up her son alone. This double vision always had the effect of making him feel disappointed and cheated. It always gave rise to painful thoughts and made him think sometimes that it would have been better if she had moved away and disappeared into memory. Right now seeing her made him think that if Kermit were alive he would be having Thanksgiving dinner with him, Mercy and his grandchildren next week instead of—

But he cut the thought off. "How have you been, Mercy?" he asked as he moved his cart out of the way of another shopper.

When she answered "fine" in a flat tone totally lacking in conviction and told him she was here ordering her Thanksgiving turkey, he blushed. He was glad he hadn't gone to the frozen food section yet. "Hope the snow holds off," he said for lack of anything else to say.

"Yes," she said, then looked him in the eye. "I often think of him. Especially on August seventeenth and on the holidays."

Pingree nodded understandingly. August seventeenth was the day Kermit was killed. "He was a good boy," he said softly, hardly realizing that if his son were alive today he would be in his late forties. For him his son would forever be the one who scored that touchdown and then, wanting to serve his country, volunteered for Vietnam.

"And he would have been a fine man," Mercy repeated, making Pingree realize his mind had wandered.

"Oh yes, he would," he said quickly. He saw that she was turning her cart. "Well, take care, Mercy."

"You too, Walt. And oh, Happy Thanksgiving."

"You too," he said to her turning back. He watched her until she disappeared down an aisle, then he headed for the frozen food section. He picked out the frozen turkey dinner and the spaghetti, which he carefully placed on top of the former, then headed for the express lane. He was tense, but the woman behind him leafed through one of the tabloids and the checkout lady was efficiently indifferent to what he bought. He packed his two cloth bags himself, carefully distributing the weight. Even so, the bag with the beef stew began hurting his shoulder before he got out of the parking lot, and in two blocks both his arms became very tired. He had often thought about buying a small pushcart, but the cheapest one he could find in a catalog Foss had was over twenty-five dollars. So he put up with tired arms and sore shoulders. For after all, an old man had to put up with such things. It was his lot in life.

Back at his building he was prepared to run the gauntlet when he went through the door, but Belcher was not at his post. Over by his door Pingree could hear the sounds of the TV and Belcher moving around, but when it sounded as if he might be walking toward the door Pingree quickly turned and went upstairs. He unpacked his groceries, then sat down feeling exhausted by his excursion. He felt lonely too, so he turned on the TV for companionship. He found some golf match from Australia on one of the sports cable channels and fell asleep in his chair before it. When he woke it was past five o'clock and time for supper. He had the can of beef stew, which he served over some minute rice, and an apple. After he cleaned things up he thought about Belcher. He hoped he'd come up, but an hour went by during which time he watched the news and still he was alone. For half an hour he paced to and fro in his narrow room arguing against his heart, which wanted to let bygones be bygones and go down to Belcher. But he prevailed. "No," he said aloud finally. "No, no, no."

He walked over to the bureau and picked up the wedding picture. He held it close to his eyes so that he could see her clearly. He kissed her. "Ellie," he whispered, "I wish you were here." Then tenderly he placed the picture back on the bureau and moved his face close to the picture of his son. "I liked you better in the football uniform," he said, still whispering. He remembered again that glorious touchdown. He remembered how Ellie felt when he hugged her, both of them filled to the brim and overflowing with happiness. He remembered how he didn't feel the wet chill of the late November day. He remembered it all as if it had happened yesterday.

And with that he went to the counter and fixed himself a cup of powdered coffee, this time using real milk. He sat before the TV and watched a Thursday night college football game on cable, all the time remembering other football games when he and Ellie watched their boy together.

Then the game was over and it was time for bed. He undressed, crawled into bed and turned off the light. Yet one thing remained to do. An old habit of mind taught to him by his deeply religious mother was to go over in his mind what he had accomplished in the day. Of course this part of his Calvinist heritage had been whittled away in the descending years. In place of the category of new things he had learned he more often than not thought of things he still held on to. But the habit persisted so that just as he relived his life when waking in the morning, he tried as he fell asleep at night to integrate whatever had come his way during the day into the entire journey of his life. Now that he was safely alone in bed he could derive satisfaction from one particular piece of work he had done today, and done so secretly and yet so openly that he almost chuckled out loud just thinking about it. That old coot Belcher didn't have a clue. Tomorrow when they made up (he was suddenly quite sure they would) he still wouldn't have a clue.

In the freezer compartment of his refrigerator his Thanksgiving dinner awaited him. When he ate it he would pretend Ellie and Kermit were with him (just as they were tonight) and together they would give thanks for all their blessings. For he had blessings. He had things to give thanks for. That touchdown his son scored. The memories of his life with Ellie. As long as he could hold on to these things he would never be completely lost. His room and his life were empty but love peopled his mind. The first blessing, then, would be that his mind was still strong.

And the second blessing? That was the best one of all, that an old man could defeat time.

Finding Out

The news literally staggered her since upon hearing it she stepped back and momentarily lost her balance. At the same time a heavy dread sank to her stomach and her heart started racing.

"But I'm not saying that proves anything," her sister said as she stood from the kitchen table and nervously began pacing.

Mercy begged to differ. Hope had just told her that she saw in the evening paper that Father Mullen of the Most Holy Trinity Church in Waska, Maine had been arrested for child molestation. Instantly she understood everything that had been happening to Jason for the past month, his sleeplessness, listlessness, moroseness and isolation, and every atom of her mother's body ached for him. Last week when she received a phone call from his teacher who told her that inexplicably Jason was losing interest in his schoolwork, she was still able to say that she had observed his behavioral changes and was much bothered by them but that she attributed them to a delayed reaction to her and Brian's divorce. Now she realized that she was really hoping that was what lay behind his personality changes—for she saw clearly that a deeper knowledge of her son had been telling her something more was at work.

She was staggered by the news of Father Mullen's arrest, then, because the news came to her as knowledge already possessed. She remembered how reluctant he was to go to choir practice and how twice on the Wednesdays when he had his private lessons with the priest he had told her he was sick those mornings so that he didn't have to go to school. She brought these facts up with Hope now. "He's been trying to avoid Father Mullen for the past month. I'm afraid now that the reason is obvious." Tears rimmed her eyes.

Hope came up and put a supportive arm around her neck. "Mercy, you can't be sure. That's the worst that it could be, but maybe it's something else…" She thought for a moment. "Maybe he saw something. Maybe he saw Father Mullen abusing the other boy. Maybe he was afraid to say anything and became afraid of Father Mullen too."

Mercy looked at her sister. Hope was crying too, belying her own belief in the rationalization she was providing for Jason's depression. "How could anyone hurt Jason? He's the sweetest boy in the world."

Hope nodded her assent. "Father Mullen is an evil man. He's a monster, morally speaking. Anyone who would violate the trust of a child and his duty as a priest is beyond the pale. I never liked it that Brian insisted he be brought up Catholic." "But how was Brian to know?"

Or was the question, how was anyone to know? They talked some more, cried some more, but nothing could be settled until Mercy spoke with Jason. He was out playing street hockey with Robbie. Hope left so that when he came in Mercy could broach the topic without any extraneous distractions to him. Fifteen minutes later he was home, but Mercy, still collecting her thoughts, let him pass upstairs to his room with only a routine greeting. Unexpectedly, she found herself confused and indecisive. She decided to get supper started first, but with her mind racing and her heart pounding she could barely concentrate on even that mundane task. She was so full of dread her hands shook. She wanted anything but to be alone with her son, and she found herself feeling guilty that the person she thought of for moral support was Kermit and not her son's father. For a while she simply stood and gathered her strength. She was fully aware that the talk with Jason could be the most important and terrible moment of her life. Yet she had to do it. She had to.

And then time seemed to disappear. She had no recollection of getting the chicken from the refrigerator and readying it for the oven or of making a salad, yet these things were done and the moment drew near.

Jason is upstairs working on music on his Macintosh. The music he writes now is dark and filled with longing for something inexplicable, inexpressible. She feels it's death he's longing for and through her tears she's trying to figure out what to say to him. She puts the chicken in the oven, checks to make sure the rice is low, and walks out to the living room. At the foot of the stairs she calls up.

"Jason, could you come down here for a moment."

He comes down looking apprehensive. He's heard something in her tone despite her best efforts to hide her fears, and already he's defensive.

He's thinner now and looks frail, fragile. She thinks: how will he ever be able to trust anyone ever again? Yielding to her impulse, she suddenly reaches down and hugs him tightly. "Oh, Jason, Jason," she sighs. "I love you so much."

He appears to be confused, embarrassed. His eyes search hers. She can see his fear. She can feel it. She sits down on the couch, gently guiding him to sit beside her.

Silence reigns while she tries to find the words. Her stomach is a tight, tense knot, and she wonders how she will be able to eat the supper she can smell cooking. She puts her arm around her son. "Jason," she finally says, "in the paper tonight there's an account of Father Mullen being arrested." She stops, for she can feel the muscles of his neck and shoulders go tense. She takes a deep breath. She hugs him more tightly. "He was arrested because he did a very evil thing—he abused a boy in your choir. Now I want to ask you a question."

Silently he looks at her, then down at the floor. His hands keep opening and closing.

"Did Father Mullen ever do anything to you? Anything he shouldn't have done?"

He continues to stare at the floor for what seems like minutes. Finally his head moves slightly, and almost inaudibly he says, "No."

"Are you sure?"

He looks at her, staring into her eyes for a moment. Then reverting his gaze back to the floor, he says, "Yes."

"Because if he did, you can tell me. If I let you down, if I didn't protect you, if you blame me, it's okay. But just tell me, please. I'll make it up to you, I swear."

"No," he says. "No." He stands. "Can I go upstairs now? I'm working on some music."

And so at supper they both found themselves wearing masks. They pretended to be a mother and son eating a meal together. Everything was held back and hidden; nothing was real. Sometimes tears sprang into her eyes spontaneously and she would get up and go to the refrigerator for something, anything—olives would do—so that when she returned to the table she could be composed. Then he went back upstairs, and before long she could hear the music again filled with longing for death, and another piece of her heart broke away and was swallowed into darkness.

She called Brian later that night as soon as she was sure Jason was asleep. But she forgot that he was attending a conference in Raleigh, North Carolina on road building, so she had to leave a message to call her as soon as he got back.

She hadn't told him much in the message, but when he called at seven thirty Monday morning he had already heard about Father Mullen and was frantic. "Is Jason the boy?" he asked before even saying hello.

She knew he was referring to the victim whose parents and the media were cooperating to keep anonymous. "No, it's some other member of the choir who's pressing charges."

Even as she heard him sigh with relief, she knew that it would be short-lived. She could sense that his response to the news was exactly the same as hers: that he instantly had understood it explained all of Jason's behavior and in a blinding flash of knowledge knew everything. She waited for a moment for him to say something, and when he didn't she said, "But I don't think that means Jason is free."

There was another long pause; then in a broken voice he said, "I didn't think so. The minute I heard about that swine and what he did, I thought of Jason."

"He tells me nothing happened, but—Look," she said, trying not to burst into tears in response to his obvious pain, "we should meet and talk about this. There's a lot I want to say, and we've got to make some decisions."

They arranged to meet for lunch that noon in a little eatery in Bedford a few blocks from the building where she worked in a law office. Brian was waiting for her outside as she came up. Awkwardly they shook hands and went inside. They had chosen the place because it usually wasn't busy, but they had to wait five minutes for a table. They both avoided talking about the subject that brought them together until they were seated, then waited further until their order was taken.

Mercy told him about her talk with Jason and his denial, and for a while they tried to psychoanalyze his behavior. They both agreed the evidence showed he was hiding something. Their lunches arrived, and after the waitress left, Mercy said, "Even if he wasn't abused, I think he's going to need counseling. He's obviously a very disturbed little boy right now."

Brian toyed with his French fries, dragging them through the ketchup but otherwise showing no inclination to eat them. "I know what I'd like to do. I'd like to strangle that puke. I never liked him. With his mincing steps, his prissy ways, his affected accent, I always had a feeling he wasn't right. But I swallowed my doubts because I wanted the best for Jason. Now isn't that ironic. This man has ruined Jason's life."

Mercy looked up. She had been almost mesmerized watching him toying with the French fries, but the phrase "ruined Jason's life" ran through her like an electric shock. "No!" she almost shouted. "I won't accept that. That man will not ruin Jason. He's too young, too intelligent, too resilient. No, his life is not ruined."

Brian put his hands up in concession. "Okay, that's too strong, maybe. But if it's true that Father Mullen abused him, then he's going to be scarred, and it's likely he'll never look at life the same way. The fact that he won't admit anything is certainly a bad sign."

For a moment Mercy tried to do something she knew was impossible: she tried to convince herself that Jason's refusal to admit he'd been abused was because he really hadn't been. But remembering the pattern of behavior, how it started suddenly in the fall and how desperately he would try anything to avoid seeing the priest, quickly disabused her of her hope. Like old friends showing up at a funeral, all-too familiar tears formed in her eyes. "We won't let him be scarred," she said fiercely. "We'll do everything possible and even impossible to save him." Then more calmly she asked, "But are you also absolutely sure Father Mullen explains Jason's behavior?"

The thought of that man made Brian scowl angrily. "Well, it does explain everything. I mean we both thought Wendy and that guy you were seeing was a factor, but nothing changed after they were out of the picture. And the fact he wanted out of choir practice and pretended to be sick on the Wednesdays he was supposed to have lessons with Father Mullen certainly is significant."

"And the music he's playing and writing now," she said. "It's so sad it makes me want to cry. It's like he wants to bury himself in a dark hole." She wiped the tears from her eyes, suddenly conscious that the waitress was looking at her from across the room.

Brian clenched his fists and tried to fight back his own tears. "Oh, I want to murder that bastard. I want him to fry in hell. That he did this to my son…"

Then he broke down, and Mercy, forgetting all self-consciousness, wept too. For a minute no words were exchanged as they both struggled to compose themselves, then Brian said, "People are talking, you know. Even my father called and asked if Jason was okay. He didn't mention Father Mullen, but obviously that was what was on his mind. Have you talked to any other parents of the boys in the choir?"

"Nell Grady called me to discuss the situation. Her son is okay. But I don't dare call anyone, and I don't think the other parents do either. We all know one boy and his parents brought charges. It would seem like prying if I called randomly. But Nell did suggest we all meet somewhere, sometime."

"Would you go to such a meeting? Do you think we should?"

Mercy frowned and considered momentarily. "I don't know. I think I'd like to have the situation with Jason cleared up first."

"How about the cops or the prosecutors? Have they called?"

"Yes. They said they'd be getting in touch with all the parents within the next month or so. You know how court cases are—slow as molasses. What did you tell your father incidentally?"

"Oh, not much. He heard about it because he gets the local paper mailed to Florida. Of course he worried the second he saw the headline. I just told him we're worried too, but that there was nothing definite yet."

Mercy nodded. "My brother's called, of course. You know what a gossip Mike is.

I didn't tell him anything. It's times like this, anyways, that I'm almost glad Mom and Dad are gone. They'd be worried sick. We must tell Jim and Alice the moment we get definite news."

Brian drummed his fingers on the table and thought for a moment. "They'll probably want to come home if we find out anything definite."

"Yeah. That will be good. Jason is going to need a lot of support in the coming months."

"So will we," Brian said. "So will we."

Nothing definite was decided at the luncheon, though they both agreed Jason shouldn't be forced into a confession as if he had done something wrong. It would be much better to use only gentle means to try to get him to talk about Father Mullen. That way, they reasoned, he would not associate them with the grown-up world that had betrayed him. For the same reason, the decision to get him into counseling was left open-ended. Both of them felt that until they learned something definite, bringing him into counseling would only alienate him. But the result of this decision not to take any actions that would bring things to a head was to make uncertainty a crushing weight almost not to be borne. Doubt and a feeling of impending doom became Mercy's daily reality. Jason, knowing or at least feeling that he was being closely watched, became even more withdrawn. A wall grew up between mother and son, and in consequence she also became isolated and withdrawn from everyone else, even to a certain extent from Hope. Their brother Mike (his real name was Miles, but since a boy everyone had called him Mike) began stopping by or phoning Mercy and asking about Jason. His prying became very exasperating, but as he was the older brother in the family she found it impossible to criticize him. Instead of refusing to tolerate his questions, she answered them evasively and became filled with resentment, which unfortunately boiled over when Hope the following day innocently asked if anything new had developed. "No, Hope," Mercy snapped, "nothing new has come along to satisfy your curiosity." Hope had colored deeply and left soon after. For three or four days she didn't call.

Her absence made Mercy's life even more difficult. Alone, except for late-night phone conversations with Brian, she felt she was on the verge of a nervous breakdown. She tried to keep constantly busy, for whenever her mind was not occupied she would begin to feel that she was in the grip of black nothingness, worse than despair and close to madness. She saw Kermit's father Walt Pingree one day at the store, and it triggered memories of her dead fiancé. He was never one to exhibit the slightest sign of self-doubt, and remembering his strength and confidence, she found herself for two days talking out loud to him, yearning for him, and only stopped when she thought that if he were alive Jason would not exist. Better to live in the world of doubt and doom, she thought, even if one step away from hysteria, for that world held Jason. She tried once again with gentle hints to get her son to talk about Father Mullen, only to have him withdraw more deeply into himself.

On Friday her boss at the law office, Perry Crompton, asked her if Jason was going to play the piano again at the annual Lawyers' Guild Christmas party, and instead of answering she burst into tears. She was deeply embarrassed at her lack of self-control, but it actually had a salutary effect. Being forced to explain her strange behavior, she unburdened herself to her boss, who turned out to be a sympathetic listener. He offered her all necessary support, told her she could have time off if she needed it, and suggested that her and Brian's reluctance to force Jason to talk was the wrong strategy. The sooner he gets it out into the air, the quicker he'll heal, the lawyer said. He also offered legal assistance in case she wished to sue the Catholic Church, but to this suggestion Mercy was noncommittal. The idea of extracting money from a church was repugnant to her.

She came away from the talk, however, feeling much better and instantly decided that as painful as it might be, Jason too would feel better when he unburdened himself. She reached Brian on his cellular phone and tried to talk him into confronting Jason with her when he came to get him that evening. Brian was cautious, however, wanting to give Jason the weekend before forcing a confrontation.

Reluctantly Mercy agreed, but on Saturday morning the phone rang, and with it all their plans, uncertainties, and delays flew away, and in their place came a new reality. It was Walter Pingree. He had, he said, some important information for her. He spoke excitedly, and as a consequence was not too articulate. It took awhile for her to understand what he was saying, but when she did her blood went cold. "My nephew, my sister's son, he's a teacher. Retired now. His school went out of business. So he's in his fifties but retired. He lives in Waska now—out on Route 5. Out in the woods when he was taking a walk he saw something. He'd like to talk to you about it. Your son Jason. He saw Jason, see? With Father Mullen, see? It's very important. He'd like to talk to you. Can he come over now, or would you prefer another time? He's with me now, see?"

Mercy, in her mind seeing Jason's face, imagined he was begging her to help him. It was difficult to think of any words to say. But looking across the dining room to where the piano sat in the living room, she suddenly found her mind clearing. "No," she said, "Jason is with his father now. This would be a perfect time. Please come now."

She was glad the house was untidy, for it gave her something to do for the five minutes she waited. She collected some of Jason's books, an electronic game, and her sewing equipment and threw them into the closet. Then she straightened the pillows on the couch and the magazines on the coffee table, and then went into the kitchen to put the breakfast dishes in the dishwasher. She kept telling herself to be calm, though she found herself trembling and filled with dread. She was looking around for something else to do just as the doorbell rang. Walter, looking both nervous and self-important, searched her eyes when she opened the door. His cloth coat was shabby, and his two-day beard gave him the look of a street person. In the past she had wished there was something she could do for him, but the thought only flitted through her mind now, quickly to be replaced by an unpleasant sense that she was being objectified by him. Somewhat coldly she said, "Hello, Walt."

He nodded and shook her hand (something he never did when they met in public) and said in a pitying, solicitous tone that made her feel a tinge of resentment at the same time the dread swelled into panic, "I'm sorry to bother you, Mercy."

She nodded. "Please come in." Her mouth was so dry it was difficult to speak. Her heart was pounding.

They went into the living room where Walt introduced his companion. "This is my nephew, Samuel Jellerson. Sam, this is Mercy."

A tall slender individual, rather distinguished and scholarly in appearance, he had large blue eyes staring out of gold-rimmed glasses and a craggy face that seemed honest and sincere. And his handshake was firm. He appeared nervous, as was to be expected, though something about his bearing told her he was constitutionally high strung.

Walt, having introduced them, took a seat and made himself inconspicuous in a corner easy chair by the piano while Mercy sat in the recliner and Jellerson on the couch directly facing her.

He sat stiffly, leaning forward and unable to relax. For a moment he gathered his thoughts, then said, "Mrs. Buckley, I'm sure you've heard about Father Mullen's arrest." He paused and waited for her to nod. "And of course that another boy and his family have brought charges."

Again Mercy nodded, and this time she found herself wringing her hands, a gesture Jellerson clearly noticed.

He hesitated for another moment, obviously nervous and unsure of how to broach his subject. His tongue licked his lips, and he took a deep breath. "May I ask you if you have any evidence that your son was also a victim?"

Mercy leaned forward and put her elbows on her knees. Looking down at the floor, she said, "Nothing specific, but I do have very grave suspicions. Is that what you've come for, Mr. Jellerson?" She looked at him imploringly. "Is there something you can tell me? Walt seemed to imply you did?"

Jellerson looked at Walt, who was watching them with intense interest, and then back to Mercy. Again he went through the ceremony of licking his lips and taking a deep breath. "Yes, I'm afraid I do. I think I saw—no, I did see Father Mullen and your son in the woods behind my house on a Wednesday afternoon in October. I know it was your son—"

"Wednesday? You're sure it was a Wednesday? Mercy asked.

Jellerson nodded. "Yes, Wednesday."

"That was the day Jason spent the afternoon studying music with Father Mullen," she said softly, and then stared at the floor. She felt numb.

"And I know it was your son," Jellerson continued, "because I saw him in a car when I was talking to Walter soon after and he identified him. Mrs. Buckley, I'm afraid I saw that beast of a priest abusing your son."

Mercy felt the blood drain from her face. Even expecting some such information was no preparation for actually hearing it. She gasped, then let out the air in a low moan. At the same time the blood rushed back to her head and made her feel hot and nauseous. Covering her face with her hands, she said, "But are you truly sure? Sure it was my boy? And…?"

"Well, I wasn't for a long, long time, mainly because I simply couldn't believe what I saw. But now…" He shrugged. "I mean after the news broke… Before I go to the police I wanted to tell you. I've been in an agony of uncertainty as to what to do. At first I thought when they arrested that man it was because of your son, but certain details I read in the paper didn't fit. First I tried to confront Father Mullen, but he wouldn't see me." He looked at Mercy and his face softened. "I didn't want to have you learn of this from the police or the newspaper. I'm going to the police station to report what I witnessed after I leave here. I think I should have done all this before now, and I hope you can forgive me. I've been cowardly and indecisive. Really, I should have gone to the police last month right after I saw it, but I couldn't believe what I saw. It happened so quickly. I saw only a glance, and yet it was burned into my mind. And I kept thinking a clergyman couldn't possibly do what I saw. But you have every right to hate me. I think I've caused your son unnecessary pain. For that I can never forgive myself."

While she listened to him, she became aware of Walt staring at her intently. Through an effort of will she managed to get her emotions under control and in a clear, even voice she said, "I don't hate you, Mr. Jellerson. On the contrary, I'm deeply grateful. Certainty is better than doubt. Now that I know, we can start to do something. You understand that Jason has been depressed for over a month, and when I heard Father Mullen was arrested I knew instinctively that must be the reason. I had been thinking his behavior—for not only was he sad all the time, but his schoolwork was falling off and he was losing interest in performing music, the love of his life—I'd been thinking anyways that he was acting this way as a kind of delayed reaction to my divorce years ago. He's a sensitive boy, though entirely normal. He plays hockey, soccer and baseball as well as study music. But I knew instantly. The thing is, he's been denying it because it was so painful."

Very gently Jellerson said, "So you asked him if Father Mullen hurt him and he said no?"

She nodded. "But I have no real idea why. He is clearly very frightened."

"I read a book on child abuse a few weeks ago trying to understand how anyone could be so evil as to violate the trust of a child. Generally it's done by people who totally lack sympathy, or more accurately empathy. These people are generally egomaniacs, totally and only concerned with themselves. Most of them, it seems, were abused when they were kids, so we see victims creating more victims. But I think I know why your son Jason denies anything happened."

She looked at him. Forgetting Walt's prying eyes, she made no effort to hide her anxious desperation. "You do?"

Jellerson nodded grimly. "Father Mullen probably threatened him. Very likely he said something about God punishing Jason if he spoke out. These people know how to use power to manipulate. He might even have said something about you and the boy's father being punished by God. I'm sure that's why Jason doesn't dare to admit the abuse." He stood. "I hope with all my heart that your son passes through this unscathed. Again, I'm truly sorry I caused your son unnecessary pain. Right now I think it is time to go to the police."

Walt stood and joined his nephew. He had maintained a discreet silence throughout the interview, but now he started talking in the same excited and hurried way he had when he phoned. "I'm terribly sorry about this, Mercy. My friend Belcher doesn't believe the priest did it. He says priests don't do such things. I told him that was nonsense. In such an unnatural position it's no wonder they do unnatural things. I could tell that Mullen only cared for himself just by looking at him. But don't worry. I won't say anything about this. I'll keep it to myself."

Mercy hardly listened to him. Her mind was already projecting ahead to how she and Brian would handle this new information. "Yes," she said, responding to his last statement, "I would appreciate that very much."

She turned to Jellerson. "I want to say again how deeply grateful I am to you for the concern you've shown for my son. Now that I know, at least we can start trying to help him." As if responding to an invisible cue, all three of them started moving toward the door. "We're going to do everything parents can do, but I think he's going to need some professional counseling."

Jellerson attentively listened to her and appeared to be thinking. Outside the door, he turned back and said, "I have spoken to my own pastor, the Rev. John Covington of the Congregational Church, about this affair, though I want you to know I was scrupulous in protecting Jason's identity. Only my wife and Walter know what I've told you. But the reason I mention Rev. Covington is because he also has a degree in child counseling and would, he told me, be glad to counsel your son if needed. He would of course charge no fee."

"Thank you. I'll discuss that kind offer with my husband." She stopped, blushed, and said, "My ex-husband, I mean." Then she thanked him once again for his help, and they said their good-byes.

Back inside the house she sat down and thought for a full fifteen minutes, going over in her mind all that Jellerson had told her and everything that had happened with Jason for the past month. She began crying again, and for another five minutes didn't so much think as feel her pain and Jason's pain. Once she had cried herself dry, she phoned Brian. He and Jason were watching a B.C. football game, and at first she could tell he resented her impinging upon his time with his son when she suggested that they had to talk right now. "We've already agreed to wait," he answered impatiently, but his attitude quickly changed when she told him about Jellerson. With her making suggestions and him guardedly answering with a yes or no, they arranged for her to come over to his apartment and have it out with Jason. He was to prepare Jason by telling him a new development in the Father Mullen affair had occurred, but he was to wait about ten minutes to attempt to synchronize it with her arrival.

Brian lived in the second story of a house owned by an elderly widow in the Camp Melton section of Waska. From his window one could see the Atlantic, though he was several hundred yards from the beach. With his business prospering he could afford a house, but he had decided instead to buy the garage and land in town where he kept his heavy equipment and supplies. Mercy often came to pick up or drop off Jason, but she rarely came inside. Her genius for decorating and renovating had no effect on Brian: his place was Spartan and untidy. A print of Portland Headlight was the only art represented. The other pictures were few in number and mostly color photographs of sports cars. The living room was large and looked larger because only two upholstered chairs and a couch, together with a few small tables and a shelf containing a sound system and a television constituted its furnishings. Likewise his bedroom held only a bed and a dresser. Only Jason's room was crowded with stuff, including a recent acquisition, a newer and better Macintosh computer. Mercy noticed all these things because that was the way her mind worked, but they had no conscious operation on her thoughts this time. Her foremost concern was the state of Jason's psyche as it could be revealed in his face.

It was not good. He looked pale and anxious, verging on terror. For the first time in her life she was aware that he wasn't glad to see her, and she had to struggle to compose herself. Brian tried to cover for her. "Your mother is here because she's your mother, Jason. Both of us have agreed that it is very important we talk to you right now."

They sat on the couch, Brian and Mercy sitting on each side of Jason to give him the strongest possible sense of physical security.

"We want to talk to you…" Mercy began.

"And you don't have to be afraid, Jason," Brian said. "We won't let anything happen to you."

"…about Father Mullen."

Jason looked up, his eyes betraying his fear. "I know."

"And you know that we both love you very much and that you're the most precious person in the whole world to us?"

Tears sprang to his eyes. Brian leaned down and kissed his forehead while Mercy hugged him more tightly. "I know you both love me," he whispered, his tears growing into sobs. "That's why I've been so afraid."

"Jason, do you remember being in the woods near Route 5 with Father Mullen?"

She could feel his pulse quicken as his eyes widened in surprise. He continued sobbing and could only manage to nod his head.

"Don't be afraid, she whispered reassuringly. "That was last month, right?"

This time he slightly inclined his head to say yes.

"Do you remember seeing a man in the woods when you were there with Father Mullen?"

His fear grew into the terror of a cornered animal. "I think so. He was on a hill looking down at us. I wanted to cry for help, but…"

She could hear Brian sobbing. Only by concentrating on the denouement could she hold herself together. "That man's name is Samuel Jellerson. He came to see me this morning."

He still looked terrified, but his eyes told her to go on. She understood that the only thing allowing him to face that terror was his desperate need to have their love. Her arm held him tightly, and Brian held his left hand. Now sobbing herself, she said, "He told me that he saw Father Mullen abusing you."

Brian groaned, but Jason was perfectly silent. He had stopped sobbing, though the tears still ran down his cheeks.

Mercy caressed his wet cheek. "My darling, my sweet boy… What did Father Mullen say to you after that? He threatened you, didn't he? But what we want you to know is that he can't hurt you. He's been arrested and is being watched closely. So he can't hurt you. Do you understand?"

"We won't let him harm you again," Brian added in a broken voice.

Jason nodded, but he didn't seem convinced.

Mercy, looking over Jason's bowed head, exchanged a glance with Brian. "Maybe he said God would punish you? Did he do that, Jason? Did he use God against you?"

His eyes narrowed strangely as he thought, as he remembered.

"Maybe he said God would punish you? Is that right?"

Still he appeared to be thinking about the time. He said nothing.

"But he won't. What Father Mullen did was evil, and God doesn't have anything to do with evil."

He started to speak, then hesitated. They waited. He looked at his father, then slowly turned and looked at Mercy. "He did. He said God would be very angry with me if I said anything. He said that because God loved my music maybe he wouldn't hurt me, but he would…"

"Would what?" Brian asked. His face was dark with unspeakable hatred. He looked as if he would strangle Father Mullen if he could see him right now.

"He said God would kill you and Mom."

Brian slapped the couch with his free hand. "He's a lying swine, Jason. He's closer to the devil than to God. That man is no priest, and he doesn't have God's ear. That I can assure you. He's a beast, a monster, not a priest."

Angrily he leaped up and started pacing, muttering imprecations at Father Mullen. Only when he saw his behavior was scaring Jason did he calm down. He sat back down and gathered him in his arms. "Sometimes," he said, "victims blame themselves. But you have to see that nothing that that monster did to you was your fault. He is evil itself for hurting you. I love you with all my heart and want you to know that we are going to get through this. You will never be alone in this, son."

As he spoke he stroked Jason's sandy hair, trying to soothe his pain away. When Jason was calm and had closed his eyes, he turned him over to Mercy and got his jacket. "My duty now is to go to the police station and report. By now Mr. Jellerson has finished."

When he was gone Mercy tried to find out if Jason had truly understood that God would not punish them. They sat on the couch with Jason nestled in her arms as they talked. She quickly discovered that he was a very confused little boy. When she repeated that God would not hurt them, he said, "But he said he could. He's God on earth. Whatever he wants, God wants. He told me so." He seemed reluctant to give up the notion, as if the evil that held him in thrall offered him something in compensation: a certainty about the world, that it was guided by divine power.

Mercy, conscious that her son's psyche was in a precarious state, chose her words carefully. "Father Mullen is just a man. He studied for his profession just like a lawyer does, but a lawyer doesn't claim he is the law. Believe me, Jason, God is not going to hurt us. If he's angry with anyone, it's Father Mullen for abusing his position and saying that the evil he did was God's evil."

"So you're saying God will strike Father Mullen down because he was lying when he told me that stuff?"

"Yes, he was lying. But also, don't expect God to punish him now for that lie."

"I'm really confused, Mom. If God is not a priest and if he doesn't punish bad deeds, where is he?"

"Well, he's not seeable by people."

"Then how do we know he exists?"

"Well, that's why faith is needed."

"What about the pope? Is he just a man too?"

"Yes. Of course your father might believe otherwise, but I think the answer is yes. He's just a man."

"Who will keep me safe if God doesn't?"

"We will, honey. That man will never get near you again. We hope he will be in jail after his trial."

They were silent for a while, and then Jason said, "Mom, can I ask you a question?"

"Of course, sweetie."

"He said God was already angry at you and Dad for divorcing. Do you think that's true?"

"No. No, I don't. Your father and I had many differences. The only thing we really agreed on was our love for you. We were just making each other miserable. God can't possibly want that."

Again he was silent for a while as he thought about what she said. Finally he stirred and looked up at her. Shyly and hesitantly he said, "I wish you and Dad would get back together."

She leaned down and kissed the top of his head. "I can't make any promises, Jason, but we will do whatever is necessary to make you feel good again. You have my promise for that."

Rumors

M ichelle Turcotte tittered and covered her mouth in embarrassment. Mr. Thibeault, the head custodian at the Bedford Rotarians hall and a man decidedly fat, had just bent over to pick up something off the floor, and the movement had exposed the top portion of his posterior hams. Sarah Henslowe, her friend, had not missed a beat in pointing and saying, "Maybe that's what guys mean when they talk about cleavage."

But she spoke too loudly, for Mr. Thibeault was not very far away. He had turned and looked sharply at them.

They moved away, still giggling, and continued searching the crowd.

They had just arrived at the Lawyers' Guild annual Christmas party, given every year in December to raise money for the poor and to allow all the lawyers in Waska and Bedford to socialize despite often being courtroom antagonists for the rest of the year. The party included the families of all the lawyers, their clerks and office help and, as a professional courtesy, the personnel who worked in the courts and the prosecutors' office, but the first event was always the raffle, to which the public was invited. Michelle and Sarah (who came as her invited guest) had arrived just as the raffle was being conducted. As a consequence the main hall was packed with people and they were unable to see any of their friends.

Sarah was Michelle's best friend. She was rather plain, with uneven features and teeth, and most boys never showed much interest in her, even though she was extremely interested in them. She was forever making silly jokes about sex like the one she'd just made about cleavage, but whenever boys were around she became almost crippling shy and to protect herself pretended indifference to their indifference. One boy in their class had clearly indicated he liked her, but he was regarded as a nerd, and she had not reciprocated his advances.

They walked up to the front of the hall and stood below the stage where later many of the lawyers would perform Christmas skits and songs accompanied by piano. Both surveyed the room for some time.

"Who's that man standing by the raffle table?"

Michelle following Sarah's pointing finger, shrugged. "I don't know."
"You sure? He looks like the guy who tutors you."
Michelle looked again and raised her eyebrows. "What? Mr. Jellerson? That guy doesn't look anything like Mr. Jellerson."
"They both have gray hair. They're both skinny. They both look old."
"So do millions of other people."
Sarah rolled her eyes and tilted her head comically. "Okay, okay. It was that he was old. It must be creepy going to old man Jellerson's house every week. I mean, you're *alone* with him."
"First of all, we're not alone. His dog Old Boy is always with us. And secondly, Mr. Jellerson's not a bad guy. At first I thought it was going to be yucky, but he knows his stuff. And sometimes I think I'm teaching him stuff. He's loosened up a lot since we first started."
Sarah screwed her face up in another comic expression. "Oh, brother. Would you rather see him or Bobby right now?"
"Bobby, of course. But that doesn't mean I don't appreciate Mr. Jellerson. Remember he offered to help you too. The man's been a teacher all his life and then his school closes on him. He really wants to help. It's quite touching how much he needs to teach."
"I'm sure it's nice of him, but I don't know what he could do for me. My grades are good but not so good that I'd get a full scholarship anywhere. At least I don't think so. I think you need straight A's for that. So even if I scored higher on the SAT's, I'm still going to Southern Maine."
"But it's not just higher SAT's that he's teaching me. He knows a lot about language and history, and lot's of times he's really interesting."
Sarah grinned and shook her head. "Boy, you really do like this guy. I'm telling Bobby."
"Don't you dare! Mr. Jellerson and Bobby are two different things."
Bobby, whose name kept coming up in their conversation, was Bobby McCartney. He had several classes with Michelle and Sarah, and as his mother worked at the courthouse, he was expected at the Christmas party. Michelle thought he was just about the cutest boy in the world. For some time they had been exchanging glances in class, in the halls, on the street. Last week he had walked to the cafeteria with her. He made it appear accidental that they happened to be coming out of the door at the same time, but she had seen him pretend to go back to his desk to look for something and then wait a few seconds to time the "accident." She observed these little stratagems because she too had been making little accidents occur that would bring them together. It was during this walk that he had mentioned he was going to be at the Lawyers' Guild Christmas party. They hadn't exactly made a date, but they had at least made the first step towards having a date. He had said he hoped to see her there, and she had said that she looked forward to seeing him.
She was just beginning to worry that she had been stood up on her nondate with him when they saw Tiffany Andrews walking by. She saw them at the same time and came up.
"What are you guys doing out here? Everyone's in the first conference room. It's the refreshment room this year."
By "everyone" of course they both understood her to mean the kids. The adults would be in the bar. The conference rooms were large rooms off the main hall that

were usually used during the Christmas party and similar functions for cloak rooms and refreshment pavilions.

"Does 'everyone' include Bobby too?" Sarah asked with a giggle.

Tiffany crinkled her nose. "Bobby? Bobby McCartney? Yeah, I think I saw him there. You guys go ahead. I've got to find my mother and tell her I'm not going to help with the raffle. They've got more people than they need."

"What's with her hoity-toity attitude?" Sarah asked as soon as she left.

Michelle started walking towards the meeting room. "I don't know."

Sarah had a notion, though. "If you ask me, she's jealous."

It took awhile for them to negotiate across the hall to the refreshment room. As they came in they could hear the loud voices of Bobby and his friends. They were showing off, though Michelle was glad to see Bobby himself didn't seem to be involved. "I can hardly wait for the old weasels to start singing 'Jingle Bells,'" one of them was saying loudly. She couldn't see him clearly, but it sounded like Carleton Ross. Another, one Billy Boudreau, a boy whom she had never liked ever since he put ice down her back in the sixth grade, then imitated an old man singing in croaking falsetto, and they all laughed. There were only a few adults in the room, so of course the horsing around was for the benefit of the teenagers.

Michelle watched them closely. She hated boys showing off, swaggering around like Hollywood heroes and making asses of themselves. It was important to her that Bobby would remain silent. Then his friends might be idiots and he might be accused of not choosing them very wisely, but he could still be someone she could be proud to be with.

Just then the boys caught sight of her and Sarah. They whispered something to Bobby that seemed to make him blush, then came over to them.

"Are you looking forward to the hokey Christmas music?" Carleton asked (for it was he).

"Hi, Bobby," she said and waited for him to shyly smile a greeting before turning to Carleton. "What would you say if I told you I was playing piano in the show?"

He grinned sheepishly. "You'd be okay. I meant the old farts doing their sing-along Christmas carols."

"Well, I'm not, but I could have if I wanted to."

She turned back to Bobby. "You guys been here long?"

Bobby shrugged and pursed his lips. "Twenty minutes or so."

"Sarah and I just got here. We came in her brother's car. She just got her license, you know."

She said this to include Sarah in the conversation. She was standing behind them listening, but she didn't say anything, nor did the boys make any attempt to talk to her.

After a moment of silence, Bobby asked, "Did you buy any raffle tickets?"

"No, my mother always buys ten or twenty. Not to win, you know, but to help the charity. What's the big prize this year?"

I think first prize is a weekend vacation at Bar Harbor. Televisions and stuff like that are the other prizes."

"Usual stuff, huh?"

"Yeah."

The other boys had drifted away as if by design, and Bobby kept glancing at Sarah, clearly hoping she would do the same. Just then, though, Michelle's mother called to her.

"Michelle, I've been looking all over for you. Could you and Sarah help me with the costumes? I got tied up at the office, and they were supposed to be here an hour ago. They're out in the car. With the three of us we can get them in one trip."

Michelle looked at Bobby and rolled her eyes.

He smiled slightly, with just enough of a look in his eyes to communicate many things—that he was sorry her mother had interrupted them but that he understood she couldn't very well say no to her and that he hoped he would see her later.

Michelle, reading all these messages, felt buoyed with pleasure. Telling her mother they would help, she smiled sweetly at Bobby and said, "I'll see you in a bit, I hope."

The costumes her mother had volunteered to deliver were the elf and Santa's helper outfits that the lawyers traditionally donned when they sang Christmas carols and did skits during the show. It only took about fifteen minutes to bring them from the car to the dressing room, but when she and Sarah returned to the first conference room a strange change had occurred. Instead of the buzz of a dozen different conversations, they found everyone was staring intently at some drama that was occurring near the door.

It turned out to be Bobby's friends showing off again, except that this time they weren't belittling adults for amateurish singing and performances; they were attacking a much more vulnerable target, Jason Buckley, and already it had turned ugly. Even before she and Sarah came up unseen behind the boys, they could hear the sneering, bullying remarks of Billy Boudreau and Carleton Ross.

"Look at the little man, would you."

"Yeah. Hey, Jason, you gonna play piano for us. Gonna tickle those ivories for us?"

Michelle could see him now. He was trying to get past them, but Billy blocked his way.

"Not so fast, little man. We're not done with you yet."

"Yeah," Carleton said. "Though the question is, are you a little man? Or are you a little fag? You queer, Jason?"

"One thing's for sure. You are a nerd. Only nerds play piano."

"I heard you're the lover boy of that priest. Is that true, little man?"

From where Michelle stood she could see Jason's face when the boys made these remarks. At first it was as if his face dropped. Every muscle went slack and his mouth opened. At the second remark his mouth closed to a thin line and his cheek muscles began twitching. Then he became smaller, clenching his fists and pulling his arms to his sides. He took a step backwards while his eyes wildly looked around for a way to escape. Finally, she could tell, he wanted to cry and was using every ounce of will power not to cry. It was awful, awful that words could have such an effect. The phrase "sticks and stones" passed through her mind, but she didn't finish the thought. The crowd was enjoying his pain; to them it was interesting, and they had no desire to interfere. She took a step forward, not sure what she would do, only knowing that she had to help him.

But things were happening too fast for her to interfere. Jason must have realized he couldn't run, and not being able to run he chose the only alternative: he fought. Though one against two and half the size of the two boys who were belittling him, he sprang on them like a miniature tornado. "You shut up!" he screamed. "You mind your own business!" All the while he was screaming at them his arms were flying, striking at them ineffectively as the boys easily warded off the blows. At least the psychological relationship had changed, since now it was the older boys who were clearly embarrassed and looking distinctly uncomfortable.

Quickly Michelle pushed her way between the boys and Jason. "Stop it!" she said to Billy and Carleton. "You ought to be ashamed of yourselves."

By now the ruckus had attracted the attention of several adults who simultaneously came up to stop the taunting. "You boys have said quite enough," Mr. Pelletier said. He was a law partner of Michelle's father and a very large man. He spoke with the voice of authority. The boys looked cowered, but again things were happening too quickly. Before they could say a word, from behind them in the main hall Jason's mother, Mrs. Buckley, rushed in, her face contorted into panic. "Jason! Jason!" she cried. "Are you all right?"

"Yes, I'm okay," he said quietly. But he didn't look it—he looked as if he wanted to make himself invisible.

Mrs. Buckley put a protective arm around him, then stared defiantly at the boys. "You boys move off," Mr. Pelletier said angrily, pointing a stubby finger. "I don't want any more trouble from you."

With everyone's attention centered on the boys guiltily retreating, Michelle went over to Jason and his mother and said, "The boys were taunting Jason, Mrs. Buckley. But don't worry. He was very brave."

She studied her face, obviously trying to recollect her. "Oh, thank you, Michelle."

"Michelle tried to stop them, Mrs. Buckley," Sarah said. "They were creeps. But I agree with her. Jason was very brave."

"Jason, if you want I'll have those boys thrown out," Mr. Pelletier said.

But Jason didn't. He explained that he didn't care now that they were gone.

With her eyes constantly watching Jason, Mrs. Buckley responded to the girls. "Yes, he is brave. At first I didn't want to come today, but he said we should. And I do want him to live as normally as possible."

Michelle, finding this remark cryptic, couldn't hide her puzzlement, for Mrs. Buckley read it on her face. She looked from Michelle to Jason, and the tears suddenly sprang into her eyes. "Somehow," she said… "somehow the word got out about what that priest did to Jason."

Michelle gasped. "You mean the cruel things those boys said were true?"

A flash of anger passed over Mrs. Buckley's face, making Michelle feel stupid and guilty for her inept phrasing. "I'm sorry. I didn't mean…" She stopped, feeling her face burn.

Mrs. Buckley, however, didn't notice; she was staring at Jason and lost in thought. Michelle waited, afraid that her thoughtless remark had deeply hurt her. But it seemed her insensitive stupidity had not so much caused pain as it had first triggered and then confirmed doubts Mrs. Buckley had about the whole enterprise of Jason coming to a public forum to play the piano.

With a sudden motion she appeared to come to a decision. "I wonder," she said, "if you'd mind substituting for Jason during the show. Play the piano, I mean. You can sight read, can't you?"

"Oh," Michelle gasped. She remembered what she had said to the boys about playing the piano. "I think so. If I had to, that is. I wouldn't be as good as Jason, of course. But yes."

She understood immediately that the request was not one that could be refused. Not only would Jason be upset after his cruel humiliation; she could see as clearly as his mother that his playing the piano was impossible. He wouldn't be the accompanist of a group of lawyers having fun while they made fools of themselves; he would be the center of attention. The party would be ruined and he would be traumatized. So instead of a semi-date with the cutest boy at Courtney Academy, Michelle spent the rest of the afternoon preparing for the show and then appearing in it. First she looked over the music for all the Christmas carols to be sung, then practiced behind the closed curtain a few of them she had never played before. Whenever she felt stage jitters creeping up on her like fire ants whose nest has been disturbed, she would take a deep breath and remind herself she was doing this for Jason. The memory of his hurt, violated face spurred her on. She wouldn't let herself think of Bobby's friends, though. Not now. It would make her too angry to concentrate.

Sarah stayed with her during the practice session. She listened and commented on the playing, gossiped, or tried to gossip, about Jason, picked up and read through the program, looked into a closet, and generally killed time. Michelle, intent upon practicing, could spare her little time, though, and eventually she wandered away only to return twenty minutes later looking lost and forlorn. Michelle, conscious of her shyness, suggested she could stay back stage during the show. "You could help put the costumes away afterwards," she said. Sarah pretended to be reluctant only for a moment. She confessed that she didn't know anyone at the party very well. Anna and Daphne Drogitos, who were supposed to be coming, had not showed up.

With the appearance on stage of the performers, her nervousness returned, but when her father came up to congratulate her for helping stop the boys and to wish her good luck (he had just heard of the events leading to her substituting for Jason because he was delayed at the office), he managed to get her to relax. Dressed as an elf, which included shorts and liederhosen on his thin legs and two rouge circles on his cheeks, he looked so foolish that she laughed out loud. Already feeling better after that, she relaxed even more when he told her that he and another lawyer had a little skit ready if there were any trouble with the music. "Besides," he said with a fatherly twinkle in his eyes, "it isn't Schumann or Chopin you're playing. You'll be all right."

And she was. She played competently and after the first song didn't experience the slightest nervousness. Occasionally when the lawyers sang a cappella or were doing a skit she searched the audience looking for Bobby, but even though with the raffle over the crowd had thinned down to about seventy-five people, she never saw him. He and his two friends had been shamed into leaving.

She saw him two days later, which was the day before Christmas, when she was doing some last minute shopping with Sarah at the mall. He was with his mother, and when she went into one store and Sarah into another, they talked.

"I bet you're still mad about the other day," he said.

Right at that moment she wasn't. She was looking into his eyes and seeing them shine in gladness at seeing her, and it made her shiver with pleasure. But a picture of Jason's hurt, violated face and his quivering lips as he struggled to control himself formed in her mind, and she said, "Yes, I am mad. Your friends were very stupid— stupid and cruel." She paused for a moment, then felt a surge of rage. "No! It's even worse. If it's true that Jason was a victim of that priest, your friends were unspeakably cruel. Do they have any idea of the pain they could cause?"

Bobby laughed nervously and shrugged his shoulders. His face went red. "They were just farting around. I don't think they really knew what they were saying. I agree with you, though. It was cruel and uncalled for. I didn't like it, but I didn't know how to say so. But honest, I talked to them later about it and I think they realized they had been very cruel. But to really emphasize it I mean to talk to them again."

He seemed genuinely repentant. And besides, he hadn't said anything to Jason. His only sin was not interfering, not telling them to be quiet. Michelle, looking into his beautiful blue eyes and thinking he was the handsomest boy in the world, decided to forgive him. "Would you?" she asked. "Would you tell them that their behavior was awful? They should be made aware of their cruelty."

He swore he would, and then he asked, "Do you think it's true what people are saying—that he was a victim of that priest?"

"I'm not sure," she said. She didn't want to spread the story any further if she could help it.

And then he changed the subject. He asked her for a date, naming a movie he would like to see. It couldn't be until after Christmas vacation was over because his family was entertaining an uncle, aunt and several cousins who were home in Maine from North Carolina, but the date was agreed upon.

So she had a wonderful early Christmas present and at midnight mass that night prayed gladly for the savior born into the world.

But she didn't forget Jason. In fact she thought of him often. Something she could not at first explain drew him to her. It was more than sympathy, though sympathy played a part; but it was even deeper than that, inexpressible like talking about the color of his soul or the sound of his thoughts, an identification that began long before his troubles did. She first glimpsed the special quality of his soul after she heard him play Schumann's "Träumerei" and he told her that whenever he played that piece he always thought about a beautiful sunset he'd seen on vacation at a lake. He said the peaceful feeling and the beauty of the music made him love the whole world. That was a couple of years ago, when she was old enough to know that probably Schumann was thinking of his love for Clara Schumann when he composed it. Still she knew exactly what he meant, for when he played it she too felt love for the whole world. From that moment on she had seen him as special. If he could make her, an ordinary girl, feel that beauty and peace in her soul, then it was as if he had been chosen by destiny. Now he felt neither peace nor love in the world. Without help maybe he never again would. An entire life hung in the balance; all his skill and knowledge as a musician could be destroyed. The thought was intolerable to her. For as long as she could remember she had been on the side of beautiful fragile things. She would always wince when a bug was killed or a flower crushed or a little bird found beneath a window with a broken neck. One of her earliest memories was of the time she snatched at a butterfly on a flower right in front of her father's lawn mower to save it. Her father had instantly stopped the mower and yelled at her for doing something so dangerous while she stood hanging her head, unable to explain the pain that the thought of a beautiful living thing being destroyed gave to her. And now that Jason was the butterfly she experienced the same pain for him. It darkened the joy that sang in her soul every time she thought of Bobby and made her feel selfish.

While she was undergoing a process of closer identification with Jason, however, the rest of the world was objectifying him. All during the Christmas vacation one of the main topics of conversation at the teen hangouts was Jason and the priest. Strangely, no one conjectured about the other victim of Father Mullen. His identity remained so well hidden that no one could have fun embellishing his story. But Jason's situation being known, it became an easy subject for wagging tongues. The rumor, which had been vague and iffy at the Lawyer's Guild party, became an elaborate edifice of assertions and counter-assertions, many of them patently false. People said the priest and Jason were on the verge of running away together to a foreign land, some saying it was Africa, other versions saying it was the South Pacific. Then another rumor had it that the two had been caught flagrante delicto behind the altar by Father Riley. Someone's mother had heard that some witness had seen them together in the woods, and a few days later Michelle heard from Sarah, who heard it from Tiffany, who heard it from someone, that the witness was Mr. Jellerson, the retired teacher. Sarah wanted to know of course if Michelle had garnered any hints about the truth of this rumor from her tutor. They were sitting in the coffee shop at the in-town mall when she was asked this, and no sooner had she said no than another girl came up and said she had heard that Mr. Jellerson was not a witness but a codefendant—that he too had been accused of molesting the boy.

This was too much and Michelle said so. It was stupid. All the rumors were stupid. The only part of them that was true was that Jason was the previously unidentified second victim. The Jellerson rumor would not, however, go away easily, though after a while the version that he was a witness and not a perpetrator did prevail. And other variations of the story continued to flourish—that Jason was converting to Protestantism, that his father was going to kill the priest, that the town's Congregational minister was counseling Jason, that the cops had discovered several other victims of Father Mullen, both here and in other states where he had been stationed.

The rumors filled Michelle with disgust, partly because she could not help but listen to them as eagerly as anyone else, but also because they filled her with a sense of unreality. She could not recognize the special boy she admired in these stories; when she pictured him in her mind, she could only see the hurt, tormented face of the victim of the boys' cruelty. Fortunately she would have a chance to see him at the holiday party their piano teacher was giving. She knew Jason was going to be present, for his mother called her mother to ask if Michelle was planning to attend. Apparently after his experience at the Rotarians' hall, she would only allow Jason to go if she were assured a friendly face would be there. The pupils ranged in age from eight to eighteen, and few among them were friends.

The party was a chance for the fourteen pupils to meet informally, since the only other time they were together was at the end-of-the year recital in May. Informal is, however, a relative term. Mrs. Cohen, the piano teacher, was too deeply committed to musical excellence to ever let her hair down. She was a slender, olive-skinned woman with a narrow face and long dark hair. It was hard to know her age, but she was somewhere on the scale where advanced middle-age is registered. She wore very stylish clothes, which always included a brightly-colored silk neckerchief around her neck except for those rare occasions when she wore a turtleneck sweater. All the students assumed she was hiding a wrinkled neck or a waddle, and the same busy tongues guessed that her face was wrinkle-free because she had had face-lifts. But all the students liked or at least respected her. She was rather artsy and affected, but almost always she was pleasant except for occasionally when she'd lose her temper because she felt a pupil wasn't showing proper respect for the music. She especially loved Schubert, Schumann and Chopin, and most of the advanced practice pieces would be by these three composers. She also loved Leonard Bernstein, whom she had met several times when a student herself. Michelle never dared tell her her father's opinion of Bernstein—that he was all flash and show with little substance and that his music was either Broadway pap or derivative, rhetorical, and shallow. At least she didn't call the music room a conservatory. It was more humbly called the piano studio and had a separate entrance from the house so that the students wouldn't bother her two grown children, who still lived at home, or her husband, a business consultant of some sort who was often in his home office but rarely seen by the students. The room held two pianos, one of them a Steinway, many chairs, shelves for books and sheet music, and a table usually piled high with piano scores but today cleared and covered with a table cloth on which hors d'oeuvres, fruit juices, ginger ale and coffee were available for the guests.

Mrs. Cohen, making her usual effort to chat personally with each guest, greeted Michelle when she arrived late. The first thing she noticed was that Mrs. Cohen was nervous. Uncharacteristically she spoke in a tentative, uncertain way. One custom that had arisen through the years at these parties was that she would always play a new piece unknown by the students. They would spend time trying to guess who the composer was, and once his or her name was known she would challenge the students to play the piece. At that point Jason would step forward and usually play the piece perfectly. Today, however, the first thing she said upon greeting Michelle was that probably no music would be played this afternoon. Instead she thought she'd play a CD of a pianist playing numerous short pieces. In place of their regular game they could try to guess the pianist's name and then identify as many of the pieces as they could. "Some are very easy, some quite difficult," she said. "Does that sound like an enjoyable exercise for the group?" she wanted to know.

Michelle was momentarily nonplused. Mrs. Cohen had never asked her for her opinion before. Finally she managed to mumble that it was a fine idea and go inside. She was the last arrival, and the others were dispersed around the room talking quietly. Almost instantly Michelle could sense that Mrs. Cohen's awkwardness was general and easily understand why. Jason was standing by himself in one corner and looking rather lost. Everyone had heard the rumors, and he knew they had, so that a mutual reticence and embarrassed silence reigned where ordinarily the sounds of a party would be heard. The tension, it seems, had even undermined Mrs. Cohen.

Michelle decided on the direct approach. She went over to Jason and greeted him, saying that she hoped he was fine. His blue eyes stared at her distractedly for a moment before he nodded. "Hi, Michelle. Thanks for subbing for me last week."

Her small act seemed to release tension, for quite suddenly everyone started talking, Mrs. Cohen invited the guests to partake of the refreshments, and in gathering by the table the fifteen individuals became a unified group. Then Mrs. Cohen put on the CD, and they all played the musical game. So the party was successful, or at least passed for successful. Only towards the end did Michelle get another chance to talk to Jason. They helped clean up and bring things to the kitchen; then while the others went back to the piano studio, she found herself alone with him. At first they skirted around the real issue, talking instead about music. Michelle asked, "Have you been playing much music?"

"A lot actually. And I've been composing."

"That's wonderful. Music for me is just a pastime, but if Mrs. Cohen has taught me anything, it's that music is the most important thing in the world for some people. I really respect that. I imagine you want music to be your career?"

"I think so. Everyone tells me I'm good at it, that I have a gift."

"Oh, you do, you do. The first time I heard you play I realized I could practice for a thousand years and not come close to what you do."

He didn't take this compliment in the spirit it was intended, however. His face clouded. "I don't want to show people up."

"Oh, you don't. It's just the difference between being a natural and being an amateur. I want to be a doctor, so my amateur status doesn't bother me."

"I'm still an amateur too, you know."

"Yeah, but just barely. Mrs. Cohen told me there's a chance you'll play a concerto with the Portland Symphony Orchestra. Grieg's, I think she said. Is that true?"

His face clouded again, and he started showing signs of agitation. "It was, but now..."

Here was an opening. She started to speak, stopped, and then awkwardly hummed. Feeling absurd, she felt the blood rushing to her face. Many people had told her that she was mature beyond her years, but now that she wanted to talk to him as one human being to another, she found herself tongue-tied. Tapping his foot and drumming his fingers on the side of his leg, he too was unable to free himself from his nerves. He also seemed afraid to look at her directly, as if he felt ashamed of himself. Only when she realized he probably felt that way because his self-image had been destroyed by that priest did she suddenly find the courage to speak directly about what was on both their minds.

"Wait a minute, Jason. I want to say something."

He had started back to the studio. He stopped and glanced at her momentarily before his eyes flitted to the floor.

She spoke slowly, choosing her words carefully. "I know about that priest..." She paused, waiting to see if he would object to the topic. When he didn't say anything, she continued. "And I want you to know you're not alone. I mean, it's not just your mother and father and Father Riley who are on your side. All decent people are. You were a victim, and you mustn't blame yourself."

His fingers continued drumming on his legs as he stared vacantly towards the door leading back to the piano studio. "Father Riley won't be able to do anything. We've stopped going to the Most Holy Trinity Church."

"Does that bother you?" she asked, responding to a wistfulness she sensed in his voice.

He considered for a moment. "No, I guess not. He's nice, but...but I'm seeing Rev. Covington at my mother's old church now. He's trying to help me."

"I hope he does. And I hope you realize that if there's anything I can do, please let me know. I think you're very special."

"Thank you, Michelle. My mother thinks I should try to live as normally as possible, but I'm feeling really weird."

"Of course you are now. But things will get better. Remember, you're a genius!"

She saw his soul catch fire so that momentarily, at least, he believed in himself, and as they walked back to the studio to rejoin the others she told herself that he was strong enough to endure.

But when the party ended and she watched him go home with his mother, he had shrunk back into himself again, and she saw that it wasn't going to be that easy. He would to have to undergo a terrible trial where the biggest battles were going to have to be won alone and inside. Even so, she sensed that somehow their separate fates were intertwined.

She was thinking of these impressions again after school started and she was walking from her house to Mr. Jellerson's for the first tutorial session of the spring semester. If the rumors could be believed, Mr. Jellerson was also somehow connected with Jason. She was resolved to ask about Jason before the tutorial was over.

Old Boy was lying outside when she came up the driveway. He yipped happily at seeing her and ambled toward her as far as his tether allowed. Without straining, he simply sat on his haunches and waited patiently, all the while his brown eyes staring at her intently. "Hi, Old Boy," she called. "How's my pal?" His tail started wagging even before she kneeled down and scratched his floppy ears. She patted him for a few minutes while whispering things like "Good boy" and "Aren't you special."

To the door came Mr. Jellerson, smiling benignly. Michelle, recalling how nervous he was during the first several weeks of tutoring, thought he was much better now that he had loosened up. From the first she divined how important teaching was to him, and seeing him so ill at ease with her and awkward, she had taken pity on him and resolved that she would work hard for him. That by no means had been her initial plan. She thought the whole idea of studying for the SAT's was absurd and had decided to just go through the motions. But with her ability (for it was an ability, a gift, she had learned) to identify with vulnerability, almost instantly she decided to put her trust in him and try to learn all he had to teach her. And it had turned out wonderfully! He was really the best teacher she had ever had, and she was learning more from him about life and scholarly procedures, about how to find and hold values while still cultivating a skeptical but inquiring mind, than she had from all the teachers she had ever had. So now that she respected and admired him, it was an extra reward to actually come to like him. She had never been friends with an adult before, but that was how she regarded him: as a friend.

So she smiled back at him, and still patting Old Boy, said, "Hi, Mr. Jellerson. It's not too cold for Old Boy?"

He didn't have his coat on, and his breath in the cold air looked as if he were smoking his pipe, but still he came out into the yard and leaned down to untie his dog. "Actually it probably is, but he likes to be out for a while every day. And the fresh air does him good. We'll take him in now, though."

They went inside and after getting Old Boy settled in his wicker sleeper set to work with some vocabulary drills followed by reading comprehension exercises. All went smoothly, thanks to Michelle's preparation, so that they finished the scheduled items early. Mr. Jellerson asked if she wanted to go on to next week's exercises on paragraph development and coherence, but Michelle said that she would rather not. "Actually, I wanted to talk to you about Jason Buckley," she said.

He nodded and assumed a serious demeanor, neither appearing surprised not distressed. She told him about the incident at the Lawyers' Guild party and about all the rumors she had heard, among them the rumor that he had witnessed something. "I wondered if that was true?" she said.

Mr. Jellerson stood and walked to the window, looked out at the barren field covered with patches of snow to the distant woods, and considered for a moment. He turned. "Yes, it is true," he said in a solemn voice that made her feel uneasy. "I witnessed something and told the police about it, but I don't think it would be appropriate for me to say anything more at this time. I will say that I know about Jason Buckley and my heart goes out to him."

Michelle, seeing the rightness of his reservation, changed her tack. "I wouldn't ask about that," she said, "but I'm really having trouble understanding those boys, Mr. Jellerson. How come boys can be so cruel?"

"Well, I've spent my life associated with adolescent schoolboys, and I certainly know what you mean. I think there's enormous pressure on teenagers—and I would include girls—to conform, to not stand out. They're trying to find out how they fit into the world so that the last thing they want is to be different in any unconventional way. Anyone like that scares them, I think. By 'them' I mean the typical teenager. You obviously are already a mature individual who sees the injustice of snap judgments. But I hope you do also see the boys were really exhibiting fear—fear probably that they might not fit in."

Michelle nodded politely, though she was far from convinced. "I suppose that's so, but it still doesn't justify their cruelty. Isn't there a difference between explaining and excusing?"

Mr. Jellerson smiled and looked pleased with her. "Yes, that's a very good insight. What exactly did these boys say to Jason?"

"Oh, awful stuff. They called him a sissy because he plays piano, a fag, a lover boy of that priest. Hurtful things like that."

Mr. Jellerson, listening thoughtfully with folded arms and hand on his chin, nodded. "I see. Hurtful is just the word. But you stopped them?"

"Yes, but not before the damage was done. Poor Jason tried to fight them even though he was half their size. Things didn't really stop until some adults broke it up. Jason was crying and awfully embarrassed. That's why he fought them, I think. He was so ashamed of his tears the only way he could recover his dignity was to fight."

"Yes, that sounds accurate. It's never a good thing for boys to fight, but there are times when one understands and implicitly approves. It's clear you do—and so do I. I can see you're his friend and you really want to help him."

She shook her head vigorously. "Oh, yes. I really feel for that kid. He's really special, you know, a genius really. I don't know why, but it's like I feel responsible for him."

Mr. Jellerson nodded in turn. Folding his arms again, he considered for a moment. "You've already helped him, of course—stopping those boys, I mean. But besides defending his good name, I'm not sure there's much else you can do. He's going through a difficult time right now. I imagine, what with this town becoming a rumor mill as far as I can tell, that he certainly needs all the support he can get. The best thing to do is not let people go wild with stories."

"I've done that. I've told people that their stories are stupid. They've heard that you're involved and talk about you too. I've told them that's ridiculous."

Mr. Jellerson's face colored deeply. "So the rumors have dragged me in too. Can you tell me what they say?"

She could see the incipient panic in his face. Old Boy felt something too, for with a sudden start he woke and stared at his master. Seeing that Mr. Jellerson's sense of personal dignity was as fragile as an egg under a hammer, instantly Michelle was on her guard. "They said things like you were planning on moving you were so disgusted with the town. Stupid things like that." She lied only to spare him. She never wanted to cause anyone pain.

The Minister

"**H**and me the monkey wrench, would you, Bill. These channel locks are useless. The slip nut's frozen."

Bill leaned down to peer at the trap under the sink where the Rev. John Covington was lying on his side, then after gauging the necessary size began poking through the tool box. He picked up and rejected a small monkey wrench before locating the ten-inch tool. "This should do the trick," he said, handing the tool to John.

Neither were plumbers. Bill Smithson was a semiretired carpenter who had recently begun attending church, and his partner was the minister. They were replacing the corroded and leaking drain trap to the sink in the basement of The First Congregational Church of Waska not because the church was impoverished—with a large endowment from parishioners over its three-hundred-year history remembering the church in their wills, it was in fact decidedly wealthy—but both men were hands-on guys who loved projects. At John's last church in Portsmouth, New Hampshire such do-it-yourself repairs had been an economic necessity, and he had gotten into the habit of fixing everything that he could himself. Bill Smithson, in turn, had found he missed work. He only worked about three months a year, stopping when he made the extra amount allowed under Social Security. So the leaky sink was a perfect project for both of them, and even though the drain connection was corroded, making for a nasty job, both were enjoying themselves.

Bill, thinking of something, started chuckling.

John tightened the monkey wrench over the slip nut and applied pressure: nothing happened. He gave a heave with all his might and still the nut would not budge.

Bill got down on his knees. "Watch out, John. I'll give it a hit with penetrating oil."

John stood and stretched the stiffness out of his bones. "Not getting any younger," he muttered more or less to himself. To Bill he said, "What were you chuckling about a minute ago. I hope I wasn't doing something foolish."

"No, it wasn't that. You asked me awhile ago what got me going to church again, and it occurred to me it was because I'm doing the two-minute drill. You know, when an older guy starts going to church, you call it the two-minute drill." He grinned. "You can use that in one of your sermons—no charge."

John smiled sheepishly and shook his head. His face assumed a comically woeful expression. "I can't use it. It wouldn't get past the censor. Years ago when the Patriots were first in the superbowl I went a bit overboard on the football metaphors that Sunday, and Wendy let me know it sounded foolish to any ears not belonging to a football fan. I vowed after that I'd avoid sports talk."

Bill, still grinning, asked, "What did you say?"

"Oh, you know. God is a coach who was preparing us for the big game. Pretty hokey stuff, I have to admit." He bent down and grunted as he applied pressure to the nut. This time it moved. "People can say a lot of things about me and probably do, but I am capable of learning from experience."

"Your sermons are fine now, John. Besides, when my buddies asked me why I started going to church again, I actually told them I was cramming for the finals."

"That's something I wish my son would do more of. I'm paying a small fortune for his college education, and he mostly gets C's."

The slip nut was off now, and he removed the old P trap. He'd bought a good brass replacement, but before they installed it they snaked the drain going into the wall. Afterwards they noticed the pipe was a bit wobbly, so Bill went to his truck for some scrap lumber while John removed the wall plate. Then they jury-rigged some pieces of 2 X 4 to brace the drain pipe, replaced the wall plate, and finally put the sink back together. What with the stubborn slip nut and the extra work in bracing the drain pipe, it was almost noon by this time, and John with a busy afternoon ahead of him briskly walked down the street to the parsonage, but not before he and Bill arranged to meet again next Monday morning to repair a window in the back of the church.

At home Wendy reminded him of his appointments. Sometimes he forgot things and she acted as an unofficial secretary, even with the church having a real secretary. But he didn't need a reminder this time—he knew perfectly well he had to make a hospital visit and then later in the afternoon have a counseling session with Jason Buckley. While he took a shower and got dressed, Wendy made some sandwiches for lunch.

They were ready when he got downstairs. As he sat down at the kitchen table, Wendy handed him a letter from their son Cory. He was attending a college in the Midwest and had only returned from Christmas vacation two weeks ago. Before he read the letter John waved his hand over it and pretended to divine its import. "I see a request for more money," he said in a solemn, otherworldly voice. "Money that is needed immediately if not sooner."

Wendy, putting the sandwiches on the table, smiled. Every letter from Cory contained a request for money, either as its main theme or as a desperate postscript. He was a perfectly stereotypical college student in this regard. "As usual your clairvoyance is breathtaking. This time it's textbooks being so expensive he spent all the book money on his first three courses."

John browsed through the letter as he began eating his sandwiches. "How come Ruthann never seemed to have these financial problems when she was in college?"

"Ruthann is a woman. Women manage money better."

"I see he's not taking European history. He claims the roster was filled from preregistration, so he couldn't transfer in. I still don't understand how political science majors manage to avoid taking humanities courses."

Wendy rolled her eyes but said nothing. Cory, a political science major, wanted to work in government. When John was at Yale the only political science course he took was political thought in the sixteenth through the eighteenth centuries. He'd read Machiavelli, Hobbes, Locke, Vico and Rousseau and had enjoyed the course. But as far as he could tell political science today was strictly a social science disconnected from history. Father and son had had many friendly discussions verging into arguments about this state of affairs. Wendy, perhaps not wishing to open that particular can of worms, changed the subject. "John, remember we're having the Daltons for dinner on Friday."

This was an item John had forgotten. "Oh, right," he said absently.

They were going to discuss the Wentworth house. Nate Wentworth, who had inherited the ancestral colonial mansion of the founding family of Waska, wanted to give it to the historical society or to the church now that he was a widower. The Daltons, who were very active in the Waska Historical Society, were working with Nate on this and had asked John and Wendy to help. Cliff and Nadine were friends from Yale and Smith—in fact the two couples met their respective mates at the same Yale-Smith mixer back in the 60's—and it was the Daltons who urged the search committee to ask John to be the new minister last year.

"Do you have any suggestions for the meal?"

John rubbed his chin and considered for a moment. "Well, with Nadine on the health food kick, how about fish? Salmon, for instance."

Wendy shook her head. "We served that last time they came."

"Well, is there a law that says we can't serve it again? It was two months ago."

When Wendy, busy looking through the refrigerator, didn't answer, he got up and rinsed his plate off. "How about scallops then?"

She seemed doubtful about this suggestion too, but the discussion would have to be continued later. Giving her a kiss, he was out the door to drive to the hospital in Bedford.

John did two days a month as chaplain on duty at the hospital, but his visit today was to see an elderly parishioner who had suffered a stroke. Widowed for many years and lonely now that her children had all moved away, Mrs. Stacey was depressed and tearful when John came in. He had gotten her involved in church bake sales and similar charity work during his year in Waska, and he tried to use these activities to cheer her up. "Your business on earth is not over, Martha. The children need you to bake your chocolate chip cookies and your brownies." But she was not cheered. She wanted to join her husband, she said, the only time during the visit that she rose above her listlessness. So they prayed together and then he left.

Walking down the hall and feeling a bit depressed himself, he was arrested by a familiar voice. "Hi, John. How are you?"

John turned to see Father Riley coming toward him. The priest was an elderly man, but still spry. Today, however, his walk seemed more halting than John remembered. "Hi, Jim. Good to see you," he said, extending his hand.

Father Riley shook his hand warmly and said, "Visiting a parishioner, I assume."

John nodded as they began walking down the hall together. "Mrs. Stacey, one of the oldest members of the church. I'm afraid she's had another stroke."

"Sorry to hear that."

"Yes, thank you. So am I. She's a wonderful lady, very good with kids. And her brownies are legendary at church socials. I assume you're on the same mission—visiting someone."

"Yes, I came to see a boy who had an appendectomy. He was rushed to the hospital last night. Of course, you know how hospitals are nowadays—if I had got here a few hours later he'd be discharged already. They're processing him right now for discharge."

John nodded grimly. "It seems money is more important than health."

They were at the elevator now. Father Riley pushed the down button and said, "Speaking of boys?"

Getting into the elevator, John said, "Yes, Jason, of course. I'm still seeing him. In fact I have an appointment later this afternoon."

Father Riley sighed and rubbed his forehead nervously. "I cannot but feel I let Jason and the other boy down."

He spoke in such a heartbroken tone that John was very moved. A feeling of profound compassion swept over him, for now he understood why the spring was gone from his friend's legs. "Oh, you certainly are not at fault, Jim. At least not personally. Perhaps all of society, each and every one of us, failed him, not just Father Mullen. He's angry, confused, hurt. He feels betrayed, but believe me he still thinks a lot of you. I'm afraid it's God's goodness he questions now. That man has a lot to answer for." Despite himself he had grown angry. He found himself spitting out the last sentence like spoiled food.

Father Riley nodded and then dropped his head into his chest. He looked even older and more spent than before. And in clearly blaming himself for Father Mullen, it was as if he regarded his whole life as a failure.

"Now, Jim," John said, laying his hand on his friend's shoulder, "no one could see what Father Mullen was. How could we? In the year I have known him, he never once really talked to me. He was secretive. We know why now, but before we found out we all assumed he was either very shy or very cold. Nobody could have guessed the burden of his sin."

Father Riley nodded politely. "Yes, but the trouble is that after it all came out I started recognizing all kinds of signs. That's what I blame myself for."

"You're just like my parishioner, Samuel Jellerson. When he saw Father Mullen and Jason he couldn't believe what his eyes saw, and now he blames himself. But really, Jim, hindsight is always perfect. Neither of you could have known what kind of man he was."

They were in the lobby now and said their good-byes. Inside his car and driving to his church, John started thinking about Father Riley, but quickly his mind turned to Jason. He had begun counseling him through the request of a surprising source—Samuel Jellerson. He had recently rejoined the church of his childhood when he retired and moved from Connecticut to the family farm in Waska. John had to admit that he didn't particularly like the man at first. He found him a cold and humorless Yankee whose suppressed nervous energy made him feel uncomfortable, and he remembered the strange questions he had asked about Father Mullen when on a birding trip with a church group last fall making him even more uncomfortable. The man had seemed to have some ulterior motive that he couldn't fathom.

But two things had caused John to gradually change his opinion of Mr. Jellerson. First he heard about his experiences in the closing of Hartley Academy and how his position had been basically decent and nonsectarian. Whatever else he was, he wasn't a small or a petty man. Having learned this, John approached his newest parishioner more openly and started to get to know him. Behind the Yankee exterior he found a man of passionate convictions, particularly about education, and a man of integrity. So he had already grown to respect him when quite unexpectedly he showed up at John's parish office two months ago. Telling the story of his involvement with Jason, Mr. Jellerson impressed John even more. His compassion for the boy and his guilt in blaming himself for not going to the police on the day he witnessed the abuse so overwhelmed him that he broke into convulsive sobs several times as he spoke. The emotional display embarrassed him, and he only recovered his equilibrium when John assured him that he totally sympathized with him and respected his integrity. Assuming his pastoral role, John reassured him that his honest doubts and the desire not to needlessly accuse a man were compelling arguments against going to the police and that therefore he should not blame himself. But Mr. Jellerson wasn't looking for comfort; he had already self-judged his actions and found himself guilty. What he wanted to do was help Jason Buckley in any way he could to expiate the guilt and to do his human duty. He asked John to accompany him while he confronted Father Mullen, but the priest refused to see them. They then separated, but later Mr. Jellerson called to ask John if he would counsel Jason, telling him he had already suggested this to Mercy Buckley, the boy's mother. Anticipating his objection before he could make it, Mr. Jellerson told him she was baptized in the Congregational Church and was still technically a member of the parish.

John had earned a master's degree in child counseling at the University of New Hampshire when he was a minister at the Portsmouth church, so professionally he was qualified to help Jason. He had seen the need to become proficient in counseling when he was confronted with several disturbed children at his church and in fact had been able to help them, but no child he had counseled had been violated and abused as severely as Jason. In his professional judgment Jason needed extensive help that was probably beyond his capabilities. Mr. Jellerson, however, explained that there was a spiritual dimension to Jason's problem. He was in danger of losing his faith. Thus, and only after much further discussion (and almost against his better judgment), he agreed to counsel Jason, adding as a proviso that he would see him for two months and if he couldn't help him he would refer him to a psychiatrist.

Not counting the first meeting a few days after Christmas where Mercy Buckley sat in and the goal was simply to get to know each other and start building trust, he had had four sessions so far with Jason and had gained enough knowledge to see that Samuel Jellerson was right: Jason's problem was twofold. Because of what Father Mullen had done to him, he was feeling extremely insecure, vulnerable, and lacking in trust, and his self-image and self-respect were virtually destroyed. But he also was experiencing an equally severe spiritual crisis. His understanding of God had been grossly distorted by the priest, who had tinkered with his mind as if it were a used car he was working on, and as a result Jason equated Father Mullen with God. He was so disturbed that he might never be right again. His life might be ruined before it had hardly begun. A priest had used his special status as a nurturer to gratify profane desires, then confused the boy in order not to be caught. Such a breathtaking example of evil profoundly affected John personally. Not only did he fear that he was not up to the task of helping Jason professionally; the evil of the priest so disturbed him that he also had self-doubts.

He had had a sabbatical a few years ago wherein he reassessed his life as a minister. All in all he had concluded that he had done a good and conscientious job as a clergyman. It was during this time that he finished his course work and wrote a master's thesis on child counseling, so no one could accuse him of not trying to improve himself in his role of helping people. But the evil he was now confronting initiated a second reappraisal that led him to make further changes in his life. A long time ago when he first became a minister a member of his congregation, a middle-aged woman with small dark eyes that seemed to bore right through him, had informed him that many in the church found him hard to take. He was too earnest, too serious, she explained. He had been hurt and embarrassed by her revelation, which had been delivered with a certain subterranean pleasure in the pain she was causing, and soon after that interview he sought out the advice of a senior minister in town, who told him his problem was a common one. Being a minister was to forever have to live up to people's expectations, he explained. The way to rescue your humanity from being a prisoner of those expectations was to cultivate other activities that gave both a respite from the calling and a perspective on it. Do that, he said, and you'll find you'll be a better person and therefore a better minister. John had always been interested in outdoor activities and sports, so straightaway he decided not to suppress that part of himself, and ever after he was an avid and unashamed sports fan, particularly of the Red Sox and college football, and he went hiking and skiing as often as he could. More recently he had taken up nature photography to combine with the hiking and cross country skiing, and to a certain extent his willingness to dirty his hands in church repairs arose from the same impetus to transcend the narrow life of a minister and achieve a fuller humanity.

So up until now the old minister's advice had been good advice—his parishioners everywhere he had served regarded him as a friend as well as a pastor—but now he found himself questioning some of the premises that had guided his career. Had he gained in humanity but lost something as a minister? Was he truly prepared for times of trouble and family tragedy when people desperately depended on their pastor? Why did the evil he felt as a living presence so disturb him? Had he grown soft? The thought that, figuratively speaking, made him gasp for breath was the idea of a fellow clergyman violating every duty in his pursuit of selfish desire. It almost made him believe in Satan's agency, though trained by liberal Protestant professors, of course, he didn't really believe in Satan. But unlike many of his classmates at the seminary he did believe in the reality of sin and evil. An impoverished, loveless childhood or terrible, neurotic parents explained a great deal of the evil in the human condition, but it didn't excuse the things people did to each other. It certainly did not excuse Father Mullen. Thus he found himself contemplating, even brooding over, the nature of evil in a conscious effort to regain some of the high seriousness that was his Calvinist heritage. During office hours when time permitted he read through his notes and papers from college and the seminary, many of them yellowed and brittle, as if searching for an intellectual answer to the evil he could feel. He gravitated especially to the philosophy of Immanuel Kant, whose writings were one of the main impetuses that led him to choose the ministry as his calling. Kant's moral philosophy, which had earned him the title of "the Protestant Aquinas" and was summed up in his famous Practical Imperative, "So act as to treat humanity, whether in thine own person or in that of any other, in every case as an end withal, never as a means only," perfectly articulated the ethical duty of every human being. To see others as Other, to use them as if they were an object, a means to an end, was recognizably the dynamics of all human evil, whether the unspeakable atrocities of the Nazis or of a child falsely accusing another of stealing the cookies he himself had stolen—or of a rogue priest hiding his rapes and terrorizing of little boys behind a Roman collar. He also reviewed many other sources from Manichaeism, Platonism and St. Paul in the ancient world, Calvin and Luther from the Reformation, up to Paul Tillich in the modern, but besides Kant the other main source of his thinking was the English Romantics, particularly Shelley, Coleridge and Hazlitt. He had been an English major as an undergraduate at Yale and had had an excellent professor of Romanticism. He remembered how well this man had articulated Shelley's central belief that the "great secret of morals is love, or a going out of our own nature and an identification of ourselves with the beautiful which exists in thought, action, or person, not our own." He liked this passage on the moral imagination because it demonstrated that ethical behavior was based on imaginative sympathy and self-transcendence. Empathy was necessary for goodness; the source of evil was selfishness. Thinking of others and doing for others was the basis of an ethical life, but to be able to live an ethical life it was necessary to escape the prison of the self. Shelley in turn led him to a passage in William Hazlitt that so exquisitely expressed the relationship between selfishness and imagination that John had actually used it for the basis of a sermon more than once in the early years of his preaching. Hazlitt demonstrated that the same power that led a selfish man to various plots and schemes for self-aggrandizement was, when properly applied, the means of considering one's fellow human beings and one's duty to them. That power was of course imagination. The selfish man could not make his plots and schemes work without making a mental projection, for the only way to know the future is by a projection of the imagination. Thus the same power that projects one selfishly into the future is the very power that makes one capable of sympathizing with others. I could not love myself, Hazlitt concludes, if I were not capable of loving others. It was because of Kant, Hazlitt and Shelley, then, and not any theologian, that John believed in the reality of evil and of human responsibility for the evil that people do.

This period of introspection had occurred during the Christmas season, and in truth it ruined the holidays for him. Joyful cries of "Merry Christmas" were uttered, and he would think of the fathomless darkness of Father Mullen's eyes; eggnog around the Christmas tree with his son and daughter at home didn't feel right whenever the vision of Jason lost and forlorn came into his mind; behind the children who came by his door to sing Christmas carols the moon loomed like Satan's eye glaring with *Schadenfreude* at the things people did to one another. And yet it was only after recovering his intellectual roots and reaffirming their truth that he felt capable of helping Jason. And helping that boy was now the most important thing in his life. He hadn't forgotten the lesson of the old minister; he was on the surface his genial self and no one except Wendy knew of the changes he had undergone. Perhaps his Christmas sermon was darker than usual this year; perhaps his reminder to the congregation to think of all those who were lost and afraid, who lived in fear and want, and who were small and vulnerable was more heartfelt than they expected, but when he shook their hands and greeted them at the door he was virtually a second Santa Claus in his *Gemütlichkeit*.

He thought wryly of that performance as he pulled into the church parking lot. Surely hypocrisy, one of the seven deadly sins, did not always wear a black mantle. He had the feeling that at this point in time his real work and his essential self were not invested in the sermons that he delivered on Sundays but in the hour that was coming up, and his conversation with Father Riley strengthened him in this conviction. Getting out of his car, he stopped for a moment and stared at the white church and steeple that since Puritan days had symbolized the spiritual aspirations of people in New England. Thinking of Father Riley's broken spirit, he recalled in the second session before Jason had grown to trust him even a little how the boy's eyes followed his every movement and how once when he had suddenly stood from his chair to get something on his desk Jason had winced and his eyes filled with terror. It was that vulnerability that had wrenched his heart, twisting it around the tears of things. By God, he would help that boy. To fail was to stand by and let win the blind forces of evil, terror and destruction, every thing that preyed upon human weakness. And to fail Jason was to fail Father Riley, whose life of selfless service to humanity was besmirched and darkened in his last years.

He took a deep breath and collected himself; then with a final glance at the steeple pointing towards the darkening winter skies, he walked up the path to his office in the parish hall, which was connected to the church by an enclosed corridor. Before getting to his essential work he would have to spend a few minutes more in the quotidian world, which is to say, he would have to deal with his secretary.

Eleanor Smallwood was her name. She was middle-aged and unmarried, with an equal number of virtues and shortcomings that were commingled together in various ways, some of which he liked and some of which he didn't. She was good with children and always kept a jar of candy available for any boy or girl who wandered in. She taught Sunday school and ran the program, choosing both the lessons and teachers with John's nominal approval, thus freeing him from those administrative duties. She was on the whole very competent and trustworthy, and having been in her position for over twenty-five years she knew everything about the church and its members—an invaluable source of information for John, who was just entering his second year as minister. It was she who told him all about Mr. Jellerson's behavior at his school's closing. But she didn't see very well and therefore didn't type very well. She also had a cavalier attitude towards spelling that John described (to Wendy and no one else) as positively Elizabethan. He had gotten her a new computer with a larger monitor, but it didn't help her typing and of course made no difference in her spelling. He had suggested several times that she use the spell checker in the word processing program, so far to no avail. But worst of all was her penchant for decorating her office for whatever season or holiday was current with a taste that could only be described as sentimentally old-maidish. John, who was not a sentimental man, had to endure the knowledge that the first impression of anyone who came to see him would be of impossibly treacly plastic or porcelain gimcracks such as the current models, a plastic Minnie and Mickey Mouse on skis and a porcelain snowman holding a puppy. The walls would also be festooned with posters of the same aesthetic level with uplifting observations such as the one that affronted him now: A SNOWFLAKE IS THE SMILE OF A CHILD. So far he had been too kind, or too cowardly, to say anything beyond an occasional ironic remark about some of these items; for instance he had observed of the Easter bunny she had on her desk last spring that it looked as if it had eaten five pounds of chocolate-covered marshmallows, and he had asked of the witch flying a broom in a Halloween poster last fall if the witch had a driver's license. But all such remarks passed over her head. He rather suspected that Christian forbearance was his only option.

But she had a good heart and he liked her. When he came in she was at her desk

going through some books. "How are you, John? Did you fix the sink?"
John took off his coat and hung it on the hook next to the door. "Yes, we were quite successful, if I do say so myself."
"Good. Everything's all ready." She was referring to the preparations for Jason's session. She meant that she had taken ice, sparkling water flavored with lime for him and orange tonic for Jason from the tiny, cabinet refrigerator and placed them on the table in his office. She had discovered last week that Jason liked orange tonic and had promised him she would get some for him.
He picked up the mail and looked through it, but seeing nothing urgent he didn't open any of the letters. "Were there any calls, Eleanor?"
"Only two. Mrs. Stacey's daughter called. She's at a motel in town and wants you to call tonight. And Bill Smithson called. He thinks he left a set of his screw drivers down in the bathroom and wants you to retrieve them for him."
John took the stickie note that had Mrs. Stacey's daughter's phone number, and saying he'd get Bill's tool after the session started going into his office.
"John, you've got a few minutes to discuss the Sunday school books, haven't you?"
He glanced at the clock: 3:15. "Yes, a few, but I do want to review some notes before Jason comes."
Some new Sunday school books were needed for next year. She had shown him three or four possibilities. Ordinarily they used the ones from the United Church of Christ, but she was very much taken with another one from an independent ecumenical publisher and wanted him to look through it for his opinion.
"Did you get a chance to look at the book?" she asked, standing and holding a copy in her hand.
"Yeah," he nodded toward the book. "Actually, no discussion is needed. If you like the book, it's fine. I read through it yesterday and see no problems."
She looked relieved. "Good, good," she smiled. "I think the children will love it." She put the book down on her desk but did not take her seat. She seemed nervous and indecisive.
"Is there something else?"
She sat down and opened the book. I was wondering something about Jason. There's a lesson in the book that made me think of him. Do you think he'll join our church?"
"I couldn't really say. It's too early."
"He's such a dear boy. I do hope…"
"Yes," John said, going into his office, but what the yes meant he was not sure. He closed the door and for the next half hour read his notes on Jason and stared at his walls more than he meant to. There were several of his nature photographs framed on the walls, pictures of a moose he's gotten by the side of the road, of waves crashing on the rocks on the Maine coast, of a flock of snow geese grazing, but it wasn't at these he stared.
He heard mother and son come in at about ten minutes before the hour. Mrs. Buckley always came with Jason and stayed in the waiting room, where Eleanor kept her company until five o'clock even though her day ended at four—which was yet another reason he liked her and forgave her her abysmal taste.
He went to the door and opened it. "Hello, Mrs. Buckley. Hello, Jason."
She maintained a certain distance, polite but not really friendly. John understood

that until she saw some evidence that the counseling was helping her son she was reluctant to go beyond a professional relationship. Last week he had the feeling some real progress had been made, and he watched her to see if her demeanor had changed. She was still a very attractive woman. She was dressed sensibly in corduroy pants, a red ski parka unzipped to reveal a heavy, gray, woolen sweater. Jason, looking small and vulnerable as usual, at least had lost the fear in his eyes. Quietly and in unison they both said, "Hi, Rev. Covington."

The greeting was pleasant and polite, but he couldn't really perceive any new warmth. He felt a bit disheartened, but fortunately he was able to recover his equanimity as Eleanor started talking.

"Cold out, huh?" she said. "At least we're finally going to get some snow, I hear." She had been very disappointed that they hadn't had a white Christmas. They were experiencing a winter drought, as it had only spit snow a few times since cold weather came in November. The only accumulation was in early January, and that melted away a few days later. But for the last week it had been very cold.

"Yes," Mrs. Buckley said politely. "I guess we're finally getting some snow." Her arm was on Jason's shoulder.

"Are you ready, Jason?" John asked.

He looked at his mother, who nodded, and followed John into the inner office.

Once the door was closed he forgot about Mrs. Buckley and concentrated all his attention on Jason. He handed him the can of orange tonic and a glass with ice cubes and said, "Have a seat, Jason."

Last week he had actually been able to get Jason to talk about Father Mullen. For the first three sessions he had only responded with a yes or no to any mention of the man. John, hoping to build upon that beginning, started the session by saying, "I want to go over some of the things we talked about last week. Is that okay?"

Jason nodded, though the apprehension in his face reminded John of the look of uncomprehending fear their dog showed when he was brought to the vet. "We can go slowly. Just tell me again what Father Mullen said to you to make you do his bidding."

It was evident that Jason had been thinking about this a lot, for without any hesitation and with only slight pauses between his thoughts he immediately began talking in a high-pitched excited voice. "He said God had given me the gift of music… He said God had given me my voice… He said God had given me my life. All these things were God's to take or leave. He said he knew these things because God spoke through him… He said God didn't just appear to him at the mass like with other priests. God was always with him. And he said…God wanted me to prove my worth. He told me I was a very beautiful boy, and then he said God had given him the gift for teaching and loving young boys… I was scared. I wanted to run away. But even more scary was that he knew it. He said, 'You're scared and want to run away. You can't.' He read my thoughts. He made me think he was telling the truth. And he said over and over God would be angry with me if I didn't… He said God could take my gift away as easily as he gave it. But he said also that God loved my music, so that…so that… that if he was angry he might take my mother and father away. He told me that when he was young and before he understood God had chosen him, he had disobeyed God and God took his parents away. It's true too. His mother and father were killed in a car accident. After that, he said, he always obeyed God. He said I would be very foolish not to do the same. So I did."

John leaned forward in his chair and looked into Jason's eyes. "Now, Jason. I hope you realize now there was nothing miraculous in Father Mullen knowing you'd be scared and wanting to run away. He has abused other boys. He knew they were scared."

"I did see that, but it was like he had me in a spell. I knew it was wrong. I didn't want to do it, but I was scared."

As he spoke, Jason looked down at the floor as if ashamed of himself. It was to work past that shame and self-blame that was John's goal for him. Very gently he said, "Was it fear of God or fear of Father Mullen?"

"Fear of God, I think."

John glanced down at his notes. Last week Jason had said it was both. "But you were afraid of Father Mullen too, weren't you?"

Jason looked up from the floor, his face ashen. "I still am. But he told me God... and he was a priest. I felt I had to believe him."

"But you know from the catechism of the Catholic Church and from the New Testament that God is love. You were confused because of the lies Father Mullen told you. I can understand that perfectly, but remember as we try to sort this out that God is love."

Jason looked as if he resented John's comment. "So where did I go wrong? Shouldn't I have trusted a priest?"

"Usually the answer is yes. It's safe to say, for example, that Father Riley can always be trusted. But what if Father Mullen was not really a priest? I mean, not really fulfilling his duties as a priest?"

Jason didn't answer. He chewed on his tongue and fidgeted in his chair from his effort to see his way clear through the confusion.

"Let me try to express it another way for you, Jason. You're wondering how the God I described can allow a man who is supposed to be his servant to do these things to you. I understand your bewilderment. People all through history have asked this question about sin and evil. In this century the Nazis in Germany murdered millions of Jews and other non-Germans. But human beings are responsible for their actions. God gave us the world, but what human beings do with it and have done with it is our responsibility. Father Mullen was selfish and evil. God did not cause him to be selfish and evil—he is responsible. Perhaps there are factors that made Father Mullen the way he is. Perhaps he was raised without love, but God is not a puppeteer pulling strings. God is love. Whenever we're kind and feel love, God is present in our lives."

He paused and raised his hand palm up. "Jason, I wish I could tell you that God could have stopped Father Mullen, but that isn't the way the world is. Do you understand that?"

Jason, who only briefly regarded John before his eyes reverted to the floor, looked up again. "I think so," he said.

"But do you understand that while you understand it intellectually, you can still feel differently? That's what I want you to see."

"Now I don't understand."

"Let me try to explain. What Father Mullen did to you was such a violation of trust that anyone, any victim of his evil, would be deeply hurt. We agree, don't we, that that describes your situation?"

By way of replying, tears welled in Jason's eyes.

John resisted the temptation of reaching over and comforting the boy. He and

Mercy had agreed that under the circumstances no physical contact would occur because Jason would not be able to distinguish benign from evil contact. Speaking very gently, John tried to hug him with words. "It's going to take time for you to heal. That's what I mean. That process, though, will also be a process of understanding more and more deeply what happened. Father Mullen is an evil man. But he's evil in many ways. He violated your trust and he violated his vows. He was so selfishly intent upon his own desires that he didn't care what he did to you. He purposely tried to confuse you about God. He did that simply to protect himself so that he wouldn't get caught. Remember, though, what I just said. God is love. God doesn't trick people. He doesn't try to make a little boy think that a bad priest is not a bad priest. He doesn't try to trick you into thinking that a man's evil and perverse desires are God's will. From a Christian point of view, what Father Mullen did was the ultimate sin—he sinned and in sinning instead of displaying penitence he displayed hubris."

"What's hubris?"

"Hubris? Hubris is overweening pride. It's the arrogance that thinks whatever someone does is either God's will or is not answerable to anyone or anything. Some say it's the sin of Adam—not disobedience but putting himself in the place of God. Father Mullen did that. He didn't care what he did to you. He only cared about himself. I suppose from one perspective we could say Father Mullen is a very sick man. It is sick and perverse and evil to think you are God. It's even worse to not be able to see the evil you are doing when you do these things."

Jason followed all he said closely, but he still looked doubtful.

"I think some other things might be confusing you, Jason. For instance, from what I understand, Father Mullen loves music. So do you. So when I say he is an evil man, I don't mean there's not a shred of goodness in him. No one is wholly good or wholly evil. Father Mullen has some good in him. It was probably the good in him that made you trust him in the first place. Am I right?"

Jason's face brightened in a moment of recognition. "Yes," he said emphatically. "He does know a lot about music, especially Bach. I admired him for that. He plays the piano and organ wonderfully too. He showed me things my piano teacher, Mrs. Cohen, didn't know."

"It is good that you see that. It's important to understand that none of us are wholly good or evil because then you can see that Father Mullen wouldn't have been able to trick you if he didn't have some good in him." He paused and briefly debated with himself whether this was the time to take things another step. He decided he'd risk it. "Jason," he said, "someday you might find it in your heart to forgive that man, not for what he did to you—for that is unforgivable—but forgive him for being a sinner. Sin is isolating, you know. In his soul I'm sure Father Mullen must be a wretchedly unhappy man. And we mustn't ever totally give up on anyone finding redemption. If you ever do forgive him, then, remember that his love of music and of Bach are the good parts to this evil man."

There was a long pause while Jason thought, and John became very conscious of the tick-tock sound of the wall clock. Then Jason said very decisively, "I know it's Christian to forgive, just as the Lord's Prayer says, but I don't think right now I can."

"I wouldn't expect you to right now. To tell the truth, I cannot really forgive him now either, even though it's my Christian duty to do so. I think you are a wonderful young man, filled with life and wonder and blessed with an extraordinary ability with music. It makes me mad to think anyone would hurt you."

John said this in hopes of making Jason see that they shared a commonality of feeling. He studied Jason's face carefully, hoping to perceive he had been reached. For a long time he pondered, staring at the floor where his foot was drumming, but then he looked up. Slowly his face broke into a smile. "I know you're on my side," he said as John's heart soared.

Old Boy

One early February evening while Jellerson was at his desk reading a U.S. history textbook the phone rang. He was about to reach for it when he heard Millie pick up in the kitchen. He waited for a moment to see if the call was for him, but when he heard her conversing, he went back to his textbook. Recently the headmaster of Courtney Academy had called him to ask if he would be available for substitute teaching. The headmaster had been very complimentary, saying his reputation as an excellent teacher had preceded him and that he had also heard many fine things from Michelle Turcotte about him. He said that he realized he was retired now, but if he understood anything about the world and particularly born teachers, they never really got out of the saddle. In maintaining the academic excellence of his school it was always his idea that a substitute teacher should be as good as or better than the teacher he replaced. So ran the headmaster's spiel, which while pleasant to hear was really quite unnecessary, for Jellerson was ready to say yes the moment he realized the headmaster's intentions. Now in preparation for the day when he would, in the headmaster's quaint phrase, be called to get back in the saddle, he was reading the textbook the school used. He was in the middle of the chapter on the Civil War, following General Grant's strategic moves at Vicksburg. Momentarily he glanced at Old Boy in his wicker basket when he made a strange sound, a cross between a whine and a groan, but before he could ask Old Boy what was the matter, Millie called him from the kitchen. "Sam, it's for you. It's Rev. Covington. He wants to talk to you about your Uncle Walt."

He had never mentioned his uncle to the minister, so Millie's statement instantly made him feel uneasy. He picked up the phone at his desk to listen to the minister urgently describe Walter Pingree's condition—he had suffered a fairly major stroke that had paralyzed the left half of his body, but having already recovered some movement in his arm and leg the doctor's prognostication was that with physical therapy he would make a good recovery. But his medical condition was only half of the problem. "Sam, he's in a bad way—I mean psychologically, spiritually especially. He's lonely and proud. Those two things I found out by his behavior, for to tell the truth getting information from him was like pulling teeth. I visited him during my chaplain hours and only learned he was baptized and married in our church much later—as I say, he's a proud man and doesn't volunteer anything. But after much effort I finally got him to tell me he had two grandnephews and a niece, all of whom seem to have nothing to do with him, and that his only other relative is you. But when I told him I'd get in touch with you, he almost panicked. 'You don't need to bother him,' he said."

Jellerson, watching Old Boy fidget in his basket, said, "That sounds like my uncle."

"Ah, yes," John said, then after collecting his thoughts continued. "His reasoning is a bit byzantine, but I think he doesn't want to be seen in a vulnerable position. The trouble is, he *is* in a vulnerable position. He is partly paralyzed and has no means except Medicare and Social Security. You remember poor Mrs. Stacey who died last week. He's in much the same state as she was— and that's why I'm so worried. Without help he's just going to give up."

"Yes, that sounds like my Uncle Walter," Jellerson repeated. "I've tried to get him out here on visits. He came for Christmas dinner, in fact, but I know what you mean about his pride. I both admire him for it and get exasperated because he makes it a barrier."

John was silent for a while. "Do you think you could help him? He's going to need a place to go after he's out of rehab. Do you think…?"

"Of course, John. We could put him up here—that is, if he'll let us."

John sighed with relief. "Thanks, Sam. That's what I was hoping you'd say."

He hadn't asked Millie before he made this promise, and yet he was certain she would concur with his decision. Things between husband and wife had been going very well lately, and not from accident either. Jellerson had been working on his relationships ever since the Jason Buckley incident bisected his life and changed him forever. When Beverly was home for Christmas he had schooled himself to avoid being judgmental. Her nose ring went unremarked; the news that she lived with another woman and two men in a communal arrangement likewise elicited no response. That she did volunteer work for the AIDS hot line in San Francisco was praised instead of queried.

All this equanimity and acceptance owed something to Michelle, for after tutoring sessions they often chatted for a few minutes, and some of the things she said had opened his eyes to the way girls and young women thought nowadays. Once she said, "It's not fair to keep people from doing things just because of who they are. Isn't freedom being fair? If freedom means some are allowed to do things but others aren't, it's not freedom; it's oppression." He had thought about that remark for several days afterwards. It was admittedly a simple thought, even sophomoric in its naiveté, and yet it made him realize that almost every difficulty he had ever had with his daughter entailed his trying to force her into his conception of what a girl should be and her resenting it. Having had an overwhelming desire to reconcile with her—it still hurt to have found out she moved to San Francisco to be free of him—he had tried to give her her own space (another phrase he had learned from Michelle), and as a result, they, father and daughter, had connected more in the brief four days she was home for Christmas than they had in the previous twenty-six years of her life. Perhaps this rapprochement would have come about without Michelle's indirect influence, for before Beverly came Jellerson had reconciled himself to Millie's new life with an equally successful result. Instead of resenting her new job and the independence and self-respect it gave her, he accepted it, at first artificially by forcing the acceptance on himself, but Millie's response had been so positive that eventually he found himself actually believing in her right to freedom. Thus independently and with Michelle's help he had nurtured his relationships with the two women in the family, and when he went out to the kitchen to sound out Millie about having Walter Pingree stay at the farmhouse, he was sure of her response and was not disappointed.

"But he will be difficult. The man's got a lot of pride," he said.

"Yes, but pride is all he has left. Besides, it's our human duty," she said.

Then he kissed her.

"What's that for?" she asked.

"For being yourself," he said with a smile.

His next task was a mental one. He knew Walt would refuse his offer when first made; the trick was going to be to anticipate all his stubborn objections. Here, however, he had a lot of history to deal with. He and his family had never been close to Walter, Jellerson's mother's brother, or to his wife Ellie. Nor had he ever been close to his cousin Kermit. He attended his cousin's war-hero funeral and remembered certain looks Walter had given him because he had been able to escape the draft, and earlier he had once attended a Courtney Academy football game where Kermit performed athletic heroics; but he was eight years older than his cousin so that it was as if a generation separated them. His younger brother Edgar had been at Courtney Academy two years with Kermit, but he also had never been close. Jellerson's clearest memory of Walt went a long ways towards explaining the gulf between them. On one of their annual, rather perfunctory Christmas visits to their relatives, when Jellerson was fourteen and Kermit six, his cousin was crying because the electric train he'd gotten for Christmas stopped working an hour after it was set up. Jellerson, from his lofty age of fourteen, had outgrown his electric train and offered it to Kermit, but instead of being gratefully accepted, Walt objected and a family squabble ensued. He said he didn't want Jellerson castoffs, and Jellerson's father took instant umbrage at his tone. The two wives sided with their spouses, and the Jellersons left the house under a cloud. For the next couple of years the families barely spoke to one another. Later Jellerson came to realize that class feelings lay behind this family alienation. In marrying his father, Jellerson's mother had moved up to the middle class, and Walter had a working-class distrust of suits and ties.

When he became an adult geographical distance also added to the mix. With Jellerson living in Connecticut, he hadn't known of his aunt's death until Millie's sister mentioned it months later in a letter. Jellerson used to send Christmas cards, but one year his card was not answered so that even that tenuous family connection was sundered. He thought about Walt when he and Millie were making plans to move back to Waska, but involved with his own burden of adjusting to a life without teaching, he had no contact with his uncle for several months after they moved home. Jason Buckley changed all that. The boy's plight began a process of awakening Jellerson from self-absorption to an almost obsessive sympathy. Like the fragrance of spring flowers permeating a room from one open window, his sympathy for Jason grew to encompass all who suffered. By this time he had seen enough of his uncle's life to know how wretched it was, and he found himself both contemplating its almost unimaginable loneliness and desiring to do something about it. He phoned him before Thanksgiving and invited him to dinner, but after an awkward pause Walt said he had made other plans.

He didn't volunteer any information on his plans, and Jellerson was too polite to ask, though he rather doubted their reality. But he did change his tactics for the next occasion, Christmas dinner. He asked him in person when they drove together to Mercy Buckley's house to tell her about Jason. Walt was waiting for him in the downstairs hall of his apartment building, sitting with another man on an old couch near the door. The other man, whom Walt didn't introduce, stared at Jellerson in a way that told him Walt had informed the man about his role in the Father Mullen scandal that the papers were full of at that time. His small dark eyes stared at Jellerson with a mixture of oily fascination and suppressed admiration for a man who was going to become the famous witness. He so repulsed Jellerson that for a time he was inclined not to invite Walt to dinner. When he had phoned him earlier to elicit his help in approaching Mercy Buckley he had specifically asked him not to tell anyone. But after the emotional scene with the boy's mother his anger abated and driving back to Walt's he did ask him. Now the dynamics were completely different, for Walt seemed to feel he would be proving something to his unctuous companion. At least that was Jellerson's impression, but regardless of his motives, Walt did come for Christmas dinner at the farmhouse.

The visit was not, however, a success. Walt's rather bizarre behavior made everyone, including himself, uncomfortable. His conduct was motivated, it seemed, by his desire not to be too beholden, or perhaps, Jellerson thought, to not have to play the role of the poor relative. His reluctance not to appear extravagant, at any rate, had everyone rolling their eyes before the day was over.

He had turkey, potatoes and peas but not gravy or cranberry sauce; he had apple pie for dessert but declined having ice cream on it despite the longing looks he kept giving Jellerson's à la mode piece of pie. And he refused wine and later at first a beer when he and Jellerson watched a basketball game while Millie and Beverly cleaned up. Throughout the visit he had the look of a man in extreme discomfort, which manifested itself in fidgeting in his chair and general avoidance of eye contact. More than just not wanting to be a bother, he acted as if he had internalized the class feelings and, fearing he didn't deserve to be treated with respect, scrupulously avoided any situation that gave it to him. Pride, yes, though infinitely sadder.

A few times he made his thought process explicit. When Millie asked, "Walter, would you like some coffee or tea?" Jellerson could see him quickly steal a glance at the kitchen counter to see the empty coffee pot. "No, that's all right," he said. "I don't want to be a bother." Only when Jellerson said he'd like some coffee and a pot was made did he consent to take a cup. When Jellerson drove him home in the late afternoon gloom and in parting said, "Well, Merry Christmas, Walt. I hope you had a good time," he only grudgingly gave his thanks. But right before he closed the car door he turned, bent his head down to look at Jellerson, and said enigmatically, "Sorry." Jellerson thought about that last word all the way home. It was as if Walt were ashamed of his behavior and was acting the way he did in spite of himself. It kept the door open.

Every bit of this history, recent and in the faraway past, Jellerson took with him into the hospital room the next day when he visited Walt. To it was added the terrible condition in which he found his uncle. His bed was elevated so that he was sitting up, and with the room very warm he had the blankets at his waist, exposing his upper body. It was pulled strangely to the right (his good side), and the left half of his face was slack as if made of melted wax. But it was the aura of depression and despair in the room that was most evident. Jellerson could smell it, though whatever he did he told himself not to show that he perceived it, nor show the slightest sign of pity. With false cheerfulness he said, "Hello, Walt. The doctors tell me you're already mending."

The remark had one positive effect—it elicited a quick and feisty response that showed Walt still had a cantankerous chip on his shoulder. Frowning darkly, he said, "A lot they know."

The nurses had told Jellerson that Walt had been slurring his words but that just this morning his speech had cleared. It was another good sign, and Jellerson was glad, though he saw John was more accurate in his diagnosis than the doctors. He stared at the picture of a rustic cabin on a lake above Walt's head and tried to find words of genuine cheer. Fighting the infectious depression that permeated the room, he found himself in a struggle whereby pity became self-pity, self-doubt, blackness. It was as if someone else, not he, said, "The doctors are doing their best, I'm sure. But we have to do our part."

Walt's right arm rubbed at his melted face. The arm was shockingly thin, as was his sunken chest covered with white curly hair exposed where his johnny opened when he raised his arm. He's not eating right, Jellerson thought. We'll have to fatten him up. The idea woke him from his impending spiritual malaise. "Walt," he said in a much more commanding voice, "you'll be better in no time. While you're healing Millie and I very much want you to come out to the farmhouse."

While Walt stared straight ahead and thought about the offer, Jellerson could see his mind working. The alternative of a nursing home as a charity case was no alternative at all. Even so, he refused the offer.

"But why?" Jellerson asked.

"Because I don't want to be a bother to anyone. I hate to feel I'm a burden. Go ahead, call me stubborn, but I'd rather not." He looked at Jellerson defiantly as if he'd been challenged to a fight. "And don't think I don't see the situation. I'm a useless old man. I have been for years. All I can do is get in the way."

His last remarks were spoken imploringly, and Jellerson recognized it was the closest he would come to asking for help.

"You won't be in the way, Walt. And if you're useless, so am I. It's not our fault we grow old. There's a poem by Dylan Thomas where he say something along the lines of 'Do not go gently into that good night. Rage, rage against the dying of the light.' Young people can have love poems for themselves, but that's a poem for us older ones. I don't mind helping you because some day I might need some help. Call me selfish, then. But you're my mother's brother. You're family. I want to help you because you're family. We have a huge farmhouse with five bedrooms. One of them, the guest bedroom, is on the first floor. It's not as if we'd be crowded. We have room for you."

Walt considered for a while. He stared out the window and rubbed his stubbly chin with his good hand.

Jellerson decided he needed a little nudge. "Remember, you helped me when I needed to get in touch with Mercy Buckley. Now I have a chance to return the favor."

Walt nodded in recognition of the justice of the observation. "If I came I'd want to pay for my board."

"You don't have to, Walter."

He raise his good arm and pointed. "See? You don't understand. It's not a question of having to. I would want to."

"Okay, okay. I do understand. You could pay for the food you eat at the house if you want. Everything else is already being used—we'd heat the house and have electricity with or without you."

"What about my stuff?" Walt asked. "I don't trust Belcher."

"Belcher? Is he the man that was waiting with you when we went to Mercy Buckley's?"

"Yeah, that's him. He's an old coot, that's who he is. A busybody. He's my neighbor. He might get at my things."

His things were pictures of his wife and son, Ellie's wedding ring, his television, some cups and saucers with a blue coronet design that Ellie always loved, Kermit's athletic awards, a chair that had been in Ellie's family for generations. They talked about these items for some time, and Jellerson, as he took his leave, promised he would get them.

He went directly from the hospital to Walt's building, finding Murray Foss, the landlord, just coming out of his apartment as he came into the hall. Explaining his mission, he chatted briefly with Murray and found him a likeable chap. It was Murray who found Walt. He was in bed, and though he could speak had lain there for hours. "I think he just wanted to die," he said sadly. "I've been looking after him for years. He's a good guy, though a stubborn and independent Yankee."

"I don't know if he'll come back," Jellerson said. "If we can, we're going to let him live with us—though don't tell him that if you see him. I know what you mean about him being a stubborn old cuss. But just in case we can't get him to stay, I want to keep his room for him."

He wrote Murray a check for two month's rent, then followed the landlord upstairs to Walt's room. It was rather as he imagined, shabby and small, with a huge stain on the ceiling, a chipped bureau, a small table with a broken chair and little else, not even a toilet, which apparently was a shared one in the hall. The "kitchen" was a tiny sink, cabinet and refrigerator unit that looked as if it had come from a camping trailer and jury-rigged into place. Murray left him, and Jellerson stood in the middle of the room for a few moments, trying to picture Walt's life. The thought depressed him, however, and so instead of pursuing it he got to work. He opened the tiny refrigerator. Some apples, half a loaf of bread, and a quart of milk was all it contained. He poured the milk away and went to the window to test it. It opened, so he got the bread, shredded it and threw it to the ground below for the pigeons. The apples he left. He checked the cabinet next. It was stocked with eight to ten cans of soup and beef stew. A box of crackers had one of its four containers opened, so he crushed and threw those crackers to the birds as well.

On the bureau were Walt's pictures. The wedding picture of Aunt Ellie and Walter had a leather frame that was worn away on the lower left hand side from years of being picked up, and though the photograph of Kermit was not framed, Jellerson was sure that it too had been lovingly fondled through all of Walt's lonely years. He wrapped them both in newspaper and put them in the cardboard carton Murray had found for him. He located the tiny jeweler's box containing Ellie's wedding ring in the bureau drawer and put it in his pocket. In the same drawer he found the scrapbook containing all of Kermit's press clippings and athletic awards and also an album of old family photographs. Walt hadn't mentioned the latter, but he packed it with the scrapbook into his box. Next he wrapped the cups and saucers with the blue coronet design in newspaper and then chose some of Walt's clothes. They all smelled musty, and

Jellerson decided he would ask Millie to wash and press them. Two woolen sweaters he placed on the top of the box. He would deliver them to the dry cleaner's on lower Main Street later. He brought the box downstairs and placed it on the couch before returning to get Walt's portable color television and the antique chair. Downstairs, Murray was waiting for him. He helped bring Walt's possessions to the car, in the process giving Jellerson some useful parting advice. Walt loved sports, Murray said. It was one of the main things that kept him interested in life. "So I hope you have cable." Thus before driving home from the dry cleaner's Jellerson also stopped at the cable TV company and arranged to have his service upgraded so that it carried more sports channels. He knew Walt well enough to know he must never let his uncle know he had done this for him.

Walt was in the hospital for four more days and then was shifted to a rehabilitation facility. While he was recovering motor ability, the Jellersons visited him most every day and at home got his room ready. Ellie's chair was placed by the window, the framed portrait was displayed on the bureau, his clothes were washed and his bedding and so forth were put in place. With the trial of Father Mullen coming up in the spring, Jellerson had to meet with the prosecutors several times as they developed their case. He also got called in to teach at Courtney Academy for three days. He covered the rise of Germany and Austria in nineteenth-century Europe in world history for seniors and the Civil War in American history for juniors, and except for a couple troublemakers in the senior classes, everything went smoothly. It was a busy time, and as a result Old Boy got less attention.

Then came a February blizzard that dumped two feet of snow on Waska. The winds during the night shook the house like a mouse in a cat's jaws and caused enormous drifts and the loss of electricity in their rural section of Waska. They woke in the morning snowbound, with the road and their long driveway unplowed, their house frigid. Their furnace was gas fired, but with electronic ignition it was useless. Jellerson got the wood stove in the living room going, but while it eventually warmed that room and heated their morning coffee, at breakfast in the kitchen they both had to wear their winter coats. While he ate a bowl of cold cereal, Jellerson was absently watching Old Boy pick at his food without much sign of appetite. For several months now he had been eating less and less, a behavioral pattern they attributed to his old age and subsequent lack of activity. They were also aware that he was losing weight, but as Jellerson watched the dog it suddenly occurred to him that he looked extremely thin. He got up and walked over to Old Boy. Kneeling down, he ran his hand from the dog's head to his rump. Under the thick fur he could feel the bones protruding. With a shock of horror he remembered several times Old Boy had acted strangely lately, lacking in pep and sometimes groaning as if in pain.

"Millie, he's not right. He's skin and bones." Feeling as if he were pronouncing Old Boy's doom, he panicked and started pacing while Millie confirmed his observation. Irrationally, he wanted to bring Old Boy to the vet's instantly, forgetting that the snow made such a trip impossible.

Millie, also taken aback by the moment of recognition when a vague realization becomes a fully conscious fact, was more stable. She agreed the situation was serious but tried to calm him with the possibility that it was only another symptom of old age. But she also agreed they should bring him to the vet's as soon as possible. The phone was in working order, so Jellerson made an appointment for the following morning, snow and roads allowing.

For the rest of the day Jellerson worried himself into such a state of nervous tension that he could not concentrate on anything but Old Boy. He lost his appetite and by mid-afternoon knew he would need a sleeping pill that night. Walt, with whom his mind had been filled for the past several days, was virtually forgotten. He would constantly go up to Old Boy to feel him as if hoping that he'd suddenly put on weight. Millie, long familiar with his high-strung personality, made only mild suggestions that he relax and wait the vet's diagnosis. She understood the love; everyone in the family knew that while Old Boy was the family dog his heart belonged to Jellerson. That this was so occurred spontaneously and by accident. He was supposed to be Bennet's dog. They chose him from the animal shelter when Bennet was twelve, thinking a dog would calm him and teach him responsibility. He was of mixed breed but predominantly golden retriever, a breed known for its gentle behavior. In that he did not disappoint. But for some reason no particular bond developed between boy and dog, and for several months as he tripped around the house and yard as a clumsy puppy he was simply the family dog. The day Jellerson and he bonded forever was the day he got his snout stuck in the fence. He had panicked and tried to work himself free with the result that a nail had cut into his mouth, making movement very painful. Though panicked and needing to be restrained by Millie, he managed to stay still while Jellerson carefully cut the nail with a hacksaw. Ever after that day Old Boy loved Jellerson, and soon the love was reciprocal, though like all relationships it didn't always run smoothly. Sometimes Jellerson would be very busy and find Old Boy's attempts to get attention by dropping a tennis ball at his feet or bringing his leash to him to be simply annoying, and the first time he was boarded during a family vacation to Washington D.C. and to Civil war sites in Virginia he sulked for two days after they returned home. But generally Jellerson picked up the ball or took the walk, and on family vacations to Maine Old Boy came along. Their bonding had one possible deleterious effect in the family. With all Jellerson's tenderness and lovingkindness focused on Old Boy, Beverly and Bennet saw only the stern paterfamilias. But the fault was hardly Old Boy's, and Jellerson had been working on making amends ever since the move back home. He often thought, and thought now, that there was always room in his heart for his children as well as his dog and that the problem had been one of expressing, not feeling, that love.

The veterinarian's examination the next day confirmed that Old Boy was seriously ill. His kidneys were failing and his blood was filled with nitrogenous waste that was poisoning him. The veterinarian explained that treatment might extend his life but that since his failing kidneys had already damaged his heart he was definitely in the final weeks or at best months of his life. He was to be hydrated every other day with an intravenous saline solution to force his kidneys to filter the blood, and he was put on a special low protein diet.

Under this regimen Old Boy did perk up at first. He was still geriatric in his behavior, moving slowly and deliberately, but mentally he was as alert as ever and clearly happier. His appetite returned, and he was eager to go outside. With high snow, walks were impossible on the roads or in the fields, but Jellerson took Old Boy for slow walks up and down the long driveway for ten to twenty minutes every day. In this way a week passed, and Jellerson began hoping that Old Boy's condition would become a long Indian summer of golden decline, but the next day when he brought Old Boy in for his hydration the veterinarian discovered his back paw was swollen and that his breathing was labored—signs that meant his heart was also failing and could not handle the extra volume of the saline solution. From that moment they stopped the hydration and Old Boy's life became a death watch.

Every spare moment Jellerson gave to Old Boy, even if it meant simply sitting by his wicker basket with a hand on his back. Far more than was his usual way, he started talking to Old Boy. Because he loved a dog, time became eternal; all things became eschatological, and his compassion, his pity and fear, extended to everything that was born and died. "Look at the little bird scratching in the snow, Old Boy. He's trying to find food. Maybe we should get a bird feeder for the little thing." And then and there he got his coat on and, allowing for Old Boy's slow, labored steps, they got into the car and drove to the hardware store to get the bird supplies. Old Boy showed some of the old enthusiasm for the trip, even wagging his tail, for he always loved to go with his master on errands. But it was a sad and somber errand, most probably the last they would ever do together, and Jellerson was ill at ease until they got back home. Later, with the full bird feeder hanging from a branch in front of his study window, he said, "Look, there's a squirrel out on the fence. He looks fine and frisky"—and then his voice caught, for Old Boy was not fine and frisky and a day would come when the squirrel wouldn't be either. Death being everywhere, it had to be battled. Meticulous and orderly by nature, he defeated that nature in welcoming any ladybugs he came across in out-of-the-way places in the house. Returning to Old Boy in the study, he would give a report. "They need a refuge from the cold, Old Boy. We'll provide it." He stopped and sank into his chair, remembering how last month during a snow squall he had told Millie that he longed for spring. Now he wanted winter to go on for infinities if seeing spring meant there would be no Old Boy sharing the greening joy. He looked out the window and across the field to the woods where four months ago they had run in panic from what they saw Father Mullen doing to that poor boy. More terrible than he felt on that day, more confused, more angry at the savagery of life, its unfairness… Tears came to his eyes. He looked at Old Boy, lying on his side in his wicker basket breathing with difficulty and apparently shivering. "Is the house too cold for you, buddy? I could turn the heat up." It would be horrible not to make conditions as comfortable as possible when these were his last days and his last hours. Tears grew to sobs that shook his frame. "Oh, buddy, I love you. I love you. I love you."

And constantly, in every context, he would tell Old Boy he was the best dog in the world. He would be at his desk, and swinging his chair around would look at Old Boy. "Do you know you're the best dog in the world, buddy?" Or in the kitchen trying to coax him to eat some more, when he locked up the house at night, in the morning getting his coffee: "You're the best dog in the world, buddy."

But the words whispered and spoken aloud changed nothing. Old Boy would raise his tired old head and listen. He understood the love: he had always known it was there and didn't really need to hear it. In his heart he was still strong; in his heart he could run for miles to be with his beloved master, wait for him for hours; he was always with him there—in his heart. So sometimes he would whine or half bark in acknowledgment at the words of endearment, and his soft brown eyes would stare into Jellerson's soul, but daily and then hourly he grew weaker so that Jellerson knew soon there would be nothing left but the love.

The thought twisted his insides like a sponge. Every night when Jellerson taught at Hartley Academy Old Boy would walk to the end of the block and wait for him. He did this at five o'clock no matter what time of year it was so that the neighbors always referred to him as the dog who could tell time. He always stopped at the curb because he was well trained never to go into the street. He would sit on his haunches perfectly still until he caught sight of Jellerson two blocks away; then he would jump up yipping joyfully and with his tail wagging furiously and circle in a curiously sidestepping way until his master came up to him, put his briefcase down, and kneeled for a lick while he patted Old Boy from head to tail. With this greeting over, man and dog would then proceed home. On those rare occasions when Jellerson was late, Old Boy would be able to maintain his still vigil for up to fifteen minutes before he would start to become frantic.

Every time Jellerson recalled those five o'clock rendezvous he visualized Old Boy waiting for him on a corner in heaven. He wasn't sure dogs went to heaven, he wasn't even sure there was a heaven, but the thought was still his only comfort.

During this time, one by one Old Boy was letting go of all the things that made up his life. The dog treat he got each evening was first to go. Jellerson would always toss it and Old Boy snatch it out of the air. But one night he let it drop at his feet without showing the slightest interest. Next he stopped taking a walk, even the abbreviated one up and down the driveway. The following day he started needing help getting into his wicker basket. Though its lip was only about ten inches high, he needed to be lifted over it to get in. And once in, sleeping or resting, he was mostly content to stay for long hours. Yet because he was still alive, Jellerson hung on to his hope. Two days later he ate a little food in the morning and drank water two or three times during the day; when evening came, however, he wouldn't eat any more. Jellerson changed the food to some fresh beef, hoping to inspire him. He cut it into small pieces and kneeled down beside Old Boy, his hand on his neck. "Come on, Old Boy. Eat a little. You need to keep up your strength."

Old Boy stared intently at Jellerson as he listened. His soft brown eyes appealed to his master, but when Jellerson, patting his head as he spoke, repeated in a hoarse whisper, "You need to keep up your strength," he did try to eat. He took a mouthful and started to swallow, then suddenly opened his mouth and let the piece of beef drop to the floor. Turning his head, he lapped at his water bowl with his tongue two or three times before backing away and sitting on his withered haunches. He looked at Jellerson with what appeared to be confusion and perhaps a touch of panic in his eyes.

Jellerson whispered, "Come on, please, Old Boy. I can't help you if you won't eat." But after a few more tries, Jellerson gave up. He simply did not want to eat. The vet had told them that Old Boy would let them know when he was ready. Jellerson looked over at Millie sitting at the kitchen table watching them. She shook her head. He nodded in acknowledgment, struggling to stay composed now that his hope was gone.

Millie made the phone call while he sat numbly at the kitchen table staring at Old Boy.

They brought him to the veterinary clinic the next morning. Millie took the morning off to be with him. Old Boy lay in the back seat too sick to even raise his head. They had had to carry him to the car. Millie was driving; Jellerson sat sideways in the front seat so that his hand could lie on Old Boy's back. He wanted to believe he was comforting the dog, but it was really for his own benefit that he felt the labored breathing and the irregular heartbeat. Guilt and a different kind of regret seized him. It would have been far more humane to have made this trip two days ago. They had had merely the ghost of his presence and he had suffered. Sometimes as they drove Jellerson thought of immediate concerns—he was dreadfully afraid he would be crying when he said good-bye to Old Boy, and he both wanted the release of tears and was terrified at being objectified by people's stares if he did cry. But he managed to get beyond his fears because they were still in the future and let his mind run over the life he had shared with Old Boy. He saw him again waiting at the corner, felt his body trembling with excitement and heard his glad yips; he saw him as a puppy tripping over his paws; he saw him sleeping peacefully in his wicker basket and heard his quiet breathing; he recalled the silent communication of eyes that spoke so deeply it was as if they shared a soul; he remembered again running from the woods in terror of the evil of Father Mullen. The day was dark with thick gray clouds and the threat of more snow. The snow from the blizzard lining the road they traveled was blackened and ugly, but the fields were still pristine. Cars passing by were hardly noticed; the radio was playing Beethoven's Spring Sonata—that too he barely noticed. Old Boy, who would never see another spring day, was not actually seeing the winter day either. His eyes were closed and he was slobbering on the vinyl of the back seat. They would visit Walt at the rehabilitation facility afterwards, and later that day—for it was Wednesday—he would tutor Michelle. She had come over Sunday afternoon to see Old Boy as if she knew he wouldn't be there today. The anticipation wasn't that insightful, of course; Millie and he knew on Sunday Old Boy wouldn't last the week even if they couldn't admit it to themselves. She had helped Old Boy into his wicker basket with tears in her eyes. That was the way with Old Boy, he thought; he inspired love in everyone who knew him.

Again he felt guilty at making Old Boy suffer. While there was life there was hope; his failure was not to see his condition was hopeless. Old Boy stirred and opened his eyes. He looked momentarily at his master, then emitted a tiny, hoarse groan. "Soon, Old Boy, the pain will be gone," he whispered.

He looked over at Millie and could see tears in her eyes. "I think we should have done this two days ago," he said. "It's my fault. I just couldn't let go."

But she could not answer him. She looked stricken, and he realized that she too was realizing that a large part of their life was leaving them today. Good-bye to Hartley Academy and all their life in Connecticut. Good-bye to a sense of well-being and goodness in life. Good-bye to Old Boy. That's what her tears meant. Good-bye, old friend.

He managed to get through the rest of the day thanks to Michelle coming for tutoring. But the next day the farmhouse was almost unbearable—huge, empty, desolate, and filled with a thousand reminders of Old Boy's presence. So frequently did tears come unbidden to his eyes that it seemed he saw every reminder with blurred vision. Often he would be overcome by such a rage against the dying of the light that he would have to pound his fist at whatever was nearby—his desk, a door, the arm of his chair—to release the rage. Every time the phone rang he hoped it would be something that would lift his spirits or that could get him out of the house. Too often it was merely some telemarketing scheme, and he would be uncharacteristically impolite in impatiently dismissing them. Every afternoon he would invent errands to get himself out of the house—a drive downtown or to the mall to get pipe tobacco, a new fountain pen, some window caulk to stop a leak.

The mornings were more bearable, for it was then he visited Walt at the rehabilitation facility. When he told him about Old Boy something strange and interesting happened. He had tried to be casual, but despite his efforts his voice broke in relating his loss. Walt had given him a strange look before muttering "I'm sorry" curtly enough to be in character. But after that his cantankerous ways had more the flavor of habit or pose than conviction. He actually smiled sometimes; sometimes it seemed as if he actually liked Jellerson. For the first time in his life Jellerson saw a Walter Pingree who was not on his guard against his middle-class relatives. He too thought that he could grow to like Walt.

On the next Wednesday, a week after Old Boy's death, he learned from the nurse that Walt could go home on Friday. She said this in front of Walt, who colored at the word "home." At first Jellerson, buoyed by the thought that his days would be less lonely, hardly noticed Walt's embarrassment. He asked the nurse questions about the follow-up therapy Walt would need on an outpatient basis and how everything at the house should be arranged for him. Only after she left them alone did he return to that embarrassment. With a smile he said, "You're going to like the farmhouse, Walt. And I guarantee, it will be home for you. You just wait and see."

To Be Worthy of Love

The cafeteria at Courtney Academy was abuzz with the story, some telling it with *Schadenfreude,* others with touches of compassion, some with know-it-all authority, others with admitted conjecture, but all with deep interest. These rumors did not, however, involve Jason Buckley or Father Mullen, for here in the middle of March, a few months before the scheduled trial began and a good four months since news of the child abuse first broke, that particular story was quiescent. Michelle had certainly not forgotten Jason; she saw him occasionally at Mrs. Cohen's and even phoned him a few times, ostensibly to ask for some musical advice but really to show him support. But as she and her three friends picked at the unsavory meat loaf, mashed potatoes and peas of the lunch, it was of Fran Hauptmann they spoke. She, the head cheerleader and the most popular girl in the senior class if not the entire school, had been absent from her classes all week, and this morning the story spread that the reason she had not been at school was because her mother had taken her to a clinic in Boston to have an abortion.

Sarah Henslowe, Bev Northrup and Cindy Carlson were Michelle's table mates on Mondays, Wednesdays and Fridays; on Tuesdays and Thursdays she sat with Bobby. They were all, in contrast to her, fair-haired and Protestant, but after these externalities the similarities began. They all had the reputation in school of being independent and nonconformists, but that was only because they were all serious, good students and regarded themselves as progressives and feminists. Because they all, with the exception of Sarah, were self-confident and pretty, they were not regarded as so weird that decent teenagers would have to avoid them, nor did they hear jokes about unshaven arm pits and legs because they openly accepted the scary label of feminist. Even so, their current interest in the rumors was far from personal. As one of the beautiful people on campus, the air-headed Fran traveled in rarefied circles that they were only allowed to view from afar. Perhaps that is why their conversation aligned more closely to those who whispered the story with more *Schadenfreude* than compassion.

"Well," said Bev, the only one of the four who in dress looked more like the typical female student—she wore skirts, blouses and pantyhose whereas her companions favored jeans and sweaters—"Well, I think Fran was a fool to have unprotected sex. Being drunk is no excuse. You have to plan ahead, and you can't trust the guys to be ready. Me, I don't go out on weekends without a pack of Trojans. I can't believe Fran was so stupid."

Michelle shrugged. She remembered how close she and Bobby were to that situation a month ago and was inclined to be charitable. "She's only human. She got carried away."

Sarah's eyes brightened mischievously. "Oh, yeah, but how many times has Ms. Gillooly in health class warned us about AIDS? Remember how she's forever drawing a revolver on the blackboard to emphasize that it's like playing Russian roulette? Fran should have seen that instead of Marty's tool!"

Everyone laughed.

Cindy, looking embarrassed, asked, "Do you think she'll get tested?" and when everybody looked at her quizzically, added—"You know, for AIDS."

"I suppose so," Michelle said.

"I wonder if she had to walk through a crowd of those right-wing fanatics? They would scare me off."

"What choice did she have? A baby would ruin her life."

Bev, who had been thinking quietly since Sarah made her joke, suddenly giggled. "I hear Marty's well hung."

Michelle stared at her. "Who would have told you *that* besides Fran herself?"

Bev giggled again. "Oh, last summer at the lake a whole bunch of guys and girls went skinny dipping. Believe me, Marty was noticed. That's all I can say."

Just then Tiffany Andrews came up to the table. "I suppose you've heard about Fran?"

"Yes," Michelle said and added, "and some other things."

Her companions giggled conspiratorially, but Tiffany deigned not to notice. "I heard it happened at Stephanie Willow's party on New Year's eve—"

"Yes," she said with a knowing air, "that's correct."

"And that she had unprotected sex in the guest bedroom?" Sarah asked.

"Obviously it was unprotected."

She turned to Michelle, but Sarah was not through. "So it's true Marty was the father? Someone tried to say it was Ted Chrestien, but that's ridiculous. She went to the party with Marty—" She stopped and giggled. "Party with Marty rimes!"

Tiffany rolled her eyes and frowned, and Michelle suddenly realized she did not like Sarah.

"Yes," Tiffany said airily, "of course Marty was the father."

She turned again to Michelle with exaggerated impatience, and Michelle asked, "Does he know about it? The abortion, I mean."

"Oh, yeah, he knows. It's what he wanted too. I'm sure you approve."

Tiffany's voice was laced with disapproval, and Michelle knew why without the help of any special insight. A month or two ago in health class abortion was discussed. While most of the girls had a rather good understanding of abortion in that they didn't like it but knew they would have one under certain circumstances, no one in class quite dared to defend the legality or morality of it for fear of displeasing the teacher, whose opinions on the subject were not known. But Michelle's mother was an activist member of NOW and several other women's organizations, and she had talked with Michelle many times about this issue. She made clear that the best thing was never to get pregnant in the first place. She emphasized that Michelle should have no secrets from her and that if she were to contemplate having sex she should practice safe sex not only to avoid pregnancy but also AIDS and venereal diseases in general. When you sleep with a man, she said, you sleep with every person he's had sex with.

Using things she learned from these discussions with her mother, Michelle defended women's right to choose what happened to their own bodies, and she attacked the shallow humanity of the antiabortionists. It was the latter that caused a sensation and that Tiffany was obviously thinking about when she said, "I'm sure you approve." Basically Michelle had questioned the depth of humanity of people who called a three-week old fetus a baby. Didn't they see human beings as abstractions? To call a collection of cells no bigger than a pin head and without consciousness human was by definition to regard a human being as an abstract thing. It implied that they didn't actually respect another human being as someone who had different opinions or as a free entity with the right to make his or her own moral choices. It revealed their own impoverished humanity because it didn't seem to dawn on these people that the essence of being human was relating to other people, needing each other, working toward common goals, planning for the future, looking for love and meaning. No, to them human beings were mere abstractions, things made by God at the moment of conception whose only duty was to obey narrow rules. They didn't believe in freedom and they didn't live spontaneously. They only wanted to impose a rigid system on themselves and everyone they saw. Like fascists they wanted to impose their opinions on all of us. That and much, much more Michelle had said in health class that day, and it had made her famous, not to say notorious on campus almost instantly. Tiffany, whose people were conservative Episcopalians, had tried to voice opposition in class, but being inarticulate she merely stumbled about foolishly. Michelle sometimes thought that for most of her classmates it wasn't what she said but that she dared to say it that had made her notorious, but she sensed in the case of Tiffany that she had made a potential enemy.

Now she gathered that Tiffany was here to find out what the notorious abortionist thought about the affair so that she could report back to her friends. Choosing her words carefully, she said, "I don't know what you're implying, but I certainly don't blame her for getting an abortion. I don't think it should be so public, but I guess that's not her fault. The same people who talked about poor Jason Buckley at Christmas are having another field day."

Tiffany shrugged with exaggerated casualness. "Well, the story is out. It isn't a secret."

The bell warning them that they had ten minutes to get to class rang. Tiffany rejoined her friends, and Michelle and Sarah walked together to the science building where Sarah had a math class and Michelle chemistry.

"Did you notice Tiffany was rather hostile to me?" Sarah asked as soon as they were outside.

Michelle nodded.

"It's because I'm not popular. She thinks I'm a dweeb." She laughed nervously and stole a sideways glance at Michelle. "I probably am. I don't have a boyfriend and never have had one."

Michelle was touched by her insecurity. They had been friends since grade school and yet such was the power of peer pressure that her best friend was afraid she might be cut. She recalled what Mr. Jellerson said about teenagers afraid to be different.

Putting her hand on her friend's shoulder, she said, "Rob Hackett likes you. Why don't you go out with him?"

Again Sarah laughed nervously. "If I went out with him, I'd really earn my dweeb stripes. A dweeb and a nerd. Tiffany would have a good laugh at that one."

"Who cares what idiots think. Tiffany doesn't like me either. Big deal. If you like him, go out with him."

"Easy for you to say. First, maybe Tiffany doesn't like you, but she either fears you or respects you. She looks at me like I'm an insect. It's not a comfortable feeling. And besides, don't you call Bobby the cutest boy in the world? Nobody would call Rob cute."

Michelle made a face that was a cross between embarrassment and mockery. Her eyebrows were raised and her mouth made an exaggerated oval as if she were saying "Oops!"

"But don't you think that when you're attracted to someone you think he's cute? That's all I mean when I say it. It's another way of saying I'm attracted to him. If you feel that way about Rob, if you have common interests and your personalities jell, then he's cute. Besides, do something with his hair and get him some new glasses and he *is* cute. You could make a project of him."

Sarah smiled wistfully. "But all he wants to talk about is Macintosh computers."

They were at the door of the science building now. Michelle checked her watch. "Just tell him it's a forbidden topic."

Sarah opened the door and held it for her and then for some other students behind them. She caught up with Michelle in front of her classroom. "But how do I do that? Macintosh computers are important to him."

Michelle slid her backpack off her shoulder and started looking for her chemistry book. "Ah, the secret is to do it with a smile. Make a joke about it. Say this Macgirl doesn't want to hear any Mactalk. Tell him you think different. Stuff like that." She grinned and tapped her friend's shoulder lightly. "With a smile, remember."

Rob was in Sarah's last class for the day, so she would have a chance to talk with him. But when they met after school at 2:30 she had to report her mission was unsuccessful. "He's so shy, all we said was 'hi,' and then he said he had to go home to install some new software on his Mac."

Michelle grinned. "Mactalk, huh? But how did he look? Glad to see you?"

Sarah laughed, a good sign. "I think so. If nervousness and a moonstruck look mean he's glad, he was glad."

They were at their lockers as they spoke. Michelle saw Bobby down the hall. "I've got to talk to Bobby for a minute. Be right back. But I do predict in a month or so we'll be double dating with you and Rob."

Bobby had track practice, so they could only talk briefly. He'd been invited to a party at Albert Jolbert's this weekend and wanted to know if she'd rather go to that or to a movie. She wasn't sure and said they could talk about it tonight when he called. He'd heard about Fran, of course, and rolled his eyes when she asked him what he thought. The nonverbal answer was clear enough to her, however: he thought they were both fools, but he also made her flush because his eyes communicated the memory of their own lovemaking. He saw her face color and his voice became husky. "I've got to go now, but…"

"Okay. I'll see you at lunch tomorrow and talk to you tonight. Sarah and I have to go out to Mr. Jellerson's now."

They touched hands lightly in parting; then still feeling the thrill of that touch, she watched him walk away. She was in love and had to admit it was the most wonderful feeling in the world. But she took care that love did not make her selfish. It did, of course, but not so much that she didn't want others whom she loved in a different way to feel this joy. Nor did it make her forget Jason's violated innocence. To be in love meant one had to be worthy of love; it meant one had to be a good person. So as she walked back to rejoin Sarah, slowly her mind turned from the intense memories of her and Bobby and the delicious joy they had discovered in each other's bodies to ways she could get Rob and Sarah together.

Sarah had been in Mr. Jellerson's class the first time he taught at Courtney Academy and had found despite her prejudices that she liked him; thus soon after that she had begun going to the tutorial sessions with Michelle every Wednesday. Mr. Jellerson was looking into scholarship money for her as well. Since Michelle didn't have a driver's license yet, Sarah borrowed her older brother's car for the trip each week. On the drive up country they discussed getting a thank-you gift for their tutor. There were only four more sessions before the SAT's were to be given. "Have you noticed the new picture in his study of him and Old Boy?" Michelle asked. She was referring to a gold-framed enlargement of a photograph from Mr. Jellerson's Connecticut days. It showed Old Boy staring at his master with a look of utter devotion and Mr. Jellerson gazing down fondly at him with a slight smile on his face.

"Yeah, touching, isn't it? And Old Boy's wicker basket is still in his study. Millie told me he can't bring himself to take it away."

"I can understand that. You never met Old Boy, but he was a really nice dog. Anyways, I was thinking we could get him a puppy for a gift. I think they're expensive, but my mother said she'd pay for it. How's that sound?"

"Pretty good," Sarah said. She was listening to a rock song about love and her mind was elsewhere.

They drove on for a while with Sarah softly humming to the song; then Michelle said, " I have an idea. Why don't you call Rob tonight. Ask him a Mac question."

Sarah looked hard at Michelle before her eyes returned to the road. "We don't have a Mac at home. We don't even have a computer in fact."

Michelle returned her stare with a grin. "I know. Say you're thinking about getting one and need advice."

"But I'm not thinking that. Would it be good to start a relationship with a lie?"

"Depends on the lie. This one's a white lie."

"I don't know. I'll have to think about it."

"And about the puppy?"

"What about it?"

"Is it a good idea? Of course we should talk to Millie first. But by the time we'd give it to him, he'd have been mourning for two months. I think he'll be ready."

"Oh, yeah, right," she said absently and then thought for a moment. "You know, I do use Macs in the computer lab for typing papers. I could ask Rob a software question. Like how do you change the margins? I was actually trying to do that last week. Do you know?"

"I think it's Page Setup or maybe there's a margin thing in the format menu. But don't take my word for it. Call Rob."

Sarah lapsed into silence again thinking about it while Michelle listened to the music. By the time they pulled into Mr. Jellerson's driveway Sarah had come to a conclusion. "You know," she said, "I think I will—call him, that is."

Mr. Jellerson was outside looking over his garden and shrubbery in anticipation of spring when they got to the house. The springlike day made him genial and avuncular. When they greeted him, he said, "Beautiful day, isn't it. Almost a shame to be inside. But you girls ready for a good workout? It's getting close now."

Michelle was glad to see him smiling. For weeks following Old Boy's death he had been morose. "How's Walt?" she asked.

He smiled enigmatically. "He's making progress every day, but he doesn't like to admit it. Or, at least, he doesn't like praise. 'I ain't a kid learning to ride a bike,' he said to me the other day at the rehab when I said he was doing great. And he only has to go once a week now."

Michelle nodded. "I've noticed he doesn't like praise. My solution is to insult him. He loves that."

Mr. Jellerson started walking towards the front door. "You can get away with that because he's crazy about you, but I wouldn't dare try that technique. Will you have time to see him later—he's taking a nap now."

"Oh, yes, though only for a few minutes this week."

"I have to cook supper at home tonight," Sarah explained, "so I have to get home early."

"That's too bad. I sometimes think you two girls get more progress out of him than the professional therapists at the rehab."

Michelle had been thinking about Walt's not liking to be praised for making any progress. In the study before they began she said, "Mr. Jellerson, I was wondering. Is Walt going back to his apartment when he's better?"

Opening his book and finding the page he wanted, he looked up. "He wants to, but I've offered to let him stay here. The back wing of the house is empty. There's a bathroom because when we rented this place it was a separate apartment. There's no kitchen, though. I've talked to Rev. Covington about running hot and cold water pipes to one of the rooms and putting in a sink. Then we could get one of those small stove-refrigerator units and he could have his own apartment and be independent. But…"

Michelle finished the thought for him. "But he says he doesn't want to be a bother."

He nodded. "Of course I tell him it wouldn't be any trouble. Rev. Covington and a couple of volunteers from the church are ready to run the pipes and extra electrical circuits— Nate Wentworth, if you know him, said he'd do the wiring. They could do it on a Saturday. I've told Walt he could pay rent so that even the cost of the kitchen unit would be no expense, and he would be under no obligation."

"I'm going to tell him that Sarah and I wouldn't be able to see him as often if he lived downtown. I'll say we'll be very disappointed if he leaves. Is that okay?"

"That's excellent. And now, young ladies, let's get to work."

They did some reading comprehension exercises with both pupils answering the questions perfectly, and then Mr. Jellerson drilled Sarah on Latin prefixes and suffixes since she had joined the tutorials late and had not had the benefit of his shorthand Latin. He had found Sarah's vocabulary weaker than Michelle's and had been giving her plenty of extra work to build up her wordhoard (which, he said, was the Saxon word for vocabulary). While they worked Michelle was supposed to be reading more passages and answering the questions on paper, but mostly she listened to the vocabulary exercises.

After another ten minutes of drilling Sarah the hour was up. They received their assignment for next week, and then while Mr. Jellerson went to the kitchen to make preparations for supper they went to see Walt.

He was living in the room that eventually was going to be Millie's sewing room. It was on the other side of the living room, not far from Mr. Jellerson's study so that they had heard him stirring about during the latter part of the tutorial session and knew he was awake. After spending a week in the local rehabilitation hospital learning to use a cane and doing exercises to get his arm back into shape, he'd been at the farmhouse for almost a month. He continued going to rehab on an outpatient basis and had made enough progress to be close to walking without a cane. At least part of his progress could be attributed to Michelle and Sarah. They had befriended him almost immediately. The first time they saw him he was practicing some walking exercises the physical therapist had shown him, and Michelle, being a hands-on person, had instantly started helping him. Now after every tutorial they spent half an hour to an hour with him. At first not used to the presence of young people, he had been quiet and self-contained, but soon he was blossoming in their presence, and Mr. Jellerson told them he looked forward to their visits as the highlight of his week.

He was sitting in his arm chair with a look of undisguised anticipation when they came into the room. "Well, you young scholars ready to spend some time with an old coot, are ya?"

"We can only stop for a few minutes today, Walt. But we'll make it quality time." The latter clause was spoken brightly, for Michelle could read the disappointment in his face.

"I've got to cook the meal at home tonight. My mother's not getting home until late," Sarah explained. "So you can blame me."

He looked at her critically for a moment, but whatever he was going to say he thought better of it. He nodded resignedly. "You've got your duties. I understand."

Michelle went over and took his arm in her hand. "But let's get you walking, Walt. I hear you're close."

A stubborn, martyred expression stole over his face and he shook his head. "No, not today. You go on. I don't want you to be held up because of an old coot."

"My Uncle Charlie's an old coot too," Michelle said. "Do you know what?"

"What?" Walt grinned.

"I'm going to call you Uncle Walt. What do you think of that?"

"I think you're a saucy young lady."

Michelle took the cane away and gently pulled him to his feet. "Come on, now. Try a step. I know you can do it."

"If I fall it's your fault."

"But you won't fall. Come on. I know you can do it."

Sarah stood on one side and Michelle on the other. He let go of the chair and momentarily held on to them. He glanced at Michelle as if for assurance, then took a step with his bad leg. He started to collapse toward her, but she steadied him. He brought his good foot forward. "Okay," he said, "you can let go." He took another small step, teetered for a moment and then stepped forward with his good leg. He turned and repeated. Both girls clapped and shrieked while Walt grinned proudly.

"Uncle Walt! You're on your feet now!"

"Well, so I am," he said, sounding surprised.

"Next week we'll have to do some dancing," Sarah said.

"And that reminds me, Uncle Walt. It would be very hard to see you if you aren't a neighbor. You've got to promise us that you'll accept Mr. Jellerson's kind offer for you to stay here. That way I can see you all the time."

Walt took two or three unsteady steps toward his chair and sat down. The stubborn look came onto his face again, but it lacked conviction. "I can't make any guarantees about that."

Michelle glanced at Sarah, who was in turn glancing at her watch. "We've got to go now, but I want you to think about staying. I asked Mr. Jellerson if you were, and he said there's an apartment in the wing of the house for you if you want it. Remember, we'll be very, very disappointed if you leave us."

A slight smile flitted across his face as he tried to maintain his stubborn expression. Obviously he was very pleased to hear a young pretty girl pleading with him. "We can talk about all that later. Now it's time for you to skedaddle."

Both girls smiled. "That means you'll be here next week," Sarah said.

"And the following?" Michelle added.

He folded his arms. "We'll see, we'll see."

Mr. Jellerson was making a salad in the kitchen when they came out. Getting their jackets on, they told him about Walt's progress and he congratulated them; then at the door Michelle asked him about the trial. "Mr. Jellerson, do you think they'll send Father Mullen to prison? I never liked that man."

He shook his head doubtfully and suddenly appeared quite nervous and ill at ease. "I think it's just as likely he'll be ordered to get psychiatric help. The prosecutors tell me it's a difficult case to prove. I'm the only witness besides the victims themselves. Justice may not be done."

Michelle nodded grimly. "I see. I was just wondering because I think of poor Jason a lot."

"So do I. I hope Rev. Covington is helping him, but of course I can't ask him such a question."

"But Walt's doing better." Michelle's face brightened. "So we can hope, we can pray."

"Amen to that," he said.

They said their good-byes, and, declining the short ride home from Sarah, Michelle walked home across the field for the first time in months. The world too was getting better, the world that already contained Bobby and therefore was wonderful and perfect until she remembered people like Jason. But it was warm enough for her to unzip her jacket; the sky was still blue even though it was five o'clock; and dried grass crunched below her feet, not snow. Under these conditions hope was not hard to find. She started humming to herself, humming a love song.

Moment by Moment

"**W**ait a minute, Hope. I think I hear something outside." Mercy rose from the kitchen table and stealthily walked over to the window that gave her a view of Hope's driveway. She and Jason were paying a Saturday morning visit to her sister while Brian was at a job site. Later they would meet and go together to a car show in Portland. While Robbie and Jason played street hockey outside, she and Hope were talking in the kitchen. The Saturday before Easter was a beautiful warm April day, and Hope had opened the window so that they could listen to the boys. As they discussed Jason's progress—just about the only thing they ever talked about now—their conversation was punctuated by the boys' cries as a goal was scored or a shot was well blocked. But suddenly Mercy had heard two other voices, and sensing trouble she had interrupted her sister.

Two boys of about twelve or thirteen, one tall and thin with a sour look on his face, the other shorter and portly with a shock of reddish-blond hair almost covering his entire forehead, were standing and talking with Robbie. Jason, playing goalie, was about twenty feet away in front of the garage.

"So you guys wanna play, or what?" Robbie was asking.

The short, fat kid seemed to be willing, but the taller one mumbled something in his friend's ear.

Instantly Robbie was energized. "What did you say? he demanded, assuming a belligerent posture and clenching his fists.

The tall boy looked at Robbie and then his friend. He seemed frightened, but being challenged he could not back down. His face flushed, and he spat out his words as a counter-challenge. "I said I don't want to play with a freak. That's what I said." He too assumed a belligerent posture and clenched his fists.

Mercy's eyes immediately went to Jason. His face dropped and he looked stricken.

Now Robbie was really angry. Ever since the troubles he had regarded himself as Jason's protector. Some sketchy reports had reached Mercy and Hope about his standing up for his cousin in the school playground and other places where boys gathered. He didn't like to talk to adults about this role, and he grew embarrassed and shrugged them off whenever the women told him they were proud of him. But the reports were clearly accurate.

"You know what you are, Wilson? You're a jerk." He started toward the boy, whose bravado suddenly deserted him. Robbie was big for his age, already five foot nine inches and 160 pounds.

"You can't make me play," the boy whined.

"I wouldn't want to play with you," Robbie shot back. "My cousin is worth ten of you, and if you did dare play with us, we'd whip you."

"Never mind," Jason called. "If they don't want to play it's no big deal." He had put on his mask, the one that showed the world he was imperturbable.

The portly kid now turned against his friend. "Don't you know when to keep your mouth shut? How would you like it if some man hurt you?" He turned to Jason and spoke louder. "I'm really sorry, Jason. Bill's an idiot."

Jason nodded slightly but did not answer.

Robbie, seeing that the Wilson boy had no fight in him, turned his back on him and bent down to retrieve the tennis ball they were using for a puck.

"Well, see ya," the portly kid said, and they continued walking down the street.

Hope had joined her at the window. The two sisters exchanged glances. "Oh, my God," Hope said, to which Mercy made no reply except to close her eyes and sigh.

They continued silently studying Jason for a long time, but the boys had simply returned to their play as if nothing had happened, so eventually they went back to the table and sat down.

"You see how our life is now."

Hope nodded sympathetically. "It's the first time I've actually witnessed this. It's awful. It's awful." Nervously she took a sip of her coffee, then made a face because it had become cold. "And you say this happens all the time?"

"Maybe not all the time. But it seems so, and Jason doesn't tell me about many incidents." She leaned forward and let her head sink into her hands. She felt utterly defeated and hardly noticed Hope reaching over to place a supporting hand on her arm. She asked herself how this could have happened, how the bright promise of Jason's musical ability could lead to nothing but pain and sorrow, and told herself that it was all her fault. "I'm so confused about what to do. I haven't thought straight in months. I thought I was doing the best for him with music lessons and so forth, but now that this has happened I sometimes think I was just being a stage mother pushing Jason so that I could live vicariously in his glory."

Hope began stroking Mercy's hand, trying to soothe her. "Mercy, that's not fair. I've watched you and that boy for years. I remember all the sacrifices you and Brian made when you had no money and still saw to it that he got lessons and a piano. You drove that old rust bucket of a car you used to have held together by duct tape. You never bought yourself new clothes. You even learned to repair to save money for a repairman." She laughed. "I remember one time you were so covered from head to foot with soot and grease that I hardly recognized you. In all that I didn't see any selfish desire to be the mother of a famous son. I saw a woman who would sacrifice everything for her son. I call that love."

Mercy took a deep breath. She licked her dry lips with her tongue and tried to blink her tears away. "Yes, maybe that's true, but look what all that effort led to." She remembered the day Mr. Jellerson had come to her house. Since then it seemed she had forgotten how to laugh, how to relax, feel free, be human. She had lost so much from Jason's violation, including her self-respect and sense of self-worth, that the woman Hope was describing seemed impossibly remote from any life she had lived.

"And things are getting better," Hope added. "From all you tell me Rev. Covington is making great progress."

"Yes. Yes, he is. Even there, though, I'm horrible. John's wonderful and he is helping Jason and I am deeply grateful, and yet..." She stopped and looked at Hope, wondering if she could possibly understand what she wanted to say. "Well, it's like I'm jealous of him sometimes. He can help Jason, but I can't. And yet I'm the mother."

If Hope was shocked by this confession, she hid it well. "Sometimes a mother can't do it all alone. Sometimes professional help is needed. But I think I understand your feelings, and I think they're perfectly natural. I think they're a symptom of the whole affair. You have to remember that you and Brian are just as much a victim of that man as Jason is. He did it to all of us who love Jason. So it's not that you're jealous of Rev. Covington. He's nurturing and healing Jason, a role that should be yours. But what's distressing you is that you've lost control. That man stole it from you. But with Rev. Covington's help you can get it back. You have to look at the long view."

Mercy knew she should feel grateful for Hope's soothing and helpful words and tried to convey that with her eyes, but still she did not feel good and therefore doubted the sincerity of her gratitude. "I sometimes think, though, that what we'll never get back is a normal life. And I don't think I'll ever quite believe in the goodness of human nature again. Honestly, people can be so cruel. Not just kids like that boy either. We go into a store and people stare. At first I didn't know how the other parents had been able to keep their son's identity a secret. Those of us associated with the choir now have a pretty good idea who the boy is, but the public doesn't. He doesn't live in Waska anymore, you see. Sometimes I envy them; sometimes I resent them, though I know I should be glad for them."

Hope rose and poured the last of the coffee into their cups. Each got about half a cup. Mixing in a little half and half, she took a sip. "Well, you're getting all the attention. Naturally it seems unfair, but I'm willing to bet they're going through hell too."

"Maybe, but I wonder if their idea of moving to another town isn't the best one."

Hope stared in disbelief at her sister. "What, you mean leave Waska?"

She nodded, then looked down at her coffee. The two cups she had already drunk were making her edgy, so she didn't plan to drink it. "You know, a fresh start where nobody knows us."

"But then you'll be having Jason live in secret. Do you think that's good?"

The remark did not please her, and instead of answering she returned the question. "Is it better that in Waska he'll always be known as the boy who was abused by a priest?"

Hope looked down and considered for a moment. She seemed close to tears, and now Mercy felt her display of pique was uncalled for. "Look," she said quietly, "I don't mean so far away that we'll never see each other. I mean Maine. I love this state and don't want to ever leave it."

"I just think it's awful that you're victimized and then victimized again by having to leave."

"Well, you can have no real idea until you live it what it's like to be the object of idle curiosity and wagging tongues. Everywhere we go it's the same. Even Keith is never himself when we're here."

Hope's face reddened and her body tensed, telling Mercy her sister understood exactly what she was saying. Keith Harris, her husband, had demonstrated the truth of her observation this very morning. He was home when they arrived an hour ago and had almost instantly gone down to his basement workshop. Then after a few minutes he had left the house with a mumbled excuse about an errand. Since the isolation that had come to them from the notoriety of the case, the only social life they had was exchanging Saturday dinner visits with Hope and Keith. Sometimes they would go in the afternoon and the men would watch basketball or hockey games before they had an early dinner; sometimes they went in the evening and played cards after dinner; but in all cases Keith showed himself to be uncomfortable in their presence. Mercy has always suspected he was afraid to say something inappropriate that would hurt or embarrass Jason or his in-laws, and in fact that is what Hope used to excuse his behavior now.

"I've talked to him about it," she said. "He knows he's acting stupid but says he doesn't know why he's always uncomfortable. He's on your side and wants to help. It's just he's so afraid of saying something stupid he can't relax."

Mercy nodded and pursed her lips. "I understand he means well. I just used him as an example of how everyone in town acts. It's that that gets me to thinking that I want to move—just so I could have some peace."

"But are you definitely planning to move?"

She shook her head. "No, it's just an idea. The word 'definite' and me don't have much in common right now. Actually, I was planning on talking to John about it. We've been meeting every couple of weeks to discuss Jason's progress. I'm going to see him on Monday. Thank God Perry gives me the day off from work so I can do this."

Hope smiled enigmatically. "So you really do trust him now, despite your worries about him and Jason."

As best she could she returned the smile, but it came to her mouth stillborn. Growing very serious, she said, "Now he's my lifeline. I think I'd go mad if he wasn't counseling Jason."

"What about Brian?"

Mercy shrugged. Thoughts raced through her mind, but she was hesitant to give them expression. Even with her sister, with whom she shared most of her intimate thoughts, she was not quite prepared to discuss Brian. The truth was that things between her and her former husband were very uncomfortable. Before Christmas they had started spending as much time together as possible for Jason's sake. They both agreed that Jason's desire that they get back together was impossible, but as a compromise they spent two or three evenings and weekends together. During the weekdays Brian would come for supper and they would sit down together as a family and spend the evening together. Sometimes they watched television; other times they listened to Jason play the piano. If some item at the store was required—new clothes for Jason or some household item—they would go together to the Maine Mall—never Waska—to get the item. When Jason did homework, Brian would use the kitchen table for his paperwork and Mercy would read in the living room. But whatever they did, at ten o'clock Brian would go home to sleep. The weekends were similar except that now Brian's apartment was home base and they did things like take outings to car shows, movies and sometimes musical events. Generally they ate out on those nights when they didn't dine with Hope and Keith. When it got to be ten o'clock and Jason was put to bed, this time Mercy would leave to sleep at her own house. This arrangement seemed to please Jason, but the former husband and wife found the situation, particularly at the time one or the other left to go home, verging on absurdity. And the four months of living this strange life had not made her feel any closer to Brian. The same things that used to grate on her continued grating—his love of cars, his indifference to beauty, his insistence that only beef was real food, and worst of all his prejudices. She would have thought that having a son victimized as he did that he would have grown in compassion and understanding, but he still made many remarks about immigrants overrunning the country and gratuitous ethnic slurs. Most of the time she said nothing because she didn't want to get into a fight for Jason's sake. One day when they both happened to be together to pick up Jason from Mrs. Cohen's piano lesson, however, he made an anti-Semitic remark along the lines that the Jews were taking over the country and she snapped. "They used to say nasty things about the lazy Irish, you know. Why can't you live and let live?" "Sure," he said, "as long as they would live and let live. But do they?" She was too angry to reply, and when Jason came out she was made uncomfortably aware of the hypocrisy necessary to hold them together as a family.

No, of all that she would not speak. Instead she chose to be neutral in her dismissal. "Well, you know, he's in the same boat as me. We can't really help each other."

Her sister nodded thoughtfully. "I see. But the better Jason gets, the better you'll be. And he is getting better?"

"I think he's at the stage where he doesn't blame himself for what happened, and he's definitely come to understand that Father Mullen is not to be confused with God. But still he has his good days and bad days. Today will be a bad one." She stood up and walked over to the window to check on him.

"You mean because of that boy?"

Without answering, Mercy watched the boys. They were playing basketball now—it looked like PIG because they were trying difficult shots and whenever one went in the other tried to match it. They seemed okay. Jason, trying a hook shot from about twenty feet away, had his face screwed in concentration. But he was good, very good, at hiding his feelings, so she wouldn't judge by appearances. If this week he had nightmares again, she wouldn't be surprised. She always heard them—his groans, sometimes cries—because she slept poorly herself. John's honest and strong face came into her mind, looking serious and intent upon helping Jason no matter the effort. She wished she could speak to him right now; it would be a relief. Sometimes she thought she was half in love with him, but the thought scared her, and she would not allow herself to follow its logic. She turned to Hope. "Listen, I'm thinking about going to the Easter services at the Congregational Church. Would you and Robbie, maybe Keith too, like to come?"

The question seemed to take Hope by surprise, and she didn't answer right off. Mercy could see the workings of her mind written on her face. A look of displeasure was quickly replaced by a slight frown that brought out the crow's feet at the edge of her eyes as she considered the proposal. Clearly she didn't really want to go but was feeling that she should. Mercy didn't want to absolutely force her to, and yet she was uneasy going alone. People might stare and make her feel objectified. If and when that happened she would deal with it much better with Hope at her side. It was even possible she might not find the courage to subject herself to those staring faces alone. So she waited, not letting her face show any weakness of purpose, until Hope shrugged in concession.

"I don't think Keith would go, but Robbie and I can."

"You don't mind? I don't think I could face all those people alone."

"No. We'll be there."

They made plans to meet at Hope's house in the morning, and then she and Jason left for the beach and Brian's apartment. Later she would allow herself the luxury of feeling guilty at forcing Hope to go with her, but now it was too important for her to have any regrets. Having Hope on board also strengthened her hand in telling Brian what she planned to do, but that could be deferred for several hours. Such was her life now, she thought: living not even day to day but moment to moment. Mentally exhausted from her effort of will, she couldn't find a way to begin discussing the incident with the two boys while they drove back to Brian's apartment. They had, however, time before Brian returned from his work site, so once home, she berated herself for cowardice and suggested they take a walk on the beach. It was cooler on the coast and a thin fog gathered in strength so that some of the distant islands in Waska Bay were ghostly shadows. Seagulls swooped about, examining every possibility of a meal, and by a rocky outcropping two cormorants sat drying their wings. The tide was low as they made their way down to the hard-packed sand. Except for a couple walking away from them a quarter of a mile down the beach they were alone.

This was no time for further cowardly delay. Abruptly, before Jason could start exploring and looking for shells and other curiosities, she said, "I heard what those boys said this morning."

Jason reached down and picked up a worn scallop shell. He examined it for a moment before tossing it into the waves. "I figured you did," he said matter-of-factly.

"You know, it may not seem so now, but a day will come when you won't have to put up with stuff like that."

He nodded and started walking again. "I know. Rev. Covington tells me the same thing." He stole a glance at her, then his eyes reverted to studying the sand. "You don't have to worry, Mom. I really do understand it, you know."

"What does Rev. Covington say?"

"He says that people act like that because of ignorance and fear. They don't understand and because they don't understand they fear."

Mercy put her hand on his shoulder. "You're a brave boy, do you know that? But I'm still angry with them."

They walked on in silence until Jason picked up a sand dollar. "These are getting rare now," he said. "Somebody told me it was pollution." He turned to his mother and looked at her very seriously. "I really mean it, you know. Something happened to me. It wasn't my fault. My days of crying about these things are over."

Mercy nodded but didn't dare speak. She looked at her watch and took a deep breath. "We'd better get back. Your father will be home pretty soon."

Back at Brian's apartment she made them tuna sandwiches for lunch and then suggested to Jason that he clean up for their outing. It was a good thing he was in the shower when Brian got home, for he had seen Father Mullen walking in the grounds of Most Holy Trinity Church when he drove down Main Street and was in the blackest of moods. He sputtered incoherently for a while before making himself clear and explaining what he had seen. "I was actually looking for a place to park. I wanted to have it out with him then and there."

His raw hatred made Mercy feel uncomfortable, fearing perhaps (she was not sure) that it might be contagious. Her own feelings about Father Mullen were by no means easily controlled. But she affected to be calm when she asked, "So what did you do?"

Brian stormed over to the sink and began rinsing his thermos out. "Well, I couldn't find any place to park and the traffic was heavy, so all I did was slow down and honk. When he looked I shook my fist at him. What I wanted to do, though, was strangle him, especially after he looked away pretending complete indifference."

Mercy felt the blood leave her face as she frowned. "Brian, don't talk like that. That won't make things any better."

"It would make me feel better."

"But would it make Jason feel better? That's what we have to think about."

His face darkened even more, and he retorted angrily, "You don't have to lecture me about my duty. I assure you I know it. Let me let off some steam, will ya."

"As long as it's just steam," she said softly in an attempt to calm him.

He sat down and started looking through the mail she'd put on the table for him. "It would make me feel better if I could bust him in the mouth a few times, but I don't expect to get a chance to do that. So you don't have to worry."

But she did worry. Through the rest of the afternoon as they attended a car show in Portland she was always on guard and tense, so much so that she developed a headache. Brian behaved himself admirably, but still she worried that Jason would sense his agitation and that it would in turn stir up demons in him that could lead to more nightmares. She was even more afraid that the incident with the two boys this morning was enough to lead Jason to have a bad night. She didn't really believe him when he told her his days of crying were over. Finally she took some aspirin for the headache, and the behavior of the two males—Brian as always positively shining in the presence of new automobiles and Jason always happy to please his father by joining in the examination of these machines—became so relaxed and happy that she finally felt free from both the headache and anxiety.

Later while they were in a restaurant having an early supper before going to a movie at the Maine Mall, she grew anxious again as she told him about her plans for going to the Congregational Church tomorrow for Easter services. Jason was in the bathroom, and she spoke quickly, hoping to have it all settled before he got back. The memory of how he had insisted that Jason be baptized a Catholic made her anxiety return. Brian was not, and since adulthood had never been, however, a churchgoer, and he merely shrugged when she told him of her plan. "That's fine. As far as I can see, Rev. Covington is a good man. And clearly Jason can't go to Trinity Church as long as that creep is there."

"So you have no objection?" she said, not hiding her relief.

Again he shrugged and then passed his hand over his thinning brown hair. "I think it's important for a child to have Christian formation so long as when he's an adult he can decide for himself. I don't suppose it really matters if it's Protestant or Catholic. You, for instance, turned out all right."

He grinned as he made the last remark. The car show really had put him in a good mood. He had not made a racist or ethnic slur all day either; Mercy wondered if there was any connection.

Jason returned. Tousling his blond hair, Brian said, "What do you say, partner. Was that a great car show or what?"

Jason grinned. Great, dad!"

"Your mother was just saying that she'd like to go to Easter services at the Congregational Church. Is that okay with you?"

He looked from his mother to his father, trying to read signals. "Are you going too, Dad?"

"Me? You know I'm not much for church."

"It would be just us, Jason" Mercy said. "Though maybe your Aunt Hope and Robbie will come too. I asked them, but Hope wasn't sure what Uncle Keith was planning."

"I don't know. I guess so." He was trying to hide his disappointment, but Mercy saw it and felt a pang of hurt and jealousy.

"You like Rev. Covington, don't you, son?"

Jason shook his head. "Oh, yeah, Dad. A lot."

"Well, then, I certainly think you should go. Me, I'll be checking on my boys. They'll be working at the parking lot for a new business in Bedford. We've got to finish by Monday afternoon."

From the restaurant downtown they went to the Maine Mall to see a movie, then drove back to Waska where Brian dropped her off at home before proceeding to the beach with Jason. It would have made more sense for Jason to stay with his mother, but Brian didn't offer, nor did she want to insist. Having passed a rare pleasant day with him, she didn't want to spoil it at the end. Besides, he was aware of the inconvenience that might arise and would, he said, bring Jason around before nine o'clock. He had clothes at the apartment so that he could be dressed and ready when he arrived. Thus Mercy was spared hearing groans from any nightmares in the night, though she wasn't spared sleeplessness from worrying about not hearing those groans.

She fell asleep sometime after two and woke with the alarm at seven o'clock, feeling very tired. After showering she spent a long time considering which dress or skirt would be appropriate. In her youth Easter Sunday was always a special day, and one wore the best and newest clothes one had or could get. Now she had to worry about being too conspicuous by overdressing or underdressing and tried on several things before deciding on a black skirt and silk blouse combination. Jason was delivered earlier than promised and wore grey slacks and a white shirt with a red tie but no jacket. Rather strangely (she thought), Brian insisted upon shooting them together with his video camera. It was the first time he had done so since well before their troubles with Father Mullen began. "You look stunning this morning," he explained, but the choice of adjectives made her feel uneasy.

But then she already felt uneasy, going as it were into the unknown. Another benefit of getting Hope to go was that it made backing out at the last moment impossible—though even as she and Jason walked in the cool morning air to Hope's house she thought about it. Her sister and Robbie were ready when they arrived, but Mercy, having already consulted her watch and made some calculations, suggested they had time for a cup of coffee. She wanted to time their arrival at the church so that they would be slightly late and most of the congregation already seated. That way any awkwardness about their joining the church—any impertinent stares, any uncomfortable conversations—could be avoided. And her timing was perfect. Only a few stragglers were hurriedly entering the church, and they were able to go in directly and find one of the few unoccupied pews without having to speak to anyone.

She recognized many faces of people about town, but those she knew included only a few old friends of her mother's as well as Mr. Jellerson, who nodded and smiled shyly when she was taking her seat—he was three rows behind her and sitting with his wife and Walt Pingree. Seeing him surprised her, and she just managed a smile and a slight wave before turning to sit. She was acutely aware that most people recognized her, though only a few looked at her and Jason longer than was necessary. Still it was those few who made her feel uncomfortable, and she put a protective arm on Jason's shoulder. He and Robbie were sitting between her and Hope as further defense against the world. Jason, however, was immediately intent upon listening to the organist play Bach preludes and seemed either unaware or indifferent to anything else. At one point when the organist missed a note and had to restart a passage, she could feel him go tense in sympathy for his fellow musician.

Presently John came up to the pulpit from a door in the back of the church. He was not one of those Protestant ministers who had taken to wearing a Roman collar and vestments; instead he was dressed in a charcoal gray suit, white shirt and dark tie. Mercy thought he looked very handsome as he surveyed the congregation and then made a small joke about not being able to help but notice many new faces. Everyone laughed since they all knew the stereotype of the Protestant who went to church only on Christmas and Easter, but Mercy felt herself blushing even though she didn't think John had seen her yet.

Everyone stood and sang a hymn; the chorus sang another; then some biblical readings alternated with more hymns. When the congregation sang Jason's sweet voice soared above all others even though Mercy knew he was singing as softly as he could. People nearby glanced at him admiringly, and she felt proud. But then it was time for John's sermon and she concentrated on the pulpit.

John surveyed the congregation, waiting for everyone to be ready, and during this survey he saw her and Jason, for his eyes lit up in recognition. Then speaking without any text, he began:

"On the day our religion celebrates the central article of our faith, I want to talk about personal resurrection. What do I mean by that? I mean all the ways big and small our lives can be renewed so that in effect we are reborn. Perhaps you have an elderly aunt or friend whom you've been meaning to visit while weeks, months, even years go by and still you've never quite found the time to see her. What would happen if you did visit her and make her feel connected to life and her family? Perhaps in the small joy you give her you will see the power you have as a human being to be a force for good in the world. Or, similarly, what if you're a businessman who has no time for his family? With little children you sometimes catch staring at you longingly? A child does not become an adult by growing physically; he or she needs nurturing. For you it is work at hand, the work you can do. Nor is it a small thing to produce a healthy child in mind and body, one who knows love and fulfillment, for then the world is a better place. Take that step. Let the love in your heart grow. You will, perhaps, see a different you in the future. These are small changes that do nevertheless lead to a new self when effected, but of course I do not exclude big changes. Some people drink too much until it becomes the consuming passion of their lives. It ruins marriages and careers and brings dreadful misery and unhappiness into the world. There is not an alcoholic alive who hasn't thought about reforming. Here redemption comes with the first step, but it is not what you do; rather it is what you think that is important. First you have to see there is a problem, and then you have to want to change your life. That first step is the biggest step."

Mercy's mind began wandering as he went on. He was talking about the English writer William Hazlitt, who said, "I could not love myself if I were not capable of loving others," and discussing, somewhat unclearly, the moral imagination for some time. She watched others, including Robbie, who fidgeted, and Jason, who listened raptly, and she glanced around to see how many more faces she could find of people she knew, and finding only a few, she thought about what she wanted to say and not say to John when they had their scheduled meeting tomorrow. She didn't really come back to the sermon until it was almost over, and John said:

"The trouble with our human condition is that we too easily get lost in our own concerns and forget we share the world with the rest of humanity as well as the animal and plant kingdoms. We are all in this together, like people in a life boat. But on this day when we celebrate the one who sacrificed his very life for human sins, it is good to remember that we all have within us the power of empathy to share the lives of others."

If the purpose of a sermon is to get the listener to take moral and spiritual stock of him- or herself, John's sermon and particularly the peroration, was effective. Mercy understood that he was exhorting people to be less selfish, and though she was aware that her condition naturally excused her from the charge of being self-involved, because she had seen Walt Pingree the charge struck home. She recalled what John had said about visiting an elderly friend. Two months ago she had heard about Walt's stroke and had thought about visiting him, but despite knowing better than most the kind of lonely life he led she had not gone to see him. For the rest of the service—the hymns, the Lord's Prayer, the chorus singing some selections from Handel's *Messiah*—she kept thinking of how her own pain had diminished her humanity. At first she was ashamed of herself, but then she looked at Jason and saw his sweet face as he sang a hymn and recalled that she would never be whole again until he was.

She was still thinking about these things when it came to be their turn to be greeted by the minister at the front of the church. John and his wife met Hope and Robbie first and were very friendly to them. John joked about Robbie's tie by saying, "Looks like you feel a bit constricted, Robbie." Then he put his arm around Jason's shoulder, making it the first time he had actually touched him as far as Mercy knew, and said, "I hope, my young friend, you liked the music."

While Jason, smiling sheepishly at the minister's spontaneous show of affection, grinned more deeply and said it was great, Mercy, shaking Millie Covington's hand and saying hello, watched carefully. His reaction seemed to confirm what he had told her yesterday: that he was getting better, that his troubles were behind him. Still she doubted.

John put out his hand. "It's good to see you, Mercy. I'm very glad you came."

"It was a wonderful service, John. Thank you." People were pressing behind her, so quickly she whispered, "I'll see you tomorrow. I have a lot I want to talk about."

Walking forward to the sidewalk, she saw that the Jellersons had stopped and were waiting to say hello. Mercy introduced her sister to them. "I've heard a lot about you and am very pleased to meet you," Hope said. Mercy, always aware of the state of Jason's feelings, saw that he tightened up when he saw Mr. Jellerson, and she knew he was remembering. How much of the trauma he had suffered, she wondered, was actually merely in hiding and not vanquished?

Mr. Jellerson, however, was too sensitive and urbane to show that he noticed Jason's discomfort. He smiled warmly and introduced his wife to them. When she'd first met him last fall she had thought because he looked severe he was severe; now she

125

was discovering that he was essentially a benign man and that his Yankee exterior hid a deeply emotional interior. Wasn't Jason the same, as if he had inherited the Yankee trait in his genes? But she had a debt to pay. Walt Pingree was standing behind the Jellersons, looking uncomfortable in an old rumpled suit. Mercy came up to him. "I was so sorry to hear about your stroke, Walt. I hope you are fully recovered."

He looked down, embarrassed, and mumbled, 'I'm fine now, Mercy."

She smiled slightly and said, "Good. I'm glad." She recalled his bitterness against the church after Kermit died as well as the pride he felt in his son before his death. A long, crooked road had led him to church today, the same church in which she and Kermit were going to be married. She made a promise to herself that she would visit him soon. Maybe, if she could find a way to say it without revealing too much she would tell him how she thought of Jason as Kermit's reincarnation.

When they got home there was a message on the machine from Brian. He was not able to get away from work and suggested Jason might like to spend the afternoon at the work site with him. He would, and Mercy took him over to the parking lot after lunch. Then feeling sleepy, she took a nap after which she found herself thinking about Kermit and what might have been to such an extent that it almost made her feel ill. Without Brian there would be no Jason; without Jason, even despite the pain of the last five months, she would be a lost soul. But, she thought, confused and close to despair from months of living without a clear future, she *was* a lost soul. Then she forgot Kermit and thought again of John.

So Sunday afternoon and evening became more moments she had to live through as she awaited a deliverance she could not perceive, and she had a bad night, dreaming when asleep of the suffocating feeling she felt during the twelve years she and Brian tried to have a baby, and thinking when awake of Kermit's death and Jason's violation until she could hardly remember there had ever been joy in her life. The only thing that made her mental torment tolerable was the evidence from Jason's quiet breathing that he at least had had a good night.

In the morning she did experience this momentary deliverance: just as the sun will rise the day after you die, so will it rise after a night of deadly torment. Once up and busy preparing breakfast and getting Jason ready for school, and with the meeting with John mere hours away, she began to feel better. The stress and feeling that she was in the grip of a blind, merciless fate did not return until she got into the car and drove to the church.

Eleanor Smallwood was all smiles when Mercy walked into the office a little before nine o'clock. She was busy taking down the Easter decorations from the walls, but stopped as soon as she saw her. She was clearly pleased to have seen her at the Easter services yesterday and talked at length about Rev. Covington's sermon and the choir. She thought John was brilliant, even when he talked over her head (she said this without the slightest trace of irony, anger or sorrow but merely as a statement of fact), and she hoped Jason wasn't bothered by the organist getting confused in one of the Bach fugues and having to restart.

"No," Mercy said, "Jason is a musician and understands these things."

John arrived, looked harried and hurried. He had overslept, he explained, because the clock radio had either malfunctioned or had not been properly set. With a self-deprecating laugh he confessed the former was his theory and the latter Wendy's and that she was probably right. He got a cup of coffee for himself and a tea for Mercy and they went into his office.

Closing the door, he pointed to a chair. "Have a seat, Mercy. It was a very pleasant surprise to see you, Jason and your sister and son at the services yesterday. I hope everything was to your liking."

"Oh, yes, it was a beautiful service. Jason told me he really did like the music."

"I think he's really starting to make progress."

"Yes, I do too. Though he's such a good actor about hiding his feelings that I worry about what he doesn't say. I know the stress of our situation is starting to wear me down. I'm told I should take tranquilizers and sleeping pills and so forth, but I hate those things. But if I feel stress, surely he does too. A lot of kids treat him like an untouchable. He's come home crying some days. This past Saturday I overheard a boy calling him a freak."

John nodded sympathetically. He leaned forward, his elbows on his knees. "I know. He's told me about some of these incidents. One day at recess the kids played a game whereby the object was to touch him—you know, as if it were a daring thing. Apparently some other kids, kids with better manners and training, stopped the game, but I know Jason was devastated."

Mercy fidgeted nervously in her seat, struggling between anger and pain. "He didn't tell me about that one," she said softly, and then the pain won out over the anger. She wiped away the tears that rimmed her eyes. "Do you think moving away from this town would be better?"

John stood and looked out the window before starting to pace. "Mercy, I honestly don't know. For one thing, he's got to face all this stuff, and moving away seems too much like running away, but I know that the children's cruelty has hurt him dreadfully, and if he's getting hurt it's hard to make progress. We've had to spend several sessions just trying to get him to deal with the way some people treat him. When I say I think he's making progress, of course I agree with you that progress doesn't mean that he miraculously stops feeling the pain. Progress, yes, but I too have noticed he can hide his feelings." He sat back down again and faced her. "Have you considered taking him out of school for the rest of the year and tutoring him for his lessons? I imagine Mr. Jellerson would be happy to help. My impression is that he desperately wants to do something. He is a first-rate teacher, so I know the school authorities would be open to the suggestion. I would be glad to talk to them for you." He paused, then added as an afterthought, "I know it doesn't seem like it, but most of the town is on your son's side. There's enormous sympathy for him."

"I know that. But it's the ones who aren't or who are ignorant that are hurtful. He claims these incidents don't bother him anymore, but I think he's just trying to protect me. Regardless, I think I do like your idea. He needs breathing room—and time—to heal properly."

"Good," John said. "I'll talk to Mr. Jellerson about it." He swung his chair around to look at something on his desk. "I have one more idea. I think with Jason's special gift for music and his intelligence, you might consider for high school a private school like Denham Academy in Leicester, Massachusetts. They have a wonderful musical program there. I know about it not because I went there, but many of my friends at Yale went to Denham, and I have plenty of contacts."

Listening to this suggestion, Mercy had two conflicting emotional responses. Of course she immediately understood that such a school would mean exalted prospects for her son's future, but at the same time it meant that separation from her would not be four years from now after high school but mere months away in the fall. The latter consideration was the one that pressed down upon her. "I don't know," she finally said. "It's hard to decide something like that. It's so sudden."

"And of course it's also rather late. If he could get in, it would probably have to be a special acceptance. Denham is like a college in that most students apply a year in advance. But I know of many cases where people have got in later. But I'm sure you see the advantages of such a place. Even right now it would give him a goal to shoot for. If kids are bothering him, or if some of his classmates are making life uncomfortable for him, the thought of a school where he could concentrate on music might be very liberating. It's like when you're doing an unpleasant job but are leaving for a vacation right after it's completed. It gives you a sense of liberation. Do you see my point?"

"I do. And of course I want the best for Jason. Let me talk to him and to Brian about the idea." It was something else she would have to do later in another moment in the cascading chaos of her present life, but it offered her the possibility of a definite future, a future of days, weeks and years instead of these fleeting moments. Brian too wanted the best for Jason. He couldn't possibly object, nor could she. So right now, thinking only of how she would miss Jason, she didn't feel better, but she could at least see a time when she would.

Decisions

They were at a bar at eleven o'clock at night and already pretty well lit, so you couldn't expect scintillating conversation, but Tony Peretti got something going by finally asking, after they had been together all day driving along the Maine coast to see sites like the famous Portland Headlights and then spending several hours at a rock club in Portland, "So, how's your old man?"

Ben Jellerson frowned and said, "Same as ever as far as I can see." He and his friend were back in Waska now having a few nightcaps before calling it a day. The rock club in Portland had been disappointing, not just the music but no girlie action. The bar was also quite dead, though they had met a large party of people just leaving as they came in. There was a couple at a back table groping each other, two women and a man talking quietly at a window table in the front, and the usual couple of loners at the bar tossing down shots with beer chasers. It was Ben's second Saturday night in freedom, for he had been discharged from the Navy just last week. But it didn't feel like a celebration. He looked over at his old schoolboy friend, who had driven up to Waska from Connecticut for the weekend, and wondered if he could make clear to him the dissatisfaction and depression that enveloped him like a fog. Tony was already drunk from the beer they started drinking in the afternoon and didn't appear to be at his mental best. Half the gulp of beer he slurped dribbled down his chin. Ben was also drunk, but he hadn't lost his coordination yet nor arrived at that blessed state where the fog of dissatisfaction and depression dissipated into gaiety.

He took a sip of his beer, then lit a cigarette. His father had talked to him about the habit this morning. Ben had stared pointedly at his father's pipe rack but had not dared express the thought in his mind: let he who is without sin cast the first stone. The self-righteousness and hypocrisy disgusted him, however, and he found he could talk about that.

"The old fart's in a tizzy right now because he has to testify in a trial next month."

Tony's eyes widened with interest. He leaned forward. "A trial? About what?"

"He won't talk about it, but my mother told me he witnessed a priest molesting a boy."

"Geez, no shit. Where would he be to see that?"

"He was taking a walk behind the farmhouse—you know, in the woods. He's taken up bird watching of all things." He drained his beer and started laughing at the mental picture of his father with binoculars in hand. "Here birdie, birdie. Show yourself, little birdie. Christ, he's queerer than the priest he saw."

Tony paid no attention to the sarcasm. With undisguised fascination, he said, "Must be a big case. Jesus, a priest. And that poor kid. Jesus."

"That's what everybody says," Ben snarled. "Poor kid, my ass. My parents talk about him all the time. I'm sick of hearing it, let me tell you."

"How come?" Tony asked, and followed it immediately with another question. "What do your mother and father say? Because your father has to testify, he talks about that?"

"No, I already told you it ain't about that. My father's going to tutor the kid. It seems he's too sensitive to go to school. The big boys pick on him, poor dear. He's a pianist and musician, you see."

Tony picked up on the sarcasm this time. "What are you saying? The kid's a fag?" He finished his beer with a long pull and banged his mug down on the bar. "Hey, barkeep, two more of the same!"

The bartender walked over to them, wiping his hands on his apron and scowling. He was a big man with a bigger belly, red-faced and balding, and always squinting as if he needed glasses but was too vain to wear them. He had been none-too friendly to them from the moment they came in and now was even less so. "You break the mug, buddy, and you pay for it."

Tony was mostly mellow when he drank, but Ben had seen him snap many times into a snarling, vicious drunk when something was not to his liking. He tensed, expecting the bartender's attitude might be the spark that set Tony off. But he was too intent upon the story of Mr. Jellerson and what he witnessed and merely shrugged. "Sorry, I got carried away. This guy here"—he indicated Ben with his thumb—"is the son of Mr. Jellerson who witnessed the priest. I imagine you've heard of him."

The bartender took their mugs and walked to the taps. Filling them, he said, "Oh yeah, we've all heard of him."

"Big doings in this here town, huh?" Ben said sarcastically.

"Well, it bothers a lot of people. He was just a boy. And there's another boy whose identity is secret. But just boys. We all feel bad."

"For who?" Ben asked with a smirk. He kept seeing the picture of his father bird watching in his mind and found it impossible to shake the sarcasm. "The fag priest?"

The bartender scowled and put the beers down. "That will be three dollars, wise guy."

Ben slid three dollar bills across the bar, and each took a long pull of their beers.

"So what did the priest do, bugger him?"

Ben didn't like the question. He frowned. "How the hell should I know? I told you my father won't talk about it. Let's drop the subject."

They lapsed into the same silence they'd often experienced in the car earlier, though now it wasn't because the road hypnotized them. Ben began examining the two drinkers he could see in the mirror behind the bar. The familiar one, Tony, had an angular face and large nose, dark eyes and hair to complement the Sicilian duskiness of his skin. His teeth were uneven, a fact that never stopped him from flashing an irresistible smile whenever he was happy—and he was often happy. That's why Ben liked him; his sunny disposition perfectly balanced his own somber and morose nature. With Tony he could often forget things and feel good about himself. Tonight was not one of those occasions, however, and that is why the man sitting next to Tony filled him with disgust. You couldn't see the light blue of his eyes, which everyone said was his best feature, but still he wasn't bad looking, though he did have a weak jaw, and his eyes looked beaten and his mouth bitter. He sat hunched up as if he were expecting a grenade to explode at any moment. You could tell he was slightly on the small side of medium height, so he didn't even have the physical presence to back up the belligerence he often felt inside, and you could tell that frustrated him. He looked to see if all the crap he had taken for the past four years showed in his face, and he thought it did.

And why not? The poor slob had spent four misfit years in the United States Navy. He remembered every single moment of those four years now as a tingling sensation, like wanting to choke someone to death while your hands were tied.

He'd known from the second day of boot camp that he had made a grievous mistake and that he was trapped and would have to see it through. Although his duties as a supply clerk were never onerous and the chief and lieutenant above him were fairly reasonable guys, he had quickly seen that he was totally unsuited to live under an authoritarian regime. He bristled at having to salute officers and call them "sir"; he had to fight the urge to spit in the face of any man who gave him a direct order. He had quit college and joined the Navy in an ill-conceived attempt to find independence. Instead of escaping from his father's tyranny, however, it was as if he had placed himself in a situation where half the people he associated with were his father. After a while he learned to live hypocritically, letting off steam by getting drunk on shore and playing a game of pretend on shipboard. He had had two slips off the ladder because when he was drunk he couldn't hide his resentment and had been insolent and insubordinate. The first incident, where he told a chief petty officer to kiss his ass, he had not been able to keep from his parents, but the second time he was able to keep secret by not telling them he had made third-class petty officer again. Thus when he was busted they were none the wiser. Six months before he was discharged he was promoted for the third time, so he left the Navy a petty officer.

He had been discharged from the Navy on a Friday and flown from Norfolk to Hartford where Tony picked him up. After a weekend with his friend in their hometown, he had hitchhiked to Maine. Tony, before going to his job as an auto mechanic at a garage, drove him to Interstate 95, and they made plans for his visit to Maine the following weekend. It was late Monday afternoon before he got to the farmhouse. Not having been to it since childhood, he had to ask directions in town and then walk the five miles up country when no car would stop for him. A dull week followed. His mother let him use her car, but except for a couple trips to buy some civilian clothes he hadn't done much. For one thing, he didn't know a soul in the town, and for another he had no clear idea what he was going to do with himself.

During his last year in the Navy he had thought about his future frequently, though he had never been able to come to any definite decision. Two things he knew: that he hated the Navy and that with only twelve credits needed for a B.A. he should return to college for a semester or two. But what then? A third thing, more vague, would be the necessity of a job. It was all very unpleasant, this thinking about the future, and finally he had decided that he would simply coast through the summer and perhaps the fall too. Thanks to his father's suggestion that he should have money deducted from his Navy pay and deposited directly into a bank account, he had saved enough money to live a year or so without working. Maybe he would visit his sister Beverly in San Francisco and if he liked the town stay there. He could get a job, perhaps a clerical job like his Navy work as a supply clerk, and after establishing residency attend one of the California state universities. Maybe he could find something in Maine that would hold him here, maybe even a girl. He daydreamed all the time about having one, though in fact he had never dated any girl in high school or college more than three times. It wasn't looks—his or hers—it was that he was wary of intimacy and trust. All his sexual experiences had been with whores or very free and unparticular girls. So even though he daydreamed about a girlfriend, he knew it was not very likely. And with his hatred of his father, it wasn't really very likely he would find anything in Maine that would make him want to stay. The trouble was that he had no place to go. Of all the people he had known in Connecticut, only Tony was not married or not moved away; in Waska he knew only his parents. As the time came closer and closer to his release from the Navy this isolation, this rootlessness, started scaring him and causing panic attacks. His answer to this anxiety was to find relief in drink. Every night he had liberty in Norfolk he went ashore and got drunk. Once he secreted a bottle aboard his ship and got drunk. He used to do a lot of drugs in college and in his early years in the Navy, but having had a couple scary experiences with bad acid on one occasion and an overdose of cocaine on another, he had been drug-free for the past year. Booze was different; he felt he could control the use of alcohol. Not that he had tonight with Tony, not that he had during his final weeks under governmental chains. Not that he had the day he was released and was drunk before he got on the airplane, and not that he had during last week with Tony. But these were all special occasions, and during the five dull days at the farmhouse he'd only had a few beers. He could handle his liquor, he assured himself.

He said this now to Tony. "You know what, Tony. Even though I'm already lit, I can still handle the booze. How about you?"

Tony grinned and fondled his beer mug. "Hey, I handle it all the time."

"In the Navy I never missed it when I was at sea."

Tony squinted at him suspiciously. "What about when you went ashore?"

Ben lit a cigarette and inhaled. He glanced at his friend, who was bent over and looking wasted. "Let me put it this way—I wouldn't want to take a sobriety test at that time."

He grinned, which caused Tony to start laughing so hard he spurted beer all over himself and the bar. Too drunk to clean it up, he had enough sobriety, if you could call it that, to agree with the bartender who came over and said, "I think you two have had enough."

"Yeah," he's right, Ben. Let's call it a night. I haven't drunk this much since your last leave. Or was it last weekend? I forget." He had another fit of giggles which were not, however, infectious. Ben returned the bartender's scowl and said, "Okay, let's blow this dump."

For sure they were too drunk to remember to stop at the head, so when they got outside and were wandering around aimlessly looking for Tony's car they took a piss against a building on the side street parallel to the bar. The trouble was a car went by just then, and they could see the shocked look of a matronly wife, illuminated by the same streetlight that captured them. They panicked for a moment before wandering on and forgetting it. At one point Tony started calling for the car as if it were a dog: "Here yellow Ford, here boy!" He thought he was being unspeakably funny and had another fit of laughter. Ben just frowned. The tingling sensation of wanting to strangle someone hadn't left him.

Tony's fit of laughter expended the last of his energy and he fell into a stupor and began walking like a zombie. In a parking lot across the street Ben saw something yellow and was propping up Tony for an attempt to reach it when he became aware of a car turning into the street and driving slowly.

Suddenly a bright blue light exploded all around them whirling dizzily. Ben became confused and panicky. He blinked, then realized it was the flashing light of a police car. It pulled over next to where they teetered on the curb. A spotlight from the top of the car drenched them in light. A voice said, "Okay, you two. Stop right there. I've received a report of two drunk and disorderlies. Looks like you're my lads."

Ben still couldn't see the voice, but the use of the term "lads" confused him so that he thought he was back in the Navy. The panic he initially felt intensified before his mind starting working. The voice was more jovial than authoritarian; the car was a police car, not the Shore Patrol.

The car door slammed and he turned to see a tall, thin police officer with very long arms coming from the shadow of the car into the light. "Looks like you boys have been celebrating. What's the occasion?"

Again the voice had a jovial quality to it which Ben mistook for weakness. "What's it to you?" he asked belligerently, then added as a wise second thought when Tony accidentally bumped into him as he too turned to face the officer, "Actually I just got out of the Navy."

"The Navy! I served on a tin can. What were you on?"

"A supply ship."

The cop nodded gravely. "We needed them, that's for sure." He reached into the car and turned off the flashing lights. "Let me see your ID's."

They fumbled for them, with Ben having to help Tony get his out of his wallet, and handed them over. The cop gave them a cursory glance and returned them. "Okay, where do you live? This is not Connecticut."

Drunk as he was, Ben could perceive the friendly intent of the question, but he could not help himself. "I hope you don't think I liked the Navy because I didn't. It sucked. Like this town, it sucks. But he's from Connecticut. I'm visiting my parents here."

A flash of anger passed across the cop's face. "Let me give you some advice, sonny. You shoot your mouth off one more time and I'll run you in to jail. Now it's up to you. Because you just got out of the Navy, and because I served too, I want to give you a break. Keep your mouth shut and all will be fine. Now, again, where are you staying?"

Ben looked at Tony, swaying like a weeping willow in a hurricane. He didn't look as if he heard what the officer was saying. He'd have to speak for both of them. He hated authority but he was also afraid of it. The officer's commanding tone had the effect of sobering him up and making him aware of the necessity for self-preservation. "Okay," he said, "it's a deal. Tony's staying at The Pine Tree Motel. I'm with my parents."

"You have a car?"

"Yeah, it's parked over there. We just found it." He pointed across the street.

"I hope you weren't planning on driving it."

"I don't know. I don't think so," he lied.

"Somebody called the station saying two drunks were seen urinating in public. I don't suppose that was you?"

Ben shook his head. "I don't think so. We took a piss right before we left the bar."

The cop considered for a moment. "Do you want to go home or stick with your pal?"

He was holding Tony up now. He was close to being asleep on his feet. "I better stick with my friend."

"A good choice. Tell you what. You leave that car where it is, and I'll drive you to The Pine Tree Motel. Then you'd better sleep it off. It's there or the town jail, in case you were wondering what the choices were."

The policeman and Ben ended up having to carry Tony into the motel room; then Ben had to listen to another lecture before he himself collapsed on the second bed in the room and fell asleep almost instantly. That didn't happen too often, so the last thought he had before blankness came was that the night's drinking had been good.

Of course come morning he paid the usual price. He woke with such a horrible hangover that even blinking, even moving his eyes, caused the pain to intensify. It felt as if his temples were being crushed in a vice.

Tony was already awake and groaning in his bed. "Hey, Ben," he said, "did we get run over by a truck last night?"

"Tell me about it. We did get run in by a cop."

"Is that how we got back here? I don't have much recollection."

Neither of them felt like eating. They got a coffee at the front desk and smoked a cigarette with it, which made them feel even worse. Unfortunately there was no time to nurse their hangovers beyond buying some aspirin in the coin-operated machine, for Tony had to get back to Connecticut to help his cousin move to a new apartment. They had to walk a mile and a half to the car. The cool morning air cleared their heads a little, but not enough to make any plans for future visits. Tony drove him to the farmhouse and dropped him off without going in. He knew the Jellersons never thought very highly of him.

His parents were just going to church, so his hope of avoiding them was frustrated; he decided he would simply brazen it out. He reeked of spilled beer and sweat and probably looked like hell. His father gave him a sharp look, though he didn't say anything. His mother diplomatically said, "Looks like you need a shower."

"Yeah, Tony and me were celebrating my release from the Navy. I think we got carried away." That stuck a finger in the dike for a while at least, and he went up to his room without any lectures. He lay down on his bed without getting under the covers and slept for a few more hours.

His head still throbbed when he woke up at about eleven o'clock, so he decided to take two more aspirin. As he waited for them to take effect, he poured the last of the coffee in the kitchen pot into a mug and strolled outside to have a smoke and in the hope that the fresh air would ease his hangover. The farmhouse had changed little since his childhood visits to his great-grandparents, both of whom lived into their nineties. It was the one familiar thing about being in Waska, and strolling about he began reminiscing. His great-grandfather was a stern and demanding man too much like his father, but his great-grandmother always indulged him with homemade ice cream, freshly baked cookies and other treats, so that some of the times he spent here numbered among his small stock of happy childhood memories. One time Beverly and he had gone to the neighboring farm with her and had been allowed to watch the farmer giving some hoof treatment to his herd of cows. Leaning against a fence, they both squealed with delight when one of the cows waiting her turn ambled over to them and wanted to be nuzzled. Beverly didn't dare to touch the cow, but he had bravely patted her on the snout. For the rest of the afternoon they were in ecstasy. But that farm was now gone; in its stead were two or three suburban colonial houses, and somebody probably had designs on the fields behind them. There was one dairy farm in operation half a mile up the road. His father had told him the farmer still hayed the remaining Jellerson pastures.

Ben walked around to the side of the house to see if he could figure out which pastures belonged to his parents, but before he could get around to the back he heard something squeal and was startled. It was only the new puppy, tethered to a post and very much glad to have some company. He regarded Ben with patent eagerness. He didn't like animals but sat down on a lawn chair next to it and lit his cigarette. He had time to kill and a head to clear, and besides, who gave a rat's ass what pastures were Jellerson land. When his parents croaked he'd sell the farm faster than you could say, "Big bucks!"

The puppy had a name, which he had forgotten. He kept trying to crawl on to Ben's lap only to be pushed away with a stern, "Beat it, puppy." This happened several times while Ben started thinking about what he was going to do with himself now that Tony had deserted him. The thought had a gravitational pull that sank him into depression, which, by a circuitous logic he could feel more than understand, made him jealous of the puppy. A picture of his father's face shining as he reached down to pat the creature came into his mind and festered.

The next time the puppy tried to crawl into his lap he slapped it away. "Beat it, I said."

The puppy whined and looked at him in confusion, his soft brown eyes not understanding the betrayal. Gingerly he approached again, only to receive a sharper blow that made him whimper in pain and back off in fright.

Just then he heard a rustle which made him look up. A pretty young woman with dark eyes and short dark hair was staring at him with a look of horror. She wore a T-shirt that did little to hide her large, shapely breasts and tight hip-hugging jeans.

He felt his face burning. "Hi," he said. "That puppy has been driving me crazy."

Her face darkened into a frown, which he could see she tried to suppress. "I see, but…" She stopped, apparently confused, trying to decide if she would leave or approach, speak to him or pass on.

His mind raced. She must be the neighbor girl whom his father had tutored and who bought the puppy for him as a thank-you gift. His mother had told him about her. He searched for her name, found it, and said, "You must be Michelle. My parents have told me about you. I'm Ben Jellerson."

"Hello," she said coldly. "Yes, I'm Michelle. Sometimes I take Buttons for a walk. That's why Mr. Jellerson leaves him out Sunday mornings when they go to church."

"Oh, I see. They didn't tell me. You want to take him now?"

"Is Walt at home?"

"Yes, he's in his pad. You want me to get him for you?"

"No, that's all right. I usually go around to the back entrance. He's my friend too."

"I know. Walt told me. He's a good guy."

She nodded. "The best."

He found himself staring at her breasts and saw that she noticed. She folded her arms across her chest.

"Well, I'll go see Walt now."

He said good-bye to her, to which she nodded.

"Well, you certainly made a great first impression on that little filly," he said out loud as soon as he heard the back door close behind her. He looked at the puppy, crouching and eying him warily. "Thanks a lot, you little shit." He stood. Out of the corner of his eye he could see the puppy cringe, but there was nothing for him to worry about. He entered the house by the front door and went upstairs to the guest room he was using. He needed a shower, but he could hear the muffled voices of Michelle and Walt below. That lucky old dog, he thought as he fantasized coming up behind the naked girl and reaching around to fondle and lift her breasts. "I'd like to be your bra for a day, Baby," he whispered to the floor in the direction her voice came from.

By the time he was out of the shower Michelle had left and his parents had returned. He could hear them talking in the kitchen. He dressed and went down to get the facing-the-music bit out of the way. His father was too excited, however, to have time to give him a lecture on the evils of too much drinking. It seemed the tutoring of the wonder boy, which had been in the planning stages since Easter, was about to become a reality. They had seen Mercy Buckley and her son at church and the outcome of this momentous meeting was that they were going to come out to the farmhouse at one o'clock to decide on all the particulars. His father was worrying himself into a tizzy about his weakness in mathematics and kept voicing his doubts. "Nonsense, Sam," his mother kept saying, "you can study the math book and stay a lesson or two ahead of him." They talked about algebra and history and everything under the sun, even about dinner plans on Mondays since that was the day tutoring was going to happen in one of the Sunday school rooms at the Congregational church, but they had nothing to say to their son who had returned from serving his country and keeping the world safe for democracy. Ben watched them with a sour feeling inside that probably was plastered all over his face while he now and then glanced through the Sunday paper on the kitchen table. He decided that he was going to get out of this house and this town and this state as soon as possible.

Only when a car drove into the yard did his mother think to mention lunch. "There's tuna salad in the fridge, Bennet. Make yourself a sandwich."

"No thanks, I'm not hungry."

When they went out to greet their guests, he made a second and lesser decision, this one that he wouldn't be polite and wait to meet them. He started to return to his room, then changed his mind and walked through the living room and into the wing of the house where Walt lived.

He tapped on the door and just barely waited for Walt to say, "Come in," before opening it.

Walt's room was pleasantly lit by two large windows. Besides his bed and bedside table, the principal pieces of furniture were an easy chair, where Walt spent most of his time watching TV and reading, a bureau and a table and two wooden chairs. Walt used the table both for a desk and an eating surface. On the bureau were his family pictures and personal possessions. The walls were decorated with a series of bird paintings that Millie had chosen and framed. A small sink and refrigerator allowed Walt to have coffee and light snacks in his room; for his main meals he ate with the family, though Ben had heard he'd had to be talked into that arrangement.

A small color television on the dresser had the Red Sox game on. The announcers were just giving the starting line ups.

"Mind if I visit, Walt? The house has guests right now and I'm in the way, I'm afraid."

"Is it Mercy Harmon and Jason? I thought I heard their voices through the window." Walt was searching the remote control for the mute. Finding it, he said, "I should say Mercy Buckley, her married name. But come in, Ben. Have a seat."

Ben looked from the bed to the table. The bed was unmade, so he pulled out one of the wooden chairs and sat down. The sports section of the Sunday paper was opened to a Red Sox story. "I see you had a visit from Michelle earlier. She asked me if you were here."

Walt nodded and looked uncomfortable. "She was a bit upset with you, you know."

He laughed nervously. "Oh? I think I know why. That little puppy kept nipping at me and after a while I slapped him lightly on the nose. Just then Michelle comes up. She probably thought I was abusing the poor thing."

He looked at Walt closely, trying to see if his story would be accepted. Nervously he crossed and uncrossed his legs.

Whatever Walt thought he kept to himself and gave nothing away in his eyes. "I see. That's what I told her. I said you were probably trying to train Buttons to behave."

"That's right. By the way, do you know why Mercy and her son have come?"

He asked the question rhetorically and expected no answer, but Walt didn't need to be told. He already knew. "I think so. Sam is going to tutor Jason. They've been planning it since Easter."

"Yeah, that's what they're here for—to make, you know, the final plans. One thing I don't understand, though. How come my father is doing this? I mean, what's in it for him? I'm guessing he's bored silly now that he's not teaching anymore. It's almost unnatural the way he regards it as so important."

Walt listened to him attentively and with a curious glint in his eye as if he felt he was being put on. He rubbed his stubbly chin for a moment, then said, "Well, don't you see, he feels bad for the little fellow. He wants to help him."

"Help him?"

Walt nodded. "Uh-huh. The boy has got quite a wallop from life. He don't trust people, seeing how that priest double-crossed him. But if you don't trust people, you're in big trouble."

That was easily answered. "Not necessarily. I don't trust people. I think it's the smartest thing you can do. Everyone's out to get what they can. You trust them and they'll nail you. I know. It's happened to me."

"It's happened to all of us, but it don't prove nothing." Walt became animated. Leaning forward and talking with his hands, he added, "Some people are like that, but you've got to trust people or you'll never get anywhere."

"Let me ask you this. Didn't you just say that Jason is hurting because of the priest?

"Yeah, I did. I'm not arguing that you should trust everybody blindly."

Ben turned and listened to the voices coming through the door from the living room. Jason's high, whiny voice could be heard, Mercy's and sometimes his father's. They were all excited and earnest, but he couldn't actually hear what they were saying. "I agree with you there, but till proved otherwise I think it's wisest to be careful. Do you, for instance, trust my father?"

Again Walt had that look on his face that suggested he felt Ben must be putting him on. "Not for a long time, but I do now. I know him now, you see. Your father is a good man."

Ben slammed the table with his fist. "No, he's not!" he shouted. "At least he's never been good to me. Whatever I did as a kid was never good enough. He never praised me once that I can remember. I know a lot of students liked him at Hartley Academy, but what good is that when his own kids were treated like dirt? It's not just my opinion either. My sister Beverly would tell you the same thing."

Walt listened to his outburst with a shocked look on his face. He shifted his weight and appeared uncomfortable. "I don't know your sister, but I don't doubt it. I suppose your father was a difficult man, what with being a school teacher and all. I've heard there's a lot of pressure on them to have kids who are good students. And I'll tell you the truth, I didn't like him years ago. What I found, though, was that he's a difficult man to get to know. Once you do, you'll find I'm not lying. He is a good man. He's trying to do the right thing, and that's why he's trying to help Jason."

Ben remained unconvinced, but he saw he wasn't going to change the old man's mind. Abruptly, he changed the subject. "How come everyone feels so sorry for that kid?"

Walt stared at him in disbelief. "I don't rightly know what you mean. Did you ask why everyone feels sorry for Jason?"

He felt his face redden. He was looking for sympathy and instead had said something stupid. Jason was a victim and everyone sympathized with him; he, Bennet Robinson Jellerson, was also a victim and yet no one had any sympathy for him. Instead he was blamed for his supposed shortcomings. But could he say that? No. At that moment Walt too became an enemy.

He was rescued by a light tap on the door. It was Mrs. Jellerson. She poked her head in the door and looked around. "Oh, that's where you are, Bennet. Walt, Mercy would like to see you. She didn't want to come all the way out here without saying hello."

Walt stood and teetered a bit, then steadied himself by throwing his arms out. "I'll come in," he said quickly as if ashamed of the disorder in his room. Ben saw him looking at the unmade bed.

His mother nodded and started to leave before having second thoughts. "Bennet, please come in and meet Mercy and Jason Buckley."

After hearing Jason talked about for a week, seeing him was a surprise. He had pictured a wimpy, effeminate scared little runt only to discover a healthy, strong boy of medium height and build. He had sandy-blond hair and bright blue eyes that stared at him fearlessly when they were introduced. Somehow the reversed expectations made Ben the one who felt uneasy and inferior, and he averted his eyes when he shook the boy's hand. While he was prepared not to like him, this being made to drop his eyes caused a strong flash of anger to pass through him. He itched with the desire to say something that would inflict pain and exact revenge. The hatred simmered as he stood in the background half listening to Walt chatting with them and only diminished when he started observing Mercy's breasts and legs where she sat on the couch with her eyes almost always on Jason. The protective mother was also a fine specimen of female sexuality, he thought, watching her cross her legs and momentarily viewing her thighs. His mother had told him Jason was a late child who came to them after ten years of trying to have a baby (she was trying to explain the depth of love Mercy felt for her only child), but she looked thirty-five or even younger.

For the next half hour the specifics of the tutoring were discussed again, and interspersed were constant signs of concern for Jason. "Would you like something to drink?" "Are you hungry?" "Would you like to listen to some music?" Not once was Ben drawn into the conversation. Even his mother, who used to be on his side, only had eyes for Jason. He watched her sometimes when he wasn't staring at Mercy. He still wasn't used to her new look, with new glasses, a different hairdo and above all an aura of self-confidence very different from the matronly faculty wife who was his mother. It made him feel lonely, so again he stole secret looks at Mercy, whose eyes as always were riveted on her son. His father left at one point and came back with several textbooks, which were then examined and discussed at great lengths. Finally, just when Ben was looking for some way to gracefully exit this happy little scene, Mercy stood up and said that Jason's father would be expecting them soon.

They all walked out to the driveway to see them off, with Ben following but holding himself apart. They stayed until the car was at the end of the long driveway; then with a final wave everyone turned back to the house.

But before they got inside Ben was surprised by his father, who put his hand on his shoulder and said, "Bennet, please walk with me for a few minutes. I'd like to talk to you."

He expected the lecture that had remained undelivered, but instead his father was strangely soft-spoken. He seemed filled with sorrow and regret and his tone was elegiac. "Bennet, you're a young man now," he began, "and yet it was just yesterday I was riding you on my knee as a little baby. The years, they just flew by. This farm, or what used to be a farm"—he swept his arm across the horizon, taking in the farmhouse, fields and woods—"has been our family's home for generations. I never thought I would live here and wouldn't have if Hartley Academy hadn't closed."

Ben looked at him with a slight frown still lingering. Only his parents called him Bennet. He hated it.

"I know. Why am I talking about this? I've been thinking of our puritan ancestors. I guess one can't help doing so when their ghosts are everywhere here. They're not exactly media stars today, and yet the work they did, the sacrifices, the integrity, the righteousness I can't help but admire. But…" He stopped and looked into Ben's eyes. "But they had their faults too, I know. They were so intent upon that righteousness that sometimes they failed in their human duties. And maybe I was too much like them, at least in that regard. Tell me, do you plan to finish college?"

Ben nodded. "Yeah. I think so." He spoke coldly even while wishing he didn't.

His father walked on in silence for a while. They were behind the house, walking in the part of the pasture with low grass. Beyond it where the high grass was the wind made waves as it blew across the long silken hay. "I know I haven't been a good father to you. It was unfair to expect so much of you as a boy. I made a lot of mistakes. Maybe I ruined your boyhood… I want to make it up to you." He looked at Ben for a sign, found none, and his eyes narrowed. "But I can't do it without your cooperation."

Ben turned and looked back to the farmhouse. He folded his arms. "I think it's too late for that now."

When his father didn't say anything, he turned back to face him. He looked hurt and angry and was struggling to compose himself. Finally he managed to speak calmly. "That's it? You don't even want to try?"

"Dad, the best thing right now is, I think, just to let me have some space. Okay?" He was lying, as he ever lied, but he held himself under tight control, tighter than his father ever could, and resisted the urge to start sobbing and throwing himself on his father's shoulder. "Okay?" he repeated casually.

His father appeared deflated; his shoulders turned in and he actually looked unsteady on his feet. "Can you tell me what your immediate plans are?"

"I think I'd like to visit Beverly. See San Francisco. One of my old college roommates is out there too, so I hope to look him up. Maybe I'll finish college in California. I don't know."

"That's a long ways away." He spoke almost in a whisper, pensively, as if speaking to himself. Then he rallied, ever the Mr. Jellerson who taught history at Hartley Academy to whom duty was sacred. "Let me at least pay for you airplane ticket," he said.

That was the kind of fatherly duty Ben could accept. "Yeah, thanks. That would be great." He turned and started walking towards the farmhouse, his father following.

The Argument

Michelle came into the kitchen wearing the thigh-length T-shirt that was her pajamas. She stifled a yawn and looked at her parents, already dressed and ready for the day—her father, in fact, was just going outside to mow the lawn.

"Good morning, sunshine," he said with a jocularity that she could not appreciate at 7:30 on Saturday morning. She had been out very late with Bobby last night and was much in need of sleep. Usually she slept in on weekends, but on this Saturday morning she had volunteered to man the Courtney Academy table at the rummage sale to benefit the Meals on Wheels program in Waska. She and Sarah had collected stuff for the past two weeks and stored it in the Turcotte garage. With Sarah and Rob expected within the hour, she had to eat breakfast, shower, dress and above all wake up before they arrived.

"How was the party?" her mother Elaine asked. "I heard you come in at about one o'clock."

She sat at the table, picked up the morning paper, then put it down, feeling too sleepy to read. "It was great. Were you waiting up for me? You don't have to, you know."

Elaine put bread into the toaster. "Want some scrambled eggs?" she asked. "You'll need a big breakfast. No telling when you'll have time for lunch." When Michelle nodded, she went to the refrigerator to get the eggs. "I wasn't waiting up, but I was awake. I can't help being a mother."

Michelle heard the lawn mower firing up and glanced out the picture window. Above the green fields and the trees she could see slate colored skies. "Did you hear a weather report?"

Don't worry. Morning clouds, clearing by noon, beautiful day with highs in the low seventies. What time are you leaving?"

"Sarah and Rob should be here before eight-thirty. We have to load the car with the four boxes and then stop at Mr. Jellerson's to get the stuff he says he's collected for us. We'll have to be efficient. The rummage sale opens at nine o'clock."

Elaine was cooking the eggs at the stove. "That reminds me. Your father told me last night there's some trouble about Jason's trial. I don't think I'm giving any courthouse secrets away if I tell you. Marcel said everyone was talking about it yesterday, including the reporters."

Michelle, her piece of toast suspended in the air before her mouth, listened to her mother. One thing was for sure. If Elaine was telling her something, it was important. She never gossiped, never belittled others. As long as Michelle could remember Elaine had always treated her with respect and as a person with a mind of her own. When she heard other girls talking about their mothers she could almost not believe the things she heard. The tales they told made her realize she was a very lucky girl to have a mother she could talk to.

"What is it? she asked anxiously. "Why did Mr. Jellerson remind you of it?"

"Because it's about Mr. Jellerson tutoring Jason. When the prosecutor heard about it he hit the roof. He thinks the defense attorney for Father Mullen will eat him alive when he testifies."

Her mouth was now full of toast and jam. She chewed and swallowed. "Why?"

Elaine brought the frying pan over to the table and spooned out the scrambled eggs onto Michelle's plate. "Have another piece of toast and a slice of cantaloupe. The defense will try to impugn Mr. Jellerson's objectivity. They'll say he's prejudiced."

"How is helping someone being prejudiced?"

"Because the person he's helping is the person the defendant is accused of molesting. He will not be a neutral witness. He won't be objective."

"I don't see that at all. They're two different things. That's just common sense."

Elaine was at the sink washing out the frying pan. "Well, you'll have to ask your father about these lawyerly things, but what's common sense to us is not necessarily so to them."

Michelle thought for a moment. "You know, sometimes my friends tease me about being the daughter of a shark. But Dad isn't like that."

"No," Elaine said, glancing through the window above the sink in the direction of the sound of the lawn mower. "No, he isn't. But defense attorneys in criminal cases will often use anything to weaken a case. They stand by the guilty-without-a-shadow-of-doubt bit. They, shall we say, specialize in shadows."

"Do they consider what happens to the victims of their trickery? If Father Mullen gets off, I think Jason would be crushed. He'll think he has no protection. Does Dad actually think he might get off?"

Elaine, kneeling down and filling the dishwasher, didn't answer at first. She got up and came to the table to clear away Michelle's dishes. "I don't think he thinks it's that serious, but he probably does think it could happen."

"I wonder what Mr. Jellerson will do?"

"Probably continue tutoring Jason. The prosecutor called Mrs. Buckley. She's like you in this. She was shocked that anyone could actually think this was a real issue, and she told him that it would look worse if they stopped the tutoring—you know, as if they had done something wrong."

"Good for her," Michelle said as she stood up. "Now I'd better get into the shower. If Sarah and Rob come, tell them I'll be down as quickly as possible."

She was glad to hear them downstairs when she got out of the shower. The half hour they had allowed for setting up that had seemed like plenty of time yesterday looked rather inadequate in the cold light of morning. She dressed quickly in jeans and a T-shirt that had Bach's benign old face on it and hurried downstairs to find Rob talking to Elaine about page layout software. He had discovered she used it in her production of circulars at her company, and he was telling her how he had laid out the Courtney Academy school newspaper on a cheap twenty-five dollar page layout application. While not exactly boasting, he was obviously proud of his achievement. Sarah, seeing that Michelle was ready, said, "Okay, Rob, enough of the MacTalk. Let's get this show on the road." She exchanged a glance and a secret smile with Michelle. The latter's advice to the lovelorn had been completely successful.

They loaded the four boxes into Sarah's car (actually her brother's car, but he was very generous). Rob and Sarah had stopped at Mr. Jellerson's house to get his contribution, so they drove directly downtown to the Congregational Church where the rummage sale was taking place. Bobby had a track meet in the morning and would join them sometime in the early afternoon.

They found the table preassigned to them and began setting up their wares amidst dozens of others doing the same thing. From friends, neighbors, classmates and family Sarah and Michelle had collected whatever things seemed valuable enough to sell. Old clothes, portable radios and other electronic equipment, CD's, tapes and records, kitchen appliances, household items, framed pictures, old garden tools, a few toys— such was the merchandise they displayed at their table and hung on one of the two chairs assigned to them. Most of the other tables had similar variety, though a few tables specialized. Baby clothes, children's toys and hand tools were three such sites they saw in a preliminary tour of the tables in the parking lot of the Congregational Church. There were even two places selling craft items. The proceeds from these two tables were to be divided fifty-fifty, as opposed to the one-hundred percent for used items. With the rummage sale benefiting the Meals on Wheels program, most of the tables were represented by churches and social clubs of a philanthropic nature. The only Christians not represented were the evangelicals, whose charity apparently didn't extend to people who lacked a personal relationship with their savior and were therefore lost souls. All in all some thirty tables (in addition to the refreshment stand manned by the ladies of the Congregational Church) were displaying their wares by the time the rummage sale officially opened at nine o'clock. Several hundred people were waiting on the sidewalk for the signal to come forward. It was given by Rev. Covington, who humorously said through a megaphone, "All right, good people, let the games begin!" Many of the early birds seemed to know exactly what they were looking for. They would pass a table and survey its merchandise in an instant, either stopping if they saw what they wanted or quickly passing on if they did not. Michelle noticed many of them had an unseemly acquisitiveness written all over their faces which indicated that they were not so much interested in helping a charity as they were in finding good deals for themselves. One of these early birds, an older man with dark hair that looked suspiciously as if it came from a bottle, surprised her by offering twenty dollars for all the records they had. She would have guessed that they were the mostly likely candidate to remain unsold; instead they became the first sale for their table.

Many more sales followed. In the first two hours, in fact, they sold over two-thirds of their goods and had made over two hundred dollars for the cause. After eleven o'clock visitors to their table, and consequently sales, became more sporadic, and they had more time to talk and people watch. While Rob went off to the refreshment stand to get them something for lunch, Sarah and Michelle started observing a man with strange little rodent eyes and a pronounced hooked nose that gave him a curiously predatory appearance. Dressed in dirty dungarees and a yellowed T-shirt, he looked rather disheveled as he walked from table to table. It quickly became obvious that he was not looking to buy anything. They saw him staring at every young female when he thought they weren't looking and even following some of them surreptitiously. His pace was unsteady, suggesting that he was drunk or high on drugs.

"That guy gives me the creeps," Sarah said. "He's raping girls with his eyes."

Michelle watched him closely. He was about twenty feet away, looking at one of the young women from the French Catholic church kneeling to get something out of a box. She wore a miniskirt. "Did I ever tell you about Mr. Jellerson's son Ben?"

Sarah, still watching the man, said, "No. What about him?"

"He looked at me like that."

"What? Mr. Jellerson's son? I wouldn't have guessed that."

"Me either. But he's kinda strange. I saw him torturing Buttons too. When I talked to him—he was outside smoking a cigarette on Sunday morning when I usually take Buttons for a walk—he was mentally undressing me."

"Yuck! But what do you mean, torturing Buttons? Why would he do that?"

"I don't know. But be careful. Here comes eyeballs."

Sarah looked up at the man and continued staring. Her technique worked, for the man quickly walked away. "What did he do?"

"Who? Ben Jellerson?"

Sarah gave her a comic look. "The man in the moon. Moon eyes. No, Ben Jellerson of course."

"I saw him slapping Buttons on the snout twice. The second time was especially quite vicious."

Rob returned from the refreshment stand with their lunch of apple juice, tuna salad sandwiches and lunch-sized bags of chips. The sandwiches made by the Congregational ladies had too much mayonnaise to be very palatable, so they didn't mind being interrupted by the second large wave of people looking for bargains. This spurt lasted less than an hour before things started slowing down again. Suddenly a commotion could be heard from the direction of the refreshment stand. There were still a couple of hundred people roaming between the tables so that they could not easily see what was happening. Sarah went over to have a look and returned to report it was that guy. When Michelle expressed puzzlement, she added, "You know, the one with the hooked nose. He's in a fight. Two men have got him down now. His face is all bloody."

Along with virtually everyone else at the rummage sale, they deserted their table and walked over to see the action, explaining as they went who the man was to Rob. It was still hard to see. Someone in front of them said, "Call the cops." The crowd was speaking all at once, a buzz that modulated like a saw going through wood and hitting knotholes. They managed to get close enough to see the man. He was screaming, "Let me go, you—" and unleashing a string of vile epithets. One of the men, a large barrel-chested man with enormous arms held the hooked-nose man down while he squirmed like a kitten having a bath. The crowd pressed, forcing Sarah and Michelle back where they couldn't see anymore. After a while Rob came through the crowd to report the man had stolen a woman's pocketbook. Someone overhearing him said it was a boom box he stole and that he tripped after he started running. This report was further corrected by a middle-aged woman with two children clinging to her skirts.

"No, I saw it. He was tackled by Mr. Johnson when he tried to escape."

It was difficult to hear these reports. Everyone was still talking at once, the captured man continued his torrent of screams and vulgar words, and then the sound of a siren filled the air. Momentarily the crowd went silent so that when one man asked, "Why didn't they just walk? The police station is less than two blocks away," everyone nearby started laughing.

The siren petered out into a whir, and the crowd swelled forward toward the street. Judging by the commotion in the middle of it, the men who had overpowered the sneak thief were making their way to the representative of the law. In the midst of all this excitement, Bobby made his belated arrival just as the cops were putting the sneak thief into the squad car for the brief ride to the police station. He found everyone laughing at the absurd aspects of the situation, everyone except Michelle that is. "Think of how desperate you'd have to be to steal a boom box in public," she said. "I saw a documentary on TV the other night where a pickpocket in Bombay was beaten by people in a market. It's their usual way of dealing with a thief, it seems. All I could think of was how pathetic and desperate the man was and how he was totally without dignity."

"Oh yeah," Sarah said, "maybe that guy in India was starving and desperate, but mooneyes probably just wanted money for drugs or booze or maybe a hooker after ogling all the girls."

"That just makes it worse. He's sick rather than evil."

"Have you forgotten how you felt when we saw him eyeballing all the girls? You weren't on his side then."

"No, I wasn't, but I am now—at least a little bit."

Rob came back from where the police made the arrest and put the man in the squad car. "It's even more absurd," he said. "Someone told me the man stole an empty pocketbook thinking it had money in it. It was for sale for one dollar."

"Well," Bobby said after things had quieted down, "it looks like this hasn't been a dull morning for you."

"We've sold over eighty percent of our stuff," Sarah said.

"How'd you do at the races?" Michelle asked.

"Not so hot. I came in seventh in the mile and fourth in the five mile. Our team came in third."

"That's actually better than you expected, isn't it?" Rob asked. He spoke slowly and tentatively, trying too hard. Though he and been assured many times by Sarah and Michelle that Bobby liked him, he never seemed to believe it.

But Bobby, who had been tutored long hours by Michelle, was as friendly as ever. "Yeah, Courtney Academy did better, but I didn't. I was hoping at least to place in one of the races and get points for the team."

An elderly lady came up to the table. Defying stereotypes, she was both friendly and assertive. With an air of someone who knew exactly what she wanted, she picked up a small portable radio. "Does this work, dear?" she asked, looking at Michelle. "So often at these rummage sales they don't, you know. They're just junk."

Michelle gave her a winning smile. "It certainly does. We tested everything. I ironed my T-shirt with that steam iron. I put batteries in the radios, plugged in the eggbeater we sold earlier." She picked up the radio and turned it on. "See, it works," she concluded.

Another sale was concluded, so that they had only five items left and over three

Parliament

hundred dollars for the cause. They agreed that if the remaining items weren't sold within the next half hour they would drop the prices—"But not too far," Sarah pointed out. The radio was five dollars. Much lower and they'd be giving the stuff away.

"If we get down to a couple of items," Bobby said, "I'll buy them." He had appeared uncomfortable and impatient since he arrived. "There's a tradeoff in time and money." He turned to Rob. "Isn't there some economic principle that says that?"

Rob didn't know. He started talking about the Cosmic Atom, the pinpoint from which the entire universe emerged. It was his theory that there were an infinite number of Cosmic Atoms and therefore an infinite number of universes. He started talking to a none-too interested Bobby about his theory.

The same elderly lady who bought the radio came back with a friend. Her name was Mrs. Biggar. Michelle knew her because her son used to work with her mother. She was a cheerful old soul. "I've heard from Dora that you have an iron that works. Would you believe I left mine on all night and burned it out?" She laughed, a girlish giggle. "My children would. They think I've burned out my brain."

Soon after Mrs. Biggar left with her iron they sold a picture frame that had deep scratches in the woodwork for one dollar, but then almost half an hour went by without the last three items being sold. They started jokingly taking bets on which item would be sold last while Bobby, still impatient and moody, remained aloof. Finally, when even the rest of them were starting to feel impatient and anxious to leave, Sarah nudged Michelle. "Look, there's the Jellersons."

They were strolling among the tables, looking things over with cursory glances that suggested they were not here to buy anything. When they got near the Courtney Academy table, Michelle greeted them.

Mr. Jellerson smiled with pleasure. "Hi, Michelle. Hi, Sarah. Hi, boys." They came up to the table. "Looks like you've had a good day."

"Are you here looking for bargains?" Michelle asked. "We've already sold all the stuff you donated, so you can't buy them back."

Mr. Jellerson laughed. "No, Millie and I volunteered for the cleanup crew. By the look of things we'll be here for several hours. Any word on the SAT's?"

"Nope, but don't worry. I feel I absolutely aced them, and Sarah feels she did real well."

"Yes," Sarah said, "and I want to thank you again for all you did for us. You were really super!"

"How much did you make for the cause?" Millie asked as her husband beamed and nodded in acknowledgment of Sarah's compliment. "Your table is about the most empty of any we've seen."

She was dressed casually in a light V-neck sweater and jeans. Michelle thought she looked quite wonderful. It seemed she was growing younger with every month, not older. "We've made over three-hundred dollars," she said proudly.

"Really? That's really a good day's work. You have every right to feel proud."

Down the path a bit and behind the Jellersons Michelle could see Rev. Covington trying to get their attention. "I think Rev. Covington's wants you," she said.

They started to leave; then Mr. Jellerson stopped. "Oh, Michelle. I'm afraid we won't have time to give poor Buttons a walk today. Would you by any chance have the time to do it after the sale closes?"

"Of course, I'd be glad to. We should be closing up almost immediately."

At Bobby's suggestion the three remaining items—a waffle maker, an ugly green salad bowl, and a rusty pair of bush trimmers—were given to another table to sell, and after turning in their money they left. Sarah and Rob were going to his house for a Macintosh lesson; Michelle and Bobby left in his father's car.

He was mostly silent as they drove upcountry, but Michelle, thinking of the man arrested and of Jason and even of the Indian pickpocket, didn't notice. They stopped in to say hello to Uncle Walt (Bobby also called him by that honorific title) and chatted for a few minutes. Walt was going to a Red Sox game with a group of senior citizens tomorrow and was quite excited. He hadn't been to a game in twenty-five years. Michelle beamed with pleasure. Unknown to him, she had been the one who asked Mr. Chilton, one of her father's partners and now semiretired and the head of the Senior Citizens Council in Waska, to get in touch with Walt.

Saying their good-byes, they wished Walt a great day tomorrow and went out to get Buttons. He was expecting them, it seemed, for he was straining against his tether the moment they came around the corner of the house with leash in hand. Michelle thought he was the most beautiful golden retriever in the history of the world, so before they got the leash on him there had to be a long greeting ceremony.

Elaine's forecast this morning had been accurate. It was a beautiful May day. The leaves, embryonic even a week ago, were fully in bloom, as were many flowers in the field they crossed on their way to the lumber road that led into the woods. Bobby was still quiet; Michelle, attributing his moodiness to his unsatisfactory showing in the track meet, kept up a steady chatter about the flowers, the beautiful day and Button's enthusiasm in hopes of cheering him up.

When at the edge of the woods she saw some small blue flowers, she changed the subject. "That blue is the color of your eyes, Bobby. It's beautiful." She looked at the yellow shirt he was wearing and frowned thoughtfully. "You know what? I think you should wear blue more often. It really accents your eyes."

The blue eyes under discussion flashed strangely. He started to say something, changed his mind and said with a nervous laugh, "But what if I like yellow?"

Michelle regarded him for a moment. "That shirt's nice. I just think you look better in blue."

"But—"

Again he stopped himself. She didn't understand what was happening. "But?"

"Nothing. It's just that you're always trying to improve me."

"Is that bad?"

He smiled strangely, enigmatically. "Not necessarily. I mean I know it shows you love me."

"Oh, I do." She leaned over and kissed him, only to feel surprised that he didn't seem to be there.

They walked on for a bit, letting Buttons examine the world new and fresh to him. Presently Bobby spoke. "Don't you think you're a little bit bossy?"

She crinkled her nose. The word in her mind was associated with a maiden aunt who at Thanksgiving came as a guest but always ended up telling everyone what to do, how to cook, where to sit. She was a family joke. "How can you say that?"

Bobby, knowing he was treading on dangerous ground, answered hesitantly and very carefully. "I mean in little things…like what we're doing right now."

"We're walking Buttons right now."

"Yes, but when Mr. Jellerson asked you if you could walk him, you didn't ask me. You just said we could."

Michelle stopped to let Buttons sniff at an old dead oak tree. He was much interested in a hole in the ground between two massive roots that probably led to an animal's den. He was excited and started barking. She watched him abstractly, all the while considering what Bobby said. He was right, of course. She tugged at the dog and they started walking again. "What did you want to do?"

"I wanted to go to the mall. I need some new running shoes."

"We can do that after we bring Buttons home."

Bobby clucked his tongue, making no attempt now to hide his exasperation. "So we can. But the point is, you didn't ask me."

She put her arm around his waist and gave him a little squeeze. "I'm sorry, Bobby. You're right."

But he was not placated. "That's only a symptom, though. Sometimes I think you're trying to make me over."

This was more serious. She looked at him, only to see he was staring at the ground. "Before I answer that, explain what you mean," she said with wounded pride.

"Well, because of you I've drifted away from Billy Boudreau and Carleton, who've been my friends since grade school. You convinced me they were immature and—"

"Aren't they? she asked hotly. It was unbelievable. They were having a fight, actually having a fight. She wouldn't have predicted it even an hour ago. She felt he was being unfair.

"Yes, yes," he said airily. "Do you know what they say of me now?"

"What?"

"They say I'm pussy-whipped."

She frowned at the hateful expression, but more than anger she felt hurt and betrayed. Afraid to start crying, she said nothing.

Bobby continued enumerating his grievances. "And Rob's not a bad guy, even though he's not really my type. Sarah I've always liked because I think she's nice and she's witty. The trouble is, you want me to see them exactly as you see them. When you fell for me, wasn't I good enough then? Why do you want me to be you?"

So that was the real grievance. She wasn't giving him enough space. He felt like her boy toy that she dressed in outfits she liked. The worst part of it was that she saw his point of view exactly. She was wrong and he was right. She knew it, yet she still felt aggrieved. When she spoke it was as if someone else was speaking. "If you feel that way, then maybe we should split up. You want some space, how about a lot of it?"

Buttons, sensing the poisonous atmosphere, whined, which was the only answer to her question. Without a word Bobby turned and angrily stalked back down the lumber road toward the house. Michelle looked down at Buttons, who was staring up at her with a sorrowful face, then turned and followed Bobby with her eyes. His body language was so hostile she stifled the cry that was in her throat. Instead it came out as a whisper: "Bobby." Just before he disappeared around the bend she had one more impulse to call after him, but something, her pride probably, wouldn't let her.

"All right," she said. "All right." Now alone, she pondered what she should do. One practical thing was to wait. She would have to give Bobby time to be gone before she got back if she wanted to avoid any awkwardness.

She began looking around. The woods were very green and very quiet. She listened for bird calls, but in mid-afternoon they were all silent. Far away she could hear now and then the muffled rumble of cars passing on Route 5. In ten minutes one of those cars would be Bobby's, driving him away from her, maybe out of her life forever. Tears sprang to her eyes. She wiped them away with her hand and looked down at Buttons. He had patiently lain down.

A thought occurred to her. She was near the place where Mr. Jellerson had witnessed the priest molesting Jason. Since she had taken Buttons down this road several times, she had asked Millie and got the particulars. After the second bend and at the point where the gravel almost disappeared the path (for so now it could be described) rose to a prominence. She walked ahead and found the spot. Looking down, she saw the clumps of small pines the size of Christmas trees. She walked down the hill to them, wondering if the police had come out here looking for evidence, then deciding that it would not be likely. She saw leaf litter, rocks and pine cones, nothing human.

She thought about Jason and human evil and began to feel sad. What was life anyways? Was sadness and pain forever a part of it? Could evil men always take advantage of innocence, then hire manipulative lawyers to avoid answering for their crimes? Was there no justice? No love? Was that the world she lived in? The tears came to her eyes again, though she was ashamed to realize they weren't for Jason but for herself and for Bobby.

"Come on, Buttons," she said, turning back to the lumber road. Walking to the Jellerson house with the tears now flowing freely, she was no fit companion for the happy little puppy who strained eagerly at his leash and whose bright brown eyes drank up the green world.

Civic Duty

Hoot Berry paused and mopped his brow with his sleeve. It was an unseasonably hot mid-May day, more like August, more like the Sahara desert over there in Africa where them Arabs wore long gowns and rode camels. That's what Charlie McKenny said awhile ago. They were working as day laborers, cash payment, thank you very much, for a paving outfit. Their backhoe had broken down and to clear a field for an access road Hoot and Charlie had been hired. Charlie with bush clippers and a small chain saw would clear the bushes, and then Hoot would dig up the roots and trunks with a pick ax and shovel. It was about two o'clock and in the high sun they were starting to wilt.

The boss, Brian Buckley, came over and with his arms folded observed them for a while. He squinted, pursed his lips, looked down at a piece of paper he had, then up to the work they had done, rubbed his chin with his hand, and finally called over the foreman. They talked excitedly for some time, comparing the paper and the land the paper was supposed to represent. Hoot, observing all this business, expected trouble, and soon enough it came.

"Jesus Christ, you guys! What did we tell you to do?"

Charlie put his clippers down and walked over to them. "What d'ya mean?"

"What do I mean? yelled the foreman. He was a big, burly blond-haired guy who had already showed his opinion of them all day by treating them like untouchables. The rest of the crew were laying down the gravel bed for the asphalt, and he'd been working with them. The day laborers had been left to themselves. So his face was red with anger now. "I mean you two assholes were told to remove the bushes and debris between the red flags. Can you see them?" He pointed. "You're in the wrong area. Stupid assholes!"

It had taken two hours to do the section that was out of bounds, and as pissed as the boss and foremen were they might decide not to pay for the work. Hoot had no steady job. He was on a list at the unemployment agency, and just like those wetbacks out west a lot of the work he did came through these temporary jobs. This was serious. If the boss got a pickle up his ass about the mistake, they could be out sixteen bucks each. So while Charlie jawed away saying it wasn't their fault, he walked over to the pile of brush they'd made and pulled out an advertising flyer that had a lot of red on it. He waved it in the air.

"Here, boss," he yelled. "This is what confused us. It ain't our fault."

He brought it over to them, making sure to be properly humble in his attitude. "We was working so hard we was just lookin' straight ahead. I think the red in this here paper confused us. Honest mistake, though, boss."

Buckley took the paper, looked at it for a second, and flung it to the ground. He muttered a curse. To the foreman he said, "We shoulda waited till the backhoe was fixed even if it did make us late." Then to Hoot and Charlie he said, "Okay, get back to work. This time make sure of the red flags. See them?" He pointed.

"Yeah, we see 'em," Hoot said. Already he had turned back to work so's to make a good impression.

For two more hours they sweated in the sun. Because they could see the end of the day close by, the work went quickly, despite the heat. They drank a lot of water from a milk jug Hoot had filled. Perhaps Charlie drank too much because at knock-off he had to pay a visit to the portable toilet to take a leak.

When Charlie went into the can Hoot seized his chance. He went over to the boss. He had the site plan in his hand and was making some mental calculations. "I'd like my wages," he said. Then thinking it had come out sounding a bit too demanding, he changed his tune to one experience had taught him to use with bosses. "I need to get some groceries for my family." This was said in the whining, wheedling way a child talked to an adult.

The boss kept looking at his site plan—a trick Hoot was also familiar with. He waited.

Finally Buckley looked up. "You've done day labor before, haven't you?"

"Yezza." Hoot nodded.

"Then you know you don't get paid till the work is over. But here"—he reached into his pocket and got out his wallet. "Here's a twenty for the groceries."

Hoot snatched it and put it in his pocket. "Thanks."

Charlie got out of the can just in time to see this exchange of money. He came over to them with a hangdog look of hunger in his eyes. It worked too, for the boss took out another twenty-dollar bill and said, "I suppose you've got to get some groceries for your family too. You guys be here at seven-thirty sharp tomorrow. We've got to have it all cleared by the afternoon."

Walking back to Charlie's old rust bucket, Hoot grinned with inner satisfaction for getting their way and tricking the boss. The beauty of it was that the boss knew he was being tricked and still came through. That was the best trick of all.

Once in the car, though, the mood changed to hostility. "That fucking puke. I had half a mind to brain him with my clippers when he was ranting at us and calling us assholes."

Hoot nodded. He'd had the same desire but had learned to keep his mouth shut. He'd known Charlie for over twenty years, but that didn't mean he was a friend. One time years ago at one of the last steady jobs he'd had he'd cursed a boss to one of the other workers, and the guy had ratted on him so's to get a better job. Hoot had been fired and had to stew in his own juices for a long time. Three months later, though, he slashed the worker's tires one night and a few months after that he'd thrown a brick through the windshield of the boss's car. So he'd gotten his revenge, but the main

151

lesson he'd learned was to keep his mouth shut.

Charlie hadn't learned that lesson, though. He cursed and cussed all the way upcountry, but Hoot hardly listened. At the outskirts of town he'd spotted a TV among the trash put out from a big house and started figuring the odds of it still being there if he went back to get it after he got home. He also figured that if a TV could be thrown away there might be some other good things. So his mind ran on about the possibility of a big haul, and Charlie's rantings went right over him.

They made a stop at the country store for each of them to buy a six pack. Hoot also bought a package of cigarettes. He usually rolled his own because it was cheaper, but special occasions like having a twenty-dollar bill in your pocket required a bit of celebration. That's the reason he bought five scratch tickets as well. He busied himself scraping them as they drove the final mile to where Charlie dropped him off. He was like a baseball player on a bad day, though—0 for 5.

Hoot lived so far upcountry that he and his neighbors hardly felt connected to Waska at all. They were all dirt poor—generations ago their ancestors had lived on self-sustaining farms, but when farming stopped paying the people that were left (and most of them moved into town or even out of the state) found themselves scratching out a living like chickens in a barnyard. His wife Olive and he had learned many ways to survive. She kept a large garden that provided them with fresh vegetables all through the summer, and home canning and pickle making got them through the winter. She also stored potatoes and stuff in the cellar for eating in winter. Hoot hunted—the folks in town would call it poaching—and fresh and salted venison made many a main course for supper.

Hoot and Olive weren't actually married, but they had been living together so long—thirty years—that common law took care of these things. They had six kids, the first when he was seventeen and she nineteen. The oldest was a car mechanic in Waska with kids of his own. The second son ran away when he was sixteen and was never heard of again. The third died of pneumonia when she was a child. Olive still grieved for her and touched the one picture they had of her every day. The fourth was now eighteen and living at home with a one-year-old brat of her own. The two youngest, a boy of thirteen and a girl of twelve, were still in school. Two or three others had been born dead, so they didn't count.

At least he had a house. A lot of his neighbors lived in tarpaper shacks and trailers. The house they had used to belong to an uncle who never married. As an old man he got sick, and Olive and he moved in and took care of him. After he died they were the only relatives still around, so the house had gone to them. It was a jury-rigged thing but closest to a cape house, small, but with two bedrooms upstairs and one downstairs. It was in bad repair, though not from lack of work, only money. The roof was patched with asphalt shingles Hoot had collected from a dumpster. They were reddish and the original roof charcoal gray, so it looked like an old quilt was thrown over the house to keep it warm in winter. He painted the front of the house last year, but the sides and back were peeling with many places down to bare weathered wood. The doors didn't close very well. In the winter, in fact, they had to brace a chair against the knob of the front door and stuff the crack with an old blanket to keep the cold out. In the winter they used only the back door, which closed a bit better. Some of the windows were replacements he'd found in dumpsters. They'd had to be jury-rigged into the frame and didn't look none too handsome.

It was no accident that Hoot's experienced eye had spotted that TV. To the extent he had a business, you could call him a junk dealer. Every week he prowled all over Waska sifting through people's junk. Much of the furniture in their house came from these siftings, some of it quite nice, for rich people (and rich to him simply meant anyone that could afford to throw away stuff he could use) were really amazing when it came to things they threw away. The couch and matching chair in their living room he'd found in town in front of one of those big houses on lower Main Street a year or so ago. They were just like new—not a rip or tear in the fabric, not a slouch to the cushions. The kitchen table was fine except he replaced the missing leg with a stud and nailed it through the top. Olive covered it with a table cloth so that you hardly noticed unless you looked real close that the table was handicapped. The radio on the kitchen counter that Olive used to play her damned country music was likewise from his usual shopping. So was the toaster, the microwave (though now it had stopped working), even the refrigerator that had given him a lot of trouble because he couldn't find some of the hardware lost when the door was removed by the conscientious rich people. But from his collection of hardware he managed to get the damned thing to close. What he couldn't use himself he sold, or tried to sell. He made a couple thousand a year, sometimes more, this way, in cash too, tax free—not that he paid much in taxes anyways; he hadn't paid income taxes in over twenty years. He made another thousand from bottle and can deposits with his kids helping him in this business. In the old barn with the swaybacked roof and gray bare wood flecked with red paint here and there that had been there long before the jury-rigged house (the original farmhouse burned down over a century ago) he had stored so much stuff that you could hardly walk into the place. Furniture, household wares, appliances, tools, a lawn mower or two, wood and other stuff from contractor demolition dumpsters, picture frames, parts for automobiles, including big stuff like car seats, old engines and doors, and tiny things like buttons and nail clippers—you name it and it was probably there. The amazing thing was, though it was all dragged in and put wherever space could be found, Hoot knew where just about everything was and could usually find it within fifteen minutes. He didn't read very well—the letters on the page did strange things and he could never make them out, so he'd only got to the eighth grade and no farther—but Olive read pretty good and she kept her eyes peeled in the classified ads of the local paper that a neighbor gave them at the end of each week. If there was an ad from someone looking for something, chances were Hoot had it in the barn. He'd go locate it and look the person up. That's where quite a lot of the two thousand came from, that and selling scrap metal and stuff to the Jew junk dealer in town.

Hoot came in the door without Olive hearing him. She had the radio on playing country and western music real loud and was singing away as she cooked supper. The door slamming made her turn around.

"Turn that damn thing off," he said. He cracked a can of beer and put the rest in the refrigerator.

Olive turned the radio off and looked at him. It was good to see the fear in her eyes. It told him things were right. "Where's Jimmy?"

"He's out back playing with Suzy."

Olive was a small woman, thin as a rail but wiry. Some people couldn't believe that scrawny body had carried six kids. Her gray hair was worn short and brushed back. It was thinning too. Sometimes he actually thought she was going bald. Whenever she went out she wore a hat. He often thought that was funny. Women were vain, even when they'd lost their looks. And she had certainly lost hers. She was 49 and had the wrinkles to prove it. Of course there were mirrors in the house, and he wasn't going to make any claims about being handsome himself. He was two years younger than her but even more wrinkled. Someone told him smokers wrinkled quicker. Well, he was certainly a smoker, but it was a small price to pay. What would life be without cigarettes and booze, he'd like to know? He had a big nose too, bigger than it should be, so that when he was young it and his crooked teeth had made him feel inferior. So he didn't expect to be living with a Hollywood starlet. In his own way he appreciated her, though he made damn sure he never showed it and spoiled her.

The only thing that really annoyed him now was that for the past three years she'd gotten religion. One of the neighboring women—Abby Moore, who lived about half a mile down the road—had started going to the Evangelical Baptist Church, and after a while she'd dragged Olive along with her. Now she kept telling him the minister thought they should be married, but he told her he wasn't going to no goddamned church with a suit on to satisfy some puke of a preacher. Common law marriage was good enough for him.

She still brought up the marriage business every now and again. From the look of her she was trying to get up the courage to do it now.

"Tell Jimmy to get his butt in here."

Without a word she went to the back door and yelled his name two or three times.

Hoot sat at the table and lit a cigarette. He tapped his fingers, figuring out how long he'd wait before the whelp got a smack.

But he came in quick enough. "You want me, Pa?"

He looked at him and rubbed his stubbly chin. Jimmy had yellow hair, the only one of his kids that did. Both Olive and he had dark hair, and sometimes he wondered. He doubted, though, that she would ever dare cheat on him. "We're goin' to get somethin'. Come on."

"What about supper?" Olive asked. "And I got somethin' to tell ya."

"It can wait. Supper can wait. This will only take half an hour."

Jimmy followed him outside. When Suzy poked her head around the corner, he said proudly as he crawled up into the cab of the big pickup truck, "We have to get somethin'."

Hoot started the engine. The fact it ran at all was due to his skill. It was thirty years old and on its second engine, but every part of it had been gone over by Hoot. Necessity had taught him to be a good mechanic—so good that his oldest son Luke didn't need any training when he got the job at that garage. The truck coughed and sputtered starting up and burned oil so that they laid down a smoke screen behind them when they were moving, but it ran as good as it could run. The fact that it couldn't pass EPA tests was not much of a problem—Luke took care of him and used a test of a good truck for him. It was called paper work, Hoot believed. Luke was a good son.

"Where're we goin', Pa?" Jimmy asked.

Hoot, slowing down to take a right turn, didn't answer. He'd know soon enough where they were going.

They drove in silence till they arrived at the rubbish he'd seen earlier. He stared intently as they approached, but it was till there.

He pulled over and parked in front of the ash cans and quickly checked the TV out. Twenty-four inch screen. Japanese made and quite new. Experience told him that it was probably either in working order and had been thrown out because the family got a new and bigger one or it needed only the smallest of repairs to make it work. Either way he wanted it. He told Jimmy to look through the trash cans. "Be sure to check all the bottles and cans for deposit" was his only words of advice.

He began tying the TV with rope to the hooks in the truck bed so that it would be good and secure. He frowned at a couple of drivers that drove by and gave him a contemptuous look, but he was so used to doing this that he didn't even feel any special hatred—just the general hatred that was always with him against rich people.

Jimmy was busy picking through the trash barrels. He found a lamp and two cans of paint that sloshed when he shook them. He'd helped his father many times and knew without asking they had passed the test. Hoot watched him without comment as he finished tying the TV down.

"That's all that's any good, Pa. There ain't no good cans or bottles."

"What about those two boards? He pointed to two pieces of 1 X 12 pine about ten inches and eight inches.

"They're too small, ain't they, Pa?"

Hoot lit a cigarette, inhaled, and stroked his chin. Jimmy was learning the trade, but he still had a long way to go. "S'pose you're makin' a repair and need a piece of wood to make a patch or fill a hole. Where would you get it?"

Jimmy's eyes lit up. "You'd get it from a piece of wood you had in the barn. Ain't that right, Pa?"

Hoot nodded as his son gathered the two pine scraps and lamp and put them in the back of the truck. The paint he took into the cab with him so that he could hold it. That lesson he'd already learned.

Hoot took a quick look through the rest of the stuff to make sure nothing else was missed, then got into the truck.

They ate supper as soon as they got back. It was a bit dry since it had been ready for almost an hour, but Hoot, washing it down with another beer, didn't care. He was in a good mood because of the television set and the fact that tomorrow he'd get over a hundred dollars for his work. Olive was very quiet and nervous and didn't respond to his good-humored remarks, even though everyone in the family knew they were as rare as hen's teeth. The kids, though, and especially Jimmy, were happy to catch their father in a good mood. But once the meal was over, at a look from Olive they all cleared out very quickly.

"Henry?" she said, then stopped.

He frowned at her. She only called him Henry when something she regarded as important was in the air. "Well?" he demanded. "What is it?"

"I was talkin' to Rev. Moore today. He was talkin' about Satan and the Scarlet Woman, the Whore of Babylon, and that Sodomite priest who's goin' to trial soon."

Hoot's frown darkened into a scowl. He thought he saw where this was going. Last year in early March when he had been out sifting through waste cans in the downtown area, he noticed some renovations were occurring at the Catholic church and that a large dumpster was filled with contractor's debris. In the dark of the early March evening he couldn't see clearly if there was anything of use, and being unsure about sifting through stuff in a church parking lot he had parked his truck on the side street and snuck through the thick bushes while staying in the shadows to go up to the dumpster. Close up and at a glance he could see a lot of studs with nails, broken wall board, scraps of lumber, electrical fixtures and even some worn furniture. He was about to start collecting some of the wood, the fixtures and one or two of the chairs that

155

looked pretty sturdy when he heard voices coming out of the parish house. He backed up and hid in a space between two thick evergreen shrubs and waited for the owners of the voices to leave. But instead they came up behind the dumpster where the thick bushes hid them from the street. They were only eight or ten feet from him where they stopped and began talking in low voices. "Remember I love you, Gregory," an adult male voice said. The moon was only a sliver, but the distant street lights of Main Street afforded enough light for Hoot to see the man had a Roman collar. This was confirmed when the other voice, that of a boy who was small, dark haired, and spoke with a slight stutter, answered, "I know you do, Father Mullen." Then the priest said, "You are my little angel from God. He meant for us to be together."

This kind of sweet-talking went on for some time so that Hoot was perfectly aware the priest was queer, a fact that didn't surprise him too much since to the extent he'd ever thought much about a Catholic priest he figured there was something not quite right about them. So the sweet-talking like lovers in a Hollywood movie didn't surprise him, but what happened next did. His eyes were perfectly adjusted to the light now and he could plainly see the sexual act that occurred. Afterwards he heard the priest remind the boy to tell his mother he was late because they had to study the score to get it just right. He said some composer's name, something like Palada or Palastrada, but of that he was very unsure. He waited for them to get into a car and drive away. Then he went up to the dumpster and took only two chairs so that he could get away quickly.

Driving home he thought about the matter for a long time. He knew that sometimes information is money and tried to figure out if he could get away with blackmailing the priest. By the time he got home, though, he came to the conclusion that his word against that of a Roman priest would not be worth a fart. So he had let it drop from his mind and hadn't mentioned it at all until the other day when Olive started talking about the trial and wondering if the priest would be found guilty. Stupidly, Hoot had told her that the priest was guilty and he knew it—he's seen him himself doing unnatural things with a boy. Now her nervousness told him that she'd let the preacher in on the secret. He asked her that now. "Woman, did you tell the preacher what I told you?"

Her eyes wide with fear, she nodded. "I did. He said it was your duty—"

But she didn't get a chance to finish the thought. His hand shot out and smacked her in the face. With a scream she fell back.

"Honest, Hoot, I didn't mean to. Rev. Moore said he'd heard a rumor that the main witness, Mr. Jellerson, was compromised because he's been helpin' one of the boys with his studies, and the preacher said that evil Sodomite might escape justice. Then I told him."

She backed away, ready to run if he came after her.

"What did that preacher say he was goin' to do?"

"He's goin' to come here tonight—soon I think—to talk to you. And one of the brothers at the church is a policeman. He's comin' with him."

He glared at her. "Woman, your big mouth has really screwed things up this time. I have a good mind to—"

"Please, Hoot. Don't hurt me. I was just tryin' to do what was right."

Her eyes got to him. They had a desperate fear in them that reminded him of the time when they first got to know each other and she was afraid of losing him because he'd gone with another woman. Since then that memory had saved her many times, and it did now. He had never beaten her anyways, just smacked her when she needed correcting.

"Okay, Olive. You get the dishes cleared. I'm goin' out to get the TV out of the truck."

He just had time to get it into the barn before he heard a car turn onto the dirt road. Quickly, though not running, he went back into the house. He listened to the car crunching over the gravel road, then turn into his yard.

He looked out the window and saw it was a cop car. He scowled at Olive but said nothing. His hands tingled and he tightened them into fists. Behind him in the corner was his shotgun. He hated cops. He didn't like the meddling preacher. He was pissed off at his wife, yet he knew he had to be careful.

"I'll go work on my garden while there's still some light," Olive said.

He nodded savagely and watched her slink away.

Jenny came into the room carrying her baby. "What's going on, Daddy? Ain't that the cops?"

"Never you mind, Missy. You and the brat clear out. Get upstairs, you hear?" He took a menacing step towards her when she didn't move right off. She turned tail and scurried upstairs after that. He could hear her muttering and cussing to herself, but the sass wasn't directed at him so he didn't care.

He listened to the clumping of feet and the creaking of the boards on the porch. A light tap on the door was followed by a louder rap.

He waited till the third knock before he opened the door.

"Yeah?"

The minister looked at him fearfully, the sniveling little swine. Then he glanced at the cop, a tall, scrawny guy, before finding the courage to speak. "Mr. Berry, we've come on a question of civic duty."

"Civic duty?" He repeated the book-learning term with a curl of his lip. He wanted them to know right off what he thought about their civic duty.

The cop was glaring at him. You could tell he didn't think that he, as a representative of the law, was getting proper respect. You could also tell that he thought Hoot was the scum of the earth. He walked into the house without being asked. "Can we come in, Sir? We do have something extremely important to talk to you about."

Hoot stood back and inclined his head like he was giving permission for the liberty the cop had already taken. He could see the contempt in the cop's eyes and glared back at him to let him know the feeling was mutual. He didn't offer a seat either. Whatever they had to say, let 'em say it on their feet. This was no time to get cozy.

The cop got out a notebook and pencil. He looked up and stared at Hoot for a moment. His face was angry-looking and official. "Information has come to our attention that you have witnessed Father Mullen of the Holy Trinity Church of Waska and a boy. As you probably know, Father Mullen is shortly to go on trial for child molestation. If you have any information that bears on the outcome of this trial, it is your duty to testify. I might also add that you can be subpoenaed to testify by the prosecutor."

Hoot folded his arms and tried to look casual. "I don't know what you're talkin' about."

"Did you or did you not see Father Mullen in the parking lot of the Holy Trinity Church sometime last March with a boy?"

Rev. Moore looked at him, trying unsuccessfully not to show fear. "Mr. Berry, your, er, wife spoke to me about—"

"My wife," he interrupted, "don't know shit."

They stared at him. The mood was growing hostile. A voice inside him reminded him to be careful. "Look," he said, "this is a big misunderstandin'. I'll tell ya what it is. Didn't you say a trial was coming up?"

"Yes," the cop answered. "It's been delayed for a few weeks but the case will be heard within a month."

Hoot nodded. "And naturally I've heard about it. And, you see, that's just it. I was talkin' to my old lady about it and wonderin' about the fag priest. She misunderstood me. She's just daft enough to think I saw somethin'. I didn't see nothin', though. I ain't got nothin' to say 'cause I don't know nothin'. Maybe I was puttin' her on a little, you know."

The cop and minister exchanged troubled glances.

He drove his point home. "You're wastin' your time. I ain't seen nothin'."

One more look was exchanged and then they gave up. "If you do 'remember' something," the cop said, " you get in touch with the police. Do you understand?"

He nodded. He understood that the cop knew he was lying but couldn't do anything about it. It was just about as good as the boss earlier knowing he and Charlie were lying about the groceries and still getting their twenty spots. He resisted the urge to grin, though. He frowned till they were in the car and the engine started.

Then he grinned.

There was enough light left to get a bit of work done, so as soon as he could hear the car pull out of the dirt road, he walked over to the barn. It wasn't wired for electricity, but Hoot had run an extension cord over. He snapped on the drop light hanging from a beam and looked the TV over. A principle he'd learned years ago was to start with the simplest thing and work to the most complex. The simplest thing was juice. He plugged the TV into the outlet in the drop light and turned it on. Nothing happened, but he wasn't surprised. He unplugged the cord and felt it. Half way down the cord he could feel where it had been pinched—probably from some heavy piece of furniture. He went to his tool box and got some wire cutters. He snipped the cord above where it was pinched and then cut away the plastic insulation to expose bare wire. Over on his work bench he kept a cord with a plug and two bare leads to test equipment. He twirled the copper leads from the test cord to the stripped wire of the TV cord, then made sure they were not touching. He plugged it in and turned the TV on. A picture, fuzzy because there was no antenna, came up. He grinned. He reached over to an antenna wire he had going to the upper rafters of the barn and touched those leads to the terminals on the TV. The picture came in perfect, sharp, and in beautiful color.

He grinned more broadly. This set was better than the one they had in the house. Tomorrow he'd move it in and set it up permanently.

For a moment he tried to fathom the kind of mind that would throw away a perfectly good TV set because of something as simple as a severed cord, but like every time he'd tried to understand the mind of rich people, he gave up and concluded that rich people were simply crazy. He was glad he had nothing to do with them.

Denham Academy

The car leaving Waska, Maine for Leicester, Massachusetts had four passengers, all attired in suit and tie or skirt and blouse—Samuel Jellerson in the front passenger seat, Mercy and Jason Buckley in the back seat, and the Rev. John Covington in the driver's seat. A year ago Sam did not know any of these people, and yet they were united today on a mission that might possibly determine Jason's entire future. They were driving to Denham Academy in Leicester for Jason to have interviews for late admission. The reason the minister and Sam were going was the same: both had worked with Jason professionally and got to know him personally, and both knew people at Denham who would, they hoped, be helpful. John knew a teacher who was a classmate at Yale, and Sam, more importantly, knew an administrator who was a former student of his at Hartley Academy. This young man, in his early thirties, was involved with the affirmative action program at the school; he worked to recruit minority students and to a lesser extent special students who could not otherwise afford to go to such a school. While not directly involved officially in late admissions, he had already been approached by Sam on the phone and had agreed to do all he could. Both John and Sam had also written glowing letters of recommendation for Jason, and his grades and attainments spoke for themselves. Jason's father, Brian Buckley, could not be free from his work at this, the busiest time of year; he was already working overtime to free up next week for Father Mullen's trial; thus it could be said of the two adult males that they were also functioning in loco parentis.

The general feeling in the car was one of sanguine expectations, especially considering that the scheduled interviews indicated the school took Jason's application seriously. To the degree the interviews with administrators, faculty members from the Music Department and the school psychologist were important, however, there was some apprehension on the part of the three adults. Jason had good and bad days. Though the good days predominated, he had had some bad ones lately which he attributed to the fact he was now seeing a psychologist the court appointed in addition to his weekly sessions with John. Last week he'd had a relapse after one of these sessions when the court-appointed psychologist of necessity asked him some probing and painful questions. He had had nightmares that night and had required sedation the next day. Though he had been fine since and appeared well this morning, the possibility of a sudden relapse had the adults in the car on needles and pins, not daring to say anything that might cause distress. As a result conversation when they greeted each other at the rendezvous point at the Congregational Church had been stilted as each passed everything he or she had to say through an internal censor. Perhaps reinforced by the early hour and the sleepiness it engendered, this led to little conversation in the car.

Sam kept going over in his mind Jason's chances. His belief that they were very good was no chimera, for he was in a perfect position to evaluate the boy's scholarly and intellectual attainments. For the past five weeks he had tutored him six hours a day, five days a week. They met in one of the Sunday school rooms at the Congregational Church, did four hours in the morning, and then had lunch with Eleanor Smallwood, the church secretary, or just as often with John and Wendy Covington at the parsonage. After lunch they worked two more hours in the afternoon; then Sam's day was done. Jason remained to spend a few hours helping in the daycare center in the basement of the parish building next to the church, and on Mondays had his sessions with John. He was dropped off by Mercy on the way to work and usually picked up by her at the end of the day, though sometimes, perhaps twice a week, Jason instead of helping at the daycare center spent an hour with Eleanor until school was out and then would walk to his Aunt Hope's to play with his cousin Robbie. Under this regimen he prospered. Though at first shy and cautious with Sam, they had quickly achieved a perfect teacher-student rapport. The breakthrough came on the second day when Sam admitted that mathematics was a particular weakness with him. His candid confession of inadequacy allowed Jason to see his humanity, and his cautious shyness disappeared. He was a natural at mathematics—it called for some of the same skills that were required in analyzing and composing music—so that in effect the student became the teacher for this subject. By the third day, then, they were fast friends. Sam had no doubt Jason could handle the classes at Denham; he was an amazingly brilliant student who understood instantly new concepts and principles and who learned facts with what Sam suspected was close to a photographic memory. When Jason told him that he could play dozens of musical pieces from memory, Sam was not surprised. Every paper and test he gave Jason was done at an A level. He was also intellectually precocious, so much so that Sam told the public school teacher who liaised for the school superintendent that he thought Jason was a genius. He said that in his letter of recommendation too, and it was not a term he would ever use loosely. Jason was a boy born to go to Denham. He'd said that in his letter as well. Thinking of all this now, he wouldn't allow himself to believe that the interviews would go badly.

At one point on the Maine Turnpike Sam caught a glimpse of Mercy's face when his head turned following a strangely painted bus coming into the state. She didn't see it or him or anything, so lost in thought was she. But she looked awful, as if stricken with horror and unspeakably sad. Feeling he was violating a deeply private moment, he snapped his head forward in embarrassment. With his head now steadfastly facing ahead, he turned his thoughts to her and her condition. The sadness he saw in her eyes was the sadness of a mother, he concluded. Her son had been violated and traumatized, and one solution—the one they were taking—was to remove him from the scenes of the trauma. That, however, meant things both good and bad. Good, if it helped heal him; bad, in that he was leaving her forever. To be a good mother meant she had to stop being a mother. For if events unfolded in the usual way, Jason would never again live at home except for school vacations. He would be at Denham for four years, then college for four more, and after that either advanced studies or the world. Her sadness was born of love and therefore doubly painful for her. He could see how divided she was, both wanting and dreading Jason's acceptance at Denham. It made him sigh for humanity, the infinite pity of it, the inescapable sorrow and loss. He thought of Old Boy, and for a moment he was in danger of tears.

And thinking of Old Boy led him to factoring his own equation of sadness and happiness. On the whole, he decided, he was probably happier than he was sad. He remembered his first months in Maine when he missed teaching with the bereavement of a man who had lost everything that made life sweet and with a despair and isolation that overwhelmed him. But in less than a year he had made a life in his hometown—or better yet he and Millie had made a life. While deeply unhappy when she first started working and gaining self-confidence daily so that her new independence had scared him and made him feel insecure, now he loved her more than he had in his whole life. It was wonderful to have an equal partnership of two free and independent individuals, neither a mere adjunct to the other. He never wanted to go back to the days when she was subservient to him. He even felt guilty sometimes remembering how she had served him and Hartley Academy so selflessly that she had had to hide away her humanity.

He still missed teaching, but almost accidentally he had found that the easiest way to forget his troubles was to think of others. In helping Walt in his need, in tutoring and befriending Michelle, Sarah, and Jason, and in doing all he could to nurture Jason back to wholeness, he had forgotten his own sorrows and found fulfillment and peace. He was also very proud that his tutoring was successful: Michelle and Sarah had done very well on the SAT's, and Jason amazed him with his insight and intelligence. He was proud of all three of them and felt for them a father's love. Another source of well-being was the high opinion the headmaster at Courtney Academy had of him. He clearly wanted Sam to teach at his school. He wasn't yet washed up and ready for the graveyard.

But Mercy's sorrow was not alien to him. He had known sorrow and still knew it. Sometimes the thought of Old Boy could still bring tears to his eyes. Like any death, Old Boy's passing engendered regrets for missed opportunities and real or imagined violations of love. He remembered many days at Hartley Academy when Old Boy was neglected, when events at the school demanded so much time and attention that a dog was not high enough on the scale of things to have his needs met, and with bitter guilt he remembered that Old Boy's response to this neglect was unconditional love. At the farmhouse he would have gotten the attention he deserved every day. Then to have died less than one year in Waska was to add regret to guilt and sorrow. At least Buttons would never know such neglect.

But the darkest cloud in his mind was Bennet. For months before his son's release from the Navy he had planned on starting anew with him, only to discover when Bennet came home that a wall separated them. Bennet could not forget the father he had grown up with; he would not see his father was a new man—the past was too powerful a reality. In the end only money had been exchanged, not love. Sam had paid for the flight to San Francisco, the flight that took his son away from him. And it got worse. After Ben was gone Walt told him what he had done to Buttons. Once or twice he had considered calling Michelle about the incident she witnessed, but he didn't have the heart to do it. He was too ashamed. It sickened him that Bennet would abuse a dog. He wondered if the reason Old Boy never bonded with him was because Bennet had done something similar to the family's first pet. He was quite sure that a person who would abuse a dog was not morally or psychologically healthy. His son was sick and needed psychological help. Every time he thought about Bennet, he was painfully aware that if he was judgmental about Father Mullen's violation of innocence, then he couldn't be less so just because his son was his own flesh. Millie said the two cases were different, but he was not so sure. He began worrying that he would vacillate on the witness stand next week at the priest's trial. He was already worried about the prosecutor's belief that it was very unwise to be tutoring Jason. If Father Mullen was found innocent, it would be his fault. Then perhaps he would have to reassess his conclusion that he was more happy than unhappy. Mercy had told him not to worry. Jason liked the tutoring and liked Sam. Because of John and him Jason was blossoming. It was more important, she said, to help him than to win the case. He tried to remember that every time he had doubts; still he had doubts.

Brooding on these matters as they drove along Interstate 95, he rather suspected the others were doing much the same. But his introspection grew tiresome and oppressive. Hoping the silence would be broken, he nevertheless did not want to be the first to speak for fear he might interrupt someone's reverie that was proceeding along more positive grounds than his had. So the silence continued as they left the Maine Turnpike, crossed the massive bridge over the Piscataqua River into New Hampshire, and proceeded for eight miles until they got into a mile-long backup at the Hampton Tolls.

The delay seemed to shake the others from their lethargy. John began first by saying that he had heard people grumble about the tolls for years.

"Because of the delays?" Sam asked.

"Sometimes they're over an hour. But what gets people angry is that New Hampshire is really guilty of extortion. People want to get to Maine and this thin sliver of New Hampshire intervenes. 'You want to go to Maine? You pay us a dollar.' Same thing when people come back—they pay the lousy buck. This delay is commuters from New Hampshire and southern Maine who work in Boston."

"I can't imagine driving that far to go to work," Sam said. "It's insane."

From the back seat Mercy leaned forward. "I've heard Brian say he's known guys so mad they'd like to blow up the tolls. Others talk about organizing a consumer action—everybody goes through the tolls and nobody pays."

John looked in the rearview mirror. "Here comes someone using the breakdown lane to ace those of us in the proper lanes."

They watched the car, driven by a young man with an intense scowl on his face, drive by.

"Usually when that happens others follow," John said.

Others followed, and Sam with a smile said, "Our minister is clairvoyant."

"We won't be late, will we?" Jason asked, sounding very nervous.

John turned back to look at him. He smiled reassuringly. "Don't worry. We'll be early. We've allowed for delays."

John had had a talk show on the radio which no one was listening to. "Would you like some music, Jason?" he asked. "I think I remember where WGBH Boston is." He began punching the seek button and they heard music. "What's that, Jason?"

It was a piano quartet. Sam thought it was Schumann's, but he let Jason answer.

"Schumann's Piano quartet," Jason said.

"Have you ever played it?"

"No, but I've studied the score."

Mercy handed John a dollar bill. She had paid the Maine Turnpike tolls and given John money for the gas. Later she planned to pay for lunch. They were only a few cars from the toll booth now. John predicted that two of the cars in front of them would either not have correct change or would ask for directions.

When only one car caused a delay, Sam said, "Our minister, semi-clairvoyant." Everyone laughed.

Through the tolls and up to speed again, Jason, perhaps revealing the direction of his thoughts during the long silence, asked how elite schools decided to accept students when everyone who applied had good grades.

"They look for other things as well," Sam said. "You, for instance, will have an advantage because you're a musician. With Michelle, she does a lot of good works—like that rummage sale a few weeks ago. Some students, I understand, do these things cynically, but not her. She's genuinely a good person."

Jason made a strange sound, rather like a squeal of delight. Sam turned to see him grinning in the back seat. "She calls me up every once in a while to ask me a musical question. But I know she just calls to show she's supportive. She's a real friend."

"And a real human being," Sam said with feeling. "I've been lucky to tutor the two best kids in Waska this year. I don't even miss teaching anymore thanks to you two."

John started on about the Red Sox after that. It was essentially a monologue, with only Jason responding occasionally. Sam and Mercy weren't baseball fans.

Right after they entered Massachusetts Sam reminded John to get in the right lane because I495 was coming up quickly. He had studied maps last night.

Another lull becalmed the conversation until the radio played the *Tannhäuser* overture, and John asked Jason what he thought of Wagner. "Wendy and I were in Seattle several years ago and saw the *Ring*. It was an unbelievable experience. Someday I'd like to hear it in German—out there they do it in English."

Jason said, "Since I play the piano I don't know much about him. I've heard parts of *Meistersinger* once and thought it was beautiful. The quintet and Walter's prize song. It was the end of the opera. Those parts were magnificent."

"I've seen *Lohengrin* at the Met," Sam said. "But I confess Wagner is not my cup of tea. I prefer Mozart."

"Who are your favorite composers, Jason?"

"Chopin and Schumann, I'd say."

"You like Grieg too, don't you, honey?" Mercy asked.

"Oh, yeah, and Grieg. Pianists, you know. Schubert's great too."

"How old were you when you first started playing the piano, Jason?" Sam asked.

"Just a little boy. I've played so long I can hardly remember a time when I didn't play."

Then, drawing close to Leicester, everyone grew quiet again. Sam was the only one of them who had ever been to Denham Academy. He attended a conference for New England private schools twenty years ago on the campus. He only remembered a few directional details, however—that the campus was on Main Street but several blocks from downtown and that the Memorial Bell Tower was the one thing on campus that could be seen from quite a long distance away. Research had yielded one other point, namely that Route 188 was Main Street. Thus when they got to the Route 188 exit off 495, they took it, drove through town, and then presently Jason, who had obviously designated himself lookout scout shouted, "There's the big bell tower, Mr. Jellerson!"

They had to stop and ask some students where visitors parking was. Getting conflicting information, they wasted ten minutes before they were parked. Still they were early. John suggested they get a coffee somewhere, but the rest of them preferred to walk about the campus, and he yielded the point. Most students were in class or in dorms, for the campus was relatively empty as they strolled around looking at buildings and the landscaping. Architecturally the buildings were a mixture of old and new, but the new had been carefully integrated into the campus to make a unified and pleasing impression. They all agreed that Denham had a beautiful campus. Jason's eyes were shining; Mercy's were sad, though Sam had to look closely to see that. John had once said to him that hypocrisy was not always a deadly sin. Now he saw the minister's point.

Nine o'clock approached. John said that his friend would only be available between nine and eleven, so they agreed to rendezvous with him late in the morning. The other three made their way to Andy Avery's office. Andy was the former student of Sam's who was working on Jason's case. Sam had talked to him several times on the phone during the past two weeks, but he had not seen him since he was a schoolboy. With his hairdo similar to the style baseball players of today favored and which in Sam's youth was called a flat top—short on the sides, back and top but brushed up about an inch in the front—and with the glasses he now wore, Sam hardly recognized him until he spoke in his slight Southern accent (he was from Virginia), "Mr. Jellerson, you haven't changed a bit!"

Sam smiled sheepishly. "Well, I'm afraid I'm a bit grayer, but you have certainly changed. You're looking very good."

"Is this our candidate?"

Sam made the introductions and was pleased to see Jason handled himself very well. He was just confident enough to appear mature and just shy enough to be appealingly boyish.

"I'm very pleased to meet you, Mr. Avery. I'd like very much to go to Denham, and I understand you can help me."

Andy nodded and gave him a reassuring pat on the shoulder after shaking his hand. He turned. "This must be your mother."

"Hello," Mercy said, extending her hand. "I'm Mercy Buckley."

"One of those Puritan names, I see. I love New England. You have a beautiful name."

Where Sam had smiled sheepishly, Mercy blushed. "I can't take credit for my parents' choices. They named my sister Hope, so you see there's a pattern. But tell me, are Jason's admission papers all in order?"

"Oh, yes." He walked over to his desk and picked up a manila envelope. Leafing through it, he said, "Yes, very much in order and very impressive too." To Jason, he added, "Young man, everyone who knows you seems to think you're an extraordinary chap."

Mercy and Sam exchanged glances at that remark. The tension drained from her face. They would be very much mistaken, very much surprised, if Andy's statement and body language didn't mean what they thought it meant.

"I've arranged for you to meet several people, Jason. Some administrators, some members of the music faculty, the scholarship people and the school psychologist. Don't worry. Everyone is anxious to meet you. We have a few moments before the interviews start. Why don't we all sit?"

When everyone was seated, Andy said, "It was terrible news to hear that Hartley Academy closed, Mr. Jellerson. I'd heard there was some trouble, then lost touch. When the news came it had closed its doors, you could have knocked me over with a feather."

"Yes, it was," Sam said in a way that he hoped would close off discussion. He felt uncomfortable talking about the religious controversies that led to the school's demise. "But Denham is certainly in no such danger."

Andy smiled as if it were a personal compliment. "None whatsoever." He glanced at his watch. "Did you do the driving?"

"No, our minister in Waska, Rev. John Covington, did. He has a friend who teaches here. He's looking him up right now."

Once more Andy looked at his watch. This time he stood, and at his signal the others stood as well. Sam accompanied them to the first meetings with the administrators and scholarship people. His presence was not really required, but a glance from Mercy told him she could use the moral support, and he didn't really mind fulfilling the in loco parentis role. The meetings were businesslike at the same time they were friendly, but they were also tediously lengthy. After they finally concluded Andy went back to his office while Sam, Mercy and Jason made their way to the music department where Jason was asked to play. He chose Chopin's "Etude in E Major," and after only a few bars both he and Mercy saw the looks of astonished approval on the faces of the two faculty members present. They recognized instantly that he was an extremely gifted musician, and during the conversation after he played they actually started more than one sentence with the clause, "When you are here." Earlier one of the administrators had said that Jason's grades and recommendations were good enough to place him among the top ten percent of applicants, and his economic situation qualified him for a full scholarship. Now with the music department showing that they eagerly looked forward to a chance to work with this child prodigy, everything should be perfect. Mercy, however, began showing by her extreme nervousness and equally by her efforts to hide it from Jason, that she regarded the final hurdle, the interview with the school psychologist, as the most dangerous part of the morning. Sam was about to excuse himself and go out for a pipe of tobacco until he saw this; thus he accompanied mother and son to the psychologist's office and only after Jason went into the inner office alone with her did he make his excuses. He told her it was close to the time to meet John, then as an afterthought also admitted he would like to have a pipe. They would meet later in the Quadrangle and decide about lunch.

He found John waiting in front of Samuel Denham Hall. His friend had talked to Andy Avery and told John that the consensus on campus was that Jason was a shoo-in, so he was not surprised when Sam reported how smoothly the interviews had gone. They settled on a bench in the Quadrangle, parallel to Main Street and fronted by Samuel Denham Hall with the Memorial Bell Tower to their left and Cockburn Chapel to their right. Students were numerous now, some playing frisbee on the lawn but most on their way to the dormitory, class or perhaps early lunch. They were of every possible cultural and ethnic background with casual dress being the unifying principle. Many wore jeans and T-shirts; only a few of the girls wore skirts or long peasant dresses. Sam thought of the contrast with Hartley Academy where an attempt to maintain a formal dress code was only reluctantly abandoned when the school was already close to dying, and the many black, brown and Asian faces he saw among the students reminded him again of the stupidity of Hartley's administrators. Denham had also started as a Congregational school.

For a while they simply enjoyed the warm May day, speaking idly of the students and the campus, the numerous robins hopping in the grass, and the incessant traffic on Main Street, the only anomalous intrusion on the peace of academia. Sam puffed at his pipe. Presently, however, the topic of education inevitably arose.

"This is a much more beautiful campus than my school," Sam said. "And the school is as academically strong as it is beautiful. This is one place where grading is not on the bell curve, where learning is genuine."

"Do you think all schools should model themselves on Denham?" John asked.

Sam shook his head. "That wouldn't be fair. They get the best here, and education has to concern itself with all students regardless of ability."

"All students means more than the three R's. There's special needs and—"

Sam interrupted. "You're absolutely right! Education is more than the three R's. When I was teaching I thought education was simply what happened in school. But now I think it's really threefold. It depends on family, society, and school. I don't mean before I didn't think family and society weren't important. It's just that education— from the Latin you know, a leading out—seemed narrower to me. We had athletics and school activities that built character. Hell, our school code for not cheating and so forth was instituted to build character. But now I realize students have to come to school already having that thing we call character."

"By 'society' I assume you also mean the church?" John asked.

"Of course. But I mean society in general too. For instance, I don't think the enormous salaries athletes make now can be very healthy. Why should a kid study Homer and Plato and Shakespeare when he can, he thinks, make millions hitting a baseball or sinking a basket? The kind of attitudes these obscenely high salaries engender say that society doesn't value learning."

John had been listening respectfully and nodding occasionally. Now he too offered an opinion. "I also think the Internet confuses students. Information and knowledge are not the same thing, but the Internet, despite it being ballyhooed as the greatest thing in the world, only offers information. Like millions of people, Wendy and I have gone on line now and explore the Web and Internet. But the claims I've seen made in the media about it are absurd. They confuse a tool that can aid education with education itself."

Sam tapped out the ashes from his pipe and got out his tool to clean it. "Yes, I agree with you," he said. "Another thing I think is that knowledge and education don't come easily. They take work. The Internet is too easy. It's perfect for lazy students who want to take shortcuts. Pretty soon so many shortcuts will lead to too many uneducated people."

"Are you familiar with Coleridge's concept of clerisy?" John asked.

Sam considered for a moment, then waited to let a large group of loud students pass by. "No, not really."

It's something we English majors learn. Coleridge thought that only a small proportion of people actually cared about ideas, philosophy, ethics, and so forth. Not a democratic idea, though perhaps an accurate one. Anyways, he used the medieval term 'clerisy' to describe them. Matthew Arnold called the same group the 'remnant.'

I have a friend from Yale who's now a professor at a Midwestern university. He thinks American society is fundamentally anti-intellectual. It cares nothing for academic, literary or intellectual excellence, only for that which makes money. He thinks only a small number of people will actually continue the western tradition. He uses Coleridge's term to describe them. 'Clerisy.' He's not happy about this incidentally—the term is merely descriptive."

Though he was unfamiliar with the terms John used, Sam had heard the argument before and was not interested in pursuing it right now. Instead he brought the conversation back towards the direction he wanted to take. "Descriptive or not, it doesn't bode well for democracy. My ideal of education is still to educate everyone. But we're already in trouble, that's for sure. The mention of money hits the nail on the head. Materialism. Society emphasizes selfishness. Think of Father Mullen. He was only thinking of himself."

"I'm afraid every society has its Father Mullens. Evil is universal for the sons of Adam and the daughters of Eve." John spoke with some vehemence. Evil was his professional domain.

"But you agree emphasizing selfishness cannot help society. Goodness is quite the opposite of selfishness, isn't it it?"

"It is. But then, not everybody buys into the Me-first mania of the media"—he smiled broadly—"if I may alliterate my M's."

But Sam found the subject too serious to joke about. "I certainly know exceptions. That young woman Michelle Turcotte is about as fine a human being as I know, and of course there are many others. But way too many learn from the behavior of their parents and society in general to care only for themselves. I don't exempt myself either. My son Bennet is a very self-centered and selfish young man. I sometimes doubt whether he even has the capacity to sympathize with others. I blame myself, of course. I was so obsessed with teaching that I'm afraid I wasn't a good father. I think the lesson he learned from my example was that teaching was my selfishness."

"I'm sorry to hear that. Do you get along with him now?"

Sam shook his head with a resignation that oppressed him. "No."

His voice cracked with emotion, eliciting from John a pastoral response. "It's never too late to make amends, you know."

"I do know. He just got out of the Navy and was home for a week last month. I tried to approach him a couple of times to say…you know, I'm sorry, but nothing happened. He wouldn't let me get close enough." He stopped, finding himself in danger of becoming too emotional. Returning to a more philosophical tone, he said, "But we were talking about society and the family. My failure is way too prevalent. If I despair more than normal, it's simply because I feel it personally, not just as an abstraction."

John was quiet for some time, lost in reflection. Suddenly his face brightened. "Let me tell you a story, Sam, a story that has the virtue of being true. I was actually thinking of it this morning as we drove here because it happened in Lawrence, Massachusetts, just down the road a bit across the Merrimack River. I remember it quite well because I wrote it down the night I heard it and"—he grinned broadly—"I plan to use it in a sermon one of these days. It's about the experience of a Cambodian boy of seventeen, an immigrant who was born in the camps after Pol Pot was driven from power by the Vietnamese, so maybe we should call him a refugee. My friend, a fellow Congregational minister, was at that time, over ten years ago, very much involved with helping the Cambodian community in Lawrence adjust to their new life in America. The boy and his family were Buddhists, but the principles that his story illustrates are universal, I'm sure."

"Is this a long story?" Sam asked.

The question made John laugh. "No, it's probably shorter than my prologue, in fact. The boy was fishing on the banks of the Merrimack River." He cleared his throat and then began speaking in a strangely effective chant:

Ponlok, now sixteen, was born in the camps of Cambodia after Pol Pot was driven from power by the Vietnamese and with his family emigrated to America. They were very poor but hard-working people determined to make it in this new land. His father worked in a shoe factory and his mother took in sewing at home. He wanted to help too, but his mother insisted that the money he made from a paper route and odd jobs be put towards his future education. He was the hope of the family, she said. It was his duty to study hard and get straight A's, which he did even though it did not make him feel as if he was actually helping the family. The one thing he did that sometimes contributed to the family was to fish. He did it for fun, but often he would catch enough fish to make a meal for his parents, him, and his little sister. One evening when he was fishing on the bank of the river he felt a tremendous tug on his line, and after struggling for over fifteen minutes, the boy reeled in the biggest fish he had ever caught. He was very pleased and excited and began to think about how proud his family would be of him. The fish was big enough for two meals, and he would be like a man providing for his family. Then he looked at the fish. It was beautiful with its scales reflecting the light of the setting sun and its eyes wild with the desire to be free, to swim once more. And suddenly he had a feeling for the fish. That was the words he used when later he told his story—"I had a feeling for the fish." Now he was in a quandary. Should he let the fish live or should he bring it home? He imagined his family proudly smiling at him as they ate the fish, and he imagined the fish swimming in the deep cool water. He could see both of these possibilities with great clarity. Finally he decided he would let the fish live, but just as he was about to throw it back into the river, a man who was fishing on the bank twenty feet away called to him. "Hey," he said, "if you're going to throw that fish back, I'd like to have it." Ponlok looked at the man. He had seen him before and knew he was from the Dominican Republic, an immigrant to America just like him. He was dressed shabbily and was obviously very poor, maybe even hungry. The boy also had a feeling for the life of the man. For a moment he wavered, much distressed at this second quandary. Finally he was inspired. "Do you wish a long life?" The man said that yes, of course he did. "Then so does this fish," the boy said and hastily released it back into the cool, life-giving waters of the river.

Sam was silent after hearing this tale. He thought about his son and wondered if he ever dreamed of his family being proud of him. He wasn't proud of Bennet, but he loved him. Pride was born of deeds. And he thought of Michelle, the only person he knew who would be capable of doing exactly what this good and thoughtful boy had done. He wished she were his daughter, then instantly felt guilty remembering Beverly driven to San Francisco by her estrangement. And he thought of the topic he and John had been discussing. It was he who said that education was wider than books. This boy had proven his thesis. Then he wondered if the boy had made it—if he had gone on to college and a career. But no sooner had he thought that than he wondered if college and a career were not somehow a shabby reward. Wasn't goodness and compassion their own reward? Was he too infected with the materialism he had bemoaned not ten minutes ago to recognize the reality of a spiritual plane? The boy was a Buddhist. Did that religion respect all of life more than Christianity? Did he have any business being proud of the western and Anglo-Saxon traditions?

"Well?" John asked, interrupting his reverie. "What do you think of this story?"

Sam glanced at his companion. His face was curiously expectant, like a proud author hoping his story would be well received. "It's marvelous, really a wonderful story. And you say it's true?"

"My friend assured me it was. He told me the boy said 'I had a feeling for the life of the fish' and 'I also had a feeling for the life of the man' with a depth of humanity as deep as the Dalai Lama's."

"And do you know what happened to the boy?"

John shook his head with resignation. "No, I don't even know his last name, nor what kind of a fish he caught."

"Well, I hope he is strong and doing well. I have a feeling for his life."

"So do I."

John's story effectively terminated their philosophical discussion on education. With the time approaching 11:30, their thoughts returned to the more concrete problem of Jason's admission to the school. They conjectured for a while on his chances, agreeing that unless something went terribly wrong in the psychologist's interview that he was as good as accepted. Sam tried to make the argument that even a breakdown with the psychologist wouldn't necessarily stop him from going to Denham Academy—at worst it might defer his matriculation.

Then they spotted Mercy coming out of Samuel Denham Hall and waved to catch her attention. She came up to them but was too nervous to sit down. "I had to get out of the office for a while," she said. "I was going crazy in there."

Sam repeated his feeling that even a bad interview wouldn't necessarily be fatal, but it didn't soothe her as she nervously paced to and fro in front of them.

"For the first time in fifteen years I wish I had a cigarette," she said. "Everything has been going great. Only this hurdle remains and I can't stop worrying."

"You're afraid he might lose control?" John asked. "Is that it?"

She looked away, staring at what no eye could see.

Sam, in an effort to get her to relax, made a weak joke. "My pipe is available, if that will help, Mercy."

She smiled wanly. "I wish it would. No, I want the best for Jason. I'm pretty sure he wants to go here. But would I be disappointed if he didn't get in? I don't know. I'm not totally sure living among strangers will be the best thing for him. So I don't know. I just don't know. I think certainty would be a relief. To have something settled would be a relief. Something definite. With the trial next week the more that is clear and settled the better. But I'm not even sure about that." With a hollow laugh she added,

"All I know is that I'm a wreck."

By now Sam's high strung nature had caught Mercy's nervousness, but it must have been very infectious, for the normally phlegmatic John also showed signs of edginess. In that state of mind the fact that everything had gone smoothly was a negative. It meant that things were going too smoothly. Having seen Mercy's face in the car earlier, Sam was sure that she had not fully resolved the conflict between wanting to keep and protect Jason and wanting him to be free to develop and pass beyond the abuse he had suffered. So he believed her when she said she wanted certainty, but he didn't believe certainty would completely end her torment.

He looked at John, trying to determine if he understood Mercy's dilemma, and decided on no real evidence except a certain intuition that he did not. John wanted Jason to be free. He had been working with the boy for over five months now, and he was the one who suggested Denham as a way out.

As suddenly as she had appeared, Mercy went back inside to wait in the outer office, leaving Sam and John to sit together in silent isolation. Sam's tension rose to such a feverish pitch that he began imagining Jason's utter collapse and ruined life as a psychological invalid. He knew the fear was ridiculous and irrational, but the knowledge did him no good. Try as he would he couldn't dispel it. Many minutes passed until the bell tower clock rang twelve o'clock and still no Jason and Mercy appeared. It was a very bad sign, Sam thought, suggesting that the psychologist was trying to put Jason back together again after his fragile psyche had shattered into fragments. Ten more minutes went by as they waited in an agony of suspense. Sam had the idea that Jason's face would tell them all they needed to know before he even spoke, so when they finally saw the door to Samuel Denham Hall open and Jason, Andy and Mercy appear, his eyes stared so hard they must have bulged.

Mercy was first out the door. Her face was an enigma; she seemed to be trying to control titanic emotions. Behind her Andy has one arm on Jason's shoulder and was talking to him in a easy and comradely way. And Jason?

Jason was smiling.

Happy Hour

M ike Harmon walked into the Washington bar with the air of a man who anticipated a pleasurable experience. Having first come here thirty years ago as an Army private on leave when he was nineteen, he was old enough to remember how the bar used to look. Back then it was a dump with dingy walls, inadequate lighting, unbalanced tables where if you weren't careful a sudden move could send your beer flying, sticky, filthy floors, and service with a grunt. Now, however, it was almost classy. It had a white oak bar with a polished brass elbow rest and marble counter. Behind it and matching it in length was a fancy thirty-foot-long mirror in which you could admire your favorite person in the place. The walls were oak-veneered paneling, and the table and chairs, though now beginning to show wear, were likewise solid oak. The renovations had been made in hopes of upgrading the clientele along with the decor, though here the new owner's plans had been frustrated. The people who frequented the bar were still mostly working class. But because it was nicer than the old days, they treated it better, felt better about themselves possibly, and as a result definitely spent more time and money in the place than in the old days—so in that way the renovations could be called a success.

The decor, however, was certainly not the reason Mike anticipated having a good time. Nor was the beer he would drink on happy hour of this Friday afternoon, nor the video games, the pool table, the free snacks, or any of the other things the bar provided for the amusement of its customers. It was to talk! Simply to talk—that was what he anticipated would be the most enjoyable couple of hours. The trial of Father Mullen was scheduled to be completed today; perhaps by now the jury had even rendered its verdict. Since the trial started last Tuesday it was all Mike could think about. The fact that his nephew Jason Buckley was involved went a long way towards explaining the deep interest he had in the case, but not the whole way. His wife Debbie often accused him of being a gossip. "Everyone always says it's women who are the gossips," she'd say, "but you're the worst I've ever seen. You're incorrigible." He did not deny the charge. How could he? He'd learned in high school Socrates' famous dictum, "Know thyself," and he wasn't likely to deny something about himself he knew to be true. He

R. P. Burnham

was a forty-nine-year-old plumber, very good at his trade and who made a good living from it; he had three teenaged daughters and a wife who loved him and tried to get him to eat properly and not drink too much; he was a happy-go-lucky guy pleased with this life of his; and one of the things that made it an interesting and stimulating life was that he liked to keep his eye on the shenanigans of other people, even as his own life was pretty dull and routine. All this he knew. He also knew that as sure as he was a gossip, the week's events had conspired to make his life delicious, like a good steak to be sniffed and savored before wolfing it down.

Before going into the bar he had stopped at the drug store and bought the evening paper. It had the transcript made from a reporter's shorthand of Samuel Jellerson's testimony. He'd quickly glanced through it and had seen that some of the rumors and conjectures he'd heard (and helped spread about himself) were inaccurate, but before he did anything else he wanted to sit down and carefully read every word about the trial.

He was pleased to find the bar was still relatively empty. He had finished his plumbing job early to get a head start on the night's discussions.

"Hi, Carl," he said to the bartender. Carl had just relieved the owner, who minded the place during the day, and was busy stocking up on liquor and bottled beer. "I'll have a draft when you get a chance."

"Did you hear the jury has got the case? Carl asked as he lifted a case of beer to the bar and started putting bottles in the refrigerator.

"No. What's the story?"

"Buck says they got it about an hour ago. The judge gave them their instructions for about fifteen minutes and now they're alone. If they can't get a quick decision, they'll be sequestered for the weekend."

"Any sense of how they're going to vote?"

Carl went over to the taps and drew a draft for Mike. "Buck says they didn't look happy, but I don't know what that means?"

Mike nodded and went over to a table near the window that allowed plenty of light. He had a pretty good idea what that meant. He took a sip of beer, reminded himself to pace his consumption, and opened the paper. His chair had a padded leather seat and back, and the arm rests were likewise padded. He felt very comfortable as he began his careful reading. He didn't expect current information—being the evening paper, it went to press in the early afternoon—but yesterday's details still offered grist for his particular mill.

He always spoke very assertively and knowingly about the trial, and as a result a lot of his friends thought he had inside information, a belief that he made no effort to dispel. His sister and nephew were, after all, among the key players in the drama. Still, the truth was much different. Most of his knowledge of how trials proceeded was gained from hours of surfing the Internet on his daughters' computer, and what he didn't learn there he supplied from all the television dramas about lawyers and court cases he watched. As far as any specific details he might have garnered from his sister or nephew—well, they were pretty much nonexistent. Mercy was still very angry with him for his nosiness when the story first broke last year, and knowing his reputation as a gossip, she had been extremely closed-mouthed with him ever since. He compensated for his lack of specific information by trying to be sure of the things he spread around and by speaking always with great certitude. Reading the paper, then, was part of his careful preparation. The other thing that kept his reputation with the guys intact was the sheer volume of rumors about the case. They were so rife that hardly anyone remembered their source or noticed that he was as innocent of hard facts as a schoolboy. He, for instance, was the source of the rumor last December that Mr. Jellerson was not a witness but rather a codefendant in the case when he'd misinterpreted the report that Jellerson felt guilty. Luckily, though, everyone had forgotten that he was the guy that started that rumor. Sometimes Mike (who remembered Socrates' dictum even in these circumstances) realized that he would make a great politician. The secret of being convincing, he'd found, was simply to convince yourself!

The paper's main story was the testimony of Samuel Jellerson, the only actual witness in the case. The prosecutor's interrogation was cream puff stuff. It only got to be interesting reading when the defense attorney got his claws into the witness. His name was William Conroy. The reporter described him as an intimidating man who constantly stared at Mr. Jellerson with a look of faint disdain on his face. At the same time Father Mullen was likewise staring at the witness, who seemed, the reporter wrote, to be made visibly uncomfortable by these two pairs of staring eyes. After a lot of routine questions, the meat of the testimony came when Mr. Conroy asked the witness how he could be unprejudiced and objective when it was a known fact that he was a friend of the boy, Jason Buckley. When the witness demurred, Mr. Conroy asked, "Haven't you been tutoring him for the past several months?"

[J]: If there's any correlation between the two, what I saw so shocked me that it made me sympathize with the boy and want to help him. But at the time I started tutoring Jason I already had gone to the police and been deposed.

[C]: Time is another point that needs clarification, Mr. Jellerson. Why did you wait so long…over a month, to be exact, before you went to the police?

[The witness didn't respond, and the question was repeated.]

[J]: Because I wanted to be sure. What I saw was so unbelievable I couldn't, couldn't…I was cowardly, I suppose.

[C]: Are you sure now?"

[J]: Sure that I saw Father Mullen abusing Jason? Yes.

[C]: Why are you sure now and weren't then?

[J]: I told you, it wasn't a question of sureness like that. It was that I didn't want to ruin a man's life and reputation. But when—

[C]: But if you didn't want to ruin a man's reputation, doesn't that imply you weren't sure?

[J]: No! I was sure but still couldn't believe it.

[C]: An interesting distinction, Mr. Jellerson. Wasn't it only after you read in the newspaper that Father Mullen had been arrested that you suddenly found your certainty?

[J]: I didn't read it in the newspaper. My wife told me.

[C]: But she read it in the newspaper, didn't she?

[J]: [The witness was quiet for some time.] Yes.

[C]: So you're really not sure now, are you?

[The prosecutor's objection that counsel was badgering the witness was sustained]

[C]: Let me ask you this, Mr. Jellerson. How were you sure it was Father

Mullen you allegedly saw in the woods?

[J]: I had seen him around town, and I've seen his picture in the paper.

[C]: But the man you saw in the woods you saw for less than a second. Have you ever spoken to Father Mullen?

[J]: No.

[C]: Yet less than a second was enough time to identify him?

[J]: Yes.

[C]: But it still took over a month to make the identification official?

[J]: Yes.

[C]: And five weeks later you were certain?

[J]: Yes.

[C]: And you're certain now?

[J]: Yes.

[C]: I congratulate you on your certainty, Mr. Jellerson, though it is a mystery to me.

After the defense attorney was through, the prosecutor redirected. He asked, "Wasn't your delay caused by your shock? Isn't it a case of seeing something and not being able to believe it because it was so shockingly unbelievable?" Mr. Jellerson answered, "Yes, I couldn't believe a priest would do so heinous a crime as to abuse a young boy."

Mike's opinion was that Jellerson had botched it, and the prosecutor's attempt to patch up the bad job was probably too little, too late. Thinking about all this and sipping his beer to make it last, he looked up to see Mark Beaulieu come in. He was some kind of a dispatcher for a trucking company whose name had been pronounced Bo-lee-o so long by the Yankees that even he said it that way now. He wasn't one of Mike's pals, but they had gone to high school together and knew each other. He was a short man with stocky limbs and a big beer belly, divorced now and prone to self-pity when he was drunk, which he often was—it was in fact the reason his wife divorced him. Strangely enough, he had been so interested in the case this week that he hadn't had time for self-pity. The case, you could say, was doing him some good.

He got a beer and came over to join Mike. "I see you've got the paper. What's the latest?"

Mike understood him to mean the latest on the trial. He wasn't alone in being fascinated by the case. "The jury has got the case now. Word is, they're not going to convict."

"Not convict? How come?"

Mike tapped the paper theatrically. "Because of what's in here. That Samuel Jellerson, the key witness, made a pretty bad job of it. The defense made him fall on his face."

Mark frowned. "If you ask me, Mike, you've been watching too many lawyer shows on TV. It's not going to be melodramatic tricks that determines the case. It'll be common sense."

For a moment Mike was nonplused. He actually had been thinking of some of the lawyer shows he watched. Then he recovered his equanimity when he also remembered some of the stuff he'd learned on the Internet last week. Thus he spoke confidently when he said, "I'm telling you, the prosecutor's got no case."

"No case?" Mark said sarcastically. "What about the victims? What about those boys?"

Mike rolled his eyes as if he were a schoolmaster dealing with the class dullard. "Word is, neither of them were very effective on the stand. But there's more. Haven't you heard of all those daycare cases where they were accused of all kinds of sexual shenanigans? All those cases were later dismissed. They called it mass hysteria like the Salem witch trials. No," Mike shook his head gravely, "a case of alleged molestation has got to have something more substantial than a 'he said' and 'I said.' I'm telling you, if the jury has doubts about Jellerson, they won't convict."

Mark took a long pull from his beer and a final drag from his cigarette before stubbing it out. "Okay, for the sake of argument, let's say that's true. The next question is, why isn't Jellerson's testimony good enough?"

"Well, read the transcript in the paper. That defense lawyer was all over him. Over a month, for God's sake. The man waited over a month before he went to the police, and that was after the story broke in the paper."

Mark, glancing through the paper, looked up. "But he explained why. It makes sense to me."

Mike smiled knowingly. "A man has to be convicted without a reasonable doubt. All the defense lawyer has to do is show there's a reasonable doubt."

"All I know is if I was on the jury I'd vote to convict."

Al Moran came in and joined them after getting a beer. He was a paint contractor and a good fellow. He was the only guy who rivaled Mike in his interest in the case. Like Mark he was short, but in his case he was slender and wiry. "You guys talking about the trial?"

Mike glanced at his watch. It was safe to drain his beer now—he'd made it last for forty minutes. He looked around the bar to see that Charlene Smith, the waitress, was busy now that the bar was starting to fill up. He rose to get a refill. "Yeah, Mark thinks he'd vote for conviction if he was on the jury. Trouble is, he ain't."

The other reason he didn't wait for Charlene was that he wanted to see if Carl had any more news. He waited at the bar while Carl filled the order for Charlene. "Any further word?" he asked when Carl came over for his glass.

He shook his head but pointed to the phone. "I've got it all arranged. We'll get a call if the jury reaches a verdict."

Mike smiled. "Great! Good work, Carl. You'll make some kind of an announcement, I assume."

Carl handed him his beer with a nod. He pointed to the lights. "I'll blink 'em," he said.

Back at the table Mark had a question for him. "Mike, one thing I don't understand. You're telling me you think the priest will beat the rap, right?"

Mike sat down and nodded. "Yeah." He took a sip of beer and, remembering Debbie, made sure it was only a sip. "I'm afraid so."

"But you don't seem to mind. You almost seem gleeful. Isn't Jason Buckley your nephew? What's going on?"

"Good question," Al said. "Whose side are you on?"

Mike frowned. He must have gotten carried away for Mark and Al to get this impression, and he didn't want that kind of opinion to get around. He put his beer down and folded his arms, making sure he looked very serious, if not hurt. "They're two different things. Father Mullen might get off because of the way the case was handled. That doesn't mean I like it. If I had my way, we'd hang that bastard by the

175

balls. Is that clear enough?"

They seemed satisfied with his explanation, and for a few minutes all three of them were content to digest it in silence. Then Mark spoke.

"So what kind of kid is Jason?"

"Jason? Jason's a really good kid. I remember when he was a little nipper how amazed he was that my name was Miles but everyone called me Mike. 'Uncle Mike, who is really Uncle Miles' he'd say. Then he'd laugh."

"Ain't he some kind of musical prodigy?"

Mike favored Mark with a knowing look. "He is. He's a pianist. He plays classical music and writes it too. But he's also a regular guy. He's a good baseball player—you should see him field ground balls—and a pretty good hockey player too. I've taken him and my other nephew Robbie fishing before. Believe me, he's a regular guy. I like him a lot. By the way," he added in a tone that betrayed just the slightest hint of self-importance, "talking about my nephew almost made me forget the interesting news Carl told me."

"Which is?" Mark asked.

"That Carl's got a friend at the courthouse. He promises to call if the jury reaches a verdict."

"That's not news," Al said. "It's the possibility we might hear some news."

"Well, it's still interesting. I told my wife I'd be home by six thirty, but if the verdict is about to come in, I'll have to be late."

Al shook his head. "Not me. The news on TV will have it. I can find out at home."

Bob Rollins came in the door. He was an electrical contractor working at the same site Mike was. They were renovating a three-story apartment building after a fire. While structural damage had been minimal, many walls were ruined by fire, smoke or water, and the owner was using the insurance money to upgrade the electrical and plumbing circuits, and carpenters and wall board guys were replacing the mess left by the fire. Mike liked him, but sometimes there was a streak of bitterness in him that could come out of nowhere and which made Mike always have the feeling of walking on eggshells when he was around.

After surveying the bar he came over and sat down at the table. "Get me a beer when you get a chance, Charlene," he said to the waitress.

"You just finishing work now, Bob?" Mike asked. "I'm working on my second hour here."

"Hey, I had to finish wiring the lights so you guys could see. And by the way, Mike. Maybe you could have used some light earlier."

"What do you mean?" Mike asked. Bob's tone made him feel defensive.

"Chuck was pissed as hell. You ran two drain pipes from the basement through the first floor, but the schematic calls for three."

Mike rubbed his chin. "I thought it was two."

"Well, all I know is Chuck was looking for you. He wanted to finish all the wallboards on the first floor and get to another job. Now he'll have to come back Monday."

"Mike had to find out about the trial," Al said. "Maybe two drains were close enough for him."

"Either that," Mark said, "or he was using the same system he uses when he pays his taxes."

Everyone laughed except Mike. He felt embarrassed. He had to admit he had been in a hurry, and maybe he didn't look at the diagrams closely enough. "I thought it was just two—one to drain the bathroom on that side and one for the kitchen sink. If I'm wrong, I owe Chuck one." Then to change the subject, he asked Bob where his partner Nate Wentworth was.

"He was working today in Bedford on another job. But don't expect to see him around much. He's got a new lady friend."

"Oh yeah? Who is she?"

"I don't really know. Those friends of his, the Daltons, fixed him up with someone, and it seems to be taking off."

He said the name Dalton with a curl on his lip. Mike, who had done some plumbing for them and found them to be nice people, couldn't understand Bob's sneer, but he decided he'd better not press it. "Did you read the paper and read Jellerson's testimony?"

"Yeah, one of Chuck's guys had it. Too bad there wasn't another witness. The one we had didn't do much."

That drew a response from Al. "Someone told me the cops knew of another witness, but he refuses to cooperate."

"Where the hell did you hear that?" Mike asked almost indignantly. He figured if he hadn't heard of it, it couldn't be true.

"I think it was that old man Tom Belcher. He knows one of the cops, some kind of relative, I think. Anyways, he told me this morning at the Swan about this witness."

"Isn't he the guy who doesn't believe priests do such things?"

"Yeah, that's the guy."

"He's not even Catholic, for Christ's sake. No, I don't believe it. First of all, why wouldn't a witness testify, and secondly, can't he be issued a subpoena to force him to testify?"

"I think they did, but there were two problems. The guy is some back-country hick, a regular swamp Yankee, so he's not reliable. And not only that, he denies that he saw anything. The prosecutor decided it wasn't worth getting him on the stand. It would just make them look bad."

"Well," Mike said, his voice heavy with a worldly resignation, "we could have used another witness. So I wish it was true and wish the guy could've testified."

Al nodded politely, apparently taking this statement to mean that Mike now believed him. "I've been hearing you say all week that you were bothered by that five-week delay in going to the cops. The defense seemed to show your fears were justified. But the trouble with Mr. Jellerson goes deeper than his word. Just like him, your sister Mercy only found out about her son after the other boy's parents pressed charges. She and Brian could also be accused of blaming a fit of adolescent depression on Father Mullen."

"Hey," Bob said, "did anyone know Gregory Hanrahan was the other boy before the trial began? I sure didn't."

Al shook his head. "I don't think so. They had moved away before the incident broke, so everybody was looking for some boy in town who was in the choir. Nobody thought to look in Massachusetts."

Mike impatiently listened to this digression. Al had made an important point, and it demanded exploration. "I think Al's point is a good one. From the perspective of the jury, it might be another nail in the coffin of the prosecutor's case."

"How do you see that?" Bob asked.

"Well, remember the defense attorney said in his opening statement that he would prove this was a case of mass hysteria and compared it to all those daycare cases. I think the prosecutor tried to answer that the cases were not the same at all, but it didn't matter. The jury had the idea slipped into their minds, which I bet was Conroy's plan all along. Now I myself remember my sister thought for a long time that Jason's behavior was a delayed reaction to her divorce from my brother-in-law. I don't think it's true—true that is that it was a reaction to the divorce. But we have to go by what the jury will think. That fat priest might just beat the rap on this thing alone."

"I think the jury has more sense than you give them credit for," Al said, then was interrupted by Charlene taking orders for the table. Everybody except Mike ordered another beer. He looked longingly at his half-finished glass but dutifully remembered Debbie's admonishment.

After Charlene had gone Al continued his thought. "Remember there are seven women on the jury. They'll be feeling more than thinking."

Bob put his beer on the table with a loud bang and stared at Al. "I don't think my wife would like to hear you say that, Al. I can see her now chasing you around the kitchen table with her rolling pin swinging wildly and fire in her eyes."

Everybody laughed.

"Is that why you're in such good shape?" Mark asked. "The wife chases you around the kitchen table, does she?"

That got a bigger laugh, and as Bob grinned sheepishly, Al said, "I just meant women feel for kids more. They'll probably see through the tricks the lawyers pull. I predict they'll find him guilty of something, even if it's not the most serious charges."

Mike, speaking with deadly seriousness, said, "Yeah, but don't forget, it just takes one guy to believe them and the case is lost."

Suddenly serious as well, Bob said, "You know, we can guess all night about what the jury is going to do. But what I don't understand is why the jury can't know about the two families in Indiana that say Father Mullen molested their sons too. Them liberals have made so many rules to protect crooks, it's a wonder anybody goes to jail nowadays."

"Are you kidding?" Mike asked. "I read last week on the Internet we have more people in prison than any other country in the world."

"Oh yeah? I don't believe it."

"Believe what you want. The reason the evidence from Indiana isn't allowed is because the case here has to be proved on its own merits. If we nail Mullen, let's nail him good. Later he can be nailed in Indiana."

"How much time do you think he should get?" Mark asked.

"He deserves life," Bob said. "Tell me he's not a lowlife. A queer priest preying on boys?"

Al nodded in agreement. "I asked one of the cops what he'd get if he's found guilty, and he said maybe five to ten."

"Shit, that ain't enough."

"He may not even get that," Mike said. "He's got to be found guilty on the evidence, don't forget, not what we think. That protects all of us, incidentally."

"You do think he's guilty, don't you?" Bob asked.

"Yeah, I do. Guilty as sin. But that's the thing about juries. They may know it too, but it has to be proved. They may find him not guilty, even when they know he's guilty."

"We're back to Jellerson again," Al said. "I don't think he did that bad."

"I do," Bob said with a sneer. "He was a wishy-washy rich guy and nothing else. He'd been teaching at a gentleman's school all his life. He doesn't have the foggiest idea what the real world is like."

They started discussing Jellerson yet again, but Mike, with his opinion already solid, hardly listened. Instead he went up to the bar to see if there was any news. Carl, however, was very busy now, and the one time he glanced at Mike it was with a look of impatience. Taking that as a hint that no new developments had occurred, he returned to the table. He noticed as he sat down that everyone had suddenly become silent. If he were paranoid, he might almost think they had been talking about him. But he wasn't paranoid, or if he was, only a little.

"What's going on?" he asked.

While the rest of them stared at their beers, Bob looked at him as if sizing him up. "Did you notice Charlene's been pretty quiet tonight?"

Mike looked over at her. She was taking an order from a table of young men and women who looked like college students just out of work from their summer jobs. She was in her late twenties, rather plain, with a bad complexion and uneven teeth and bleached blond hair. It was known she was unmarried with a three-year-old daughter, though she never talked about her child. At work she was quiet, efficient, and businesslike as opposed to friendly. Except for one thing, she made little impression on the regulars. That one thing, however, was very noticeable. She had enormous breasts, which were often the subject of jokes among the guys.

"I haven't noticed anything special," Mike said. "Isn't she usually quiet?"

"So you haven't heard about her arrest for soliciting?"

"What? Charlene?"

Bob nodded gravely. "It happened in Portland last weekend. She asked a guy if he was looking for a good time, but unfortunately the guy was an undercover cop, and he nailed her."

"What will happen? She'll get fined, I guess."

"Why don't you ask her?" Bob said.

Mike was doubtful. "I don't know. I don't want to embarrass her." Despite all the jokes they made about her breasts, none of them ever said anything to her about them. They recognized a certain dignity about her that wouldn't tolerate such a freedom. That's why Mike was so shocked at the news—it seemed so unlike her.

But then he heard Al Moran wheezing as he tried to suppress a laugh, and he looked up to see all of them laughing at him. He felt the blood rush to his face.

"Jesus, Mike, you'll believe anything," Bob snorted, very pleased with himself. He was obviously the ringleader for their joke.

"Well," Mike said, attempting to recover his dignity, "you'll notice that I didn't really believe it."

"But you were only sure when we started laughing," Al said. "You're just like Jellerson. Only really sure when everyone else is."

"Okay, I'll be a good sport," Mike said and grinned to prove it. But he wasn't and the grin took a lot of effort. Truth to tell, their little joke took all the fun out of the night. When, fifteen minutes later, Carl flashed the overhead lights off and on and announced that Father Mullen had been found innocent of the serious charges but guilty of the lesser charge of lewd and lascivious behavior, he heard the news in a dull, lethargic state of mind.

"That will mean a fine and probably he'll be made to have psychological counseling," Al said.

"And I'll bet someone will sue him in civil court. I'll bet that pig doesn't get off as easily as he thinks he will," Mark said.

"I hope he burns in hell," Bob added, "and that he gets nailed in Indiana."

But Mike said nothing. Suddenly all he could think about now was Jason. It wasn't a game anymore. It was real, and Jason was still the victim.

Pity and Terror

"**S**o Mr. Jellerson blames himself?" Sarah asked. They were sunbathing in Michelle's backyard on the Saturday after school got out for the summer. Later, in the afternoon, they were going to a beach party comprised mostly of junior-year classmates who would move up to the exalted position of seniors in the fall. Both of them were very pale, as befits serious students who had been studying for finals and completing papers during the sunny month of June, and Michelle had suggested that getting a little color would make them stand out less at the party. She buttressed her suggestion with the observation that both were starting summer jobs next week where they would have little opportunity to sun bathe. Sarah had a job at a candy shop at the beach, and Michelle was going to do clerical work at her father's law office—he hadn't completely given up on her pursuing a career in law even though she was still committed to a life in medicine. Her dream, or one of her dreams, was having a clinic in Africa or India and helping the poor. She would have preferred a summer job in the health professions, but they were hard to come by whereas with a lawyer father a job in a law office was easy to get.

Michelle rolled over on her back. "Yes," she said, "Millie told me that he feels awful."

"Do you feel it was his fault?"

"No, not really. The defense made him look wishy-washy and indecisive for not going to the police instantly, but I can understand his thinking."

"I can't."

"Why not? Haven't you ever seen something so horrible you couldn't believe it?"

"Aside from my calculus final, not really. Have you?"

Michelle shifted to her side. "Actually no, but I can imagine it. Can't you just see Mr. Jellerson coming upon Father Mullen abusing Jason, seeing that it's a priest and a boy, and not being able to really believe what you saw?

"Sorry, but again the answer is no. If I saw it I think I'd know what I saw."

Michelle was a little annoyed with Sarah for saying this. "You mean, then, that you agree with the people who say it's his fault Father Mullen isn't going to jail?" She spoke rather sharply. She could so easily imagine Mr. Jellerson's point of view that every time she thought of him coming upon the priest and Jason her heart would start pounding and her breath would quicken as if she were actually there.

"I also agree with Mr. Jellerson himself, don't forget. He blames himself too."

"That's why it's up to his friends to support him. Let me ask you this. How would you feel if people blamed you for something terrible, and yet you had done the right thing—only human weakness, honest doubt, or whatever you want to call it, kept you from doing it right away? What if this trial ruins Jason's life? How would you like to have that burden on your conscience?"

Sarah rolled onto her stomach, then reached back to unfasten her bikini top. At first Michelle started to get angry again at the utter casualness of her friend. What kind of response was that to a serious and important question? But then she saw that Sarah was thinking about what she said. She waited.

"Do you think the trial will ruin Jason's life?" she asked in a tiny voice.

"I don't think so. But it could. He could begin thinking that society can't or won't protect him. He might never trust people again. He could start feeling so insecure he wouldn't be able to function."

"I hope not. Jason's a good kid."

"He is a good kid."

"What does his mother say—about Mr. Jellerson and the trial, I mean?"

"She doesn't blame him. Millie told me that she talked to her and Mr. Jellerson for a long time after the trial and understood why he did what he did. She thinks it's more important simply to get the whole thing behind Jason."

"Well," Sarah said, turning and leaning up on one arm and looking at Michelle, "if you put it that way, I hope so. And I hope Mr. Jellerson doesn't blame himself. I'm trying to understand his position." Then, responding to Michelle's widening eyes, she looked down at herself and, incorrigible as ever, started laughing. Her unfastened bikini top had slipped down and exposed her breasts. "Oops! I hear that Tiffany Andrews sunbathes topless, but I'm not such a cosmopolitan girl as her." She adjusted the top and fastened it, but not before making a quick self-examination of the progress of her tan. With a comically exaggerated look of shock, she said, "I don't think we're making much headway with this tanning idea. I can't help noticing there's no different in color between my arm and the places no profane eyes may see."

Michelle examined her arm. "I see what you mean. I'm still pale as a ghost. Maybe the morning sun isn't strong enough."

Sarah stood and, shading her eyes, looked at the sun. "Yep, it looks pretty sluggish to me. Maybe it was partying too hard last night and hasn't woken up yet."

Michelle joined her on her feet. "My mother doesn't think tans are healthy anyways.

"How do you think Tiffany gets her tan? I bet she has a tanning light."

Michelle started putting on her shorts and her T-shirt with a Greenpeace logo. "I wouldn't be surprised. She has everything else. But let's go inside and have some lunch."

Michelle's mother was helping her own mother rearrange her condominium after the purchase of some new furniture and had left tuna salad for them along with instructions to clean everything up after they were through. Her father was working at the office.

While they ate their lunch, Sarah asked about Bobby. "What will you say to him when you see him?"

"I don't even know if he'll be there."

"I bet he is. So what will you say?"

"I told you before, I don't think we'll get back together."

Sarah chewed at her sandwich while staring abstractly out the window. She took a swallow of apple juice. "I'm still surprised every time I hear you say that."

"I wouldn't have said it at first, but I've had almost two months to think about it now. At first I moped around like I'd lost my shadow, but the more I thought about it the more I saw we should split up. If I kept trying to change him, it must mean that I didn't like him the way he was. If it was just some things, not all things, it would be different. But he was trying to be a different person than he really was. He stopped seeing his best friends—who are, I think, immature ninnies—and tried to be a person he wasn't. We argued about little things like the color of his shirt, but it was really big things that made us different. One thing good came from it, though. I got you and Rob together. You two fit nicely together."

"You know, we do actually. I'm the luckiest girl in the world. I don't see that he is different from me. We see the world quite the same way."

"I'll tell you what else besides time helped me see that Bobby and I weren't meant for each other. It was Jason."

"Jason! Isn't he too young for you?"

Michelle felt herself blushing. Sarah's face looked so surprised she had dropped her jaw and was looking at her with her mouth wide open. "You misunderstand me. I mean when I was feeling sorry for myself and moping around, I thought of Jason's troubles. Mine in comparison were so trivial that I, I...well, it gave me perspective, shall we say?"

"In what way?"

"I mean that as long as I just felt sad I could only think that being happy was having Bobby back. But when I saw that my troubles were trivial compared to Jason's, suddenly the things that Bobby said I could analyze objectively. We were really too different to make it together."

"I see," Sarah said doubtfully. "But how could you be objective about love?"

She thought for a moment. With Bobby she had discovered that it was very hard to communicate the real you. Love was such a strong need that through its eyes corners looked round and wiggly lines seemed straight even when they remained corners and wiggly lines. But here was her best friend also not quite seeing what she was trying to say. One consequence of this was rather scary. She saw a vision of human isolation so powerful that neither love nor friendship could ever be complete or perfect and where people never quite connected, and suddenly it was very important to make Sarah understand how she felt.

She leaned forward resting on her forearms. "It wasn't being objective in a cold sense. It was seeing that even if we made up there would be other differences—many, many of them—that would arise. I mean, then, that I can clearly see that even if we got together again and were happy for a few months, eventually we wouldn't be. He can't always prefer yellow when I like blue. He can't pretend to be a feminist and a progressive when really those things don't mean anything to him. Suppose we got married? Would he like it that I want to be a doctor and go to Africa to help the people? Or suppose he wanted to vote for some right-wing Republican? Would he lie and pretend he supported a progressive candidate? Do you see what I'm saying?"

Sarah nodded. A dreamy look came over her. "Too bad Rob has to work today and can't make it to the party. You know, he doesn't care much about politics. He just accepts me for who I am."

"Rob is different. He's open-minded. Do you know what I think of Bobby?"

"That he's not open-minded?"

Michelle nodded.

Sarah stood and brought her plate to the sink. I remember something in civics class that puzzled me. We were reading Peter Singer's "Animal Liberation." Mr. Ulanov and the class discussed all the points—how if a creature can suffer he or she deserves ethical regard, the economic arguments about how it takes three times as much grain to feed a cow for meat than just using the grain to feed hungry humanity, all the stuff about factory farming and experimenting on animals, all of which just about made me a vegetarian then and there. Well, after all these discussions Bobby raises his hand and with this really perplexed look on his face asks, 'But it's just food, isn't it?' He didn't get a single point from the discussion."

"See what I mean?" Michelle said as she brought her plate over to the sink and started cleaning up.

After that was done, Sarah asked how they could kill the next hour.

"I was thinking the same thing. I haven't walked Buttons for over a week. I haven't seen the Jellersons since last week either. What say we walk across the field and see if we can take him for a walk."

"If that makes us late, it's okay. We can be like Tiffany, fashionably late and having everyone in agony about when the lights of the party are going to show." She slunk across the kitchen floor like a high fashion model on the runway to emphasize her satiric sally while Michelle laughed.

At the farmhouse there was a delay before their knock was answered. They could hear a voice inside and were about to knock again when Mr. Jellerson opened the door. He looked shocking—older and with a dullness to his eyes that suggested defeat.

"Hi, Mr. Jellerson. We've come to see if Buttons needs a walk."

"Oh, hi girls. Yes, I think Buttons could use a walk. Would you like to come in?"

Michelle looked at Sarah, who half closed her eyes and turned her head slightly. She too had noticed how nervous and distracted Mr. Jellerson looked. The invitation was polite but lacked all conviction. "No, we won't disturb you. Is Buttons at his tether?"

For a moment he seemed lost in thought, then shaking himself out of his torpor, he said, "Yes, I seem to have forgotten to take him inside when the sun got high. When you bring him back, please bring him inside. I'll leave the door unlocked for you."

"We will," Sarah said.

They started to go, but Michelle turned and said, "We'll pop in and say hello to Walt first. We'll use the side entrance."

"Okay, thank you, Michelle."

Going around the corner of the house and seeing Buttons suddenly jump up eagerly when he spotted them, Michelle said in a quiet voice close to a whisper, "Did you notice something wrong?"

"Yes, maybe Walt will tell us."

They stopped and patted Buttons for a few minutes. He rolled on his back while they rubbed his belly, then leaped up and ran in circles, all the while his tail wagging furiously.

"We'll be right back, Buttons. We have to see Uncle Walt first."

He had heard them. He was at the door and greeted them soberly. "Hi, Michelle. Hi, Sarah. I take it you've heard the news."

"No. We did think something was wrong, though. What is it?"

Walt's face grew very serious. "The Jellersons' son, Ben, is missing. He hasn't been seen for two days in San Francisco. Beverly called last night and this morning, and we're expecting her to call again as soon as there's news. At first the police weren't involved, but I think now they're looking for him." He shook his head. "It's bad, very bad, I'm afraid. Ben has got mixed up with a friend from his past and has started doing drugs again, hard drugs. We're all very worried."

"Oh my God! Then they're waiting for news. Poor Millie. Poor Mr. Jellerson."

Sarah nervously shifted on her feet, swaying back and forth. "I notice you're not limping, Uncle Walt. You're walking perfectly normally."

He nodded gravely. "I hadn't noticed. I guess I was favoring the leg from habit."

"Well, we're going to take Buttons for a walk now. Bye."

"What do you suppose it means?" Sarah asked as soon as they cleared the house. They were walking across the pasture to the woods.

"I'm not sure. He is a strange boy, troubled I think. Have you ever wondered what a street person looked like when he was young? I've sometimes thought he looked like Ben."

"What do you mean? Ben is middle-class."

With sandals on their feet, they were both walking through the deep grass very slowly. Michelle spoke with her head down, carefully seeing her way before stepping forward. "So are plenty of street people. That famous dog man of Waska—that guy who used to go around town with five or more dogs? I read in the paper his father owned a factory. They were estranged. Ben was like a street person in one way—he was strange and he didn't relate to people. When he looked at me that time I told you about, what was so creepy about it wasn't just that he was looking at my body. He was looking at my body and not seeing me. That's what gave me the creeps. But when that guy got arrested at the rummage sale, I saw something else. I saw that Ben was also a miserable and unhappy human being. It must be horrible to be lonely and not see people."

"But what does that have to do with his disappearing?"

Michelle stopped to let Buttons investigate a bush. He sniffed at it with intense interest and grew excited.

Moving again, she said, "I'm not sure. Maybe he wanted to disappear. Maybe it wasn't drugs, or not just drugs. Maybe he just wanted to disappear. Maybe he'll become a street person."

They moved out of the hot, bright sun and into the cool woods. The scent of pine and more faintly of some flowering tree permeated the air. It was beautifully inviting and refreshing. Sarah said, "And maybe he's dead—that's what everyone is really afraid of."

"I hope not, but I agree that is why Mr. Jellerson is so tense. It must be horrible."

"What do you think of Walt?"

"You mean about the limp? I think he just got into the habit of favoring his right leg from when it was weaker."

Buttons barked at a squirrel, and they stopped and watched it scold the puppy from a branch.

"Walt told me that Mr. Jellerson was very upset when Walt told him about Ben hitting Buttons," Michelle said.

Sarah walked on in silence, her eyes staring at the ground. She seemed lost in thought.

"What are you thinking about?" Michelle asked.

"Poor Mr. Jellerson. Poor, poor Mr. Jellerson. Why does life have to be so sad? It makes me feel guilty to be so happy."

"I know what you mean," Michelle said as she lightly and tenderly touched Sarah's cheek and they exchanged a glance of wordless communication. "Let's go back. I think Buttons has walked enough."

They returned hurriedly, both of them feeling nervous and apprehensive, and would not let Buttons stop to investigate things. His whines of protest were hardly acknowledged. At the house when Michelle leaned down to take his leash off and hang it on its hook in the hallway she found herself trembling. At first the house seemed strangely quiet, but then they heard an unearthly moan and became aware of another sound, like that of water gurgling over rocks. They exchanged a panicked glance, then stepped into the kitchen.

Buttons scurried over to his master, who was standing in the doorway from the kitchen going into the front rooms, only to be ignored. Once again he whined plaintively and still was ignored. In the meantime Sarah and Michelle found themselves reaching for each other in horror. Mr. Jellerson was as one released from the gates of hell. His face was contorted, his mouth gaping as if in the act of howling, his eyes bulging, his face deathly pale. He seemed to have trouble breathing. It came as gasps interspersed with words they could not at first understand. Michelle looked over at Millie to see that she had covered her face with her hands and was weeping and trembling. She felt terrified and at the same time profoundly embarrassed to be witnessing this pain. She felt she had no business being part of such an unspeakably private moment. She looked next at Sarah and saw on her face the same mixed feelings of horror and pity, uncomfortable embarrassment and helplessness. Then for the first time she saw that the phone had dropped from Millie's hand and lay on the floor. She could hear a voice coming from it but stifled her impulse to pick it up. Now what Mr. Jellerson was saying became comprehensible: "Oh, no! Oh, no!" he kept repeating over and over as he gasped for air.

She knew without being told that Bennet had been found and that he was dead. Still she was at a loss for what to do. She wanted to hug them both but didn't feel she should—not yet at least. She hoped they would hug each other to share this terrible pain.

Walt came out of his room and stood behind Mr. Jellerson. "Sam, is it Ben?"

He nodded, and without another word tears sprang into Walt's eyes too. She remembered that years ago he had lost his son. In this way several seconds passed. Michelle moved closer to the phone to hear a frantic voice continue to yell, "Mom! Dad!"

She picked up the phone and looked at Mr. Jellerson. She was conscious that the tears were flowing from her eyes now, though she could not remember when they started. He nodded, so she spoke quietly into the receiver. "Hello, this is Michelle Turcotte. I'm a neighbor."

She looked at Millie and Mr. Jellerson (and why didn't she call him Sam, why the formal Mr. Jellerson when he had said it was all right?) and wished they would go to one another. She kept looking, even as her tears continued flowing, from one to the other, and then, thankfully husband and wife clasped each other in their arms.

"Our boy is dead," he sobbed.

Beverly's voice impinged upon her consciousness. "Are they all right? Are my parents all right?"

Speaking very softly, Michelle said, "They're in shock, I think. Your brother has...?

"His body was discovered this morning under a wharf... An overdose of bad heroin... He had been dead for two days."

R. P. Burnham

The Day After You Die

When Jason Buckley woke up on a Sunday morning two weeks after the trial of Father Mullen, he soon realized something was different. Since that black day last October the usual sequence of waking consisted of passing from a state of comfortable and warm sleepiness to an awakening consciousness of the self where images of his mother and father, family and friends, would cascade through his mind; he would think of music, usually what he had last played or studied or composed, a Schubert impromptu one time, a Beethoven sonata another; he would have a pleasant feeling of well-being together with a sense of purpose and identity as a musician; he would feel himself as much a living part of music as he was the son of his parents, the friend of his friends, and it was all very good. Sometimes this state lasted just a few seconds; other times for up to a minute he would bathe in the warm waves of well-being; but always at some point the face of Father Mullen would flash into his mind: he would hear the black priest telling him that God would be angry with him if he did not obey; and the feeling of well-being, of living in a world of order and harmony, would melt away into nothingness while he would be plunged into a state of panic, uncertainty, ambiguity, vulnerability, terror, fear, shame and degradation.

An intense struggle for his body and soul would ensue. His stomach would go heavy, his heartbeat would quicken, he would break into a cold sweat, the pressure of his fear and loathing would make his nerves vibrate like an out-of-tune violin string, and with his jangling nerves making him want to run, his thoughts would be hard to control and would race. These physical symptoms that wracked him exactly duplicated the way he had felt alone with Father Mullen in the woods. At first the relived memory so dominated him that he feared it would be his permanent condition, and thoughts of suicide were his only relief. All day at any time the feeling and its effects could overtake him, and he would be powerless to resist it. But eventually he found a way to fight back. The panic and the feeling of total vulnerability were the result of his being alone and defenseless with Father Mullen. It followed that the less he was alone, whether in his mind or in the world, the more he would feel secure and protected. So his first line of defense was the love his parents had for him. Early on his condition was so desperate that he asked his parents to get back together even though he understood that they regarded themselves as incompatible. Later, after Michelle Turcotte had talked to him at Mrs. Cohen's Christmas party, he found that her wonderfully supportive words when repeated in his mind like a mantra could make the panic go away. She had said, "I know about that priest, and I want you to know you're not alone. I mean, it's not just your mother and father and Father Riley who are on your side. All decent people are. You were a victim, and you mustn't blame yourself... I hope you realize that if there's anything I can do, please let me know. I think you're very special... Things will get better. Remember, you're a genius!"

When Rev. Covington started counseling him, he added some of the things the minister had said to Michelle's supportive and compassionate words, and in contemplating them found they too had the power to make him feel that Father Mullen could not dominate him forever. He especially appreciated the time Rev. Covington made clear in his mind the way the priest had manipulated and tricked him: "God gave us the world, but what human beings do with it and have done with it is our responsibility. Father Mullen was selfish and evil. God did not cause him to be selfish and evil—he is responsible. Perhaps there are factors that made Father Mullen the way he is. Perhaps he was raised without love, but God is not a puppeteer pulling strings. God is love. Whenever we're kind and feel love, God is present in our lives... It's going to take time for you to heal... That process, though, will also be a process of understanding more and more deeply what happened. Father Mullen is an evil man. But he's evil in many ways. He violated your trust and he violated his vows. He was so selfishly intent upon his own desires that he didn't care what he did to you. He purposely tried to confuse you about God. He did that simply to protect himself so that he wouldn't get caught. Remember, though, what I just said. God is love. God doesn't trick people. He doesn't try to make a little boy think that a bad priest is not a bad priest. He doesn't try to trick you into thinking that a man's evil and perverse desires are God's will. From a Christian point of view, what Father Mullen did was the ultimate sin—he sinned and in sinning instead of displaying penitence he displayed hubris."

For over a month he thought of these two every time Father Mullen slipped into the inner sanctuary of his mind. His memory was so good that he remembered virtually every word just as they said it. Finally, and, with his sense of humor starting to return, in hindsight perhaps too obsessively, he had written a musical composition to embody the emotional journey the love and support of people other than his parents had allowed him to take. It was to him a journey of freedom, and naturally he connected it to music—the one thing he did that made him feel most free. Music was a world of peace. It was orderly and within its safe boundaries it offered him free expression of the deepest feelings. Returning to the tonic key made him feel there was place in his soul that was unassailable. Thus in his composition he used basic sonata form even though he was writing program music. The first theme in B major represented Michelle's comforting support, and at times was literally a musical version of her words, which he could sing to the music. The second theme in the dominant F key represented Rev. Covington's support. In the development section he merged the two themes in a contrapuntal fantasy. In the recapitulation, with the minister's theme now in the tonic key of B major, he repeated the themes. Later after Mr. Jellerson started tutoring him and he realized how deeply committed his tutor was to his welfare, he added a coda to his composition that represented Mr. Jellerson's support more abstractly than the specific themes for the others.

On easy mornings he only had to hum a few bars of the themes or simply hear them in his head to dispel his soul's desolation; on bad days he would go through the entire composition verbally and musically, recalling Michelle's words and seeing her sweet face and compassionate dark eyes when she said them and the minister's kind face when he explained how evil had tricked him, and he would almost always recapture the security they gave him.

But this morning he did not even have to hum a bar of his secret composition. This morning was different.

The sequence of events that led to his peaceful Sunday morning began on Friday night. His father was scheduled to leave for his annual fishing trip to upstate Maine with three of his cronies, but he didn't want to go because Jason was still upset about the trial. Jason, not wanting to keep his father from a trip he had been making for over twenty years, said, "It's all right, Dad. I would feel better if you went." His parents had been fighting about the trial and what to do about its outcome. They had tried to keep their disagreement hidden, but Jason had heard enough bits and pieces of it to know what the issues were. His father wanted to sue Father Mullen in civil court where there was a much better chance of success. His mother took a diametrically opposite view. She wanted to have the entire affair put into the past so that they could get on with their lives. For a long time Jason was not really sure which side he was on. He had had fantasies of hurting Father Mullen. Sometimes they were so violent they scared him. He talked to Rev. Covington at his weekly sessions about them, and the minister told him they were perfectly normal at the same time he counseled that it would be better to forgive the man who had trespassed against him. He saw, then, both points of view while believing his mother's was probably the best one. What bothered him more than the conflicting issues, however, was the tension that existed between his parents. Believing that the absence of his father for a few days might be a relief, he had insisted that his father should go on his trip. He perfectly understood that his generosity was a mixture of altruism and selfishness. He also understood that his desire for a few days of relief from domestic tension placed him on his mother's side of the argument. Neither had directly asked him what he wanted to do. If they did, he was prepared to side with his mother even if it hurt his father's feelings. What he really wanted was for his father to come around to his mother's opinion. He needed them both.

After his father left he started feeling guilty, and Saturday became one of his bad days. He spent a lot of time upon first waking up going through his musical composition both musically and, when that wasn't enough, verbally, and he struggled all day against the omnipresent image of Father Mullen. With his mind racing trying to outrun the priest, he was a nervous wreck. He had no appetite and found it difficult to sit still.

Somehow he got through the day, which included a visit to his aunt Hope's house and some basketball with Robbie. As a treat they had pizza for supper. He ate enough to keep his mother from being worried—or so he thought, for he should have known he couldn't hide anything from her. At bedtime she came into his room. The first thing she asked him was what he wanted to do about Father Mullen. Here at last was the question, but for a long time he couldn't quite bring himself to take sides. Still, still he wanted both his mother and father to be on the same side. Finally he did tell what Rev. Covington suggested.

"He told me to remember the Lord's Prayer where we ask for strength to forgive those who trespass against us. He thinks that's the best way."

"So do I," his mother said, stroking his cheek lovingly.

"But, Mom, more than anything I want to get rid of the picture in my mind."

"The picture?"

"The picture of Father Mullen. He's like a monster I carry around with me."

His mother had stood and paced in the narrow space between the bed and bureau for a minute or so before coming to a decision. Then she sat back down on the bed and told him the story of Kermit Pingree.

It was a revelation. He never realized his mother had had a life before she became the person who was his mother. She told him everything about Kermit, how he was a star football player for Courtney Academy, how he was as handsome as a movie star with his long blond hair and blue eyes and a tall, muscular body, how he was not a good student but still did everything with a larger-than-life flair, how he had joined the Marines to fight for his country and in joining how he had volunteered for the front lines. He was a dreamer, she said. He pictured himself as a war hero in the same way he was an athletic hero. He made their future married life in a house with a white picket fence in the front and a backyard filled with kids sound like a Hollywood epic—the fulfillment of the American dream. He was totally decent and never belittled those who were not star athletes or bright glittering stars in the night sky of high school society. She said that he could not stand bullying and that once she saw him stop some of his football teammates from belittling skinny, scholarly students. He was optimistic, extroverted, sweetly naive and trusting.

All this was very interesting to Jason, but what she said next took his breath away. She told him of the long bleak years she and his father had tried to have a baby and how when he was born it was for her like emerging from a dark, dank cave into a beautiful sunny day. "I wanted to call you Kermit, but your father didn't like the name, so we compromised on Jason. But I have always associated you with him, despite the fact in most ways you are completely different."

"How are we different, Mom?" he asked, wanting to hear the differences so that he could learn the ways they were the same.

"Well, you're imaginative and intellectually brilliant. You're a musical prodigy. Kermit was nothing like that. But—"

She paused, and he waited, concentrating all his attention on her, for now she would tell him how they were similar. "But both of you have the capacity to dream, to strive for a different and better world, to work to bring that world to reality."

"It must have been awful when he was killed. How did you feel?"

Again she stood and paced between the bureau and bed to collect her thoughts. When she sat back down she regarded him tenderly. "That's why I thought it was a good time to tell you about him," she said. "The news almost killed me. It took everything I had been living for for five years away. It made me feel my life was over."

She looked away, thinking, while he waited patiently. His nerves were tingling with the excitement of discovery.

"Someone once told me that the day after you die the sun will rise. When the morning after I heard the news came and I saw the sun coming through my window, I cried and cried and cried. I felt my life was over. But what I want you to understand now, Honey, is that it wasn't over. I met Brian and from Brian I had you. Do you think now I would change a thing? You are the treasure of my heart, the life of my life. The only connection now is that sometimes I think secretly—and you must not tell your father this—that you are in some ways Kermit reborn. When you came dreams of the future came with you. Life was wonderful again because you were in the world. When your musical abilities were discovered, I realized I would do anything to help you fulfill yourself. Your father feels the same way."

Lying in bed, he recalled the whole conversation, still experiencing it as a new revelation. The principal lesson he learned from his mother's story wasn't even discussed explicitly. He saw that his mother had suffered a terrible blow that almost destroyed her, and yet it did not. He saw that life was ever redeeming. He saw that from ashes hope could rise. He saw that he was going to be well. He knew—for he could feel it as a pulsing presence—that he could get his self-confidence back.

After his long inward journey he returned to his room. Even though it was Sunday, with his father away he was in his room at his mother's. There was his Macintosh on the desk, and on the small table near it his electric keyboard that he used to try out tunes he was writing, which were then recorded on the computer. They were fine; what he examined critically were the decorations. With the exception of a Boston Red Sox pennant and a picture of him and his parents, the rest of the pictures and figurines were all dinosaurs. He got out of bed and walked over to the shelf beside his desk. He picked up and examined a Tyrannosaurus Rex and a Stegosaurus. Then he looked at the pictures, one again being a Tyrannosaurus Rex and the others scenes with many different dinosaurs. He remembered the delight he used to feel looking at these pictures and models. Now quite suddenly the delight was gone. He started to tear down the poster of the T-Rex but stopped after pulling the tape off of one corner.

He went downstairs. His mother was at the kitchen table with a cup of tea in front of her and the Sunday paper in her hand. She put the paper down and smiled. "How did you sleep, Honey?"

"Mom, I've been thinking. It's time to make a change in my room. Would it be all right if I took all the dinosaurs away?"

"Of course, if you want to. But why do you want to take them away?"

He sat down at the table and studied her face. He smiled. "I slept wonderfully last night, to answer your question."

She reached over and stroked his hand. "That's great, Honey."

He frowned, just a little, but it was a frown. He could see that she saw it. She regarded him with a worried, puzzled look on her face. "It's just that dinosaurs are kids' stuff. I've got those posters—the Beethoven one and the Boston Symphony Orchestra one. I'd rather have them on the wall. Robbie has rock posters on his wall. It's only right that I have classical music stuff. And you know that picture of the Denham Academy campus they sent us? Could we get a frame for it? I'd like to have that on my wall too. And, Mom, one more thing. Aren't I too old now to be called 'honey'?"

She smiled again, this time a smile of relief. "Yes, maybe you are," she said.

They had breakfast and then it was time to get ready for church. He only had time to strip the walls and pack the dinosaur models in a box. Later in the afternoon he would give the room its new look. It was fun to think about it, though it made him laugh to find this out. Maybe he inherited his mother's love for renovating and decorating after all! There had never been any signs of it before. But he knew the happiness and sense of contentment went deeper. He felt he was making a passage into manhood. "When I was a child, I spake as a child, I understood as a child, I thought as a child: but when I became a man, I put away childish things," St. Paul wrote in a passage in Corinthians that Rev. Covington read in church last week. The passage also said that love was the most important thing in the world. He had to agree with that. Love had saved him. At church, however, they received some very bad news. Mr. Jellerson's son Bennet had been found dead in San Francisco. Rev. Covington did not say what the cause of death was when he announced it from the pulpit, but when he talked to Jason and his mother after church he told them it was from a drug overdose. Jason had a few bad moments when he heard this news. The loneliness of death presented in a mental image of Ben Jellerson dead reminded him too much of the loneliness he felt when defenselessly he had had to submit to Father Mullen. And Mr. Jellerson's undoubted pain made him feel the support structure that existed in his mind was in danger of collapsing. He shook himself out of this black mood by playing in his mind Michelle's theme and by recalling that his mother had found the strength to survive: on the day after you die the sun will rise. He wanted to have the strength to always remember that. He was also ashamed that his first thought upon hearing of Ben's death was a selfish one. From the talk with his mother last night he was starting to see that he would never be whole until others' pain could be shared. Pain makes you selfish and self-regarding, yet if others had been selfish he would not now be strong enough to be free from the image of Father Mullen as God demanding his obedience. The day after you die the sun will rise; it will shine on others' pains and joys, for the world was bigger than any one individual and we needed one another. So he saw the way, even if less clearly he saw the way to get there. But his thoughts had a direction now, and he would work at thinking his way out until he found it.

Driving home with his mother, he reached his first decision: "I think we should go to Bennet Jellerson's funeral. Mr. Jellerson needs our support."

His mother smiled and patted his knee. "I'm glad you feel that way, Honey. I agree." Then she had laughed. "I mean Jason."

He thought a lot about Mr. Jellerson during the next three days. He had been a great teacher when he tutored him in the spring. He always grew excited and beamed with pride whenever Jason showed insight and intelligence during a lesson. But he also reminded Jason that subjects like history, philosophy and literature required understanding that only came through experience in life. One time when they had been discussing civil rights during a civics lesson and Jason had criticized Lincoln for being slow to issue the Emancipation Proclamation, Mr. Jellerson explained how one had to be careful about making categorical statements about actions. Lincoln was constrained by political factors, by northern racism, by the need to keep some of the border states in the union, and so forth. "You are a very precocious and intelligent young man, Jason, but don't forget that you are still very young. The more you live and experience the world, the more you'll understand how all kinds of factors constrict the decisions we make and actions we take." He had made this observation not to criticize Jason but to help him grow. He wasn't just teaching facts; he was teaching him how to become an adult. That's when Jason realized that Mr. Jellerson was the kind of teacher who inspired students to strive for excellence. To come to a lesson unprepared would be to let him down. Now the lesson dealt with life and experience, and Jason wanted to make sure that when he saw Mr. Jellerson at the funeral that he did not let him down.

After three days, during which time his principal activity was to think, often while he played music and sometimes while he composed it, and in which his only accomplishment was to finish redoing his room, the day of the funeral came. It was sparsely attended. Millie Jellerson's sister and brother-in-law, a few distant family members, a group of some half a dozen to ten people from out of town who were possibly colleagues from the school where Mr. Jellerson used to teach, the headmaster and a few teachers from Courtney Academy, and certain members of the congregation and some personal friends—all in all about thirty people came to the Congregational church for the services. Among them and of interest to Jason were Michelle Turcotte and her mother. He had learned from Rev. Covington that Michelle was helping out at the farmhouse during this time of trouble and had hoped she would be here. He wanted very much to talk with her. He could say things to her he couldn't comfortably say to his parents. She and her mother were dressed in white blouses and dark, knee-length skirts, and were sitting with Mrs. Covington and Eleanor Smallwood, who were attired rather more frumpily in full-length dresses. The Jellerson party arrived last. Mr. Jellerson looked awful. He and his wife had to support each other as they came into the church. Once he even stumbled and was caught by an old man Jason recognized as Walt Pingree. Walt walked stiffly and didn't appear to see very well. He peered about him, nearsighted and awkward. But Mr. Jellerson, though much younger than his uncle, looked older. His face was drawn, there were bags under his eyes that indicated he hadn't been sleeping well, and his chest was caved-in as if he hadn't eaten in a week and, much worse, as if he had given up on life. His tutor seemed to have aged a decade since he last had seen him. Jason was shocked at the transformation. He had been able to hide his own pain from everyone except his parents, but here was pain so overwhelming that nothing could hide it. Jason remembered Mr. Jellerson's face when he confessed to him his mathematical deficiencies. He had been so sincerely concerned and ashamed that he was not good at mathematics that he appeared boyish. To Jason his earnestness had appeared almost comic. It had made him instantly feel sympathy for his teacher, and afterwards they had become friends.

The fourth member of their party, a young woman, must be the daughter, Beverly. She had short brown hair, was slightly overweight, and while not pretty was attractive. She wore a tight navy-blue dress. When she turned as she sat down, he noticed she wore a nose ring. She looked uncomfortable, probably, he guessed, because she hardly knew anyone in the church.

On the dais was the closed coffin surrounded by flowers. He looked at it next, then glanced at his mother and saw the same faraway look in her eyes he had seen through the years. Now he knew she was remembering another who had died young and unfulfilled. For some reason Rev. Covington was delayed. Five minutes or more went by after everyone was seated, and Jason had plenty of time to examine the church. He was still getting used to it. Its simplicity contrasted sharply with the ornate decor of The Most Holy Trinity Church. At first he found it strange, but now he was beginning to see a certain nobility in it. He had told Rev. Covington about this conclusion. The minister had smiled broadly and told him he was starting to think like a Protestant, explaining that the founders during the Reformation wanted to have direct spiritual communion with God. In order to contemplate the awesome power and magnificence of the Creator, nothing should distract the mind. Then he cited the Shaker hymn, "Simple Gifts," and Jason understood him perfectly. Be single-minded. Clear out the distractions. Direct your thoughts to something higher than the day. His thoughts, however, were soon directed back to the coffin. It contained the central mystery of faith; it was in fact the reason human beings searched for faith. He contemplated these mysteries even after Rev. Covington arrived and gave the service, only fully participating when hymns were sung and the Lord's Prayer was said. He looked around at other faces, some bored, but most very serious. Mr. Jellerson wept almost continuously; his wife was more controlled but she cried too. Beverly sat motionless with an inscrutable expression, without tears, but he did see her cheek muscles twitch several times, suggesting she was keeping herself under control with great effort. It that were true, he could recognize in her similar propensities he himself shared. He found that interesting.

After the church services everyone got into cars for the trip to the cemetery, but when they gathered at the grave site he noticed that Michelle and her mother weren't among them. He whispered a question to his mother, and she whispered back that probably they had gone to the farmhouse to get the refreshments ready for the group.

To his relief, his mother's conjecture was correct. Michelle and her mother, acting as hostesses, greeted them at the front door of the farmhouse. Michelle had changed out of her skirt and was wearing a very attractive outfit consisting of the same silk blouse that she'd worn with her skirt, tight, dark slacks with a matching jacket and a crimson tie. She looked like a waitress at a fancy restaurant or like a professional woman, he was not sure which. But she looked pretty—that he was sure of. He knew Mrs. Turcotte from Mrs. Cohen's, but his mother had only occasionally met her. While they chatted he had a chance to talk with Michelle.

"I hear you've been helping Mr. and Mrs. Jellerson this week."

"My mother has done most of the work. We've cooked for them. I've walked their dog, and done some of the arrangements and stuff. But, Jason, how have you been? I missed you at the recital at Mrs. Cohen's party."

"I've been really fine, though at the time of the party I wasn't. This week I cleaned out all of my boy's stuff—dinosaurs and stuff, and put up posters of the BSO and Beethoven."

She smiled. "That's great. Congratulations on your acceptance at Denham Academy, by the way."

"Thanks, I'm real excited. They have a great music program there. It's just what I need."

"I'm sure you'll love it." She looked behind him to see Rev. Covington, his wife, and Eleanor Smallwood coming up the walk.

He nudged his mother. "I hope I have a chance to talk to you later, Michelle."

"Yes, me too."

He was a little displeased with himself. Telling her about his new room decorations was meant to signal that he was no longer a boy, but the way she smiled made him feel embarrassed. To announce you were no longer a boy was to be boyish. He would not make that mistake again.

They went into the living room. Extra folding chairs that had been placed against the walls wherever there was no furniture remained empty, for they were among the first arrivals. The emptiness of the chairs gave the room an abandoned and lonely-sad appearance. He followed his mother up to the Jellersons and offered condolences, but that too was disappointing. He felt he was too perfunctory in saying, "I'm very sorry to hear of your loss." Both Mr. and Mrs. Jellerson thanked him in a conventional way, thankful for the sentiments expressed but with hearts untouched. He hoped he would have a second chance to speak to them, but in the meantime his mother brought him over to Walt Pingree. Though he had seen him scores of times when he was with his mother downtown or at the store, this was the first time he'd met him with the knowledge that he was the father of the man his mother was going to marry.

His mother brought it up. "I think of him at times like this," she said, her voice sad and her eyes faraway.

Walt nodded sadly. "Poor Sam is heartbroken. It doesn't help him for me to say I know how he feels."

"What kind of music did Kermit like, Mr. Pingree?" Jason asked.

The question was unexpected, and Walt gave him a quizzical look. "I remember he played the Beatles all the time. Ellie said it was the most god-awful noise, but Kermit defended them and said they were the greatest band in the world. Do you know the song "Here Comes the Sun"? It was his favorite. He hummed it all the time when he wasn't playing it. When he played it he sang along."

Jason saw his mother nodding in recognition. "He told me once he wished he could play guitar like George Harrison. It was his favorite song."

"Did he like the Moody Blues?" Jason asked.

Walt rubbed his chin. "I don't rightly know. Maybe. I can't recollect that group."

"My mother told me he was a great football player."

Walt's eyes shined. "Oh, he was! I'll never forget the time he scored the winning touchdown for Courtney Academy in the state championship game. It was the happiest day of my life. He carried three tacklers into the end zone with him. He was not going to let anything stop him. Ellie and me were so proud we were bursting."

More people were coming in now. The group from Connecticut, comprised mostly of people of advanced middle-age, came in first. At the same time they came through the front door Beverly Jellerson came down the stairs. Concentrating on her nose ring, he watched her talking with these people. He had seen others wearing them before, but for some reason hers fascinated him. He wouldn't have expected such a thing from the daughter of Mr. Jellerson, whose political and social opinions were much more conservative than his mother's. He suspected that it was a sign of rebellion. He also couldn't help comparing her to Michelle, whom he could see at the door. Michelle was much prettier. Her business suit was very attractive, and he liked how he could see her bra through the diaphanous silk. No sooner did he think this, however, than the idea made him blush. He could feel his cheeks burning and turned away so that his mother wouldn't observe him.

The people from Connecticut moved into the room and went over to the Jellersons. A slender woman of about fifty dressed inappropriately (he thought) in bright colors, and who was at the tail end of the group, started a conversation with his mother and Walt. Before he could join in Beverly came up and introduced herself. She held out her hand and he shook it.

"Yes, I'm Jason Buckley," he said to her query. "Pleased to meet you. I'm very sorry about your brother."

She half closed her eyes and sighed. "It was a terrible shock. Years ago he got in with a bad crowd. I tried to talk him out of hanging with them, but he wouldn't listen. Drugs, you know. Then he joined the Navy and stopped taking drugs after a bad trip, or so he told me in a letter. I think I believed him, though. Once he got to San Francisco he stayed with me for a while, but we didn't have much room—he had to use a sleeping bag on the living room floor, so pretty soon after that he went to stay with one of his friends from the bad crowd who now lived out there. I wish my apartment was bigger. I wish he wasn't so indifferent about himself, you know, self-destructive and not caring."

She spoke rapidly in an uncensored stream. He was amazed she was telling him all this. He guessed it was therapeutic for her, but all he could think to say was "I see" as he watched Michelle moving across the room. She and Sarah were now beginning to get the refreshments out and putting them on the table.

Beverly followed his eyes and for a moment also observed Michelle. She seemed distracted now, suddenly unsure of herself. Then with another sigh from half-closed eyes she said, "Michelle told me about you. She says you're a remarkable young man. I don't doubt it, but what do you think of her?

"What do you mean?"

She smiled conspiratorially, eliciting from him a grin. He was beginning to like her, but then her face darkened as she said, "Some people seem to think she's remarkable too. Do you?"

Responding to the hard edge of her voice and the strange look in her eyes, he became more guarded. "Don't you?"

She glanced at Michelle and appeared to be carefully contemplating her response. "Well, some people might find her hard to take. I mean, isn't she a bit too good?"

He shook his head emphatically. "I don't think so. How can you be too good?"

She shrugged her shoulders, and with that gesture her mood changed. "I suppose you can't. Actually, I have to admit she's been wonderful to me. We got to know each other on the phone before I even came. Did you know she's been doing everything for my parents. She was here when I phoned about Ben. She's cooked, cleaned, made arrangements with the airline, everything."

He watched Michelle placing a tray of finger sandwiches on the table, then arranging napkins and toothpicks. "That sounds like her. She told me her mother is helping too."

"She is, but it's mostly Michelle. She's just being modest. She's a big fan of my father. Not surprising, I suppose. Millions of his former students worship him. Let me tell you, though, it's not easy being the child of a dedicated teacher. Just like Ben I've had my problems with him. We hit it off pretty good last Christmas, but you can guess who's been working to bring us even closer together."

"Michelle?"

She nodded, then said rather flippantly (and making him again revise his roller-coaster opinion of her downward), "You *are* a genius, I see. She told me, anyways, that I wasn't being fair to him, that I couldn't see him clearly because of all the bad memories. She said he was really a good man who cares about everyone. He helped her and her friend Sarah for the SAT's. She said he'd tutored you and that you would agree with her."

"I do," Jason said, glad to be able to get a word in. "Your father has been very, very kind to me. He and Rev. Covington got me accepted into Denham Academy. Your father knew people there and put a lot of work into it. I'm very grateful to him."

"I think Michelle wants to talk to you about my father. He's taking my brother's death very badly."

"I know—about Michelle that is. We plan to talk later."

An hour went by before they could talk again. In the meantime he and his mother mixed with most of the people in the room and had something to eat. Jason had several finger sandwiches and lots of pickles, which he loved. For dessert he had two date bars and would have had more, but he didn't want to appear childish. The people from Connecticut and the representatives from Courtney Academy left, after which the atmosphere changed to a more informal one. Rev. Covington spent a lot of time ministering to Mr. Jellerson. He did most of the talking while Mr. Jellerson would only nod occasionally. It was scary to see a man being devoured by despair. Jason reminded himself again that he had a duty not to let his teacher down. He had other very important things he wanted to talk to Michelle about, but the first thing he brought up was his desire to help ease his tutor's pain. "I want to help him, you see. I owe him so much. But I don't know what to say to him."

Michelle looked over at Mr. Jellerson and considered for a moment. "Just say what you feel. I found out very quickly that though he doesn't look it, he's actually a very emotional man. He feels and feels deeply. He appreciates sincerity. He's also prone, I think, to self-blame. I think he blames himself for his son's death. But he is too harsh on himself. Each of us has to take at least some responsibility for our actions. Bennet taking drugs makes him responsible just as much his unhappy childhood."

"That's true," Jason agreed. Her observation so neatly meshed with the directions his thoughts had been going lately that for a moment he wondered if she were clairvoyant. But of course she wasn't. The remark was simply typical of her.

"What he needs now," Michelle went on in a low voice, "is to feel he has the support and gratitude of his friends and people who know him. Jason, let me ask you something."

They were interrupted by Sarah, who came up to them. "Hi, Jason," she said and to Michelle: "Should we start cleaning up. Nobody seems to be eating anymore."

"Yeah, you could start. I'll join you in a sec."

She sat down on one of the folding chairs and patted the seat next to her. When he joined her, she went on. "I think another thing he blames himself for is Father Mullen's trial. Is it all right if we talk about that?"

He nodded, feeling a little uneasy.

Naturally she noticed his hesitation. "Are you sure?"

"Oh, yes. Don't mind me." He smiled, attempting to put her at ease.

"Well, it's just that I think he blames himself for how the trial ended. You don't, though, do you?"

"Oh, no, not at all. Both my mother and I understand, you know. My father is angry. He wants to make Father Mullen pay. But I'm trying to be free of him."

"I see. So you could tell Mr. Jellerson that you don't blame him?"

She was listening so sympathetically that it engendered an idea. "Michelle, later if you could..." He felt himself getting tongue-tied and began again. "I agree with my mother, you see. She thinks it's best to get Father Mullen behind me."

"I understand. I think it's best too."

She leaned forward, her face close to his. The intimacy made him feel very comfortable and unafraid. "Because if I tried to get revenge a year or more would go by and he'll still, you know, be calling the shots."

She nodded, her face a perfect picture of sympathy.

He looked around, hoping that nobody would interrupt them. He saw his mother watching him while she talked to Sarah. "One way to get him behind me is to confront him. That's the conclusion I've come to."

She was surprised. "Oh, Jason, are you sure? You mean you want to speak to him?"

"No, no. I have no desire to do that. But the place where...it...happened is near here. I'd like to go there. Do you know where it is?" He found himself as nervous as an adolescent asking a girl for his first date. He was amazed he had actually dared ask her.

She understood him completely. "But you could use some company. Jason, I'd be honored. And I do know how to get there. Millie—Mrs. Jellerson—told me where it was awhile back."

"You would!" he said too, too excitedly. He still couldn't hide the boy in him.

She nodded and smiled sweetly, and in her smile he thought he could see all the beauty of her soul. "When things calm down here, we can take Buttons for a walk. Okay? Before that, though, we have to talk to Mr. Jellerson."

After she left him he went over to his mother and told her what he and Michelle planned to do. She looked dubious, almost panicky, until he explained how important it was to him; then she gave her assent. At the same time he could see Michelle telling her mother and Sarah about the plan. They showed surprise.

He left his mother and went over to help Sarah and Michelle clean up. In the kitchen Sarah told him she thought he was brave, but he shrugged it off. If he was brave, he'd be going alone. They were wrapping the sandwiches in clear plastic and discarding what couldn't be saved. He brought the trash out to empty in the containers in the barn, and on the way back stopped and met Buttons. The puppy was glad for the company. Jason patted him for a while, then told him he would see him in a bit.

Back inside he decided this was the time to see Mr. Jellerson. He went into the living room and was glad to see that while his wife sat on one side of him the seat to his left was empty. He sat down beside him, and remembering Michelle's advice said, "Mr. Jellerson, when I told you before I was sorry to hear about your son, I didn't express myself very well. Believe me, it hurt me as if I had lost a brother even though I didn't know him. But I know you, and I want you to know that I appreciate all you've done for me. You and Rev. Covington have been so helpful I regard you as my second fathers. I especially know that I wouldn't have been accepted at Denham Academy without your help. I will remember that help with gratitude for the rest of my life. And I consider it a privilege to have been tutored by one of the best teachers and best men in the whole country."

At first Mr. Jellerson listened to this silently and with an expression suggesting puzzled curiosity, but then by degrees his face started betraying emotion. The longer Jason went on the more he saw that his words were affecting his teacher profoundly. Tears welled in his eyes, his face softened, and his burden seemed to be lighter. One other thing might lessen it even more.

"Also, I want you to know that I really, really appreciate your concern for me ever since the thing with Father Mullen happened. Without the support of you and Michelle and Rev. Covington and others, I don't think my family and I could have got through these days. The way the trial ended isn't anywhere near as important as that support."

"Thank you for that, Jason" was all Mr. Jellerson could say, but it was from the heart and said all that needed to be said.

Everyone, including Michelle and Sarah, had gathered around, though he was not conscious of their presence until after he had spoken. Mrs. Jellerson, who sat on the other side of her husband and heard every word of Jason's tribute, rose and hugged him; then Mr. Jellerson did the same. Eleanor came over for a hug, during which she whispered, "You're an angel." As if inspired by Jason, everyone started soothing Mr. Jellerson with similar remarks, and as voice was added to voice the dignity and self-possession that Jason associated with him started reasserting themselves on his face.

His mother came over and put her arm around him. Nearby he heard Beverly whisper to Walt Pingree, "It's a regular love-in." He looked at her, trying to see if the tone of sarcasm he heard was real or imagined. Imagined, probably, for she looked serious. Walt took this opportunity to awkwardly thank his nephew for his help last winter after he'd had his stroke. It occurred to Jason as he listened that in comforting Mr. Jellerson no one ever actually spoke about Bennet. No one said anything about him being a young man who would have made the world a better place or some similar pleasantry. For the first time he felt a true sadness for the life of the dead boy. Because he lived, suffered, and died, he deserved to be mourned.

Mrs. Jellerson offered everyone a drink, and when most accepted the offer Beverly took upon herself the task of getting the wine, sherry and mixed drinks prepared. Jason glanced at Michelle, who nodded slightly. Sarah, seeing this exchange, volunteered to finish up the cleaning alone, and the way was clear for him and Michelle to take their walk. Instantly a cold sweat came over him and he felt himself tremble. His mother was regarding him with an expression of unspeakable yearning and worry, as if trying to call him back. It was too late for that, however, nor could he say his nervousness surprised him. Of course he should be nervous: he was going to face a demon.

Outside Michelle tested the air and decided it was warm enough in the late afternoon sun to remove her jacket and tie. He did the same, and they hung their clothes over the porch fence; then he waited while she got the leash and collected Buttons.

Walking across the field, with Buttons leading them at the end of his twelve-foot leash, she told him she thought his words had comforted Sam.

"You call him Sam?" Jason asked.

She nodded nonchalantly. "I have for ages—since last Saturday to be exact." Then she laughed, exactly the medicine he needed, for he felt himself relax.

"I followed your advice. I spoke sincerely. I told him he and Rev. Covington were like second fathers to me. I think he liked that."

"It was a good thing to say."

Entering the woods now, his nervousness returned. They walked for some hundred yards before he asked, "Are we getting close?"

"Pretty close. Are you okay?"

"I'm a bit nervous," he admitted before lapsing into silence. Up ahead he recognized the hill and its accompanying valley, the valley of the shadow of death. The image of Father Mullen loomed in his mind, casting a shadow over him. His breath quickened and suddenly, unexpectedly, one of his violent fantasies of beating the priest with a stick sprang into his mind. Blow after blow descended on his face until it was unrecognizable, and then with a rock he pulverized the rest of him into pulp. He could feel his hands tingling with the desire for blood. The blood lust was a kind of madness, so powerful he was not sure he could control himself. Now he was scared for a different reason.

"This is the place, isn't it, Jason?" Michelle said softly.

He looked into her compassionate, dark eyes. Last year, long before Father Mullen had poisoned his life, she had told him the story of how when she was a little girl she had jumped in front of her father's lawn mower to save a butterfly. "I don't know why," she had said, "but I can't stand for anything to die unnecessarily."

It would be better to forgive him, to take with his daily bread redemption and forgive…

They walked into the lowland and over to the pines the size of Christmas trees. He wasn't sure he wanted to tell her where the exact spot was. He saw it. It would be better to forgive…but he wasn't quite ready for that yet. He walked about, trying to control his breathing. Michelle, respecting his inner solitude, remained silent. The only sound was that of Buttons digging at a pile of leaves.

No, not forgiveness, though maybe a bit of pity. He was a miserable, pathetic little soul, contemptible more than menacing. He had had to lie, and yet he called it love.

He looked at Michelle.

"Are you all right?"

"Yes, let's get out of here. I've seen enough."

He wanted some distance to get between them and the place before he would talk about it. As soon as they turned into the slow bend in the lumber road, he spoke. "For months I tried to imagine what I could have done differently."

"Could you?"

"Not really. Now knowing what I know, I could, but not then. He told me he spoke to God. You're Catholic, aren't you, Michelle?"

She laughed. "Not a very good one, I'm afraid."

"Well, me neither now. In fact I'm not Catholic anymore. I'm a Congregationalist, I guess. But then I was. And I believed it all—how the pope was God's representative on earth and how priests got their authority from the pope. Rev. Covington has shown me that it was sophistry Father Mullen was using. He said no decent priest would make a claim like the one he made. But all the time when he said he spoke for God and that God would hurt my parents if I didn't obey him, it made sense. So believing that, how could I have acted any differently? He said God would kill my parents, you see."

"You couldn't," Michelle said gently. "You just couldn't have." She looked close to tears and added angrily, "What a creep that man is."

"But at the time I couldn't act differently, my body was telling me something else. It told me to run. The thing that bothered me and still bothers me is that that was the right thing to do. My instinct was right, but I didn't listen to it."

"But you had your reasons. Your parents."

"Yes, he said God would kill my parents."

"What a creep he was, that priest," she repeated even more angrily.

"Yes, I clearly see that now. Just like I see God isn't like he said. Rev. Covington said to me that whatever God is, God is love. God is goodness. He explained that God made us free, that he doesn't interfere in human affairs. He gave us free will."

"That sounds right to me."

Jason stopped and looked at Michelle, who had to tug at the leash to restrain Buttons. "But you know what that tells me? It tells me that prayers do nothing."

"Well, maybe not directly. Maybe we draw strength from faith."

They started walking again. "Rev. Covington tells me not to be bothered by doubts. Faith implies doubt, he says. It's not a condition of certainty but a striving. I'll tell you the truth, though. I'm starting to doubt God exists, at least as a white-haired and benign man on a throne in heaven. What I'm starting to see is that in beautiful music I can hear God."

Michelle smiled. "When you play, so can I. But I think no matter what, we have each other. No matter if there's a God or not, we human beings are not alone. I've thought of the same things about prayers. God watched the Nazis murder millions, but human beings could have saved them, or should have. So I say, we can stand by each other."

He nodded grimly. "But still it bothers me that my instincts were right and I didn't listen to them. You see, don't you, how I could have felt God betrayed me."

"But it was understandable why you didn't run. Father Mullen was the one who betrayed you. You, according to what you knew at the time, were protecting your parents."

"According to what I know now, I was wrong. But, yes, that's what I thought I was doing."

"So the way I see it, you were heroic. You were noble. If I was you, I'd be proud of myself."

But he couldn't accept that. He remembered one thing more. "There's something else, though. I was afraid of the woods here. I didn't know where I was so that if I ran I would get lost. What if that fear was the one that made me disobey my instincts? What if it was self-deception?"

"At my house when we say something like that my mother always says, 'Thinking in a circle gets you dizzy.' I think it's understandable you would be afraid in all kinds of ways, including being lost. That's the reason the creep brought you to the woods—so that there was nowhere to run."

"Okay, that sounds right. Maybe I'm trying to blame myself."

"Yeah, when it's Father Mullen who's to blame." She paused to let Buttons pee on a tree. He sniffed his handiwork, seemed satisfied, and started trotting happily again. They followed.

Up ahead they could see the opening in the shady woods where the pasture began. It was bright and sun-drenched. Jason began thinking of his mother's remark: "The day after you die the sun will rise." Now he saw that every day was the day before the day you would die, and you had to live that day in full knowledge of tomorrow. Even if tomorrow came and you lived through it, you still had to know that one day out of an inscrutable calendar of tomorrows really would be the day you died. The question then was finding the strength and faith to face that day. Thinking that Michelle might not understand this vision—thinking, that is, that while he was wise beyond his years she was young and though certainly not naive was still maybe not tough-minded enough to understand what hard experience had taught him—he refrained from speaking his thoughts in the belief he was protecting her.

Almost immediately he realized the absurdity of thinking himself superior to her in wisdom. Didn't she just say that no matter if there's a God or not, we still have each other? Tomorrow he would think of some way of converting that thought to musical expression and adding it to his composition.

a note about the writer

*R. P. Burnham edits **The Long Story** literary magazine and is a writer. He has published fiction and essays in many literary magazines. He sets most of his fiction in Maine, where he was born and raised and has deep roots. **The Least Shadow of Public Thought**, a book of his essays that introduce each issue of **The Long Story**, was published in 1996 by Juniper Press as part of its Voyages Series. He was educated at the University of Southern Maine (undergraduate) and The University of Wisconsin–Madison (graduate). He is married to Kathy FitzPatrick, an associate professor of biology at Merrimack College in North Andover.*

Wessex Books in Print

(available from Amazon, Ingram, Baker & Taylor, Wilson & Associates,
your local book sellers or direct from us)

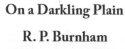

R. P. Burnham   **On a Darkling Plain**
208 pages   **$12.95**

Samuel Jellerson, 56 and forced into early retirement, is walking in the woods behind the family farm in Maine one fall day when he witnesses a priest molesting a boy. From this one event all the action in the novel follows and draws a wide cross section of the town—a frantic mother, an idealistic teenage girl, a brooding, alienated young man, a priest, a minister, a swamp yankee, a lonely old man, a happy-go-lucky plumber, and many others— into a theme that explores the nature of evil and its antidote empathy, the force that creates community, fellow-feeling and a sense of responsibility to others.

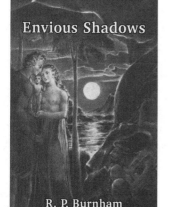

R. P. Burnham   **Envious Shadows**
228 pages   **$11.50**

Envious Shadows is a deftly crafted, engrossing contemporary novel, one of those works that is not afraid to face the grim realities of life and the cruelties of society as well as the redeeming power of love... A beautiful work that depicts life in all its grim realities, *Envious Shadows* is a rewarding read.
> —Mayra Calvani, *Bloomsbury Review*, Vol. 25, No. 4 (July/August 2005)

In *Envious Shadows*, R. P. Burnham has given us a full blooded novel, driven by plot, character and issues of racism, sexism, infidelity, the struggle to survive economically in a small Maine town, and the overarching love that can redeem us from sorrow and loss. This is a book that will provoke thought, feeling and rage at hatred and inequity. Surely this is the most we can ask of any writer when we pick up his book.
> –Laurel Speer, poet and former columnist for *Small Press Review*

Brian E. Backstrand
176 pages

Little Bluestem
$12.95

Little bluestem is a vigorous, drought-resistant native bunchgrass. It is well known in the Great Plains and in other places in America's heartland where it frequently is found with other prairie grasses. Most of the people in Brian E. Backstrand's first collection of stories, *Little Bluestem*, would know this hardy plant by sight. They would see it surviving in the ditches and volunteering on the hardscrabble places of the rural landscapes in which they live. They would understand it to be an ordinary grass which persists and endures.

Backstrand's stories from rural America chronicle often small but important moments of the lives of ordinary people from the farms and the small towns of middle America. Memories—healing or disruptive, constant or denied—often play an important role in the stories of *Little Bluestem* which link together rural people from various generations, caught in the midst of struggle or in a moment of recognition or healing. Backstrand's intention is to lift up ordinary people from rural contexts and place them squarely before his contemporary and often urban readers. His stories come as an invitation, asking his readers to consider once more their rural counterparts who, like the common, native bluestem grass, often are overlooked.

William Davey
224 pages

The Angry Dust
$24.95 *hardback*

This exquisite novel tells the story of Prescott Barnes and his family leaving the dust bowl for golden California, but there its similarities with *The Grapes of Wrath* end. The grandson of a wealthy preacher who disinherited Prescott's father, Barnes, despite his cynical black humor, unwavering hostility to religion, and his illiteracy, possesses a fierce integrity and passions that make him larger than life at the same time he is perfectly human. Told with perfect command and in a brilliant style, this is a novel of tragic grandeur in the fine high style of old with the action inevitably leading to tragedy, and tragedy totally flowing from character. In Prescott's case, it is his poverty and hostility toward religion that leads to his tragic mistake. Every character, even the minor ones like Rev. Eberstadt (a con man who nevertheless grows in sincerity and in capacity to love) are revealed in such detail that we get to know them like old friends. The plot unfolds as inevitably as an eclipse, and the forces of nature, like the tornado that strikes them, are vividly and unforgettably described. Most importantly, Prescott Barnes's tragic confrontation with the world compellingly reveals how common people can possess power and grandeur.

Sandra Shwayder Sanchez   Stillbird
126 pages $9.50

What a pleasure to read this inventive, intelligent new novel by Sandra Shwayder Sanchez. *Stillbird* has the resonance of an epic tale and the immediacy of a gripping storyline. Sanchez reveals an acute sense of place and season as well as a rich appreciation for history. Through nuanced characterization and dramatic suspense, Sanchez draws us into a complex and fascinating world. *Stillbird* shows us that Sandra Shwayder Sanchez is a writer to watch for.
> —Valerie Miner, author of *Abundant Light and The Low Road*

An epic in less than 200 pages, Sandra Shwayder Sanchez's lovely *Stillbird* holds every fiber of the reader's attention from beginning to end, and, like her character Mary, dances "with more joy than a body could bear."
> —Jennifer Heath, author of *The Scimitar and Th Veil: Extraordinary Women of Islam, On Th Edge of Dream: The Women in Celtic Myth nd Legend*, and other works

Ita Willen   The Gift
106 pages $9.50

The close of the Nazi death camps was a beginning rather than an end for those who survived. Told through the eyes of a child of Holocaust survivors, *The Gift* lets us feel the pain and the courage that reaches into the decades beyond the war. Compelling and insightful. A memorable read.
> –Barb Lundy, poet

Every time I read this memoir (and I have read it several times) I am awed by its beauty and insight. Every time I read this memoir I increase my own insights about how I can live my own life more fully.
> –Sandra Shwayder Sanchez, author of *Stillbird* and *The Nun*.

Forthcoming from The Wessex Collective

Sangre del Monte   Roberto Lucero

Paul Johnson called this novel a "miracle of a book." It is a classic tale in the mode of the warrior quest. Jose Maria, a sixty-two-year-old farmer is shaken from his "unremarkable" life by a vicious attack on his son in the forest. As a result of having to deal with this incident, he is forced to struggle with the problems of reality vs. illusion regarding physical and spiritual life and death. The narrative is set in the north central mountains of New Mexico, between early summer and the first snowfall in October 1842. The story proceeds from Jose Maria's change of perception that life is plain and ordinary to a realization that the accumulation of daily events creates a rich and remarkable spiritual life for those who meet its challenges.

Roberto Lucero was born in an isolated mountain valley in northern New Mexico in 1937. He has worked for a publishing company, been a reporter for *El Grito del Norte*, a liberal newspaper, and earned a liberal arts degree from the University of Colorado. He later earned a Master of Arts degree and is currently a clinical counselor. He has been writing short stories, essays, and poetry since high school. *Sangre del Monte* is his first novel. He is currently working on a collection of short stories.

The Marble Orchard   Paul Johnson

After living all over Africa and South America, earning his itinerant living as a painter (sometimes of art, sometimes of houses) Carl Larson returns to the small town he couldn't wait to leave for a brief visit to get his elderly, widowed mother settled in a nursing home. Once back "home" Carl has encounters with several ghosts from his past (some figurative and some literal) that in vintage Paul Johnson style combine serious tragedy with laugh-out-loud comedy. Johnson has a particular gift for making each and every character—even, in this book, a neighbor's dog—come alive and stick around.

Paul Johnson was a political activist in the 1960s, a homesteader in the 1970s, later lived in Brooklyn where he supported his writing habit with carpentry work, was a founding editor of *Win* magazine, won a war resister's award in the early nineties and moved to Las Vegas, New Mexico where he now resides with his wife, Fran, an art therapist. He has drawn upon his broad life experiences to create in-depth portraits of his generation in books that involve readers emotionally in ideas and issues that matter. Robert Miner in *The New York Times Book Review* said of his first novel, *Killing the Blues*, "The voice in Paul Johnson's first novel is tough, amusing, cantankerous and sometimes astonishingly gentle," and *The New York Times* called his second novel, *Operation Remission*, "remarkable as much for its subject matter as its literary flair."

The Clockmaker and Other Tales   Sandra Shwayder Sanchez
A Collection of Modern Mythical Fiction

In this collection of three short stories and two novellas, a medieval nun escapes the massacre of her convent and memorializes her dead sisters in stone, a shoeshine boy in 21st century Cuzco solves a murder and gets a job in the movies, the friendship of half brothers Isaac and Ishmael is tragically sabotaged by real-estate developers in Appalachia, a developmentally disabled man rescues various people and animals from an apocalyptic flood in a row boat and walks them all to safety in northern New Mexico and the maker of an astronomical clock in the Old Town Hall Tower of a mythical city very much like Prague is blinded to prevent him from recreating his masterpiece and walks back home across the centuries.